CAROL FINCH
CAPTIVE BRIDE

ZEBRA BOOKS
KENSINGTON PUBLISHING CORP.

ZEBRA BOOKS

are published by

Kensington Publishing Corp.
475 Park Avenue South
New York, NY 10016

First printing: February 1987

Printed in the United States of America

To the hero at home

Part I

By the time you swear you're his,
Shivering and sighing,
And he vows his passion is
Infinite, undying—
Lady, make a note of this:
One of you is lying.

—Dorothy Parker

Chapter 1

Rozalyn DuBois rearranged her clothing after Jeffrey Corday had practically twisted it about her neck in his insistent attempt to detain her. Forcing a pleasant smile, she then swept into the oversized solarium where her grandmother sat amidst a jungle of prized potted plants. Although the *grande dame* of Rabelais was a mite hard of hearing she would be able to detect Rozalyn's irritation. Rozalyn told herself she must approach Lenore with a cheerful word of greeting, and she hastily ran her hand across her mass of unruly raven hair, settling it back into place as best she could.

Lenore caught sight of the blue-eyed lass who sailed into the sunroom to mingle with the pastel flowers lining the glass windows and dangling from the ceiling. Twisting in her wheelchair, she surveyed her granddaughter and then frowned bemusedly at Rozalyn's somewhat ruffled appearance. Her perceptive gaze ran the full length of Rozalyn's velvet green riding habit, noting a few telltale wrinkles and the renegade strands of ebony hair that had come free of the bun atop Rozalyn's head. Lenore was certain her granddaughter had not employed

9

a carriage to transport her to the stately manor that overlooked St. Louis for Rozalyn's coiffure was in disarray and bright pink stained her creamy cheeks. Judging by her appearance, Lenore concluded that the girl had straddled her flighty steed and thundered across the meadow to reach the mansion.

Heaving a disapproving sigh, Lenore once again scrutinized her lovely, but disheveled granddaughter. If Aubrey DuBois had spent more time with this child he would not have such a feisty misfit on his hands, Lenore mused sourly. Rozalyn's father was so engrossed in his fur-trading ventures and speculative expeditions into the Rockies that he had permitted Rozalyn to run wild. There was nothing this hoyden hadn't attempted since she had returned from finishing school in New York four years earlier.

The child came and went as she pleased, cavorting with all sorts of unsavory characters. They had taught her a multitude of things a sophisticated young woman from a prominent French family should have known nothing about.

Indeed, Rozalyn DuBois was a fun-loving adventuress, a free spirit who insisted upon living life to its fullest, no matter what the consequences. She breezed through St. Louis like a devastating whirlwind, leaving no stone unturned, setting the gossips' tongues to wagging with her wild antics and madcap adventures.

Each time Aubrey grumbled that his daughter had become rebellious and unmanageable, Lenore scolded him for not taking a hand in the child's upbringing. She insisted that Aubrey's lack of interest in his daughter was the true cause of her scandalous behavior, but Aubrey considered himself the reigning royalty of St. Louis. He refused to be lectured on any subject, especially one that centered around his high-spirited daughter. So, though he would not become involved in Rozalyn's life, he frequently complained about her unruly behavior.

What Rozalyn needs, Lenore surmised, is a strong-willed man to curb her wild shenanigans and to mellow her temperament. With scrutinizing eyes, Lenore watched Rozalyn glide up to her, looking very much like a cherub who had just flitted down to Earth. But she was not! Rozalyn DuBois, the most-sought-after debutante in St. Louis, had a bit of the devil in her. An endless string of young men came to her doorstep, for Rozalyn was always between fiancés, one beau after another having fallen from her good graces and been shuffled out with the clutter. Yet another would-be fiancé was always itching to pursue her.

To say this blue-eyed temptress was fickle was an understatement, Lenore begrudgingly admitted to herself. Rozalyn seemed to know what she expected and desired in the man who would become her husband, but she, quite simply, could not latch onto a man who fit her rigid specifications. The child was virtually impossible to please.

Lenore had informed her capricious granddaughter that she was making a grave mistake by searching for a custom-fit in a tailored world. Rozalyn had never been able to stroll into a boutique to select a gown to fit her curvaceous figure without necessary alterations. Why then did she expect to meet a man who perfectly matched her expectations? Rozalyn had sniffed distastefully at her grandmother's comparison. She'd further declared that if she could not secure a custom-fit in a husband she would have no qualms about becoming a spinster. At least, Rozalyn rationalized, that way she would remain happy. Her friends had made the tragic mistake of attempting to reform the irresponsible rakes they had married, and Rozalyn refused to follow in their foot-steps.

An argument had ensued between grandmother and

11

granddaughter, and when Lenore had informed Rozalyn in no uncertain terms that she would see her properly wed before she departed from this world, Rozalyn had insisted that there was no great rush since her grandmother was going nowhere. Then, with plain-spoken eloquence, Rozalyn had announced that she would not marry until she was damned well ready and she was not ready yet!

Since that heated exchange six months earlier, Lenore no longer bothered with a greeting when Rozalyn faithfully came to check in on her. She simply cut to the heart of the matter, firing the same tiresome question. It was her hope that Rozalyn would select a husband, if only to end that constant badgering.

"So tell me," Lenore demanded. "Have you lighted upon a man to your liking? Pray say yes and give this crippled old woman an ounce of peace." Lenore drew attention to herself by tucking her lap quilt around her legs and clasping her bony hands over her chest. Her melodramatic gesture was meant to remind Rozalyn of a lifeless soul lying in state, eyes fixed in a sightless stare. "I am not getting any younger you know. This aged body of mine is deteriorating so quickly that I may not be alive when next you come to call. My dying request is to see you wed."

Rozalyn's gaze soared toward the ceiling. Heaving a frustrated sigh, she silently muttered at the beldame who had acquired a single-minded purpose these past few months. Every other day Rozalyn paid Lenore a visit, and every other day she was met with prying inquiries about her love life . . . or lack of it. She would have been in a huff if anyone but her grandmother had dared to hound her so relentlessly, but out of respect for the aging *grande dame*, Rozalyn bit her tongue and swallowed the caustic rejoinder that ached to fly free.

She had had her fill of scheming fortune hunters like

12

Jeffrey Corday. It was easy to spot a man who was courting her solely for the DuBois fortune. Indeed, Jeffrey had been so obvious the past month that Rozalyn had become cool and aloof when he approached her. She had hoped he would take the hint and pursue some other heiress, but Jeffrey had only pressured her for an answer to his marriage proposal. Since this mule-headed man had not responded to tact, Rozalyn had been forced to tell him exactly what she thought of him. She had vehemently protested his underhanded strategy of trying to snare a wealthy young woman who could afford his expensive tastes and his feather-weighted coin purse.

Jeffrey Corday was a prime example of the kind of man Rozalyn detested. She had lost what was left of her patience with him that very morning, and their confrontation had left her smoldering. The nerve of the man, Rozalyn thought furiously. Did he honestly believe she could be swayed with humble apologies or deceptive excuses? Rozalyn was a great many things, many of which her grandmother did not approve, but she was no man's fool.

Her overzealous suitor's first mistake lay in making a grab for Rozalyn when she was on horseback, after she had requested that he leave her be. His second blunder was his lack of ability to keep his seat when Rozalyn had retaliated. Her temper, already sorely put upon, had burst loose when Jeffrey had clutched at her clothing to keep his balance, and she had given him a forceful shove that toppled from his perch into the shrubs.

He has fallen head over heels for me, Rozalyn mused with wicked amusement. But he has received his just reward.

Jeffrey was up to his neck in debts, and he saw Rozalyn as his salvation, but her association with him had only given her another bitter taste of the hazards she faced in courting. There seemed to be not one man on God's green

13

earth who could look her in the eye without seeing dollar signs.

"Well, have you no encouraging news for your decrepit old grandmother?" Lenore queried impatiently.

"Grand'mère, I hardly consider you in your dotage," Rozalyn chortled good-naturedly. "Inside the body you label as decrepit is an energetic young woman who will undoubtedly outlive us all."

"No, my dear child, inside this body is a brittle bag of bones and a shriveling heart that aches to see you happily wed," Lenore contradicted.

"I do wish just once you would greet me with something other than '*Where is the man of your dreams and why haven't you married him yet?*'" Rozalyn grumbled, her tone harsher than she'd intended. The morning had not gone well and Lenore's badgering was not improving her disposition.

"Someone has to remind you that you are sorely in need of a husband," Lenore countered. Wagging a thin finger in Rozalyn's unconcerned face she continued. "If your mother and grandfather were alive they would be appalled by your impulsive shenanigans and your stubborn refusal to take a husband. You are twenty years old, for God's sake! You need a man to care for you, one who will look after you. Your father is too busy counting his money to see to your future, so I am left with no choice but to intervene."

With great difficulty, Rozalyn dragged in the trailing reins of her temper. Lenore never had kind words for her son-in-law; Aubrey DuBois had barely met with Lenore's approval while Jacqueline was alive. After his wife's death, he had completely devoted himself to his work, having no regard for anyone but himself. His obsession for making money preoccupied him, and Lenore considered it disgraceful, that he ignored his daughter after his wife's death.

14

Aubrey freely admitted his penchant for making a fortune in furs by selling them to the trading companies in New York. He had never taken time for anything else, not even for his wife. Nonetheless, Lenore constantly belittled Aubrey for neglecting his daughter, who was sorely in need of guidance.

Rozalyn had been hurt by her father's disinterest, but she had come to realize there was no changing him. Now she amused herself while Aubrey spent every waking hour at his warehouse on the waterfront, conversing with the trappers, rivermen, ex-soldiers, and drifters who swarmed in the taverns and grogshops. He employed these rowdy adventurers to trap beaver and mink, and he encouraged his employees to trade with the Indians in exchange for the valuable furs that brought high prices in the East. His only goal in life was to monopolize the fur trade west of the Mississippi. Rozalyn had no doubt that her father had already accomplished his aim, for he set his own prices and virtually controlled the fur business.

Each summer Aubrey led a caravan, heaped with merchandise, to the rendezvous at the foot of the Rockies. He bought pelts from trappers and sold them necessary supplies for the following year. DuBois also enlisted ex-soldiers to construct trading forts in the wilds in order to promote trade with the Indians. It seemed to Rozalyn that her father had sewn up every facet of fur trading and that he reigned supreme, thwarting all competition that sought to cut into his vast profits.

Aubrey was known as the king of fur trade, but he could not relax and enjoy his prestigious position. Something drove him, some ambition that Rozalyn had never quite understood. But she had been forced to accept his obsession, along with the depressing fact that he had no love to offer anyone, not even his only child.

"Father is a very busy man," Rozalyn said defensively. "And I am quite capable of fending for myself. I

15

have learned to adjust to the situation and I have no complaints about my life," she added with a careless shrug.

"Of course you don't!" Lenore railed. Then she wheezed, unable to catch her breath after her over-zealous outburst.

Damn that Aubrey. He's never cared a fig for his wife or his child, Lenore thought bitterly. It seemed he had felt it necessary to take a wife and produce an heir, but his family meant no more to him that the rest of his possessions.

"You have been left to run wild and your father has conveniently forgotten that he has a daughter. He was married to his business long before he wed Jacqueline, and he shut both of you out of his life. I firmly believe Jacqueline died of a broken heart, rather than from the grippe, but I will not be satisfied until you find a husband and begin to lead a life of your own."

Lenore's overheated rebuttal seemed to drain her failing strength, and she collapsed in her chair, exhausted and out of breath. Rozalyn peered at the *grande dame* with growing concern. It was obvious the dowager was ailing since she had taken to her wheelchair the previous month, claiming she no longer trusted her wobbly legs to support her, and her health had deteriorated drastically the past few weeks. Her face had become chalky and her shoulders drooped noticeably. It was apparent that Lenore's health was escaping her; she seemed to grow steadily worse with each passing day. The old woman was prone to violent coughing spasms, and her strength failed her when she exerted herself to give boisterous lectures. Although Rozalyn considered Lenore to be overdramatic at times, certainly the dowager had enjoyed better days.

Rueful gray eyes lifted and focused on the shapely maiden who was poised in her velvet riding habit. "Do you wish me to rest in peace when the heavenly chariot comes for me, child?" Lenore inquired in raspy spurts. "Answer my only prayer, Rozalyn. Find a man who can fill the emptiness in your life, the emptiness you disguise by gallivanting all over town in those outlandish breeches. You scare the wits out of good citizens when you thunder down the streets on that barely manageable stallion you insist upon exercising in the most unlikely places." Lenore drew a shuddering breath and then plunged on before she lost her raspy voice. "And for heaven's sake, stop cavorting with the undesirables who swarm the streets." When Rozalyn compressed her lips to prevent a guilty smile from blossoming on her lips, Lenore mellowed slightly. It was difficult to remain angry with this lovely sprite, and Lenore found herself basking in the warmth of her granddaughter's impish grin. "This city is thick with kidnappers and thieves, Rozalyn. I do wish you would be more careful of the company you keep. One day you might find yourself held for ransom by those who live a hand-to-mouth existence. The riffraff you dare to call friend could easily turn on you."

Suddenly the beldame's wrinkled face assumed a strange, pained expression, and she seemed to have great difficulty drawing a breath. Rozalyn fell to her knees and clasped her grandmother's hand in her own, becoming more concerned by the minute. Could it be that Lenore's condition *was* far worse than Rozalyn had allowed herself to believe? How could she deny the dowager her dying request when it seemed to mean so much to her? She would never forgive herself if *she* were the cause of Lenore's distress. The beldame of Rabelais was one of the few who fussed over her, and Rozalyn dearly loved the old woman, despite her tendency to harp on the same annoying subject.

"Does it mean so much to you to see me happily wed?" Rozalyn reached up to smooth silver strands of hair back into place; they had tumbled loose during Lenore's violent coughing spasm.

"It means everything to me, child," Lenore breathed hoarsely. Then she gave her granddaughter's hand a weak but loving squeeze. "You are all I have left in this world. My last wish is to see you wed to a man you respect and admire, one who will not cast you aside for the sake of his fortune, one who will shower you with love. You have been so long deprived of true affection."

Rozalyn noted the sentimental mist that clouded Lenore's eyes, and she could not bring herself to disappoint her *grand'mère,* not in the woman's weakened condition. Indeed, she would have promised Lenore the world if she'd thought that would boost her failing spirits. Lenore had lost her husband and her daughter, and her son-in-law had been no comfort to her in her declining years. The beldame fussed over Rozalyn to fill her lonely days, insisting that her granddaughter behave like a proper lady, and she chastised Rozalyn each time a talebearer came to the door to tattle about her lively granddaughter's latest prank. Although she gave lectures aplenty, the *grande dame* also showered Rozalyn with love, the only affection she had known since her mother had died nine years earlier.

Rozalyn had grown up like a wild flower. Only her grandmother had attempted to offer her direction. If Rozalyn lost Lenore she would have no one who truly cared about her. Rozalyn suddenly realized this, and she vowed when the day came for her to relinquish her earthly claim on this good-hearted old woman, Lenore would go in peace. She decided to give Lenore what she wanted, even if it was not in her power to do so.

"Do you want to know a secret, Grand'mère?" Rozalyn whispered confidentially. "I think I have found a man much like Grand'père, one who can make me as happy as Philippe made you."

A smidgeon of color worked its way into Lenore's

18

waxen features. "Have you truly, Rozalyn? Do not lie to me, child. It would break my heart to live on false hope," she wheezed, emphasizing her poor health.

Rozalyn did not bat an eye. Was it so wrong to deceive Lenore when this meant so much to her? Was it wrong to give her hope when her strength failed her and her days were numbered? She could not blurt out the truth, not now. She would never allow Lenore to know that the man of her dreams remained a fantasy, out of her reach.

"*Oui, Grand'mère,*" she insisted. As Rozalyn pasted on a love-struck smile, her vivid imagination began to conjure up a most dashing gentleman, one who probably didn't even exist. "He is tall, dark, and incredibly handsome, a fine specimen of a man who takes my breath away when I look upon him." Rozalyn cast her grandmother a discreet glance, overjoyed that the news was having the same effect as a magic potion. Lenore had straightened in her chair and had inclined her head, intending to miss not one word of Rozalyn's confession.

"Tell me more, my dear," the elderly woman said enthusiastically. "I want to know everything about this new man in your life."

Rozalyn closed her eyes and dreamed up a Prince Charming, a man who surpassed all those she had met. "He walks with a confident stride, and is a mite arrogant perhaps, but rightfully so, Grand'mère. He is powerfully built, with sturdy broad shoulders a woman could lean on for consolation and compassion, and his handsome face is framed with thick, dark hair and his eyes"—she paused and then thought better of giving a specific color, in case her next beau could not perfectly fit the description— "his eyes dance with a living fire, while his smile is so warm and contagious it can melt a woman's heart."

"Even one encased in ice . . . like yours, child?" Lenore taunted, her eyes taking on the sparkle Rozalyn had not seen in them of late.

"Especially mine," Rozalyn gushed like a bubbling volcano. "My heart flutters beneath my breast as if it might leap out when I am near him." She was spreading it on a mite thick, but her words had done wonders for Lenore's condition. They had given the old woman a breath of hope, a sense of serenity she lacked.

When Lenore noticed the glow in Rozalyn's cheeks she readjusted her spectacles to ensure that she was not imagining things. "So you have, indeed, met a man to your liking," she surmised.

"*Oh, oui, Grand'mère,*" her granddaughter insisted with a positive nod, playing the role of a love-smitten maid to the hilt. "I think this time I have found a man who can make me happy. I will even relinquish my wild wandering ways if he asks for my hand. He does not want to change me, you understand," Rozalyn hastily added when her grandmother's eyes narrowed skeptically. "He accepts me as I am and he has no need of Papa's money. For him, I could be true/and I would never think to embarrass him with some impulsive shenanigan."

Lenore's graying brows formed a dubious line over her eyes. She found herself becoming more suspicious of her granddaughter by the second. If Rozalyn had discovered true love, why hadn't she mentioned this mysterious gentleman before when she'd been given the third degree? And what kind of man could make this rambunctious hoyden sacrifice her freedom for the sake of love? He sounded too good to be true. That made Lenore skeptical of his existence. She would have to see him in the flesh to believe there was such a perfectly matched beau for this sprite nymph.

"Then I should like to meet this one," Lenore demanded in a tone that anticipated no argument. "When I see the two of you together I will know for certain that he is everything you say he is and that you truly care for each other."

Rozalyn wilted back on her haunches like a delicate flower drooping in the blistering summer sun. "You want to meet him?" she chirped, inwardly cringing as her lie tumbled down around her like a rockslide.

Lenore gave her gray head an affirmative shake. "Today . . . now . . . as soon as you can fetch him to me."

Good God! Rozalyn thought disgustedly. Now what the devil am I going to do? How can I talk my way out of this mess?

Her grandmother would have a fit if Rozalyn suddenly admitted that she had made this all up. The truth could cause another setback in Lenore's deteriorating health. The *grande dame* would begin to rant and rave, and that could well be the last lecture she ever delivered. It seemed Rozalyn was to be the death of her grandmother, one way or another.

Stall, Rozalyn advised herself. She had to allow herself enough time to collect her wits and determine how to wade out of this gigantic lie after she had sunk into it neck deep. Oh, why hadn't she kept her mouth shut? Her good intentions had not been an ounce of help.

"I would . . . uh . . . very much like you to meet him," Rozalyn stammered. After climbing to her feet she presented her back to Lenore, concealing her troubled frown. "But he is quite busy at the moment and I seriously doubt he—"

"Too busy to pay his respects to a dying woman who may not live to attend the wedding? *Mon Dieu*, surely he could spare me a few minutes of his time," Lenore scoffed and then gasped for breath. "Look at me, child! I have one foot in the grave and I am living on borrowed time. We cannot delay. I would despair if I fell asleep never to wake. I demand that I be permitted to meet the man you have described. I want him here, *tout de suite!*"

21

"Mais, Grand'mère, it is quite impossible—" Rozalyn muttered, only to be cut off by Lenore's annoyed sniff.

"Fetch him posthaste. I may not see another sunrise, but I will damned well meet your intended. I have something to say to your new beau . . . if indeed there is one," Lenore added and then tossed Rozalyn a dubious frown.

"Of course, there is," Rozalyn adamantly insisted.

The gleam in Lenore's gray eyes warned her granddaughter that she was determined to have her way in this matter. Rozalyn must produce living proof of the man she had conjured up and *now!* Sweet merciful heavens. Where was she going to find this chivalrous knight on such short notice? Lord, she could use a miracle. Rozalyn lifted her eyes heavenward, wondering if she were asking the impossible and knowing in her heart that she was.

Finally, she heaved a defeated sigh and nodded in compliance. There was naught else to do but walk calmly from the mansion. Once outside, Rozalyn would dash madly through the streets of St. Louis until she located a man who closely resembled the description she had given Lenore. My, what a tangled web she had woven for herself this time.

"I will fetch him to you, but do not despair if I do not return within the hour. I will bring him to you as soon as I can."

God, what was she saying? She couldn't fish such a man from this melting pot of humanity if she had one year, much less one hour!

"Time grows short," Lenore wheezed, feeding upon Rozalyn's sympathy. She fully intended to force Rozalyn's hand on this important issue. If Aubrey would not see to the child's future, she must. She would see Rozalyn properly wed . . . if it was the last thing she ever did, Lenore promised herself. If this man met with her approval, she would accelerate the courting process. Rozalyn would be wed . . . as soon as arrangements could be made. "I only pray that I do not breathe my last before you return." Lenore clutched her chest and coughed hoarsely. "God forbid that I do not endure the hour. If I am not here when you come back . . . always remember that I love you. . . ."

Rozalyn was frantic. Lenore's last plea was nearly her undoing. The smile plastered on the young woman's face slid off her lips when she breezed down the front steps, and she frowned grimly as her gaze circled the abandoned street. What was she going to do if she could not find a man who met her description? Prince Charming thought *he* had trouble, Rozalyn mused resentfully. He had only to find a foot to fit a glass slipper. Rozalyn had to locate an entire body, one with a muscular physique, crisp raven hair and bright, intelligent eyes. *Mon Dieu!* She had embroiled herself in such a wild lie that she feared it would swallow her up.

Her full skirt swished about her as she scampered across the ground. Despite it, she vaulted into the saddle, then sent the stallion racing down the street. Her pale blue eyes scanned the surroundings and her mind buzzed with apprehension as she thundered toward the heart of St. Louis in the hope of finding a man who would suit. She prayed the good Lord would deliver such a man in her hour of need. Her thick lashes fluttered up and her gaze soared skyward as she clung to that thought.

"It *was* a necessary lie," Rozalyn declared self-righteously. "I only told Grand'mère what she needed to hear, to lift her sinking spirits. I could use some divine assistance down here." When the sun hid its head behind a fleeting cloud, casting a shadowed frown on Rozalyn, she let her breath out in a rush. "Oh, very well, I will see to this grisly business myself."

She had found herself in many scrapes because of her impulsiveness, but she had always been able to rescue herself from trouble. This time, however, she had waded in much too far for she had not expected Lenore to force her hand. It would kill the *grande dame* to learn that there was no such man and that her most recent suitor was still entangled in the shrubbery. Jeffrey had been abruptly dismissed, rejected, and anyway he was blond. Rozalyn could not have rounded him up and dragged him to Lenore's doorstep, not even if she'd dyed his hair and padded his waistcoat to make him appear more muscular. The man Rozalyn had conjured up, quite simply, was everything Jeffrey Corday was not.

Why hadn't she promised Lenore that she would take courting seriously in the future instead of spewing forth wild tales about a man she couldn't produce? Rozalyn chided herself as she leaned against the bay stallion's neck, urging him into his swiftest gait. Damnation, if she managed to escape from this catastrophic lie she vowed never to tell another one. But Rozalyn had the sinking feeling that her tall tale would cause disaster.

This is not the time for depressing thoughts, she told herself. Surely she could find a man to fit the description. She would convince him to assist her and she would be willing to pay a king's ransom for his time and trouble. It would be money well spent.

With that encouraging thought whipping through her head, Rozalyn veered toward the main street of St. Louis. She was anxious to begin her search for a man with jet-black hair and a powerful body, not to mention a darkly handsome face that would turn any woman's head. God, was she mad? Rozalyn gulped hard and then silently answered quietly, but unequivocally . . . yes.

Chapter 2

Dominic Baudelair straightened his tailor-made jacket and then eased a shoulder against the supporting post by the mercantile shop. His dark, craggy features wore a pensive frown, his keen gaze inspecting the thriving city that had sprung up on the banks of the Mississippi.

Odd, he mused as he peered toward the wharf where he had spent the past two days. It was inconceivable to Dominic that the city could have changed so drastically the past five years. Because of his isolation in the Rockies it had taken him two full days to adjust to such a swarm of people.

Although St. Louis still retained the sophisticated ways of the French who had settled it, crime ran rampant in the streets. Since Dominic had shed his buckskin garb and donned the trappings of a gentleman he had endured one near brush with disaster. It was most ironic, he mused pensively. He had survived encounters with hostile Indians and had ridden the treacherous waters of the Missouri in a keelboat, but when he'd set foot in so-called civilization he'd very nearly had his scalp split open for the sake of the coins he carried in his pockets.

Thieves and thugs prowled the avenues of St. Louis; Dominic could attest to that fact after his painful encounter. Although the good citizens complained that it was dangerous to venture out after dark, they had yet to organize a regular police force so scores of ruffians swarmed up from the raucous waterfront to prey upon the wealthy French aristocracy. A gentleman took his life in his own hands when he dared to venture out alone at night.

Keen green eyes swept the faces of the stylishly dressed crowd milling around him as Dominic smiled quietly to himself. It was still difficult to adjust to a congregation of so many people. He had been too long in the wilderness. Pushing away from the supporting beam, he ambled down the boardwalk. After his self-imposed isolation, Dominic hungered to appease his urge to hold someone soft and feminine in his arms. Then he intended to turn his mind to his purpose, the one that had brought him from the precipices of the Rockies to the crowded streets of St. Louis.

Aubrey DuBois . . . when the man's face materialized before him a disgusted scowl appeared on Dominic's dark features. For the past several years DuBois and his agents had brought their caravans to the rendezvous at the foot of the mountains. They carted supplies to hard-working trappers, like himself. DuBois' floating version of the company store was welcomed, but not without reserve. The furrier bought up pelts and then transported them back to St. Louis; so, instead of traipsing back to civilization with their furs, the trappers could return to the mountains. It was a seemingly honorable effort on DuBois' part, Dominic thought resentfully.

Actually, although DuBois pretended to send the caravan to save the trappers valuable time, he was far more concerned about himself. Another sour frown etched Dominic's features when he remembered the sky-high prices DuBois demanded for his supplies and he cursed the man. Whiskey sold for thirty cents a gallon in

St. Louis, but DuBois charged three dollars a pint at rendezvous. Coffee and sugar were ten cents a pound, lead was six cents, and gunpowder was seven cents . . . but not at the foot of the Rockies. There, the price was as high as the altitude. DuBois demanded two dollars a pound for each item. One would have thought the man was selling gold instead of coffee and gunpowder!

Other much-needed merchandise was marked up as much as two thousand percent. Dominic considered DuBois' scheme to be nothing more than highway robbery. Aubrey seemed to have some personal grudge against the very men who supplied him with furs.

By the time the trappers sold their fur pelts at low prices and bought their essential supplies at ridiculously high ones, they had very little profit, and they spent their last few coins on the Indian maidens who came to trade at rendezvous. Oftentimes, this was the only opportunity for the men to appease needs that had built up for ten months or more while they were hunting in the mountains.

Because of the hardships DuBois imposed on trappers, Dominic had made the journey to St. Louis. Having refused the low prices offered at Green River, he was determined to find a profitable market. He had collected more than six hundred pelts during the winter and spring of 1836. It seemed foolish to settle for two dollars a pound for beaver pelts when he could sell them in St. Louis for eight dollars a pound. After his business transaction, Dominic had stashed more than fifty thousand dollars in the bank. It angered him to think that many of his friends would have found trapping rewarding if they had accompanied him back to St. Louis where they would have gotten the top price for their fur pelts.

Things are going to change, Dominic promised himself. If DuBois refuses to lower his outrageous prices, I will compete with him.

Dominic dearly loved the mountains. Indeed, although he had inherited his grandparents' estate he chose to leave its vast wealth untouched while he roamed the wilderness. But if Aubrey would not listen to reason, Dominic planned to invest some of his money in a floating trade store that would charge the trappers much lower prices than DuBois did.

Who the hell did Aubrey DuBois think he was? God? Dominic snorted disgustedly. DuBois was a powerful man who controlled one of the largest fur companies in America. He dominated a half-million-square-mile fur empire, but he could be cut down to size. The man had stooped to selling illegal whiskey to the Indian tribes to entice them to trade, and he thought nothing of sending his henchmen to bribe Indian agents, thereby saving himself the necessity of providing the tribes with the supplies government treaties specified when white men bargained with Indians for furs. DuBois had also instructed his henchmen to scare off rival traders with threats and, occasionally, robbery.

In short, DuBois was a scoundrel in every sense of the word . . . and his daughter was an unruly misfit, or so Dominic had heard. He had never met the chit, but the grogshops on the wharf were thick with stories about this wild-hearted termagant who had taken St. Louis by storm. Like father like daughter. Dominic smirked. Why, the entire DuBois clan was probably reprehensible. Rozalyn DuBois had made an infamous name for herself in civilization, just as Aubrey had made a name for himself among the trappers. Although Dominic had seen Aubrey each summer at rendezvous, he had steered clear of the man as much as possible. But now he had come to St. Louis to confront the furrier with his grievances, and he was not leaving until they had come to terms.

Suddenly, Dominic heard hooves thundering toward him. Jolted from his contemplative deliberations, with the agility of a jungle cat, he leaped onto the boardwalk. His condemning glare sought the inconsiderate rider who had very nearly trampled him. That reckless son of a . . . Dominic's disrespectful epithet trailed off when his piercing green eyes skipped over the rearing bay stallion's flailing hooves and came to rest upon its rider.

His astonished gaze locked with a pair of light blue eyes that danced so spiritedly they held Dominic spellbound. They were the strangest color of blue he had ever seen, so pale and sparkling that they unnerved him. Dominic could not drag his glance away from this young woman. A fringe of thick, black lashes surrounded those laughing pools of blue that lit up her exquisitely beautiful face. And she had a dainty upturned nose, wild raven hair, high elegant cheekbones, full sensuous lips, and . . . Dominic felt desire kindle in his veins as his all-consuming gaze swam over the voluptuous curves of her breasts and then resettled on her soft, inviting lips. He blinked bewilderedly but continued to stare at the nymph who had brought her stallion down on all fours. Her steed now pranced in a tight circle while she studied Dominic from all angles. I must be dreaming. I have been too long in isolation, he told himself. Yet, before him was the most gorgeous creature he had ever laid eyes on.

While Dominic was hungrily devouring Rozalyn, she was scrutinizing him for an altogether different purpose, but even while she was reminding herself that her interest in the man was born of desperation, she found herself instantly attracted to this darkly handsome stranger. Tall and raven-haired, he towered above the other passers-by, like a stately pine dwarfing the trees of a forest. When his long, confident strides took him across the street, Rozalyn was impelled to view this male specimen at close range, and she charged toward him before he reached his destination. To her relief, she found him to match the description she had given Lenore almost an hour earlier.

His black velvet waistcoat stretched across his wide shoulders and strained over his powerful chest as he dodged the stallion's prancing hooves. Crisp, wavy hair, as black as midnight, framed his craggy features, and he had prominent cheekbones, an aquiline nose, and a strong jaw. Green eyes that sparkled like priceless emeralds peered back at her from beneath a veil of long, sooty lashes—lashes that any woman would envy. And there was an arrogantly confident look about this swarthy rake, a stamp of wild nobility in his bronzed features, an aura of primitive maleness about him. Rozalyn was suddenly vividly aware of his masculinity.

The sun had darkened his handsome face. The forces of nature had eroded and hardened the laugh lines that strayed from the corners of his vibrant green eyes so that when he smiled deep slashes cut through his cheeks and enhanced his attractive features. His brows were dark and thick, as if to protect his eyes from harsh weather, and his lips were full. . . . Rozalyn suddenly wondered what it would be like to experience the touch of those lips, yet quickly she corraled her wandering thoughts. She was here on an urgent mission and kissing a total stranger was the least of her concerns!

Determined to continue her careful appraisal of this candidate, she allowed her discerning gaze to run the full length of his hard, muscular torso, finding not one flaw to criticize. Indeed, this dashing gentleman was the epitome of masculine grace. Rozalyn found herself attracted to him, simply because it was impossible not to be.

There was not an ounce of flab on his virile body. Although he dressed like a wealthy aristocrat, his physique more closely matched those of the drifters she had seen milling about her father's warehouse. His gaping white shirt exposed the dark matting of hair on his

30

chest and accented his dark tan. Rozalyn caught herself wondering if his torso had been fully exposed to the sun and if his tan covered every inch of his . . . Banish the thought! Again she berated herself for permitting her mind to drift in such an intimate direction. Such wicked musings should never have entered her head. It was shameful and most improper to visualize how a man might look if he were stark naked.

After discarding her sinful musings, Rozalyn gave the man another scrutinizing glance, and when the rake broke into a disarming smile, Rozalyn knew her frantic search had come to an end. This stranger had magnetic charm and dashing good looks. Lenore would be properly impressed by him if Rozalyn carted back to the solarium and introduced him as the light and love of her life.

"You will do nicely," Rozalyn announced with an approving nod. Extending her dainty hand, she silently requested that he climb up behind her on the bay stallion.

Isn't it supposed to be the other way around? Dominic asked himself. He mentally thumbed through the fairy tales he had read after his father had dragged him from the mountains at the age of thirteen and had deposited him on his grandparents' doorstep to receive a proper education in St. Louis. Knights on white chargers were supposed to sweep lovely damsels up into their arms and then tote them off, weren't they? But there he was, approached by a disturbingly attractive lass. Her soft, husky voice turned him into a heap of senseless mush. Her feminine fragrance drifted down to warp his senses.

Well, perhaps this dream was a strange one, but Dominic Baudelair was not a man to question good fortune. His large hand enfolded her small one, and he gave not a second thought to refusing the invitation of joining her in the saddle.

"I will do nicely . . . for what purpose?" Dominic questioned, grinning with roguish anticipation. He

31

stuffed his booted foot in the stirrup and swung up to settle himself behind this mysterious bundle of beauty. This may evolve into a very interesting morning, he thought delightedly. His lovely companion was far more intriguing than the painted doxies who waited in the brothel.

The rich, mellow resonance of his voice, so close to her ear, sent a shudder through Rozalyn, and the feel of his hard torso, fitted against her feminine curves, made her tremble. This is absurd, she told herself. *Mon Dieu*, I don't even know this man! Why does his nearness have such an unsettling effect on me? She had not counted on being so physically attracted to the man she was hauling to Lenore's solarium. That changed everything! She would have to keep a watchful eye on this rogue. There could be nothing between them. This stranger was only a temporary prop who would serve her purpose until she could devise a way to untangle the mess she had made.

When his muscled thighs crowded her hips and his brawny arms enveloped her waist, Rozalyn gulped down her apprehension and gouged the bay stallion in the flanks. The steed made a tight circle, reversed direction, and then lunged forward as if struck by a lightning bolt. Unprepared, Dominic very nearly toppled off the bay's rump. A startled squawk erupted from his lips and he clung to the only stable thing within reach—Rozalyn. Once he had squirmed back to an upright position, he clamped one hand on the pommel of the saddle, the other tightly around her waist. As he molded himself closer, Rozalyn's anxiety rose another notch.

"Damnation, woman, slow this nag down or I will provide a corpse for the mortician. Where the hell are we going in such a rush?"

Rozalyn refused to allow the stallion to break stride, and the amused onlookers parted like the Red Sea, permitting her to thunder off on her urgent mission. She maintained her reckless pace to ensure that the rogue she had picked up off the street would make no advances. It was far easier to have him holding on for dear life than to have him attempting to seduce her, she decided.

"I request a favor from you, *monsieur*," Rozalyn threw over her shoulder, pleased that her tone sounded cool and indifferent though her emotions were in turmoil. "If you will do exactly as I tell you, you will be well paid for your inconvenience."

When the stallion veered around the corner and finally streaked down the open road, Dominic eased his grip on the saddle horn. Grabbing the handful of raven hair that had been slapping him in the face, he tucked it beneath her collar. "You have piqued my curiosity, *chérie*," he murmured. His fingers absently brushed through her lustrous ebony strands, and he inhaled the delicious scent of lavender that clung to this mysterious minx. "I am waiting to hear how I might assist you."

Rozalyn purposely ignored his velvety tone since it had such an unusual effect on her. Obviously, this handsome rake thought she was requesting the use of his body for some seductive tryst. Rozalyn intended to set the matter straight posthaste. "I have been caught up in an unfortunate lie and I ask that you help me untangle it. You are the only one who can aid me in my hour of need."

A puzzled frown plowed Dominic's brow. If this was her idea of an explanation, it left a great deal to be desired. He didn't have the foggiest notion what she was talking about or how a total stranger could solve her problem.

"What sort of lie are we discussing here, or dare I ask?" His voice was laced with suspicion and Rozalyn was quick to detect his skepticism.

Heaving a frustrated sigh, she formulated her thoughts and attempted to list them in logical order. "My grandmother has become ill. It is her last wish to see me properly wed," she explained as she slowed the stallion to a walk. "But unfortunately, I have found no man who suits me, much to Grand'mère's chagrin. She is determined to seal my future before she passes on."

A wry smile slid across Dominic's lips, his gaze wandering over her shapely figure. He would have no complaint about marrying this bewitching beauty and he seriously doubted that any other man would either. Indeed, what was there about her not to like? She was the epitome of grace, the picture of loveliness . . . a bit unconventional perhaps, but distractingly attractive. Realizing that, Dominic wondered if the fault might lie with the lady, rather than with the male population of St. Louis.

"I can only assume by your remark that you are a mite particular," he chortled against the velvety softness of her neck. "And dare I say it . . . fickle?"

Rozalyn took no offense at the truth, but she felt she had just cause for remaining unattached. The men in her life had made her cautious and mistrusting. "I suppose that is an accurate account of the situation," she admitted with a nonchalant shrug. "But that is neither here nor there. When my ailing grandmother had one of her sick spells I was prone to say anything to boost her failing spirits. I confessed that I had recently met the man of my dreams and I described him as tall, dark, and handsome. Never in my worst nightmare did I expect her to demand an immediate introduction to the man who was simply a product of my imagination. Nor did I anticipate that she would shuffle me out the door and insist that I drag my beloved beau back to her within the hour."

Dominic chuckled at the exasperation in the young woman's voice. "Let me guess, *amie*. You climbed onto your steed and raced into town to find someone to fit the description. And *violá*, I was close enough in size and stature to pass as an impostor." As Dominic pressed closer to her curvaceous hips, his breath whispered over the nape of her neck, sending chills through her. "I am flattered. Thank you for noticing me."

"You are welcome," Rozalyn tossed back at him and then gave his crowding legs a subtle nudge. "And you are very astute." Her gaze drifted toward the mansion they were nearing. "I did come in search of a man who fit the description of this imaginary character. To satisfy Grand'mère, you and I must act as if we are very much in love. I ask you to leave the *grande dame* with the opinion that, because of this compelling attraction between us, we will soon be wed. She is very determined when it comes to seeing to my future."

"You wish me to play your doting admirer, your loving suitor? You want me to bestow my affection on you in her presence?" This could well be the easiest task he had ever undertaken and the most pleasurable one. If Rozalyn had seen the outrageous grin on his face she would have been leery of dragging Dominic to Lenore's doorstep, for his mischievous smile indicated that he would carry her request much further than she intended.

"This may well be the most important role you have ever played. You haven't by chance had any experience in the theater, have you?"

"No, I am afraid not," Dominic confessed, stifling another merry chuckle. "But I promise to put forth my best effort."

"I shall count upon you to be convincing." Rozalyn reined the stallion to a halt in front of the sprawling mansion and then gestured for Dominic to climb down. "You can bring a worried old woman a meager amount of serenity. Is that asking so much?"

Dominic reached up and helped Rozalyn down. Allowing her shapely body to brush familiarly against his, he stared down into those sparkling blue eyes that reminded him of sun beams dancing on a clear mountain stream, and his knees went weak. He was drowning in their colorful depths. "If this charade may save grandmother from many sleepless nights, I am only too happy to assist you," he assured her, his voice raspy with desire.

"*Merci.*" Rozalyn smiled beneath his warm regard, but she removed herself from the circle of his arms before the odd sensations trickling down her spine clouded her thoughts. This stranger's nearness aroused her and she could not fathom why. After all, she knew nothing about him.

Sweet merciful heavens! The color seeped from her flushed cheeks when she realized the blunder she had very nearly made. She had come dangerously close to dragging this man into the house without asking his name! Lenore would have seen through her scheme immediately, and would have been furious when she realized Rozalyn had purposely set out to deceive her.

"What is your name, *monsieur?* I cannot expect to convince Grand'mère that we are hopelessly in love if I cannot even call you by your given name." Wide eyes focused on him, pleading with him to supply his name.

Dominic stepped away, and sweeping his top hat from his head, he bowed elegantly before her. Then he struck a sophisticated pose and flashed her a wide smile that displayed even white teeth. "Dominic Baudelair at your service, *mademoiselle.*"

A thoughtful frown settled onto her exquisite features. Baudelair . . . The name echoed at the back of her mind. It was well known in St. Louis, just as DuBois was. But her father had permitted no one to voice it in his home. Although Aubrey refused to discuss the matter, Rozalyn knew he had some kind of grudge against the Baudelair family. He would not approve of her associating with anyone by that name, but Dominic was the only man she'd found who would suit her purposes. Besides, Aubrey would never learn of this incident.

"And by what name shall I address such a lovely vision as you, my beloved?" Dominic inquired, his eyes hungrily devouring her.

"My name is Rozalyn DuBois." She curtsied primly before him. Then, spinning on her heels, she sailed up the marble steps.

"Du—" Dominic swallowed quickly and almost choked. His eyes bulged as he stared incredulously after the saucy chit who was gracefully floating up to the entrance. DuBois! The name rang in his ears like a clanging bell.

The taverns on the waterfront were abuzz with tales of Rozalyn DuBois. So this was the elusive ice maiden, the sought-after heiress of a fur empire. It was rumored that she had cast aside more eligible bachelors than the ocean had fish, and she was said to be as wild and impulsive as the wind. It would take a strong man to bring this feisty hellion to heel. Dominic had listened to a half-dozen men spin yarns about this free-spirited sprite. She traveled in such diverse social circles that neither gentleman nor thief would dare to cross her—out of respect and sometimes out of fear. She had established a rapport with both aristocrats and ruffians. Indeed, it was claimed that the lady was never out of her element. She possessed the uncanny knack of relating to people from all walks of life, to prince or to pauper, and Rozalyn DuBois never had to fear going about St. Louis after dark. For some strange reason even the ruffians held her in high esteem. Rozalyn had become their legendary princess.

Dominic had assumed that this wench's reputation had been built on the foundation of her father's prestige, but now he was beginning to think Rozalyn had earned her own reputation. As a matter of fact, Dominic wasn't sure he would put anything past this lively young beauty. Although she had the face and body of an angel, there was a daring sparkle in her wide blue eyes, a mischievous gleam that warned there was more to the lady than shallow beauty.

The stories about Mademoiselle DuBois were almost too incredible to believe, but Dominic wondered if he had been a mite too skeptical. A sly smile rippled across his lips as he reassessed the vivacious beauty who had thundered down the street and demanded that he climb into the saddle to assist her with an urgent mission. No, it would not be wise to underestimate this lovely chit, he advised himself.

He was beginning to believe the rumor that Rozalyn had challenged one of her overzealous suitors to a duel when he'd attempted to take outrageous privileges with her. No doubt, the lady was as adept at handling firearms as she was in managing the flighty stallion she rode. Rozalyn had been furious with the man, so the story went. She had insisted that they row out to the local field of honor—Bloody Island, a small mound of land in the Mississippi River. Although the young man protested the absurdity of dueling against a woman, Rozalyn forced him to pace into position. She insisted that, since she was the one who had been offended, it was her right to defend her honor. She was not about to have a man fight her duel for her. The gentleman refused to fire against a woman, but Rozalyn had no qualms about facing a man. She was infuriated with this bold rake; who had dared inflict bungling embraces on her after she had made it clear that his touch repulsed her. She was determined to have her revenge. So, to assure him that, lady though she was, she could blow him to smithereens if she had a mind to do so, she blasted the pistol from the man's hand at twenty paces. Needless to say the young man became a believer.

He promptly voiced his apologies and swore never to go near Rozalyn again, especially without a protective suit of armor.

Dominic had suspected that this temperamental hoyden, who was the subject of several other wild tales, was so ugly that men only approached her because of her vast wealth. But this lass who cavorted with ruffians, raced her stallion against worthy opponents and won, and who indulged in many other wild antics, was a far cry from a wealthy witch. It still baffled Dominic that the feisty hellion, whose name was frequently spoken in the grog-shops, and this dazzling nymph were one and the same. Aubrey DuBois may have been a scoundrel, but his daughter was—

"I suppose you have heard that I have a notorious reputation. Perhaps you are apprehensive about associating with me," Rozalyn speculated as she saw conflicting emotions cross his bronzed features.

A low rumble rattled around in his massive chest. "I cannot lie to you, *chérie*. I have not been in the city long, but I have heard about your unusual behavior. Such talk does leave a man to wonder what is in store for him."

When Dominic made no further remark but only stared at her, Rozalyn asked impatiently. "Well, are you coming or not? I have no intention of blowing holes in your expensive jacket if our scheme fails against my grandmother . . . if that is what you are thinking."

"Then, by all means, let us commence with the first act," Dominic chortled as he swaggered up the steps. "I can think of nothing more worthwhile than humoring an old woman. And I can think of nothing more entertaining than carousing with a young woman who has a reputation of being . . . shall we say, a bit unconventional? Especially since she has granted me amnesty," he added with a subtle wink.

A wary frown puckered Rozalyn's brow as this lion of a man strode up beside her. He had an ornery look about him, a twinkle in his emerald eyes that most likely spelled trouble.

"Why are you grinning at me like that?" she demanded to know.

"Like what?" His devilish thoughts were suddenly masked behind a mock-innocent stare.

"You know very well what I mean." Rozalyn sniffed. Warily, she sized up the powerfully built rogue who stood more than a head taller than her five foot-two-inch frame. "I don't know what you are thinking, but let me assure you that I will not tolerate—"

Dominic clamped his lean fingers around her elbow and herded her toward the door. "Come, my love. It is impolite to keep our elders waiting. I do wish to make a good impression on my future grandmother-in-law." He leaned close to Rozalyn as he opened the door, and when he drew her around in front of him, his moist breath skimmed her ear. "I assure you the *grande dame* will be convinced that I am smitten with you. Have no fear of that."

"Thank you for coming to my rescue. I shall be eternally grateful," Rozalyn murmured, no longer fearing that Dominic intended to blurt out the truth and get her into more trouble with the beldame. "I promise you will be well paid for this inconvenience."

"The pleasure will be all mine . . . I'm sure," Dominic insisted. Soft laughter tumbled from his lips while he followed the shapely lass through the foyer.

If Rozalyn had known what lusty thoughts were whirling through his mind, she most certainly would not have granted him amnesty. Indeed, she would have carted Dominic back to the brothel and deposited him on the very spot on which she had found him. Earlier, she had been guilty of visualizing how Dominic might look in the altogether, but his imaginings had progressed far past the stage of visualizing the curvaceous lass before him without a stitch of clothing. Dominic was immersed in a most delightful fantasy that would have made Rozalyn blush deeply had she been able to pluck thoughts from his mind!

Chapter 3

Rozalyn cast her supposed beau a discreet glance as they rounded the corner and stepped into the solarium. There was a fascinating aura about this handsome stranger, a subtle charm that piqued her interest. It wasn't only his dashing good looks and masculine physique that had caught her attention. No, there was something more, some inner driving force, a bold confidence, she perceived in him. He was different, somehow, from the other aristocrats she had met. Rozalyn was reasonably certain that he was not the kind of man who would be content with attending social functions, the sedentary gatherings of the idle rich. He looked as if he could endure a hard day's work and show no signs of fatigue. Perhaps if she and Dominic had met under normal circumstances they could have . . .

Her straying thoughts trailed off when her gaze landed on her grandmother, and she snapped to attention, determined to play her role with convincing sincerity. Lenore was a perceptive old woman who could spot an impostor. They would both have to concentrate on their roles, and she prayed Dominic would uphold his end of the bargain.

"Grand'mère?" Rozalyn slipped her hand from the

crook of Dominic's arm as they moved into Lenore's line of vision, forcing a happy smile onto her face. "This is the man I was telling you about."

Lenore adjusted her spectacles to study the swarthy gentleman who towered over her granddaughter. *Mon Dieu!* A most handsome specimen, Lenore observed. Then she berated herself for doubting that Rozalyn had a new beau, much less one as strikingly attractive as this rake.

"Dominic Baudelair, this is my grandmother, Lenore Rabelais." Rozalyn smiled adoringly at the towering mass of muscle beside her.

Dominic sorted through his repertoire of charming smiles. Presenting the old woman with one of the highest quality, he clasped her hand and pressed a fleeting kiss to her wrist. "Madame Rabelais, it is an honor and privilege to meet you. Rozalyn has told me a great deal about you."

"Nothing insulting, I hope," Lenore wheezed as she flung her granddaughter a teasing grin. "I have been harsh with Rozalyn of late, and I would not be surprised to learn that she had taken my name in vain on several occasions."

"*Au contraire,*" Dominic contradicted, breaking into another disarming smile that melted the beldame. "Rozalyn has the utmost respect for you and she speaks fondly of you." His sinewy arm slid around Rozalyn's waist, drawing her against him, as his lips grazed her delicately arched brow. Then he refocused his attention on the old woman who was drinking in the scene. "She may be a bit feisty at times, but besides her high spirit, she possesses a heart of gold. I adore her for both."

Rozalyn allowed the close physical contact for the sake of the charade, but she could not explain the strange sensation that surged through her when her senses were invaded by the musky scent of him. You are only caught up in your role, she told herself, determined to stand her ground when strong, confident hands wandered over her ribs to settle familiarly on her waist. These hands have mapped the contours of a woman's body on numerous occasions, Rozalyn thought resentfully, even as she forced a smitten smile and laid her head against Dominic's sturdy shoulder.

Novice he was not! He seemed at ease touching her, and Rozalyn had the sneaking suspicion this rogue intended to portray her doting beau even more convincingly than she had requested. Unfortunately, she was in a ticklish situation. If she attempted to put him in his place in her usual manner, Lenore would know this was a deceitful charade.

Now she knew why he'd been grinning so smugly when he'd pranced up the steps. Sidling closer, Rozalyn bided her time until she could retaliate suitably.

"Isn't Dominic everything I said he was, Grand'mère?" she purred. Her sooty lashes fluttered up to peer into his handsome features, certain that beneath his charming exterior lurked a snake. No wonder he was so charming since he was a serpent.

When his adventurous hand strayed across her hip to sketch the curve of her derièrre, Rozalyn inwardly flinched and gritted her teeth. How she would have loved to slap him silly! But if she dared, her grandmother would swear she had lost her mind. The old woman didn't have any idea what was going on behind Rozalyn's back. Her view of it was blocked and Dominic was taking full advantage of that fact.

Rozalyn silently fumed as Dominic's fingertips splayed across her buttocks. Two could play his game.

"Dominic does seem to be everything I hoped you would find in a man." Lenore watched the two lovebirds hover close, seemingly enamored of each other.

"He is far more than I expected and I am most fortunate," Rozalyn insisted. A sticky sweet smile glazed her lips. She was most thankful her riding habit reached to the floor so Lenore could not see her grind the heel of her riding boot into Dominic's foot. "I am very happy, Grand'mère . . ." She tilted her face as if to offer Dominic her waiting lips.

"And so am I." Dominic bit back a grimace when the mischievous imp's boot heel mashed his foot, but he recovered in time to note the invitation of her soft, sweet mouth.

But he learned quickly that Rozalyn did not mean to offer pleasure, only to inflict more pain. As his mouth slanted across hers, she bit into his lower lip, silently daring him to yelp in pain and spoil her charade. Dominic took it like a man, however, and he quietly, patiently, waited to get even.

When he lifted his raven head, Rozalyn's eyes were glittering with deviltry. It was all he could do to prevent clamping his fingers around her swanlike neck and shaking the stuffing out of her.

Naturally, Lenore was not aware of Dominic's bold caresses or of Rozalyn's painful retaliations. She did not know how difficult it was for Dominic to remain silent when he experienced a kiss that was, in actuality, a vicious bite—the first such in his vast experience of women. Lenore was warmed by the touching scene, and her spirits soared with pleasure. At last Rozalyn had met her match. Dominic Baudelair was everything Lenore had wanted for Rozalyn, and it was obvious her grand-daughter adored the man or she would not have openly invited his kiss. Never had Lenore seen Rozalyn pay such adoring attention to a suitor.

"You cannot know how pleased I am to see that the two of you are so fond of each other." Lenore beamed at the couple before her, living proof that looks could some-times be deceiving. "You cannot know how long I have prayed for this day."

"And I dream of the day I can make Rozalyn my own," Dominic murmured. His lips brushed against her neck and then he nibbled at her ear, just as mercilessly as she had bitten his lip.

Rozalyn did not dare pull away, but she swore her earlobe would be completely chewed in two if Dominic persisted. Reaching up to pull a hairpin from her shining mass of raven curls, Rozalyn tucked the makeshift weapon in her hand. Inconspicuously, she brought it around behind Dominic, a spiteful smile rippling across her lips as she anticipated her counter tactic. She stabbed the rake in the back and watched him wince uncomfortably at the prick of her jeweled hairpin.

"You do plan to wed? And soon?" Lenore straightened in her wheelchair, her eyes lighting up like candelabra.

"Bien entendu," Rozalyn assured the beldame. After extracting the pin from his spine, she jabbed Dominic between the shoulder blades.

"The sooner the better." Dominic smiled through gritted teeth and then sucked in his breath when the little imp situated the hairpin between his ribs. Damn, Rozalyn had certainly made her point. "Forgive my boldness, madame, but I cannot wait to have Rozalyn all to myself. . . ." He did not explain for what purpose. Indeed, the old woman would have been shocked to learn that it was torture he had in mind, not romance.

That will be the day! Rozalyn thought smugly. Dominic deserved exactly what she had given him, and she was not about to allow him the chance to seek vengeance. After all, if he had behaved himself she would not have found it necessary to inflict pain on his person. The lout!

"It would certainly seem so," Lenore observed with a smile. "The two of you appear to be anxious to repeat the vows and even more anxious to . . ." Her voice trailed off, leaving the insinuation in the air.

"Oui, madame, there is a compelling attraction between us," Dominic insisted, baffled by his overwhelming urge to strangle the ornery chit and then kiss her senseless. How could he be stung by two contradicting emotions in the same moment? "I fear I cannot resist your granddaughter. She is like no one I have ever known."

"That is a fact." Lenore sniffed. She cast Rozalyn a curious frown, wondering if the high-spirited sprite could give up her wild ways . . . permanently . . . even for such a man as this.

Desire overruled Dominic's need for revenge when his eyes locked with dancing pools of blue. Like a moth flying into a flame, knowing full well he would get his wings singed for taking unfair advantage, Dominic lowered his head to capture her lips. His kiss devoured and yet savored the sweet taste of her.

Shock waves of pleasure flooded over Rozalyn, astonishing her. She had expected flames of indignation to leap through her when he bent her into the hard contours of his body, but they did not. Instead, she experienced a sensation comparable to nothing in her somewhat limited experience. Jeffrey Corday had repulsed her with his forceful embrace, but this handsome stranger had breached her defenses. The manly scent of him wrapped itself around her senses as her traitorous body melted into his, reveling in the pleasure he wove about her like a warm, protective cocoon.

Rozalyn had been kissed, but never like this! Dominic was teaching her things she had never known about kissing, things that intrigued her. His questing tongue traced her lips and then probed deeper, but only for an instant. He was tempting her, silently assuring her that she was only being offered a foretaste of pleasure. Rozalyn had only begun to discover the difference between a kiss and a *kiss.*

Strong, capable arms cradled her, and his warm lips continued to mate sensuously with hers, leaving her knees weak from his devastatingly tender assault. His black magic was more potent than any forceful embrace. Dominic Baudelair could make her feel as if they were making love though they shared no more than a kiss in broad daylight with the beldame as an audience.

Rozalyn was no fool. Naïve? Well, perhaps a little, she conceded. But she did know when she had been skillfully seduced. Dominic was more man than she could handle.

Dominic dragged his lips from hers and then brushed a feathery kiss across her flushed cheek, leaving her with a warm, giddy sensation trickling down her spine. *"Pardonnez-moi, madame,"* he apologized, his voice heavy with disturbed desire. "I seem to have forgotten myself." Good God! Had he been so long without a woman that the feel of this soft, delicious nymph had driven him to distraction? The kiss had served only to whet his appetite, creating a monstrous craving that he was hard pressed to ignore. This raven-haired minx had a strange effect on him. A kiss and a few caresses set off a chain reaction in his male body, and the far-reaching side effects of their embrace had set every nerve and muscle to tingling. "As I have explained, I seem to have tremendous difficulty resisting your lovely granddaughter." A sheepish smile pursed his lips as he ran his knuckles over Rozalyn's delicate jaw and surveyed her bewildered expression. "Were we to wed tomorrow, I am not certain it would be soon enough to satisfy me."

The delighted grin that crinkled Lenore's aged features was bright enough to lead a wayward traveler through a blizzard, and there was an unusual glow in Rozalyn's eyes, a flicker that Lenore had never detected in them until this moment. Usually, boredom was etched on Rozalyn's features when she was in the company of one of her suitors, but not today. It was as if the poor child had been struck by a bolt of lightning. Dominic's kiss seemed to be as intoxicating as wine to her granddaughter.

Rozalyn DuBois, the free-spirited butterfly, had finally lighted on a man who seemed capable of matching her quick temper and her zest for living. Lenore was beside herself with happiness. She felt better than she had in years. Rozalyn and Dominic had done wonders for her spirit. They had turned her dreary world around and now she was delighted to be a part of it once again.

"If there can be no wedding tomorrow we will at least celebrate the upcoming, joyous event with an engagement party. I want the two of you to come to supper on Friday," Lenore insisted enthusiastically. "I will invite a few of our friends." She clasped her hands together and said delightedly, "Ah, I have so many arrangements to make for the celebration."

"But, Grand'mère," Rozalyn gasped, her wide blue eyes flying to the beaming old woman who suddenly appeared ten years younger, "that is quite impossible!" Rozalyn didn't trust herself to spend an entire evening with Dominic, not after the damage he had inflicted on her in the span of thirty minutes. There was no telling what he might do! "Dominic is a very busy man and I could not ask him to—"

"I am never too busy to enjoy the *grande dame's* delightful company," he cut in, bringing quick death to Rozalyn's hasty excuse. "We will be happy to join you."

Biting back a wicked smile, he glanced around to detect the dismayed expression that momentarily crossed Rozalyn's bewitching features. Let the little spitfire steam and stew, he thought devilishly. She brewed up this lie and it serves her right to be simmering in her own juice. He was thoroughly enjoying this escapade. He would gladly spend an evening with this raven-haired beauty at his side, doting over him . . . even if it was just an act. If it were not for Lenore, Dominic knew Rozalyn would never consent to keep company with him, not after he had taken advantage of her blind side.

Rozalyn DuBois fascinated him, nonetheless. He dearly loved challenges. Indeed, he lived for them. That was why he chose to hunt and trap in the wilderness instead of living on the wealth his grandparents had accumulated. Every day in the wilds was a daring adventure. Although courting this ebony-haired hellcat would not be as difficult as confronting an unfriendly tribe of Blackfeet or tangling with a grizzly, it would serve as an amusing pastime, he told himself.

"Then I shall expect you at seven on Friday," Lenore declared. Wheeling her chair around, she rolled across the solarium, dodging the maze of potted plants and amazing Rozalyn with her sudden display of strength and agility. "I have not hosted a dinner party in years, but now I have the perfect reason to do so."

"Grand'mère!" Rozalyn wailed, distressed that her white lie had snowballed into catastrophe. "You are not well enough to entertain a houseful of guests . . . are you?" A curious frown knitted Rozalyn's brow. My, but Lenore's burst of energy was astonishing. The previous hour she had voiced doubts that she would survive the day. Now the beldame looked as if she could challenge an opponent to a wheelchair race and emerge the victor.

"I feel better than I have in weeks," Lenore insisted exuberantly. "The distraction will be good for me. I would much prefer to die from overexertion than boredom." It was all she could do to keep from catapulting herself from the chair and dashing into the foyer. "Now where is that confounded servant? He is never around when I need him. Hawthorne! *Venez ici, tout de suite!*"

Lenore's miraculous recovery was soon forgotten when the old woman sailed out of the room to summon her servant and give instructions for the dinner party. Despair crowded in on Rozalyn from all sides. Sweet mercy! How was she to endure a full evening with a man who seemed to have as many arms as an octopus. Why, it was heroic to tolerate Dominic for thirty minutes! How could she endure him for an evening? Grumbling over her disastrous luck, Rozalyn stormed toward the door. Dominic followed in her wake, grinning like a weasel about to make a meal of a delicious dove.

Chapter 4

Once they were out of earshot, Rozalyn let loose with both barrels. "Now see what you've done," she snapped furiously. "This ridiculous engagement party will kill her. Why couldn't you have left well enough alone? Isn't it enough that you took unfair advantage of me in her presence? What kind of man are you? How dare you fondle me right under Grand'mère's nose!"

Her voice was becoming higher and wilder by the second so Dominic clamped his hand over her mouth to shush her before she brught the servants to the stoop to investigate the cause of her ravings.

"You told me to sound convincing," Dominic reminded her, his tone laced with wicked amusement. "I upheld my end of the bargain and now you must uphold yours. You promised that I would be compensated for my time and trouble and I intend to hold you to that vow, *chérie.*"

The devilish grin on his sensuous lips evoked a suspicious frown from Rozalyn. She had the sinking feeling that Dominic lacked moral fiber and he anticipated something other than gold coin in payment for services rendered. He was crazed if he thought she would submit to some outlandish request.

When his hand dropped away from her mouth, Rozalyn flung him an icy glare, but Dominic showed no sign of frostbite, much to her dismay. He merely shrugged and flicked an imaginary fleck of lint from the sleeve of his waistcoat.

"Well, what price do you demand?" Rozalyn asked tersely. "I will decide if it is reasonable compensation. And once you have escorted me to Grand'mère's dinner party, we will associate no more."

"No?" One thick brow tilted to a taunting angle. "And how will you explain that distressing news to the *grande dame?* You saw for yourself that the possibility of seeing you wed took ten years off her life. Your disappointing announcement will have her teetering with one foot in the grave."

A deliciously wicked grin rippled across Rozalyn's lips as she raked Dominic with a scornful glance. "You know of my infamous reputation, *monsieur.* It would be a shame if you met with a fatal accident on the eve of our wedding. My grandmother would be heartbroken by the news, but she would be too busy consoling her bereaved granddaughter to think of herself."

It was Dominic's turn to eye this feisty chit warily. He could have sworn by the devilish gleam in her eyes that she would derive sinful pleasure from disposing of him. He had heard enough about Rozalyn DuBois to know that it was suicidal to underestimate her. The only way to counteract her threat was to turn the tables on her, and he intended to do just that. Without bothering to respond, he promptly spun about and marched back up the steps to Lenore Rabelais' manor.

"What do you think you're doing?" Rozalyn questioned.

"I'm going to inform your grandmother that you and I are strangers and that you dreamed up this scheme to deceive her," he threw over his shoulder.

Rozalyn made a face at his departing back, muttered several disrespectful epithets, and then heaved a defeated sigh. "Very well, Dominic, it seems my hands are tied. You leave me no choice but to become a victim of blackmail."

Instantly, Dominic reversed direction and, beaming with self-satisfaction, strutted down the steps like a haughty peacock out for a morning stroll. Rozalyn was itching to pluck out his tail feathers, one by one. The scoundrel! He had incredible nerve. Damn him for backing her into a corner and stalking about her like a mountain lion toying with his prey.

"What is it you expect for playing my beloved beau?" she queried, her tone acrid with anger. "And do try to be reasonable . . . if that is possible for a man like you."

A sly smile slid across his full lips, and cupping her chin in his hand, he brought it down a notch. "My dear Rozalyn, I am not in a position that dictates compromise. You are." He chuckled at her exaggerated pout. "I will inform you of the sort of payment that will satisfy me and you will reimburse me for my trouble. If you don't, I will march back to Madame Rabelais and expose you for the liar you are. And that, *amie*, will break the old woman's heart."

"You, sir, are no gentleman!" Rozalyn hissed venomously, struggling not to scream at him.

"Nor did I claim to be," Dominic calmly reminded her. "If that was one of your qualifications you should have inquired about the matter before you hauled me up behind you and carted me to your grandmother's doorstep. Really, *amie*, you are much too impulsive to be so particular."

Her eyes burned with scorching blue flames. "Oh, how I would love to—"

"Temper, temper," Dominic scolded in an infuriatingly mocking tone.

Temper be damned! Rozalyn bared her claws and stalked toward him, but he flung up a hand to forestall her. Nodding his raven head toward the front door, he silently reminded Rozalyn that he was still within shouting distance of Lenore. When Rozalyn begrudgingly retracted her claws, Dominic arrogantly drew himself up in front of her. Then, clasping his hands behind him, he addressed her with a taunting smile. "Now, love, will you pay me for my time and trouble or shall I run and tattle to Grand'mère?"

Rozalyn clenched her fists in the folds of her skirt. Oh, how she itched to put this conniving rascal in his place. But Dominic, scoundrel that he was, had backed her into a corner, leaving her no way to retreat. How she detested being outmaneuvered, especially by a man. It infuriated her to watch him gloat over her predicament. He was taking pleasure at *her* expense and Rozalyn deeply resented it.

"I will pay cash for my mistake in summoning your assistance," she grumbled, fishing into her purse to retrieve sufficient funds.

Instantly, Dominic's long, lean fingers folded around her wrist to restrain her, and an ornery smile dangled from one corner of his mouth. "I cannot be bought with cold, hard cash, my dear." Meeting her perturbed glare, he told her bluntly, "It is *you* I want and I will settle for nothing less."

Rozalyn had been afraid he was going to say something like that. The blackguard. Her temper came to a boil and her eyes blazed up like a forest fire. Yanking her hand from his grasp, she fumed. "Surely you don't think I will become your human sacrifice. If you do, you are utterly mad!"

Again her voice rose until she was all but shouting into his grinning face. Dominic pressed his index finger to her pouting lips before she drew a crowd. "There must be a first time in every woman's life. I see no reason why this shouldn't be it. That seems fair compensation for portraying your devoted lackey. And for your information, *chérie*, I am as sane as you are," he assured her with a smug smile.

"That has yet to be determined." Rozalyn glared daggers at his broad chest. "If you think for one minute I will allow myself to be hornswoggled into your bed to serve your lusty needs, you'd better think again, Dominic Baudelair. I want nothing to do with you!"

"Then you did not enjoy our previous embrace?" His tone implied that he would not believe her if she responded negatively, not after the way she had melted in his arms. "Come now, Rozalyn. Be honest with yourself." She could deny the attraction to appease her stubborn pride, but Dominic had known the moment his lips met hers that a spark of passion had leaped between them.

"I would have vehemently protested your kisses and bold caresses if Grand'mère had not been sitting there watching us," she declared. "Regardless of your high opinion of yourself, you are not God's gift to women. Indeed, you have the personality of a snake!"

Without preamble, Dominic pulled her into his arms, intent on proving her a liar. His mouth swooped down on hers, stealing her breath and the objection she most certainly would have voiced.

"The *grande dame* is watching us from the window," he whispered. "Be convincing, Roz. We don't want Lenore to see us having a lover's spat on her front lawn."

Rozalyn melted against him like snow thawed by a campfire, her arms curling instinctively about his broad shoulders, and before she was aware of what she was doing she was kissing him back! *Mon Dieu*. What was the matter with her? She and Dominic had been in the middle of a trenchant argument. She had only to *pretend* that she enjoyed his fiery kiss. But no, the flame of anger had been transformed into passion, and she'd instantly warmed to this roué's touch. Rozalyn wondered if she actually felt something for him. That is impossible, she told herself. She had just met Dominic and she wasn't even sure she liked him.

As his arms tightened about her, pulling her full length against his muscular frame, his blazing kiss ebbed, and lips as gentle as the summer wind whispered over hers, eliciting an unwilling response. He had abandoned forcefulness for tender seduction. His probing tongue traced the inner softness of her lips and then intruded into the sweet darkness of her mouth. Tiny shards of pleasure tingled beneath her skin as Dominic's masculine body moved sensuously against her, allowing her to feel the hungry need she'd aroused in him.

A knot of desire uncoiled deep inside Rozalyn, but the sensation baffled her. She chastised herself for surrendering so easily to his embrace when she knew full well what he expected in return for portraying her beau.

When Dominic abruptly broke their kiss, Rozalyn blinked bewilderedly, and when he withdrew his supporting arms, she had to regain her equilibrium. My, but his kisses had a strange effect on her.

"I will be expecting you to come to me tonight, *petite nymphe*," he murmured, his flaming emerald eyes holding her hostage. "I am staying at my grandparents' estate. I will send a coach for you."

Rozalyn could not seem to take her eyes off his bronzed face. He held her captive with his probing gaze, forcing her to consent, though her mind was screaming *no*. Had she lost what little sense she had been born with? She couldn't traipse off to a stranger's home, knowing full well what he expected of her. Yet could she refuse when this scoundrel would go straight to Lenore and spill the truth?

A thoughtful frown knitted Rozalyn's brow while she studied the smile lines that crinkled his tanned features and considered her alternatives. Despite a long line of suitors she had kept her innocence intact by using her wits, she reminded herself. There were ways to deal with men who used women for their lusty purposes. She would somehow maneuver this rakehell into agreeing to escort her to her grandmother's party. All she had to do was give the matter serious consideration. She would approach it calmly and rationally, but once she had maneuvered Dominic into doing *her* bidding she was going to have him strung up on the tallest tree in St. Louis. He deserved no better for treating her so badly. It would be interesting to see just how arrogant Dominic Baudelair would be when his neck was stretched out like a giraffe's.

"I will await your carriage," she promised, determined not to part on a sour note since she desperately needed his assistance.

"Shall we say eight o'clock?" Dominic curled his index finger beneath her chin, tilting her face to his and noting the flareup of mischief in those mystical blue eyes. She was scheming, he realized. What prank did this fiery beauty have in store for him? *You will find out soon enough,* he warned himself. He made a mental note to be prepared for whatever deviltry this witch was brewing.

"Eight it is," she confirmed. Her curious gaze drifted to the window above them. Had her grandmother truly been spying on them or had Dominic manipulated her into his arms like a spider spinning a treacherous web around a defenseless fly?

His face brightened with mischievous glee when he noticed where her eyes had strayed. Chuckling, Dominic pivoted away to swagger down the street. "I lied," he confessed in an unrepentant tone. "The beldame wasn't really watching us. I wanted one last kiss to sustain me until tonight."

Furious red splashed across Rozalyn's cheeks, and she glanced hurriedly about in search of some weapon to hurl at the cunning Dominic, but she found nothing, not even a rock. Muttering under her breath, she mounted her stallion and flew down the street, silently listing the flaws in Dominic's character—and there are plenty of them, she thought.

Dominic dived sideways as Rozalyn thundered past, not about to risk having hoofprints on his back. He figured only a fool would underestimate Rozalyn DuBois. After she had galloped away, her skirt billowing in the wind, her raven hair trailing behind her, Dominic rolled to his feet. Snickering, he watched the tempestuous Rozalyn disappear around the corner. He had stumbled upon a most unusual woman, the like of which he had never known. This lovely hoyden had blown into his life like a misdirected whirlwind, sweeping him into the eye of a storm.

Yet this blue-eyed spitfire fascinated him. She was a strange concoction—part desirable woman, part temperamental child. The freshness of youth sparkled in her sky-blue eyes, and her smiles radiated like the sun. Still, Rozalyn DuBois was a contradiction of everything he had come to anticipate in a woman. She was a curious enigma. The fairer sex had always come willingly into his arms, and often uninvited. But not Rozalyn. She was fighting her attraction to him, stubbornly, defiantly. What was she so afraid of? Why was she so defensive? Dominic had expected to find a cold, impassive maid in his arms after the rumors he had heard. But he had discovered that beneath her heavy coat of armor lurked a warm, passionate woman. He knew he would not be satisfied until they had shared far more than a kiss.

A grin of roguish anticipation rippled across his lips. Tonight he would sample that gorgeous vixen's charms.

After he had played the charade for Lenore he might even . . . Dominic shook away such thoughts. He would let tomorrow take care of itself. After all, tonight was foremost in his mind. Once he had shared intimate moments with this young woman from the St. Louis' *debutante,* he might become bored with her. Few women held his interest for any length of time. He had been born under a wandering star and he wanted no entangling bonds to trip him up. He was an adventurer who thrived in the wild. He had an aversion to being hobbled by a female. Still, Rozalyn had piqued his curiosity, she was a challenge. Once he had satisfied his curiosity he would be on his merry way.

Dominic broke stride and very nearly stumbled over his own feet, when a troubled thought shot through his mind, sending his soaring spirits plunging. Christ, he had thought himself so clever in his dealings with Rozalyn yet he'd failed to realize he had waded in over his head. He had been so distracted by her beauty that he had neglected to consider that he was not dealing with just any woman. How could he force Rozalyn into his bed when he had important business with Aubrey DuBois? The last thing he needed was to have Rozalyn running to her father and claiming that he'd made improper advances. Then he wouldn't be able to persuade Aubrey to lower his prices.

Confound it, that changed everything! Dominic had backed this lovely sprite into a corner, but he had failed to notice that he had crowded himself into one. Why the devil had he consented to assist her in this harebrained scheme? Because the beast within him had been drawn to her curvaceous body and flawless face. Fool! Dominic berated himself. How the devil was he going to worm his way out of this mess without alienating Rozalyn? Dammit, he needed her assistance as much as she needed his.

Grappling with these disturbing thoughts, Dominic aimed himself toward the Baudelair estate, intending to spend the afternoon considering the repercussions of dallying with this raven-haired she-cat. He was playing with fire, and if he wasn't careful, he'd get burned. Like it or not, he would have to handle this blue-eyed hellion like fragile crystal. That had never been his way in the past, but circumstances were forcing him to turn over a new leaf in his dealings with women—Rozalyn in particular. She stood squarely between him and Aubrey DuBois. However, he could not allow her to know that, for she would use that knowledge as a weapon. And, judging by what Dominic had learned about this wily vixen in the taverns on the wharf, Rozalyn DuBois needed no more weapons at her disposal.

Wouldn't it be ironic if she fell in love with him and then aided him in his dealings with Aubrey? Dominic began to consider the possibility. If he set out to charm this minx, her attachment to him would make her vulnerable. Then she would do exactly as he commanded. It would serve such a free-spirited lass right to find herself infatuated after she'd left a string of broken hearts in her wake. A wry smile slanted across Dominic's lips. He would play the perfect gentleman, cater to Rozalyn, dote over her without wallowing at her feet. He would woo her, become her champion in her hour of need. Then she would return the favor without realizing that Dominic had carefully sought to obtain her allegiance.

Grinning in satisfaction, he veered toward his estate, intent on planning his encounter with Rozalyn. Before I finish with that wildcat I will have her purring like a kitten, he promised himself. I will do so for an important purpose, Dominic rationalized when his conscience flared. He was the spokesman for the hunters and trappers. Their livelihood depended on him. So, on the wings of self-righteousness, Dominic strode up the steps of the huge stone manor. Quietly, he shut the door behind him, then he began to calculate his tactics for the upcoming evening.

Rozalyn had very nearly worn a path in the plush carpet of her boudoir with her frustrated pacing. Her good fortune in finding a rake to fit her description of the man of her dreams had, in actuality, been a stroke of rotten luck. If Dominic Baudelair had an ounce of decency he would never had insisted that she compromise her virtue in payment for his assistance. The longer she paced, the more furious she became.

How could she pretend to be civil to Dominic when she must constantly fight the urge to pound him flat and float him down the Mississippi? The cad! How dare he suggest that she spread herself beneath him to compensate for his time and trouble. How dare he threaten to expose her to her grandmother.

He wasn't dealing with some simple-minded twit who could be manipulated and who would not think to retaliate when he became familiar with her right under Lenore's nose. This rogue will not outmaneuver me, Rozalyn thought belligerently. She was strong willed and she had a temper. She was not about to allow a conniving rake to twist her around his little finger.

She crossed her arms beneath her breasts and impatiently tapped her foot, waiting for a scheme to hatch in her mind. There had to be a way out of this mess. If she didn't panic, an idea would eventually come to her. This wasn't the first time she had found herself in a scrape, she calmly reminded herself. She must somehow win Dominic's affection, keep him dangling like a puppet on a string until the engagement party was over. Then she could tell him exactly what she thought of him and of his skullduggery. After wishing him a one-way trip to hell, she would then run to her grandmother and play the betrayed, heartbroken lover. Lenore would think no less of her granddaughter if the *dis*engagement was presented as Dominic's idea.

But how was she to keep Dominic at arm's length when he approached her like cavalry responding to a bugle call? Dominic Baudelair was as bold as he was handsome, and it was obvious that what he wanted from a woman he took. And what he wanted from her had nothing to do with love or affection. Not that she gave a fig whether or not he fell in love with her . . . the possibility lingered in her mind and a deliciously mischievous smile caught the corners of Rozalyn's mouth, lifting them upward. That was the answer! If Dominic found himself attracted to her, that attraction might evolve into affection. He would be more considerate of her feelings then, wouldn't he? She would love to have that lion of a man eating out of the palm of her hand instead of licking his lips in anticipation of devouring her. But Rozalyn was not in the habit of manipulating others to achieve the ends she desired. She had always been bold and direct, not underhanded and scheming, so her conscience bothered her. But I am not dealing with the usual situation or the normal breed of man, she hastily reminded herself.

As Rozalyn peeled off her clothes and sank down into the tub, she let her thoughts flow, contemplating her plan of action. When Dominic came at her, hungry to satisfy the beast within him, she would confess that she had felt some warm emotion when they'd first kissed. She would ask to become better acquainted with him before rushing into a situation that might leave permanent scars on her tender, innocent heart.

That should do it, Rozalyn thought smugly. Surely Dominic had been born with a smidgeon of conscience. He wouldn't stoop so low as to force himself upon her when all she asked was a little time to allow her affection for him to blossom. She would woo him as she had no other man, making him fall in love with her, giving him no reason to doubt her sincerity. And if her plot was successful, perhaps she would consider a career in the theater. Rozalyn giggled to herself. Indeed, to smile and bat her big blue eyes at Dominic would require a magnificent pepformance. Rozalyn would prefer to shake the man until his teeth rattled. After all, he deserves it, she thought huffily. She ignored the tiny voice of conscience that was berating her for attempting to manipulate this man for her own selfish purposes. She was only doing what had to be done.

Let Dominic think it had been love at first sight, if he believed in such sentimental notions. Let him think that, in time, she would surrender to his embrace without protest. Let him think she might offer him what no other man had claimed. He would soon realize there was one woman on earth who refused to be dominated by a man.

Satisfied with her counter tactics, Rozalyn scrubbed her face until it shined. Then she selected the most provocative gown she owned. A sly smile pursed her lips when she wormed into a pink silk affair with a plunging neckline, and she peered at her reflection in the mirror. This will make the rake sit up and take notice, she thought wickedly. Once she had his attention, she would set her plan in motion. Carefully, she pinned her ebony strands on top of her head, to create a sophisticated appearance, but she let a few ringlets dangle about her oval face. She wanted to retain some appearance of youth and innocence, just to remind Dominic that she was at least ten years his junior.

After her painstaking preparations, Rozalyn spun away from the mirror. If this scheme failed to keep that bold rogue in his place, perhaps she would beg the assistance of some of her rough-edged friends. Rozalyn snickered spitefully at the thought of several ruffians leaping out of the shadows to pound some manners into Dominic. If he couldn't understand tact, maybe he would respond to forceful persuasion.

As was the custom in the DuBois mansion, Rozalyn was on her way out for the evening when Aubrey was returning from another long day at the warehouse. Although Aubrey had only been home two weeks since his yearly journey to the rendezvous, he had spent not even an hour with his daughter. He traveled to the foot of the Rockies each summer to trade with trappers, and Rozalyn had grown accustomed to his uneventful homecomings. She no longer anticipated a cheerful greeting from her father. She was like a stick of furniture he veered around. Aubrey had never paid attention to her.

When she descended the steps, garbed in her stunning gown, Aubrey did, however, notice that he was not the only person in the foyer, much to Rozalyn's surprise. When he spoke to her they never truly communicated. Aubrey just made a few inconsequential comments and asked some innocuous questions so he would not have to listen carefully to her responses.

"Where are you off to this evening?" Aubrey veered toward the study to pour himself a tall drink, forcing Rozalyn to follow him if she intended to have her answer heard.

A disappointed frown clouded her delicate features, for she realized Lenore was absolutely right about Aubrey. He made only meager attempts to be social to his daughter, as if she were no more than an obligation. Aubrey pretended an interest in her, but he was not concerned enough to await her reply before he ambled away. Rozalyn doubted that he even listened when she supplied an answer.

Determined to test that theory, she swept into the elaborately decorated study where her father spent his evenings, laboring over his ledgers. "I have a most exciting evening planned," she gushed as she threw back the drapes and peered out into the darkness. "I thought I would take a drive along the wharf and then set your warehouse afire."

"That's nice," Aubrey mumbled stoically as he plopped down at his massive desk. After rummaging through a drawer, he located his ledgers. "Try to be home at a reasonable hour. The streets are not safe after dark these days."

What did he care if she were brutally assaulted and left in an unconscious heap in an alleyway? Aubrey didn't even know she existed. He really *didn't* give a fig what she said or where she went. It was a crushing blow to Rozalyn's pride that her father would not even spare her five minutes of his precious time. What had she done to deserve such disinterest?

Hurt by his indifference, she ambled out of the study without saying farewell. Why should she? Aubrey was paying no attention. He'd already buried his nose in his ledgers and had blocked out the rest of the world.

Rozalyn burst through the front door and then planted herself on the bench that sat in a corner of the porch that stretched across the front of their home. Tears triggered by wounded pride swam in her eyes, but Rozalyn refused to release them. She had spent the past nine years braving her father's lack of concern so why should she fall to pieces tonight? He didn't care about her. If she faded into the woodwork, never to reappear, he probably wouldn't even notice she was gone.

A pensive frown puckered her brow. Was it because of Aubrey's cool indifference that she played her mischievous pranks? Did she hope to make him notice her? Most likely, Rozalyn decided as she considered the past few years of her life. She had led a boisterous existence: chased her own rainbows, followed her every whim, and cavorted with lively characters whose way of life varied greatly from hers. Yet she had not gained her father's attention. Although she had failed to do so, she had learned a valuable lesson. Money does not make the man nor credit him with morals. She had met many delightful characters in the streets. Although most of them were desperate for coin, by and large they retained a certain amount of goodness and conscience. They focused upon survival, and Rozalyn often helped those who were less fortunate. Then, too, she spent many a night listening to the tales and joining in the adventures of the raucous waterfront crowd.

Indeed, her association with so-called ruffians had earned her a scandalous reputation in the sophisticated social circle of the French aristocracy. But her friendships with the earthy men of the streets were more gratifying than her association with the shallow gentility.

Dismissing these thoughts, Rozalyn pricked her ears at the sound of an approaching carriage. She had important matters to attend, she reminded herself. Gracefully she descended the steps to accept the groom's supporting arm. Then, breathing a thankful sigh that Dominic had remained at his estate, Rozalyn settled herself on the tufted seat. Staring at the opposite wall, she concentrated on her purpose as the carriage rumbled down the street. She had to tame this lusty beast who had suggested they become intimate since they were supposedly head over heels in love with each other.

She must *pretend* to be enamored of this tall, dark, ruggedly handsome cavalier, though he could never truly steal her heart, especially after he had attempted to blackmail her into his bed. If he were a noble gentleman he would expect nothing in return for aiding a damsel in distress. But Dominic Baudelair is a philanderer, she thought resentfully. She would flirt with him and string him along for a while, but she would not allow herself to be seduced. Someday the right man would come along, and Rozalyn would offer him all the love she had to give, the love she had kept bottled up inside her all these years. Until that day came she was not going to experiment with passion—and especially not with Dominic. She wanted no part of him. She'd had enough trouble keeping his straying hands corraled in front of her grandmother. She couldn't even imagine what he might do while they were alone. . . .

Rozalyn squeezed her eyes shut, squelching the traitorous sensations that spilled through her when Dominic's handsome visage arose in the darkness. Only an arrogant fool would discount his charm and persuasiveness, she cautioned herself. She could not give an inch. She would have to stay one step ahead of him or she might . . .

Don't think about that, Rozalyn chided herself. You have enough to fret over. Clinging to positive, determined thoughts, Rozalyn eased back into the carriage seat, mentally plotting her moves. When she appeared on center stage to face the charismatic but dangerous Dominic Baudelair, she would be well prepared.

Chapter 5

Rozalyn was jolted from her contemplative deliberations when the brougham in which she was riding came to a screeching halt. As the sound of muffled voices came through the open window, she poked her head out to see the groom holding his hands high above his head while three men aimed their pistols at his chest.

A robbery, Rozalyn thought disgustedly. She was anxious to confront Dominic and to begin her performance. Indeed, she had spent the past few minutes rehearsing her soliloquy. She did not need her train of thought derailed.

Hastily, Rozalyn flung open the door and hopped to the ground, only to hear the groom's shocked gasp.

"Mademoiselle! Stay inside!" Mosley instructed her as he nobly positioned himself in front of his assailants to protect this lovely maid from harm.

Rozalyn disregarded the groom's instructions. Boldly, she marched up to one of the masked men who looked more than a little familiar. Harvey Duncan's plump physique and short stature gave him away.

An impish smile pursed her lips as she fished into her purse and then tucked several coins into Harvey's vest pocket. "You truly should find a more respectable occupation, *monsieur*," she chastised in a tone laced more with amusement than irritation.

"Rozalyn!" Harvey gasped when he recognized the lady's soft, throaty voice. "What the devil are you doin' in this coach? It ain't yers. You know we never would have stopped it if it was."

The groom's jaw sagged on its hinges as he listened to this attractive young lass converse with the thief who had ordered his men to surround the carriage and who, until a moment ago, had held his pistol to Mosley's chest.

"The gentleman with whom I plan to share the evening sent his groom and brougham for me," Rozalyn explained before wheeling around to climb into the carriage. "Now, if you good men will excuse us, we have an appointment to keep." Before she could reach for the door latch, Harvey was beside her, graciously offering his assistance. "*Merci, monsieur.* You are too kind."

Mosley half-collapsed in relief when the circle of thieves retired their weapons and flocked to the carriage for one last glimpse of the lady before she disappeared into it. Sweet Jesus! This was the strangest robbery attempt Mosley had ever seen. He stared at Rozalyn's departing back, his weather-beaten features skewed in astonishment.

"Coming to yer assistance is always my pleasure, *mam'selle,*" Harvey chuckled. After tucking his pistol in the band of his breeches, he wrapped his stubby fingers around Rozalyn's arm to lift her into the brougham. "We're havin' the usual game at Sadie's Tavern tomorrow night," he whispered confidentially. "You ain't gonna miss it, are you?"

As Rozalyn sank back onto the seat and primly tucked her full skirts around her legs, a mischievous smile skittered across her lips. "Me? At the gaming tables? Really, *monsieur,* I think you should know the answer to that." She reached out to straighten the mask that had drooped on the left side of Harvey's cheek. "I wouldn't miss it for the world. What are the stakes?"

"A week's wages on the wharf and whatever collectables we have in our pockets." Harvey grinned. "Perhaps even a few stolen jewels if some of the men have enjoyed a prosperous week."

"I see no reason why we can't play merely for the sport of it," Rozalyn admonished lightly. "Did you ever stop to realize that your life of crime might be supporting your penchant for gambling? You could be a wealthy man if you didn't drain your purse at Sadie's gaming tables."

Harvey laughed out loud at Rozalyn's attempt to lecture him. What a delightful lady she was. Rozalyn had the face of a seraph, a sharp-witted mind, and an ornery streak as wide as the Mississippi. And Lordy how she thrilled to adventure. Rozalyn had no qualms about garbing herself in men's clothes and joining Harvey and his friends, but although Harvey and Rozalyn shared the same unquenchable thirst for excitement, there was a vast difference between them. Rozalyn could easily afford to drop a few coins at the gaming tables and she played for sport. Harvey played to survive. He envied Rozalyn's wealth, but he could not begrudge it to the feisty young lass who had stolen his heart the first time he had laid eyes on her. And he was not the only man who would have given the world for this young woman's affection. This daring sprite had won the hearts of every scoundrel in St. Louis. Because Rozalyn did not consider herself better than her less fortunate friends and she was overly generous, the code of the streets demanded that she be granted amnesty. When she heard that one of her friends was down on his luck, sufficient funds mysteriously found their way into his pocket. Rozalyn expected nothing in return except the opportunity to mingle with men who knew how to appease her thirst for adventure.

Smiling quietly to himself, Harvey gave her hand a

fond squeeze before it fell away from his face. How well he remembered the sad, lonely look on this young girl's face the day he'd halted her carriage almost four years ago. He hadn't had the heart to steal from the young beauty and he'd sent her on her way, but Rozalyn had jumped from the brougham to follow him. Harvey had melted like butter too long on a stove when he'd whirled around to find her staring up at him with those mystical blue eyes. Rozalyn had wanted to know what life was like for those who didn't live in monstrous rock mansions, those who had to scratch and claw for enough coins to afford their meal.

Harvey had taken the curious little nymph under his wing and had introduced her to a life that had been inconceivable to her. From that day forward, Rozalyn had come to him when her spirits were heavy. Harvey helped her survive the loneliness of living with a father who gave her wealth but nothing of himself. She had even sneaked Harvey into the mansion when he had been wounded by a man who had come at him with a butcher knife. Right under her father's unobserving nose, Rozalyn had nursed him back to health; she'd stashed enough coins in his pocket to see that he didn't miss a meal while he was recuperating.

"You be on yer way, missy. I'm sorry for the inconvenience." Harvey backed away and gestured for the groom to climb back onto his perch. "And give my humble apologies to yer new beau for the delay."

The smile faded from Rozalyn's lips, and she eased her head back against the seat and turned her thoughts to her "new beau." If only Dominic were as agreeable as Harvey, she mused whimsically. She had the uneasy feeling that manipulating a man like Dominic would be a difficult matter, especially so since she had very little experience in such matters. Dominic had an air of confidence and he was very quick-witted. Rozalyn had only a brief acquaintance with the man yet it had led her to believe that he refused to take no for an answer. She would have to keep a watchful eye on him. He was a conniving rascal who made Harvey Duncan appear a saint in comparison. Although Harvey was desperate for coins, he did have scruples, whereas Rozalyn wasn't at all sure Dominic did. He was opportunistic and mercenary, a wolf in gentleman's clothing.

Dominic peered out the window of the parlor. After rechecking his timepiece, he frowned worriedly. What the devil was keeping Mosley? Had Rozalyn locked herself in her room, refusing to come down? Dominic knew the minx had something planned for he'd forced her into a corner. He wished he could read her complicated mind.

Hooves clattering against the cobblestoned street drew his attention and he spun away from the window, his long, impatient strides taking him to the porch. Mosley hopped from the driver's seat and hastened toward him, but not before casting one last glance at the young woman who remained enclosed in the coach.

"Forgive the delay, Master Baudelair," he apologized breathlessly. "I just had the strangest experience of my life."

Thick eyebrows formed a line over Dominic's green eyes. "You were accosted by thieves," he predicted. He wasn't the least bit surprised since they swarmed the streets at night.

"That we were," Mosley affirmed. When Dominic started down the steps to ensure that Rozalyn had not suffered from the harrowing experience, Mosley grabbed him by the arm. "But they didn't hurt the lady. It was the oddest thing I ever did see. The lady hopped out of the carriage while four men were holding me at gunpoint. I

73

thought sure they would make away with her so I told her to get back in the coach. But she waltzed right up to one of the thieves and scolded him for living his life of crime. Then she tossed him a few coins and he helped her back into the carriage." Mosley let his breath out in a rush, then shook his head in disbelief. "There that robber was, apologizing to her for the inconvenience. They stood there visiting like they were old friends."

Dominic chuckled at the bemused expression on Mosley's face. So the rumors about this she-cat were true, he concluded. Even muggers and thieves wouldn't lay a hand on this spellbinding witch. This saucy, spirited creature held court in the streets of St. Louis. Even the ruffians rolled out the red carpet when Rozalyn DuBois appeared. Dominic spitefully wondered how she would fare when set upon by panthers, bears, and unfriendly Indian tribes. She might have charmed the entire male species of the civilized world, but she wouldn't have a prayer in the wild, he decided. The little chit probably thought she had the world in the palm of her hand since she had been spoiled by everything in breeches, but if she were taken from her element and deposited at the foot of the Rockies, she might not be so all-fired sure of herself. And he would enjoy watching Rozalyn DuBois fumble her way through an environment that was as foreign to her as China.

Flinging aside his spiteful thoughts of throwing this gorgeous wildcat to the wolves, Dominic pasted on a charming smile, as he swiftly strode across the lawn to open the carriage door.

"*Ma chérie,* I have been fretting about whether or not you would come after I behaved like an ass this morning. The hours that have separated us have been . . ." Dominic's voice trailed off in the breeze when his eyes beheld the enchantress who emerged from the brougham.

A tiara of rubies and diamonds was set amid her upswept

raven curls, and a matching choker adorned her throat. The moonlight gave her a mystical appearance, but it also drew Dominic's attention to her shapely figure which was wrapped in silk. The daring bodice of her gown displayed the creamy swells of her breasts with such devastating effectiveness that Dominic had difficulty thinking. As he feasted on the bewitching sight presented to him, he suddenly had difficulty breathing. Rozalyn had assaulted his senses, and they had surrendered without a fight. Dominic was stung by an arousing need to lose himself in the sweet scent that invaded his nostrils, to touch and taste this delicious morsel who had appeared from the dark confines of the carriage.

"Will you help me down, Dominic?" Rozalyn murmured coyly, pleased that she had captured his undivided attention and had seemingly left him dumbstruck. Her first step in dealing with this philanderer was successful. Now she must charm him. "I pray that your attentiveness means you approve of my gown. I dressed to please you."

A skeptical frown furrowed Dominic's brow when his mind digested her soft words. What had happened to the contrary little minx who had practically run him down that very morning? His lean fingers folded around her trim waist and he effortlessly lifted her from the coach. In doing so he was distracted by the luscious fragrance of jasmine and the feel of her firm, ripe body. Lord, this shapely witch could tear the very thoughts from his mind, not to mention the disastrous effects she had on the rest of him. Dominic had an overwhelming urge to engage his lips in something more arousing than conversation, and he yielded to the temptation.

His warm, full lips took Rozalyn's hostage, and her feet never touched the ground when he swept her from the carriage. She was plastered against the rock-hard wall of Dominic's chest, chained to him by arms as confining as steel bands. His devouring kiss made breathing impossible, and Rozalyn was becoming more lightheaded by the second. How could she keep her wits about her when Dominic's crushing embrace immobilized her mind?

To her dismay, Rozalyn found her traitorous body responding to his intoxicating kiss. As her lips opened to allow his probing tongue to explore the dark recesses of her mouth, he enfolded her, molding her quivering body to his muscular contours. Her heart was thundering about her ribs like a runaway stallion, and Rozalyn feared it would beat her to death before Dominic released her from his clutches.

The musky scent of him bombarded her senses, and Rozalyn felt her resistance drop. She didn't want to feel this delicious knot of desire unfurling within her. She didn't want her arms to loop over his broad shoulders, pulling him closer. She didn't want to experience the tantalizing shock waves of pleasures that were splashing over her, swamping rational thought and drawing it into the swirling currents of passion.

Rozalyn kept telling herself she would use all these sensations to advantage. Dominic had to know her heart was pounding furiously since her body was crushed to his. Let him think she was strongly attracted to him, that his touch aroused her. That was her intention, wasn't it? To convince him that she was warming to him?

"Dominic . . ." Rozalyn whispered in a half-strangled voice. Only when he dragged his lips from hers did she realize that he had set her feet to solid ground. "I have the oddest feeling the lie I told Grand'mère is coming true. Ironic, is it not? We are only strangers, yet I experience warm, giddy sensations when I'm near you." Her long lashes fluttered down to caress her cheeks, and coyly, she let her fingertips skim the expanse of his chest. "I must confess that I was perturbed with you earlier. But I must also admit that I have been unable to put you from my mind all day." Her eyes lifted to lock with his intriguing emerald pools. "Do you believe in love at first sight? I mean, do you suppose there is truly something to the notion that one can tell at first glance when one has met one's destiny?"

Do I appear awestruck? Rozalyn wondered. Have my soft, inquiring words touched the tender side of this mountain lion?

"I didn't . . . until this morning," Dominic murmured, bringing her dainty hand to his lips. Things are going splendidly, Dominic thought to himself. Now that Rozalyn has mellowed slightly I will set about convincing her that my intentions are sincere. "You take my breath away, Roz, and I crave you when I am near you." Dominic peered into her eyes and then smiled sheepishly. "I am very ashamed of the way I behaved this morning. Can you forgive me?"

Rozalyn forced back the smug grin attempting to surface on her lips. Her ploy was working. Dominic was becoming infatuated with her. By the time the evening ended she would be leading this lusty dragon around on a leash.

"If you can forgive me for my temper tantrum," she cooed sweetly.

Curling her hand into the crook of his arm, Rozalyn peered at the towering walls of the Baudelair estate. This mansion had been without its master for several years, but servants had cared for it. Rozalyn knew very little about the mansion's owner. It seemed he had taken to the wild years ago and had not been heard from since. Rozalyn was curious about Dominic's connection to the grandparents he claimed had owned this huge estate. Had he lived with them for a time? And what of his parents? Why had he returned? Where had he been all these years?

Her discerning gaze took in Dominic's granite shoulders and the hard contours of his thighs which were encased in brown velvet. Had Dominic been born in the wild? If he had, why was he so sophisticated? How could he move so easily from one kind of life to another? Although Dominic appeared domesticated and docile at the moment, Rozalyn doubted this sleek black panther could purr . . . permanently.

Dominic moved with agility and masculine grace. Yet there would be a few rough edges beneath his elegant clothes if he had grown up in the wild. Taking all things into consideration, Rozalyn decided it would be wise never to let her guard down with him, and she would not if he would kindly refrain from kissing her senseless and crumbling every defense she sought to construct.

Dominic led Rozalyn into the sprawling parlor that boasted expensive furniture imported from Europe. After pouring them both a drink, he offered Rozalyn a stemmed wine glass. "I propose a toast to the vision of loveliness who has come to fill the emptiness in my life." His emerald eyes deliberately worshipped her as they worked their way over her curvaceous figure, not missing the smallest detail.

The bewitching nymph is what dreams were made of, Dominic thought. He could almost feel her soft, feminine curves brushing against him, taste her lips—lips that were as addictive as the cherry wine he was sipping.

"When I take my place by your side at Madame Rabelais' dinner party, there will be no pretense, *ma belle enchantress.*"

Rozalyn batted her pale blue eyes at Dominic. Her blinding smile would have melted a lesser man into his boots, but Dominic was as immovable as the Rock of Gibraltar. Rozalyn knew it would take more than warmth to thaw his heart. She set about adding more fuel to the fire.

"I drink to my good fortune. Fate graciously smiled

upon me when I happened onto you, Dominic Baudelair. You are the most fascinating man I have ever met." Rozalyn raised her goblet in silent toast, an impish grin blossoming on her lips. "And also the most attractive. I find myself wanting to know everything about you."

Dominic swallowed a self-satisfied smile, along with his sip of wine. He silently gloated over the fact that, by placing his best foot forward, he had charmed this temperamental hellion into submission. The evening was progressing marvelously. By the time he bid Rozalyn adieu, she would be willing to do whatever he asked of her.

After setting his glass aside, Dominic drew Rozalyn into the circle of his arms. He applauded himself for managing this feat without evoking a fiery protest. No ice maiden this, he mused. His lips feathered over hers, savoring the delicious taste of her kiss as he inhaled the tantalizing fragrance of jasmine. The men who approached this minx and met with defeat had obviously employed the wrong tactics, he decided. His arms involuntarily tightened about Rozalyn and his heart beat in double time when he felt her full breasts against his chest. Dominic paused momentarily to remind himself that he was only playacting and that his strong reaction to this captivating beauty had evolved from his role.

Take advantage of this blackguard in his weaker moment, Rozalyn bade herself, and willfully ignoring the arousing sensations coursing through her when his hard male body moved intimately against hers, she concentrated on her purpose. Delicate fingertips traced the lapel of his jacket, then Rozalyn pushed herself back as far as his encircling arms would allow before she lifted her face and blessed him with the most adoring smile she could muster.

"Dominic . . . I . . ." She paused for dramatic effect, as if the emotions he'd stirred were playing havoc with her thoughts. And they were! But Rozalyn would not allow herself to believe that for a minute. "What I feel for you is like nothing I have ever experienced," she confessed softly. "That which you asked in payment for your assistance would be readily given . . . if I knew in my heart that what I feel for you is eagerly returned." Her long, sultry lashes swept down and then drifted up to meet his probing gaze. "What I am trying to say is that I think I may be falling in love with you. But it is much too soon to know. It has happened too quickly. I beg time to accept these sensations. If I give myself to you, body and soul, this night . . . so soon . . . well . . ." Rozalyn hesitated as if wary of baring her heart. "I don't want to be hurt, Dominic. I suppose I am a bit of a coward when it comes to love. I want to be very sure of the man who steals my heart. I want the moment to be right." Heaving a sigh, Rozalyn peered beseechingly at Dominic. "Can you possibly understand how I feel, what I am trying to say? I know nothing of men, and I am overwhelmed by you because you seem so worldly and experienced. I would feel nothing but shame if I could not satisfy the only man who has truly stirred me." Rozalyn reached up to trace the bronzed features of his face. "Perhaps I am a hopeless romantic who lives with childish dreams, but I want my first taste of love to be special. I have rejected other men's advances, saving myself for the one man who truly cares for me, not my father's money or prestige he might stand to gain in the joining of our two families."

Rozalyn had rehearsed her soliloquy all the way to Dominic's estate, and now she was reasonably pleased with her performance. Her voice had trembled slightly; and she felt she had appeared sincere. But had she convinced Dominic that forcing her to his bed might spoil what could become a beautiful relationship?

He clasped her hands in his and smiled tenderly into her bewitching face. "I am ashamed of myself for insinuating that I would steal your innocence, *amie*," he whispered repentantly. "I will not deny that I crave your delicious body for that would be a lie. But I would be less than a man if I allowed my desire for you to destroy the fragile bond that has begun to grow between us." He cupped her face in his hand, staring deeply into her fathomless blue eyes. "Love is the one emotion that has escaped me all these years, but I can feel it taking root when I touch you. I will wait for you to come to me, Roz. I will gently teach you the pleasures of love. And they will be special. I promise you that, *chérie*."

While guiding Rozalyn toward the door, Dominic took a mental bow for his performance. "Ours will be a proper courtship. Tonight you and I are going to view a play." He winked down at Rozalyn, his eyes twinkling like priceless emeralds. "Perhaps we can pick up a few pointers from the actors, to aid us in our performance at Lenore's dinner party. But, for myself, I doubt I will be acting when I proudly stand at attention, waiting to be introduced as your most devoted admirer."

When Dominic steered Rozalyn through the hall and back outside, she half-collapsed in relief. My, hadn't she handled this mountain lion with finesse? She had appealed to his sense of decency and he had responded accordingly. A smug smile rippled across her lips when she considered her flawless performance. But she was too pleased with herself to notice Dominic was sporting a self-satisfied grin, one bright enough to replace the sun if it ever burned out.

He had played the role of the enamored beau to the hilt, and as his tall, muscular frame entered the carriage, he was satisfied. Aubrey's lovely daughter was infatuated. By denying his lusty appetites, he could earn her trust, and when their evening ended she would consider him the man of her dreams. Then, when Dominic approached Aubrey, Rozalyn would insist that her father comply with his demands.

Silently and separately, Rozalyn and Dominic gloated all the way to the theater. While they viewed the play, she kept reminding herself that, although the actors were professionals, their acting could not hold a candle to the performance she had given. Pehaps she should consider an acting career. She had pretended to be hopelessly in love with a man she detested. If she had not appealed to his tiny thread of conscience she would have been stripped of her innocence, yet with feminine persuasion, she had managed to coil that rascal around her finger, so tightly that he would never come unwound. Now Dominic would play her doting suitor at her grandmother's party and no one would be the wiser, especially not Dominic.

A perplexed frown captured Rozalyn's features as she absently applauded the second act of *A Midsummer Night's Dream*. Just how the devil was she going to explain this interlude to Lenore once Dominic had been sent on his way? Well, she would fret over that after the engagement party. Surely a workable solution would come to her when she allowed herself time to consider the alternatives. In the meantime, she needed to keep Dominic dangling so he wouldn't cause her trouble—and he could cause trouble if he got out of hand. At that distressing thought, Rozalyn glanced discreetly at her companion. When she found him staring at her, she blessed him with an adoring smile to pacify him.

The evening progressed without a hitch. Dominic showed himself to be a perfect gentleman, and Rozalyn was her bubbly, enthusiastic self, chattering about the play and pretending to delight in Dominic's company. Her mood soured when they exited from the theater to find Jeffrey Corday blocking their path.

"I must speak with you, Rozalyn," he insisted. "I have come to—"

"I told you this morning that we have nothing left to say to each other." Rozalyn turned up her dainty nose and veered around the annoying obstacle that stood between her and the carriage.

Jeffrey's splindly fingers clamped around her arm to detain her. "You did not allow me to apologize. I care deeply for you. You must know that." His scratched face wore a humble expression, but Rozalyn's attitude toward him had not mellowed a smidgen. "It isn't your father's money I want. It is you. It always has been."

Dominic faded into the background when Rozalyn jerked her arm from her persistent suitor's grasp. It was amusing to watch this spitfire in action when he wasn't on the receiving end of her fury, and he was curious to see how the gangly blond would fare when he pitted himself against this she-cat.

"Is it truly me you care about?" Rozalyn sniffed caustically, raking Jeffrey with scornful mockery. "And what if I informed you that my father has become so miserly with his wealth that he does not intend to offer a dowery? Would you still be eager to wed me?" When Jeffrey floundered for a reply, Rozalyn laughed bitterly. "It is true, you know. That is why Papa is in no great rush to see me marry. He does not plan to incorporate my future husband into his business. Indeed, I doubt he'd take the time to select a wedding gift. And I trust you can support me in the manner to which I have grown accustomed because financial aid from my father will not be forthcoming."

The young man looked as if he had had the props knocked out from under him. Although Rozalyn was breathtakingly lovely, the woman Jeffrey selected for his wife had to be wealthy. If not they would be wallowing in debts, those Jeffrey had been unable to pay. He had lived beyond his means and was dangerously close to financial disaster. He wondered whether Rozalyn was telling him the truth or whether she had made those remarks to spite him.

Dominic stood quietly by, listening to the conversation. He detected the hint of bitterness that seeped into Rozalyn's voice when she mentioned her father, and he was also quick to note Jeffrey's pallor when Rozalyn assured him there would be no financial transaction when she wed. No wonder this fiery misfit had remained unattached. If all her beaux lusted after her wealth, she had every reason to be cynical about a man's attentions. Dominic made a mental note to assure Rozalyn that he was not like the rest of the men in her life.

A stab of conscience struck him at that thought. Wasn't he using Rozalyn? Although it wasn't Aubrey's money that interested Dominic, he was anticipating a favor. His pensive musings dissipated when Rozalyn drew herself up in front of her speechless suitor.

"I must assume from your silence that you can ill afford a wife who lacks financial backing. But it is no matter," she added with a careless shrug. "You see, I have met someone else, Jeffrey." She indicated Dominic, who seemed huge compared to the skinny blond whose face and hands showed that he'd fought his way from prickly shrubs that morning.

Jeffrey's face fell like a rockslide and his eyes glittered menacingly. He was a desperate man. The sharks from whom he had borrowed money need not know that her father would not assume his debts, only that he and Roz would soon be wed. That possibility alone had kept Jeffrey afloat these past two months. The last thing he needed was for news to spread that Rozalyn had turned her attention elsewhere, and the fact that she had openly acknowledged some affection, no matter how small, for this towering mass of brawn infuriated Jeffrey. He did not need competition. He had enough trouble wooing this temperamental heiress without some stranger waltzing in to stake a claim to her.

Without stopping to consider the repercussions, Jeffrey doubled his fist, fully intending to plant it in Dominic's tanned face, but his gesture proved to be disastrous. Before his fist could make contact with Dominic's jaw, his arm was halted in midair and caught in a bone-crushing grip that made him yelp in surprise.

Rozalyn's mouth dropped open in disbelief. Jeffrey was behaving like a crazed idiot, taking punches at a man who could have torn him to shreds if he had so desired. And outside a theater!

The scuffle was over almost before it began. Rozalyn gaped as Dominic, with the quickness of an uncoiling snake, struck Jeffrey on the jaw. He then jabbed him with a booted foot, sending the stork-legged blond skidding across the grass to bounce off the theater wall.

For a moment, Rozalyn and every other onlooker stood paralyzed. Dominic's fighting tactics were like nothing they had ever witnessed. He'd sprung at Jeffrey—half-man, half-beast, and his lightning-quick moves had had Jeffrey dazed and downed before he'd even known what hit him. Dominic's entire body had become a weapon of defense. Rozalyn wondered if Dominic could be subdued, even if the odds were ten to one.

Awesome respect dawned in her eyes as he straightened his jacket and then strode back to offer her his arm, and she instantly decided that it was better to have Dominic as an ally than as an enemy. However, she cautioned herself never to engage in fisticuffs with this so-called gentleman.

"Mademoiselle? Shall we go?" Dominic inquired as if nothing out of the ordinary had happened.

He wasn't even out of breath.

Rozalyn cautiously laid her hand in the crook of his arm and nodded mutely, still too dumbstruck to locate her tongue. As they strolled past Jeffrey, who lay in a crumpled heap like a misplaced doormat, Dominic paused to stare down at him.

"If you ever lay a hand on me or harass this lady again, I will do far more than merely gain your attention, *monsieur*," he told Jeffrey in a voice that indicated he was making no idle threat. Indeed, his tone was deadly calm. Although Jeffrey's vision was blurred, there was nothing wrong with his ears. He retained enough of his senses to surmise that flying at Dominic a second time would be inviting his own demise. "Consider your alternatives, Jeffrey." The name rolled off Dominic's lips like a mocking taunt. "A life of poverty might not seem so distasteful when measured against having every bone in your body broken . . . at least once."

Not until Dominic had lifted Rozalyn into the brougham was she able to untangle her tongue. And when she did, she fired the questions at Dominic.

"Where did you learn to fight like that? Were you raised by a pack of wolves or have you lived among the savages? How long have you—"

Dominic brushed his index finger over her lips to quiet her, and then he flashed her a wry smile. "Which of those questions would you like me to answer first?"

All of them, Rozalyn thought. Her curiosity was eating her alive! She didn't know anything about the man riding in the carriage with her. She didn't know if he had been hatched from an egg or if he had a mother. She didn't even know if he took his coffee black, if he was just passing through town, or if he took his jacket off in a methodical way.

"I would like to know where you learned to fight and then I want to know everything about you," she insisted. "Start from the beginning and do not omit anything."

Dominic chuckled at the lively curiosity in her intelligent blue eyes. "I learned to fight from the Crow Indians, and I have sharpened my abilities by facing unfriendly beasts. I am a half-breed, Roz. My mother was a Crow maiden and my father traveled with Lewis and Clark when they explored the western boundaries of the Louisianna Purchase. When a man chooses to live in the wilds, he learns to defend himself or perish." Dominic could tell by the astonished expression on Rozalyn's exquisite features that she was becoming more apprehensive by the second. Perhaps fear will keep the little minx in line, he told himself. Yet he didn't want Rozalyn to be petrified of him. Gently, he reached out to smooth away the wary frown that puckered her brow. "I have faced wolves, grizzlies, and hostile Indians who were eager to add my scalp to their coup. But my taste for violence does not include abusing beautiful women, if that is what you are thinking."

Rozalyn breathed more easily, but his explanation did not fully satisfy her inquisitive nature. She wanted to know what motivated a man like Dominic Baudelair, she wanted to know why he had returned to civilization, and why he seemed properly educated. She was under the impression that trappers were a wild, illiterate breed of men like the ones she'd met on the wharf. But Dominic was different.

"I returned to St. Louis to complete my business transactions after rendezvous," Dominic went on to say. "Unlike your blond friend, Jeffrey, I am financially independent. I live in the wilderness because I enjoy its challenges—or at least I did until I met you." His hand curled beneath her chin, tilting her face to his light kiss. "Now I find myself pitted against the beast within me. There is no greater enemy than one's self. I confess that controlling myself when I am near you is one of the most difficult tasks I have undertaken."

When Rozalyn surrendered to his kiss, she told herself she was still playing her role. But her body had difficulty accepting that. And when his wandering fingertips sketched the lacy bodice of her gown, making arousing contact with the full swells of her breasts, her weak protest died beneath a quiet sigh of pleasure. Dominic was weaving dreams about her, crumbling her defenses, immobilizing her mind, and it seemed a collection of butterflies had been set loose in her stomach. She could not draw a breath without them fluttering against her thundering heart.

As his lips abandoned hers to glide over her bare shoulder and investigate the creamy skin along her collarbone, Dominic told himself he should tread carefully with Rozalyn. The primitive male needs channeling through every nerve and muscle in his body could be appeased after he deposited this innocent maid on her doorstep. But it wasn't just any woman he wanted. It was this fascinating vixen who had left Jeffrey bruised and battered that very morning.

But his body refused to heed his warning. Rozalyn had been on his mind all day, and the dangerous game he was playing now haunted him. It wasn't enough to kiss her sweet lips. Dominic ached to know this ebony-haired enchantress by touch. He wanted to mold his body to her lusciously soft contours. He longed to lose himself in the fantasy that had hounded him since he had consented to play her love-smitten lackey.

Rozalyn felt herself being pressed into the velvet cushions, and Dominic's hard, muscular thigh insinuated itself between her legs. Something is very wrong, Rozalyn warned herself. Why didn't she protest when his roaming hand slid beneath her petticoats to map the generous curve of her hips? Why wasn't she devising a counter tactic to keep Dominic at a safe distance? That was what she had intended, wasn't it? No answers came to her. Thought was impossible when skillful hands flowed over her quivering flesh, causing passion to burst forth like a disturbed lion. If she demanded that he take his hands from her, she would be denying herself the giddy pleasure that was like nothing she had ever experienced.

His hot kisses tracked a trail of fire across her breasts, and when his tongue flicked one taut peak, a tantalizing tremor vibrated through Rozalyn. Then desire blossomed, like a rose opening its petals to the warmth of the sun. Helplessly, she surrendered to the rapture that overshadowed rational thought.

While his lips skimmed her flesh to give the same titillating attention to the other pink bud, his inquiring hands glided gently over her calves, tracing an erotic path to her inner thighs. Then knowing fingers intruded into her womanly softness, teasing and caressing her, while his moist mouth returned to hers, devouring her with hungry impatience.

Rozalyn was on fire, and her inhibitions fled from the blaze that threatened to consume her. She had never wanted a man the way she wanted Dominic, yet she couldn't fathom why. Was it her adventurous spirit that had led her down this wayward path? Why could this one man release her carefully controlled desires and make her passion burn out of control?

Her arms involuntarily wound around his sturdy neck. Then her lashes fluttered up, and her gaze trapped in the vivid color of his eyes. Like green meadows rippling in the wind, they danced with golden sunlight, and her heart leaped with excitement as he whispered her name with such pained sincerity that she felt the last barrier of her deteriorating defenses buckling with his plea.

"Roz . . . I made a promise I cannot keep. To seek out another woman when it is you I crave would only be torture," Dominic groaned, his voice tormented. "God forgive me, but I want you though I know you are not a woman to be trifled with." Rozalyn not only heard his raspy words she felt them for his sensuous lips were tracing the slim column of her throat. "Tell me to leave you alone. Order me away before I lose what little sense I have left."

A sea of tears swam in the back of her eyes. Overwhelming sensations fell upon her like an avalanche. Order him away. . . . Rozalyn could not seem to voice the thought. The words that formed on her lips were a contradiction of what he was asking of her. His touch was like warm summer sunshine, and she found herself moving closer to the solid mass of strength that pinned her to the seat instead of pushing him away.

"Show me the pleasures that have eluded me," she invited, lifting her face to his, then welcoming the pressure of his demanding mouth on hers.

Dominic moaned as her hand slid between the buttons of his shirt to make timid contact with the naked wall of his chest. He was ablaze with desire and Rozalyn's touch fed the flames. He could not seem to get close enough to her, he resented the garments that separated her flesh from his.

Like a man who had been stranded on a desert for days on end, and deprived of nourishment, Dominic took her lips and the sweetness within. His lean fingers splayed across her thighs, pushing her skirt away to allow him free access to her sensitive flesh.

"Master Baudelair? We are here, sir," Mosley called after reining the steed to a halt and waiting a few minutes for Dominic to bid the lady good night.

"Damn." He cursed his poor sense of timing. What the sweet loving hell did he think he was doing anyway? A young woman's first encounter with a man should not come about in a carriage.

Mosley's voice dragged Rozalyn from the potent crosscurrents of emotion back to reality. She was humiliated that she had behaved so shamelessly. Had she been a harlot in another lifetime? Her passions had burst free the moment she had met a man unlike those with whom she had dealt in the past. Sinful soul, she chided herself as Dominic pulled her up beside him to rearrange her clothes.

"Roz . . . I—" Dominic began, only to be interrupted by her agonized wail of mortification. Before he could continue, Rozalyn had flung open the door and had scrambled from the carriage to flee up the steps.

Dominic slumped back onto the seat and raked his fingers through his hair. His breath came out in a frustrated rush. Then he assured himself that the incident had turned out for the best. After all, he had not intended to deflower this wild rose when he desperately needed her assistance. He would simply have to relieve his cravings at the brothel. There he would find a woman who asked no more than a smile and moments of his time.

Clinging to that thought, Dominic poked his head out the window to order Mosley on his way. He stared at the wall that met his gaze. The lingering fragrance of jasmine and a vision of the lovely creature who had been so close returned to haunt him. It is better this way, Dominic again told himself, but his body was paying no attention. He had wanted Rozalyn as a man hungers for a woman who has kindled the fires of desire in him.

Chapter 6

Rozalyn collapsed against the door after she had locked it behind her. *Mon Dieu,* she had come dangerously close to . . . She squeezed her eyes shut, fighting the emotional tug of war going on within her. Dominic's darkly handsome face rose before her mind's eye. She could almost feel his hard thighs pressing intimately between hers. He had ignited a spark as ancient as time itself and had left her with a gnawing craving that wouldn't go away. Having taken her past the point of no return, she was aching to satisfy needs she had never understood until Dominic had introduced her to the dark world of passion. Now she had yearned for his touch, reveling in the sensations that . . .

Enough of this! Rozalyn told herself. Then she bolted through the hall and leaped up the stairs two at a time in her haste to escape the phantom who tormented her.

"Rozalyn, is that you?" Aubrey called from his study, though he didn't come to the door.

"Oui, Papa," Rozalyn replied and then continued on her way.

"Did you enjoy your evening?" came Aubrey's absent inquiry.

"No, it was the most unsettling evening I have ever

experienced," she muttered bitterly, knowing exactly what her father's response would be.

"That's nice. *Bonne nuit.*"

Heaving an exasperated sigh, Rozalyn trudged up the remainder of the steps. Tess, the plump, round-faced Negress who was in charge of keeping the DuBois mansion in order, was in the hall, and when Rozalyn requested a steaming cup of tea laced with brandy to help her sleep, the old woman eyed her curiously.

"You got somethin' troublin' you tonight, girl?" Tess pried, her piercing gaze probing into Rozalyn's as if she meant to read her mind and pluck out the disturbing thought. "It ain't that new beau of yers, I hope."

"I seem to have contracted a headache after watching the play," Rozalyn hedged, refusing to divulge that it was a six-foot-two-inch headache with laughing emerald eyes and hair the color of midnight.

"Well, it don't s'prise me a bit," Tess sniffed as she waddled down the hall. "Considerin' the hours you've bin keepin'. You do so much comin' and goin' that I git dizzy just watchin' you."

A quiet smile grazed Rozalyn's lips after Tess wheeled around the corner and disappeared from sight. The housekeeper did her share of lecturing, but Rozalyn was quite fond of her, though she wouldn't have been surprised to learn that Tess was her grandmother's informant. The two of them fussed over her like mother hens, and they both kept abreast of every rumor in the wind, especially those pertaining to Rozalyn. Yes, Rozalyn was willing to bet Tess and Lenore traded information. How else would Tess have known about her "new beau"?

When Tess returned with the brandy-laced tea she presented Rozalyn with a short lecture on the necessity of getting the proper amount of sleep, instead of rising before the crack of dawn and staying out until all hours of the night. Rozalyn was too weary and frustrated to argue

93

with the housekeeper. All she wanted to do was adjourn
to her room to sip her tea and grapple with the events of
the day.

They had begun with an innocent lie, one meant to
appease Lenore and bring her peace. Later, to make matters worse, Rozalyn had tried to lie to herself, thereby
dragging herself deeper into the web of deceit. Like a silly
fool she thought she could resist Dominic's magnetism,
his subtle wit, and devastating charm. She had even told
herself that her reaction to his embrace was part of her
act. But she knew for certain that she had not been acting
a few minutes earlier in the carriage. Her heart had overruled her head, and she would have surrendered to
Dominic's persuasive gentleness if they had not been
interrupted. Dominic had even begged her to deny him
and she could not. *Could not!* Rozalyn groaned miserably,
then gulped down another sip of her spiked tea. Her heart
was obviously as wild as her spirit, she realized. Why else
would she have kissed Dominic with reckless abandon
and then offered herself to him? She had always been
impulsive, chasing rainbows and whims without fore-
thought. But why did her will power fail her only when
she was with that raven-haired devil? Rozalyn cursed
when no answer came to mind. She couldn't fathom why
she was so drawn to that well-formed mass of brawn and
muscle, even when she knew the results of her attraction
could be disastrous. She was on shaky ground, but she
couldn't reverse direction because of the foolish lie she
had told Lenore.

Sighing tremulously, Rozalyn set her empty cup aside
and peeled off her gown, letting it flutter into a careless
heap around her ankles. The caress of the light autumn
breeze wafting through the balcony door reminded her of
Dominic's tender, coaxing touch. She had learned a great
deal more about this handsome stranger in one day than
she'd learned about the men who had escorted her about

town. Dominic was as ornery and playful as a little boy; yet he possessed a mature man's charm and clever wit. He was an ominous foe and a potentially dangerous lover. But he employed gentle, persuasive tactics, against which Rozalyn had no defense. His warm, protective embrace had proven itself to be more potent than force. Rozalyn was accustomed to retaliating against the energetic assaults of men, but she had been totally unprepared for Dominic's brand of passion. And he was a composite of the things Rozalyn had admired in numerous men, but had never confronted in such a fascinating combination.

A demure smile hovered on her lips as she wriggled into her nightgown and then stretched out on her satin sheets. At least she knew Dominic had no intention of using her as other men had attempted to do. He had openly admitted that he had already acquired a fortune and he had no need of hers. What he wanted from her was only that which a man and woman share. If she had not been so sensitive about men courting her father's money she might have been indignant that Dominic wanted her. Oh, she had protested his proposition in a fit of temper, but when after spending an evening with him, during which time he behaved as a gentleman until passion got the best of him, she considered his suggestion more of a compliment than an insult. After all, what woman would want a man who had no physical interest in her? Dominic found her desirable. Was that so wrong? And if it were, why did it feel so right when she was in the sinewy circle of his arms?

At least he has been honest, Rozalyn told herself. Unlike Jeffrey who lied through his teeth when he professed to love her instead of Aubrey's money. If she were to give herself to a man, why not to Dominic? He did care for her. Hadn't he said so? Hadn't he apologized for being so blunt in his intentions and hadn't he tried to hold himself at bay, leaving the ultimate decision to her?

After years of searching she had happened upon a strong, fascinating man, who possessed a certain boyish charm, and he had proved to be a delightfully amusing companion.

A drifting shadow caught Rozalyn's attention, and when she realized she was not alone in her boudoir she bolted straight up in bed. It would have been easier to deal with any intruder but the man who stepped from the shadows to peer into her soul with those incredible emerald eyes.

Dominic had managed to remain in the carriage for all of three minutes after Rozalyn had fled to the house. But his vision of her and the jasmine fragrance that remained in the air overwhelmed him. No amount of rationalization could convince him to settle for another woman when he knew it would be Rozalyn's face he would see when he closed his eyes and surrendered to passion. Another woman could relieve him but not satisfy him.

After shedding the jacket that had absorbed her alluring scent, Dominic had ambled aimlessly along the street, letting his thoughts wander where they would. His footsteps had followed the train of his thoughts, and he'd found himself standing beneath her balcony, staring up at the beckoning shaft of light shining from her second-story window. Like a moth fluttering toward the flame, Dominic had scaled the lattice and crossed the balcony until a breathtakingly lovely vision stopped him.

His body had caught fire as he'd watched his enchanting nymph pull the pins from her hair, allowing it to tumble down her back in a waterfall of glistening ebony, and he had groaned inwardly when she'd drawn away the pink silk wrapper, revealing ivory skin and the body of a goddess. The high, thrusting peaks of her breasts had begged for his touch, and her trim waist had seemed so narrow he'd been sure he could wrap his hands around it.

His gaze had drunk in her curving hips and her shapely legs, worshipping the sight of her.

Dominic was burning alive with a fever and Rozalyn was the cause of and cure for his soaring temperature. His pleasure in looking upon her perfect body was so intense it made him ache. He couldn't have turned and walked away, not if his life depended on it. His male instincts had been deprived too often during the course of the day, and he could no longer suppress his primitive urges.

Dominic had not meant to come back; his intentions had been honorable. However, his flesh was weak. Now his eyes drank in a captivating goddess dressed in sheer and revealing blue muslin. His hands and lips craved to touch the body it silhouetted.

"I should not have come back," he murmured, but he came around to the edge of her fourposter bed.

"No, you shouldn't have," Rozalyn agreed.

Her gaze settled on his gaping shirt, taking in the dark matting of hair she had only begun to explore earlier. Her brief investigation had only served to pique her curiosity. Now, in the flickering lantern light, she realized she would never overcome her infatuation for this power-fully built rogue until she proved he was only a man, not some image from an illusive dream.

Dominic sank down on the side of her bed as if he belonged there. His emerald eyes flamed with a hunger only Rozalyn could appease as he reached out to tunnel his fingers through the silky tendrils that cascaded over her shoulder. "I tried to leave you, you know," he whispered huskily. "But I could not bid you adieu so abruptly, not after what happened in the carriage. I need to apologize."

"Apologize for what?" Her brow arched questioningly. She was the one who had scampered off like a frightened rabbit, though she had never been one to run from trouble. In the past she had squared her shoulders and confronted it.

"For doing this . . ." Dominic's head lowered deliberately, his eyes focused on her lips as if they were the first pair he had ever seen.

Rozalyn didn't realize until too late that she had accepted his apology and had also invited him to continue where he had left off a half-hour earlier. The brandy had impeded her thought processes, and it never occurred to her to resist him. Instead of asking herself why she had allowed this bold man to invade her home in a most inappropriate manner, she wrapped her arms about his neck, and drew him with her to the satin sheets.

Lips as soft as summer rain melted beneath Dominic's kiss, and for a long breathless moment he was content just to taste her honeyed response, to inhale the enticing scent that was so much a part of her. But, as before, a kiss was not enough, would never be enough. It only whetted his thirst for this spirited beauty. His hands began to glide to and fro before slipping over her shoulder to cup the full swells of her breasts. Then, with heart-stopping tenderness, his caresses slid beneath the gossamer gown to map the silky curve of her hips.

When his bold caresses ventured along her inner thighs, Rozalyn's breath lodged in her throat, but her traitorous body arched instinctively toward his seeking hands. And when his caresses enfolded her soft mound, Rozalyn swore she had inhaled her last breath. Dominic's lips abandoned hers to grant her air, but it was not enough to sustain her when he again assaulted her with tantalizing kisses. Flames leaped across her flesh in the wake of his moist lips, and a tiny moan bubbled in her chest when he took a throbbing peak into his mouth, suckling, arousing, teasing her until she was mad with wanting him.

He seemed to have an extra pair of hands as he

explored the unchartered territory of her body, discovering each sensitive spot, his touch triggering shock waves in her. Rozalyn surrendered to the sensations he aroused. Hers was not to reason why, only to respond to his wondrous caresses and to enjoy the pleasures of love, pleasures she had never before allowed herself to experience. Dominic's practiced hands and warm lips melted her resistance and subtly demanded a response, until Rozalyn felt as if she were drifting on a sea of indescribable rapture. His touch was black magic, leaving her soft and pliant.

While his tongue tasted her flesh and his skillful hands spun her nerves into a tangled web, Rozalyn breathed a ragged sigh. She craved more of this sweet torment, even as she wondered at the emotions erupting from somewhere deep within her. She cried out softly as his probing fingers invaded her womanly softness, but he silenced her cry with his mouth, stealing her breath and then giving it back in a most satisfying way.

He smells so good, so clean, like the outdoors, she thought deliriously as she nuzzled against him. His lips were like soft velvet, his body a warm mass of strength that she longed to feel pressed, full length, against her. As if he sensed her needs, his hard male frame settled over hers, and she felt a gentle pressure as his legs urged her thighs apart. The solid weight of his body blended into hers, and Rozalyn eagerly accepted him, longing to satisfy the compelling urges he had instilled in her.

Then a sharp stab of pain splintered her dreamlike trance, and she instinctively shrank away, choking on her breath. Dominic's arms slid beneath her hips, lifting her to him and then slowly withdrawing before she could protest.

"One moment of pain will lead to timeless moments of splendor. Yield to me, Roz," he murmured breathlessly against the rapid pulsations of her throat. "It is not my want to hurt you. Never that. I only seek to please, to satisfy. . . ."

Her body relaxed in response to his coaxing words, though she was not at all certain she believed him. But he did not lie. As he began to move carefully within her the pain ebbed and then blossomed into a strange new kind of pleasure. That sensation grew until it had become yet another exquisite sensation, the one building upon the other, taking her higher and higher still.

His full lips rained a sea of kisses on her bare shoulder as he drove into her, his male body aroused by the feel of her feminine flesh joined intimately to his. Their love-making blocked out all thought, but Dominic could not have recalled other moments that compared with these. He was winging his way toward heaven, an angel in his arms, feeling the warmth of each star as they soared past. As he was swept into a dark world of rapturous sensations that played havoc with his sanity, he realized he had sacrificed part of himself when he had dared to introduce this innocent sprite to passion. Yet Dominic was discovering a universe so delightfully fulfilling that he didn't care if he ever charted his way back from this ecstatic journey into eternity.

He felt Rozalyn's nails digging into the taut muscles of his back, her body moving in perfect rhythm with his, and he tasted the hint of brandy on her lips before he died a slow sweet death as love's pleasures overwhelmed him. Raw emotion swelled in him like a melodious crescendo until Dominic was completely absorbed in the taste and feel of the woman in his arms, driven onward by primal desires that numbed his mind and freed his emotions. His passion flowed like wine, sending streams of rapture in all directions.

Then shuddering tremors claimed him and he toppled from his towering perch. He clutched Rozalyn to him as if he never meant to let her go, couldn't let her go. He could feel her heart beating in wild, frantic rhythm with his as, together, they plunged helplessly through time and space, recalling each wondrous sensation that had gripped them, not yet ready to collide with reality.

When Dominic's powerful body relaxed against hers, tears of ecstasy misted Rozalyn's eyes. His lovemaking had satisfied her craving, but she still longed to touch him as he had touched her, to return the pleasure his hands and mouth had given her quivering flesh. She had not yet known him by touch and feel, and she knew she would never be content until her inquiring hands had sketched the hard, lean terrain of his body.

When Dominic eased down beside her, Rozalyn half-rose to lean on an elbow and her curious gaze ran brazenly over the naked length of him. Her fingertips traced the firm line of his jaw and then trailed down the corded muscles of his neck to circle each male nipple. Then her hand splayed across the crisp, dark hair that covered his laboring chest and she felt a deep rumble of laughter beneath her palm.

Rozalyn's wide innocent eyes swung back to his shadowed face to see a raised eyebrow and a boyish smile.

"My, but you are an inquisitive imp . . . and not easily satisfied," he chortled, his voice still husky with the after-effects of passion.

A becoming blush stained her cheeks, but her roving hand continued to follow the furring of hair that descended across his lean belly. "Shouldn't I be?" she parried. "After all, I have never been with a man before or dared to touch . . ."

Her explanation was cut short by Dominic's quick intake of breath. Her adventurous hand brushed across his lower abdomen and the sensitive part of his anatomy, making him flinch uncontrollably.

"Did I hurt you?" Rozalyn questioned, concerned. She glanced up and noted his odd expression.

Dominic could not contain the soft laughter that bubbled from his lips. Rozalyn was so naïve and innocent that she was delightfully amusing. It was obvious that what she knew about men could easily have been stored in a thimble. She was unlike any other woman he had taken in his arms, for those in his past had taken many passionate journeys and not all of them with him. Rozalyn was inexperienced, but she was quickly learning to become a seductress.

"You were sensitive to my touch," he reminded her. Dominic grinned when a crimson coloring swept over her cheeks. "Men and woman are not so different."

Rozalyn's blue eyes scanned his hair-roughened flesh and hard, muscled thighs. "Men and women are not so different?" she repeated incredulously. From where she sat there seemed to be noticeable differences between them!

"Perhaps you should peek in yonder mirror," she advised. "It would seem you have not looked closely of late. You and I are as different as night and day."

Another tremor of laughter shook his broad shoulders and then died into silence when her inquiring hands trailed lower. Dominic had intended to make a clever rejoinder but Rozalyn's dedicated investigation of his body had ripped the words off the end of his tongue. Her thumb slid over the bulky muscle that enlarged his thigh, then it rose to examine the scar that curled around his ribs.

"Mountain lion or grizzly bear?" she questioned.

"A hungry pack of wolves that intended to make a meal of my horse until I interrupted them," Dominic supplied, although he had to fight to keep his mind on their conversation when her gentle hands were transforming his brain into mush.

"And this one?" Her light caress flowed down to his right hip to another telltale sign of a painful encounter.

"That was a starved panther. He invited me to dinner. Needless to say, I declined," Dominic told her.

Rozalyn giggled at his remark and then allowed her hand to trickle across his left thigh. "And what caused this?"

"A ruthless white man." His voice quivered with long-harbored hatred.

"And how did he fare in the scuffle?" Rozalyn queried curiously.

"You don't want to know."

No, she probably didn't. Rozalyn had witnessed the result when Jeffrey had dared to assault this angered lion of a man with nothing more lethal than his fist. She hated to venture a guess as to the fate of the man who'd attacked Dominic with a dagger.

When Rozalyn's butterfly kisses skimmed across Dominic's chest and then skipped across his ribcage, he lost all interest in conversation. What she is doing to me should have been considered a crime, he mused. She was draining him of his strength and leaving him a quivering mass of desire. Her innocent, inventive techniques were wildly sensuous and Dominic was amazed at how quickly she had aroused him. He had thought his passion completely consumed after he'd made love to this playful sprite, but now it blazed anew, feeding on the embers that smoldered within him, and on memories of moments so wild and sweet they fueled the sparks to flame.

Her tender hands caressed, her soft lips whispered across his quaking skin, exciting him, dragging a moan of torment from his thudding chest, and he allowed Rozalyn to take the initiative when he had granted that privilege to no other. He had always instigated lovemaking in the past and, once his needs were appeased, he left his lover's arms. But tonight he remained in her silken arms, adoring the feel of her caresses, the light touch of the warm feathery kisses that tasted his flesh. Dominic was too immersed in pleasure to consider why he was in no hurry to leave this raven-haired enchantress or why he allowed her to dominate their lovemaking. He could only respond to the exquisite feelings her touch evoked.

Dominic caught his breath when her hand folded about him, stroking him, arousing him until the dancing flames became an inferno of desire. Then her caresses began to roam once again, touching him everywhere until Dominic was engulfed by such fierce, driving needs that he craved to fulfill them before they shattered his sanity. He had meant to be gentle with Rozalyn, but the savage yearnings that compelled him were more than he could bear. Like a great tiger rolling upon all fours, he pressed Rozalyn onto her back and crouched above her, his body taut, his eyes ablaze with desire.

Rozalyn's breath lodged in her throat when she met his tortured gaze. It gave her a warm sense of pleasure to realize that her touch had such a devastating effect on such a powerful man. She welcomed the feel of his lean, muscled length, the sinewed columns of his legs blending into hers; losing herself in the sea of turbulent sensations he created. His male body burned against hers and with the desperation of two lovers reaching for each other from afar, they came together, hungry and impatient to ease the wild yearning that consumed them.

Dominic could not seem to get close enough to the maddening flame that burned him inside and out. He moved against Rozalyn, seeking the ultimate intimacy, instinctively driven toward that one glorious moment of pulsating numbness that blocked out all except sublime pleasure.

Their storm of passion was so intense that Dominic felt like a weightless feather flung high into the churning clouds, whipped and tossed in a tempest so furious that he could not fathom how he could survive it. Savage splendor whirled about him, echoing like the crashing roll of thunder, and just at the moment when he swore his very soul would split asunder from the overwhelming sensations swirling within him, he found sweet, satisfying release.

Then, from the depths of the dark, rolling clouds of passion, came shards of golden light, illuminating the bright, shining moments that transcended reality. His soul touched the pure essence just beyond his reach, and then every part of his being vibrated. He was soaring on pinioned wings, unsure whether he had forfeited his life or been caught up in some fantastic dream.

Rozalyn was suffering from the same feeling of disorientation. She could not seem to sort reality from the blinding rays of light that sparkled before her eyes, and strange sensations splintered through her. Somewhere beyond rational thought, she dangled in the timeless universe of emotion. And then, ever so slowly, she seemed to fall through space, to come gently to rest on a puffy cloud.

A soft, shuddering sigh tumbled from her lips, and her eyes fluttered open to see the shadowed face only inches above hers. The contented smile that rippled across her lips faded when Dominic dropped a feathery kiss to the sensuous curve of her mouth.

No words were spoken. Their fulfillment was silently communicated. And, in that moment of tranquility, Rozalyn realized that she was staring love in the face.

It cannot be, Rozalyn lectured herself. It is the aftereffect of passion that provokes such thoughts. She decided when she had the opportunity to sit back and contemplate these moments she would realize that Dominic was just a man, not the man of her dreams.

As Rozalyn's heavy eyelids fluttered down to rest against her cheeks and she surrendered to sleep, Dominic quietly inched away from her to don his clothes. But his eyes lingered on her shapely contours, bathed in moonlight, and he again longed to caress the feel of her silky skin. Fighting the battle of self-conquest, Dominic bent over Rozalyn to draw the sheet around her bare shoulders.

She stirred slightly and then moved toward the pillow that had cradled Dominic's head, her senses still filled with the fresh, clean scent of him. Even in sleep she found herself in his sinewy arms, yielding to the pleasures of passion, soaring like an eagle in a cloudless sky, drifting . . . diving . . . spiraling.

With grim determination, Dominic turned away from the sleeping beauty who had responded so wildly in his arms. It took a great deal of will power to walk into the shadows instead of easing back down beside her and following her into her dreams. But the last thing he needed was to be caught in that lovely temptress' bed, he reminded himself. He quickened his step, threw a leg over the balcony railing, and shinnied down the supporting beam. Aubrey DuBois would probably have him shot before he could voice a word in self-defense.

"Damn," Dominic muttered as he rammed his hands into his pockets and ambled down the street. He had openly invited trouble by taking Rozalyn's innocence. But Lord, how could he have resisted her? The attraction between them was like the spark that ignites a forest fire, and nothing could contain the blaze until it burned itself out.

A quiet smile grazed Dominic's lips as he aimed himself toward the Baudelair estate. He had known his share of women, but not one of them could hold a candle to the captivating vixen who had very nearly trampled him with her stallion and then had taken him on a passionate journey beyond the stars. Perhaps I am asking for trouble, but it is worth it, Dominic assured himself. A sea of memories flooded over him, sweeping him back into moments mere words could not describe. No ice maiden this, he chuckled as Rozalyn's bright blue eyes and raven-haired visage materialized in the darkness. Beneath her cool exterior was a woman capable of unbelievable passion. Like an arrogant fool, Dominic had thought that once he had sampled this bewitching minx's charms he would be content to walk away, but leaving her had been one of the most difficult tasks he had undertaken. Now he wondered how in the devil he could forget the way it had been between them, the way her lips melted like rose petals beneath his, the way her satiny skin trembled in response to his exploring caresses?

Dominic scolded himself. He had returned to civilization to confront Aubrey. Now he would simply have to tread carefully with Rozalyn lest she confess a fond attachment for him. Damnation, why hadn't he kept his distance? He had complicated matters by allowing his desire to overshadow his purpose. He had made wild sweet love to an innocent maid, and the repercussions of that passionate tryst could be disastrous!

"Confound it, don't think about that either!" Dominic muttered. He leaped up the front steps and headed for the study to pour himself a stiff drink. With bottle in hand, he plopped down in a chair and proceeded to chase down his troubled thoughts with brandy. It took some doing, but after two hours Dominic did manage to elude the shapely genie who kept rising from his bottle.

It took two servants to haul Dominic up the steps to bed. Neither of them breathed a word about the master of the house falling flat on his face at the foot of the stairs, but they could not contain their grins when they had settled the inebriated lord in his bed. Dominic pried one glazed eye open to mumble grateful appreciation. Their amusement did not come from their master's slurred voice, but from the name he gave his assistants. It was very feminine and unfitting for the two bulky men who had pulled off his boots and tossed him onto his bed.

"I think the master must have fallen beneath a witch's spell," John Chadwell snickered, closing the bedroom door behind him.

"It would certainly seem so." Chuckling, Mosley started down the steps to return to his room. "And I only know of one witch by the name Master Baudelair was calling us in his time of need."

Chadwell nodded in agreement. "There is only one Rozalyn who could cause a man so much trouble . . . so I've heard."

"That's the one," Mosley declared. "She single-handedly drives off thieves—and she drives a man to drink to excess. I've got the uneasy feeling Master Baudelair will be wishing he hadn't come down from the mountains. That woman has already turned his world upside down and they have only just met."

"But she is quite a beauty. If I were twenty years younger . . ." Chadwell sighed whimsically.

"If you were twenty years younger you would also find yourself lying abed in an unconscious heap, just like the master," Mosley snorted. After ambling across the hall, he stood beside his bedroom door. "I've heard the rumors about the woman Dominic toted off to the theater tonight, and I've seen enough to know those wild tales are true. Master Baudelair will wind up like all the rest of the men who thought to tame that girl's wild heart. He stands a better chance fighting a mad grizzly."

"He's young," Chadwell argued. "Dominic will bounce back."

"Right back into that woman's arms," Mosley declared. When Chadwell scoffed at the prediction, Mosley's mouth stretched into a wide grin. He drew a ten-dollar gold piece from his pocket, and dared Chadwell to match it.

Chadwell eyed the old groom for a long thoughtful moment before fishing into his pocket for a coin. "This gold piece says Dominic Baudelair will have another woman draped on his arm by this same time tomorrow. No blue-eyed witch will bring a man like Dominic to his knees. Why, I'll even bet he marches back to the mountains without giving the lady a second thought."

"You've got a bet." Mosley pivoted on his heels and walked into his room. "You're going to lose your money, Chadwell. I'll even bet you double or nothing that Dominic winds up marrying that feisty lass."

Chadwell hooted in disbelief. "Dominic married? You heard him say he has no time for romance. In the mountains, he's as free as a bird and he'll stay that way. Marriage isn't his cup of tea."

"We'll just see about that," Mosley grunted sarcastically as he shut the door behind him. "He won't be the first bird to have his wings clipped."

"Dominic Baudelair?" Chadwell guffawed. He was still chuckling when he clambered into bed and snuffed out the lantern.

That old fool Mosley would soon be parted from his money. Dominic Baudelair was a restless breed of man who had never been able to stay put. He soon tired of civilization, and he longed for the wilderness and the challenges it presented. No, Rozalyn DuBois was only a pleasant diversion. Before long Dominic would yearn for the mountains. He would go where the wandering winds took him, and it would probably be another five years before Dominic ventured to return to St. Louis. Dominic married? Why, that was the most preposterous statement Chadwell had ever heard, and it would damned well cost Mosley twenty hard-earned dollars for making it!

Chapter 7

An amused grin skittered across Chadwell's lips when he strode into the dining room and saw the disheveled Master Baudelair sitting alone at the table. Dominic's head was propped on his hand, and his eyes were streaked and red from his bout with brandy. He looks a mite green around the gills, Chadwell observed.

"Good afternoon, sir," the servant said, all too cheerfully to suit Dominic whose sensitive head vibrated with each word.

"Is it? I hadn't noticed," he grunted and then groaned miserably when his temples pounded against the sides of his eyes like an overzealous drummer hammering on a percussion instrument. "Coffee . . . bring coffee." His voice was low and raspy, an attempt to guard against increasing the throbbing in his head.

Chadwell scampered back to the kitchen to retrieve a cup and quickly returned to set steaming coffee beneath Dominic's nose. "A bit under the weather, I see," he mocked lightly.

Dominic grumbled an inaudible response and, lifting the cup to his lips, cautiously took a sip.

A thoughtful frown settled on Chadwell's fair features. "I have always maintained that the best way to forget a woman is to quickly latch onto another one. It is more practical than drowning oneself in one's brandy bottle.''

Narrowed green eyes glared at Chadwell from beneath a veil of tangled lashes. "I don't recall saying that a woman was my problem," Dominic muttered grouchily.

Chadwell's shoulder lifted in a nonchalant shrug. "That was easy to assume since you called me and Mosley by a certain lady's name when we put you to bed last night."

Had he? Dominic couldn't remember. The whiskey seemed to have saturated his brain. The last thing he recalled was stuffing Rozalyn's tormenting vision in the empty brandy bottle and corking it in before she could escape to haunt him again.

Since Chadwell had every intention of winning his bet with Mosley, he pursued the subject Dominic would have preferred to drop. "As I was saying, it seems a better solution to distract oneself with another beautiful woman. I've heard a good many tales about Rozalyn DuBois. If a man knows what is good for him, he would have no further association with that young lady. Rumors suggest she is not to be tamed. You are not the first to find difficulty in courting that spirited maid. It seems futile to go off in search of the sun when one knows one might be singed."

"It isn't that simple," Dominic snorted before he took another swallow of coffee. Absently he reached for one of the fruit tarts Chadwell had brought to him to settle his churning stomach.

"Nothing is simple when it comes to women," Chadwell prophesied. Bracing his arms on the table, he stared pointedly at Dominic. "But need I remind you that, even as a stripling, you were prone to variety when pursuing females. I have no doubt that Rozalyn DuBois will be long forgotten when another lovely face catches your eye. If I may be so bold, I would suggest that you turn

111

your attentions elsewhere and leave Mademoiselle DuBois to her unruly ways."

With that parting remark, Chadwell took his leave. He hoped Dominic would give it a moment's consideration.

Dominic chewed on the servant's advice and then eased back in his chair to stare off at the far wall. Perhaps Chadwell was right. What he needed was a distraction, something to take his mind off his problems. It will be best to avoid Roz until I escort her to Lenore's party, he told himself, not consciously admitting that he couldn't trust himself alone with the blue-eyed minx who could ignite his passions with a mere kiss.

Determined to test the theory that the best cure for wanting one woman was to seek another, Dominic unfolded his tall frame from the chair. He went upstairs and soaked in a hot bath before venturing to town. Although he had been unable to think of holding another woman in his arms when they ached for Roz the previous night, Dominic vowed to drive his craving for that feisty chit from his mind. If he could look into another woman's eyes without seeing those fathomless pools of blue staring back at him, he would know he was cured of the spell that raven-haired witch had cast upon him.

Dominic garbed himself in buckskins and then aimed himself toward the waterfront, intending to patronize a woman whose profession it was to ease a man's needs without tying his thoughts in knots.

Dark, disapproving eyes appraised the ragamuffin garbed in baggy breeches, a stained vest, and a soiled cap pulled down around her ears. "Jest where do you think yore goin' dressed in that ridiculous getup?" Tess demanded as she stepped around the corner to block Rozalyn's escape route.

"Into the streets," Rozalyn informed the housekeeper.

Determinedly, she marched toward the plump barricade.

"Yore gran'mammy would keel over dead if she got a look at you," Tess scolded, wagging a stubby finger in Roz's unconcerned face. "Besides, yore an engaged woman, so I heard. And I got a notion yore man wouldn't approve of yore gallivantin' about town in that garb."

"Consider it my last fling before my joyous day of wedlock," Rozalyn smirked. Then, before Tess could grab a handful of her shirt, she darted away.

"Blast it, chile! Yore gonna git yoreself in a peck of trouble if you don't stop this nonsense." Tess let out her breath in a rush when the door slammed in her face. Grumbling in exasperation, she stomped up the back steps to finish her chores. "There ain't no holdin' the reins on that girl. She jest runs wild!"

Outside, Rozalyn breathed a sigh of relief when the cool evening breeze swirled about her. This distraction was just what she needed to elude the memories that had preyed so heavily on her during the day. She had awakened to find Dominic gone and she had berated herself for submitting to him like some common trollop. When she paused to consider how brazenly she had touched him—aroused him, encouraged him to make love to her a second time—her face flushed six shades of red.

What did I expect to feel the morning after? Rozalyn asked herself as she led the prancing bay stallion from the stables and reined him toward the wharf. Certainly not this warm giddy sensation that lured her back to Dominic. Heavens! Had she so easily become a slave to her own passion? It is just that the experience is so new, Rozalyn rationalized, desperately trying to keep their tryst in proper perspective. But she was different somehow. It would take time to adjust to the feelings Dominic had stirred within her.

During the ride to the wharf, she assured herself that it

was only fascination that tugged on the strings of her heart—not love. Besides, Dominic had made no promises, nor had he confessed any deep feelings for her. She had to keep her emotions under control. After the dinner party, she would keep her distance from him. Giving herself time to reflect on their whirlwind affair, she would see if Dominic sought her out again or if he was content to go his own way. She was certainly not going to chase him, she vowed as she slowed the stallion to a walk and aimed herself toward Sadie's Tavern. She had carefully guarded her heart these past few years, and it would not do to have it broken by a green-eyed devil with a charismatic smile. Dominic had led her to believe that what he felt for her was more than fleeting desire, but could she be sure? If she bared her heart to him would he respond with true affection, or would it be unwise to be open? After all, he was a man and her past experiences warned her to proceed with caution.

Flinging aside her pensive deliberations, Rozalyn ambled into the smoke-filled tavern. Harvey Duncan was seated at a corner table, dealing cards to three other men.

The sight of Rozalyn, even in her outrageous garb, made his hazel eyes light up, and a broad smile cracked his face. Eagerly he gestured toward the unoccupied chair across from him. As Rozalyn threaded her way through the crowd to take her seat, several familiar faces turned to greet the notorious lass who made a weekly appearance at Sadie's.

When Rozalyn was settled in a chair, Harvey dealt her into the game and Gilbert Powell shoved a mug of ale in front of her. Rozalyn glanced dubiously at the tall stack of coins at Gil's elbow and then she arched a curious brow.

"It appears that you have enjoyed a productive week," she said mockingly.

"I should say," Gil chuckled. After scooping up his

cards, he thoughtfully chewed on the end of his cheroot. "Some dandy was generous enough to hand me a donation. Right kindly of him, it was."

One delicate brow arched higher as Rozalyn studied him from beneath the brim of her dingy cap. It was doubtful that Gil had related the incident exactly as it had happened. "Did this dandy need forceful persuasion or did he readily donate to your cause, Gil?" she asked point-blank.

An ornery smile rippled across his lips as he held his cigar between his teeth and rearranged his cards. "Fought like a wild man, he did," Gil admitted. "But since the odds were seven to one, he finally decided that it was far better to give than to receive . . . Christ!" Suddenly Gil slumped down in his chair, yanking his hat low upon his forehead to shadow his face.

Rozalyn had the sneaking suspicion that one of Gil's victims had entered the tavern and he feared being recognized. She swiveled around in her chair to glance at the newcomer, and her eyes popped in disbelief when they landed on the tall figure of a man dressed in buckskin. Dominic looked ruggedly attractive in doehide and fringe, she decided before she twisted back around and slumped down in her chair, just as Gil had. Damn, what was that rogue doing in Sadie's? Rozalyn groaned and wished she could sink into the floor.

"Are you two gonna bet yer hands or curl up for a nap?" Harvey snorted impatiently.

Rozalyn looked as if she had swallowed a pumpkin, and Gil looked as if he were choking on one. Harvey darted a glance from one to the other, frowning bemusedly at their odd behavior. Rozalyn hurriedly glanced at her hand and then tossed a few coins into the center of the table.

Damnation, it was impossible to concentrate on the game when her gaze kept straying to the dashing frontiersman who had seated himself nearby. Rozalyn was irritated when the buxom blond barmaid sashayed over to take Dominic's order.

Molly sized up the handsome rake whose buckskin shirt strained across his massive chest, and he eased back in his seat to give her the once-over. Her heart fluttered wildly beneath her breasts when his bronzed features melted into a flirtatious smile.

"Is there something I can do for you?" she asked, her voice sultry, her smile willing.

Dominic's piercing gaze sketched the woman's shapely contours. Then one dark eyebrow lifted suggestively. "I suppose I could force myself to be content with a mere mug of ale," he murmured, his voice a seductive caress, "but it would only quench my thirst."

Molly leaned over the table. Pretending to brush the crumbs away, she displayed the full swells of her breasts revealed by the low neckline of her thin white blouse. "I wouldn't think to turn one of our customers away hungry," she informed him provocatively. "I have a room upstairs. . . ."

As his emerald eyes glided over the comely blonde's appetizing figure, Dominic silently cursed himself for making comparisons. The wench was attractive, but her beauty could not hold a candle to that of the raven-haired enchantress who seemed to have taken up permanent residence in his mind. Blast it, he had come to the wharf to assure himself that he could still find pleasure in another woman's arms, that was what he was going to do!

His index finger trailed over Molly's bare arm while his hawkish gaze wandered over her exposed breasts. "I should like to see your room, *chérie,* but you are what interests me most."

Rozalyn pricked her ears, silently fuming as she listened to Dominic and the harlot proposition each other. The nerve of him! The previous night he had whispered that it was she who made him burn with desire. Obviously Dominic was a walking keg of kerosene. Any woman could cause a spark that would set him ablaze. The two-timing, lying scoundrel! She applauded Gilbert for robbing Dominic of his coins and she spitefully wished he had disposed of the lout.

As Molly sauntered toward the stairs, Dominic arose to follow. He stopped dead in his tracks, however, when his gaze locked with a pair of fiery blue eyes that fried him to a crisp. Now it was Dominic's turn to wish the floor would swallow him. Of all the rotten luck!

Molly's sticky-sweet disposition turned sour enough to curdle milk when she glanced over her shoulder and saw Dominic staring at the feisty hoyden who stepped down from her pedestal each Thursday to brush shoulders with the peasants of St. Louis. The dashing rogue had lost all interest in her, and it infuriated her to lose such a handsome client, and the forthcoming coins, to Rozalyn DuBois.

"Haven't you heard?" Molly smirked, gesturing toward the improperly dressed wench. "That one does not indulge in the finer pleasures in life."

Rozalyn vaulted to her feet and slammed her cards on the table, fully intending to place a stranglehold on Molly's skinny neck. But before she could pounce, Harvey grabbed her by the elbow and yanked her back into her seat. As he did so, the cap tumbled from her head, allowing her raven curls to spill down her back like a shimmering waterfall.

"Don't pay the chit no mind," Harvey advised. "She's always bin jealous of you and it's her only way of retaliatin'."

Rozalyn was still boiling like an overheated teakettle, and Harvey's calm assessment of the situation did little to ease her flaming temper. She desperately wanted to put Molly in her sluttish place, but Harvey still held her arm

117

and he refused to free her.

"Perhaps that is true," Dominic quietly acknowledged as he dragged his eyes from Roz's fuming face and settled them on the sneering wench. He felt a strong compulsion to defend Rozalyn against slander, though he was certain she could make mincemeat of the shapely blonde. "But maybe it is just that she is a lady with discriminating taste. With her, I would not be left to wonder how many others had already sampled what was offered."

Molly shrieked indignantly at that insult, and swung her arm to retaliate. When Dominic ducked away, the barmaid's forward momentum caused her to spill the pitcher of ale she was carrying in her other hand and the frothy brew tumbled down the front of her blouse.

Rozalyn was bombarded by conflicting emotions as she observed the scene. Although she was pleased that Dominic had stood up for her, she despised him for dallying with this snippy tart in the first place. When Molly stormed off to change her clothes, Roz turned up her nose and scooped up her discarded cards, focusing her attention on the one-eyed jack grinning up at her. Before she could make a play, however, Dominic's awesome shadow fell over her and Gil slid down in his chair, as if his backbone had evaporated.

"May I join your game?" Dominic asked, his hand folding around Rozalyn's rigid shoulder.

Although the gesture appeared to be a silent apology, Roz shrugged it away, stifling the ripple of pleasure that coursed through her. Damn him! He is not going to waltz up to me with that disarming smile and make everything right, she fumed.

A curious frown crept onto Harvey's weather-beaten features as he watched Rozalyn and the handsome stranger exchange glances. Something was going on here, but he couldn't ascertain what it was.

"You can take my place," Gil mumbled as he crawled

118

out of his chair, cautiously keeping his back turned to the man he and his friends had relieved of coins three days earlier.

A wry smile trickled across Dominic's lips as he planted himself in the vacated chair. The rogue had looked faintly familiar and Dominic knew why he was slithering away, but this was not the time or place to point an accusing finger at one of Rozalyn's thieving friends, especially since he had propositioned another woman right under her nose.

"I doubt you will find our gaming table as stimulating as Molly," Roz sniffed sarcastically. After raking in the cards, she shuffled them so vigorously that she very nearly wore off their numbers.

Dominic's shoulders lifted and then dropped, making the long fringe on his massive chest quiver. When he had dragged in his cards, he eased back in his seat and cast Rozalyn a discreet glance. "I always did prefer a challenge. The wench did not present a real one," he told her flatly.

One eyebrow arched as Rozalyn glared at the scoundrel. Had he insinuated that once she had surrendered in a moment of madness he had tired of her as well? "That which comes easily does not hold your interest, *n'est-ce pas?*" she inquired, careful not to allow any emotion to seep into her voice.

"Not necessarily," Dominic contradicted with a soft chuckle. "I am only saying that the gaming table and those surrounding it are far more intriguing." His eyes wandered brazenly over Rozalyn's concealing garments, and he made no attempt to disguise his interest in what lay beneath them.

Harvey peered first at one and then the other, wondering what the devil was going on. Rozalyn seemed as skittish as a colt, whereas this handsome stranger was making blatant overtures that would have earned any

119

other man a hard slap on the cheek. Could it be that this dashing rake had piqued her interest? He did seem a far better match for this feisty misfit than the straight-laced dandies Harvey had seen hovering around her.

Casting aside his wandering thoughts, Harvey inclined his head toward the stack of coins in the center of the table. "Toss in yer ante," he commanded sternly. "We don't play for sport."

Dominic fished a few coins from his pocket and then pushed them across the table. "Cutthroat cards?" he chuckled. "I don't believe I've played it like that."

Harvey beamed in satisfaction. Perhaps he could pluck this pigeon clean. The stranger might soon find himself wishing he had accompanied Molly to her room. At least there he'd have reaped some reward for forfeiting his coins.

After half an hour, Dominic had lost all the coins he had set before him so Harvey raised the stakes, determined to drain the rogue of his money and send him on his way. That idea also appealed to Rozalyn, and she encouraged Dominic to dip deeper into his purse when he announced that he intended to withdraw from the game.

"Well, if you insist, *mademoiselle*." He sighed and then retrieved another stack of coins. "But I fear the competition is much too fierce."

Rozalyn continued to sip her ale, grinning smugly at the thought of Dominic being outsmarted at the gaming table. She knew Harvey was beating Dominic by sleight-of-hand tricks, dealing his opponent hands that tempted him to bet, but hands that must bow to Harvey's. Rozalyn kept silent, certain Dominic deserved to lose his money because he had come to the tavern to find a wench to appease his voracious appetite.

When Dominic was allowed to deal, the tide suddenly turned and the other gamblers' profits dwindled to little or nothing. And within another hour, Harvey was glaring. The evening hadn't gone as he had anticipated. He knew he'd been hornswoggled but he could not accuse this rogue of cheating since he'd indulged so heavily in the underhanded tactic himself. His eyes narrowed when Dominic unfolded himself from the chair and clamped a hand on Rozalyn's arm to hoist her from her seat.

Rozalyn glowered at Dominic, then she pried his long fingers from her forearm. "I am going nowhere," she insisted, her voice noticeably slurring the words.

The little imp has been sitting there sipping ale until she is swimming in it, Dominic thought sourly. She had been giving him the cold shoulder since he'd invited himself into the game and, to numb herself to his annoying presence, had consumed enough brew to make her wobble like a newborn foal.

"I intend to escort you home, *mademoiselle*," Dominic gritted out through a tight smile. He did not want to make a scene and invite the wrath of Rozalyn's devoted friends.

"I can find my own way home, thank you," she snapped as she glared in Dominic's general direction, wondering which of the two blurry images she saw was the real Dominic Baudelair—whoremonger, roué, and scoundrel. Damn, why did I try to drown my irritation in that confounded mug? she asked herself.

"He is right, you know," Harvey chimed in. Leaning back in his chair, he resentfully studied the stack of coins on Dominic's side of the table. "A lady shouldn't be wanderin' around the wharf at night, especially when she's bin dippin' heavily in drink."

Rozalyn had not expected Harvey to side with Dominic and she would have told him so if she hadn't been herded out of the tavern so quickly her head was spinning.

"You are making me dizzy," Rozalyn groaned as Dominic hustled her toward her horse and then promptly deposited her in the saddle.

"I would like to do more than that," Dominic snorted

derisively. Placing his foot in the stirrup he swung up behind her. "You should have your backside paddled for cavorting with swindlers and drinking like a sailor."

"Swindlers?" Rozalyn hooted in disbelief. "It seems to me that the pot is calling the kettle black. Don't think I don't know what you were doing. Harvey kept a few cards in his sleeve, but you were dealing from the top and bottom of the deck. And speaking of double dealing"— she twisted around to glare at Dominic—"for a man who only last night professed to be content where he slept, you were certainly singing a new tune!" She sniffed distastefully and then swiveled around to rein the bay down the wharf. "Molly Perkins? Really, Dominic, I never dreamed you would stoop so low. That harlot has spent so much time on her back that she is completely disoriented when she finds herself in an upright position. She was slobbering all over you and you—"

Dominic clamped his hand over her mouth to shush her. "Lower your voice, Roz. You will surely raise the dead." He chuckled, and his warm breath tickled her neck as he leaned close in case she felt the mischievous urge to topple him off the horse's rump. "I was not particularly impressd with the company you were keeping either, minx. And I know damned well who robbed me when I arrived in the city. It was your dark-haired friend who graciously offered me his chair."

"It's a pity Gil didn't do more than relieve you of your money," Rozalyn grumbled spitefully after she ripped his hand away from her mouth. "It might have saved me . . ." Her sluggish voice trailed off as six masked men swarmed them, blocking escape in any direction.

Dominic cast her a disgusted glance. "Did you sic your pack of guard dogs on me?"

"I didn't plan this," Rozalyn protested.

"Spare me a proclamation of innocence," Dominic scowled as he reached for his flintlock, but his hand

122

remained poised for he thought it best to let the weapon stay in his belt.

"Climb down, mister," one highwayman ordered brusquely. "Yer jinglin' pockets are like a bell calling people to church on Sunday. It ain't healthy for a man to be toting such a heavy purse."

As Dominic grudgingly swung to the ground, Rozalyn caught the deadly gleam in his eyes. She had witnessed that same dangerous expression in them when Jeffrey had made the foolish mistake of pouncing on him outside the theater. Nervously, she gazed back and forth between Dominic and the six men who were closing in on him. She knew the raven-haired devil was sizing up his competition. His powerful body was tense. Like a jungle cat he awaited the appropriate moment to attack, even when he was so outnumbered.

"You caught me off guard when last we met," Dominic said evenly, his cold green eyes boring into Gil's mask. "But not tonight. Call off your pack of wolves, Rozalyn. They may eventually get the best of me, but I swear I'll take at least half of them with me."

Mocking laughter echoed through the crowd of men and Harvey stepped forward to aim his pistol at Dominic's heaving chest. "My, ain't we the arrogant one," he snickered. "Do you fight as well as you boast?"

With a lightning move, Dominic kicked the pistol from Harvey's hand, and it sailed through the air, discharging when it bounced on the ground. As Dominic recoiled, like a rattlesnake preparing for his second strike, the startled thieves fell back, attempting to decide whether they should believe what they had seen. Harvey just stood there, his empty hand tingling from the force of the blow, his jaw sagging beneath his mask. Dominic had sprung so quickly that he'd had no chance to pull the trigger before his pistol was gone.

Apprehension flooded over Rozalyn and she hurriedly

fished into her pocket to retrieve enough funds to compensate the losses the men had sustained at Dominic's hand. "Take the money and leave," she hurriedly ordered when the men recovered their composure and stalked toward Dominic once again. "It isn't worth fighting over."

"Are you sure you want to let this stranger escort you home?" Harvey croaked, his eyes widening incredulously.

Harvey was certain Rozalyn would approve of their retaliation. Indeed, the only reason he had allowed this bewitching lass to be led from the tavern by this rogue was to set the man up for a robbery. Harvey was flabbergasted because Rozalyn wasn't encouraging them to attack.

"I have witnessed Monsieur Baudelair's fighting tactics," Rozalyn informed him. "Dominic makes no empty threats. I do not relish seeing my friends torn to pieces for the sake of a few coins. When Dominic claimed he would take three of you with him when he fell, he was being modest." Her gaze focused on Harvey's dubious frown. "My prediction would have been four. Which of your men will you select to be the two who will walk away unscathed?"

The silence was so thick Rozalyn could have stirred it with a stick. Finally, she breathed a sigh of relief when the men backed away, eying Dominic with considerably more respect now.

This lady was not one to blow the truth out of proportion, Harvey mused as he knelt down to retrieve his flintlock. If Rozalyn swore the brute had the tough hide of a rhinoceros and the disposition of a disturbed grizzly, Harvey would be prone to believe her. And to confirm her claim, Dominic had used his entire body as a weapon of defense.

A faint smile sparkled in Harvey's eyes as he tucked

the coin pouch in his pocket and nodded his thanks to Rozalyn. "We was intendin' to take up a collection for Corbin after the card game. His wife and kids will be most grateful for yer contribution since he's laid up."

Rozalyn rummaged through her vest for some remaining coins and then tossed them to Harvey. "Don't let them go hungry while Corbin recuperates."

"Yer a saint, my lady," Harvey murmured as he ambled over to grasp Rozalyn's hand in his own. His hazel eyes searched hers for a long, thoughtful moment before he whispered confidentially, "Are you sure you don't want us to follow you home? Just in case this fellow gives you trouble?"

"No," she insisted. "My concern was for your welfare. He is very agreeable when no one crosses him."

"But what if he—" Harvey tried to argue.

"I will be fine." Rozalyn cut him off, and then gestured toward the bulging purse Harvey carried in his pocket. "Deliver the donations to Corbin's family and let me worry about our friend."

Reluctantly, Harvey pivoted away, but not before casting Dominic a warning glance. "If you hurt that girl, you will answer to me, Baudelair. I may need to recruit an army to get my revenge, but I promise you will pay if you harm a hair of that angel's head."

Angel? Dominic rolled his eyes heavenward as the men faded into the shadows. It was obvious that the love-struck thief had overlooked Rozalyn's cantankerous qualities. As far as Dominic could tell, Rozalyn was a strange mixture of seraph and witch. She bestowed warmth, compassion, and affection on her unruly friends, but Dominic had been on the receiving end of her temper once too often not to know there was far more to the feisty lady than Harvey perceived.

It still amazed him that this heiress was drawn to the unfortunates who swarmed on the wharf. Although

Rozalyn was rich and beautiful, she seemed to thrive when she was mingling with the common people of St. Louis. What is it about Harvey Duncan that draws her allegiance? he wondered, and his gaze circled back to the improperly dressed lass who sat atop her bay stallion.

"Don't you have any normal friends?" Dominic's tone was mocking.

Rozalyn looked down her nose and bristled at his inquiry. Indeed, if Dominic had not grasped the reins, Rozalyn would have left him afoot, his question unanswered.

"There is nothing wrong with my choice of friends," she declared hotly and then flinched when Dominic hopped up behind her. "We look out for each other. We care about each other. There is no pretense of friendship in the streets." Her sharp gaze riveted over Dominic as she turned in the saddle. "I cannot say the same for a certain aristocrat whom I have recently met."

Dominic breathed a frustrated sigh and then snatched the reins from Rozalyn's hand. "I suppose you are referring to the incident with Molly Perkins," he grumbled as he aimed the steed down the street.

"Precisely." Her back stiffened when his hard contours came into contact with her.

"Naïve little nymph," Dominic chortled, and his arm slid around her waist, drawing her closer to his solid strength. "Must I confess what was troubling me when I went in search of another woman? Can you not guess my purpose?"

"I know very well what motivated you." Rozalyn tried to free herself, but his sinewy arm tightened about her, making it impossible for her to move or breathe normally. "You have an insatiable appetite. It was your lust that led you to Sadie's Tavern, naught else."

Dominic nuzzled his cheek against the soft, silky hair that streamed over Rozalyn's shoulders. "You are very wrong, chérie. I was running from your memory. The feelings you stirred within me were frightening to a man who has learned to fear little in life." Dominic sighed heavily when he felt her body go rigid against his. "Condemn me if you must, Roz, but my worst punishment lies in realizing I was lying to myself. When I looked at Molly I could only compare her to you. It was you I wanted, and I could only see your smile on her face. I would have much preferred to fight your guard dogs than the emotions raging within me. My torment comes in the form of pure, sweet memories of the time we shared. They constantly hound me while we are apart."

The bay stallion pranced uneasily as Dominic lifted Rozalyn in his arms and turned her to face him. As he took her lips, like a man savoring a thirst-quenching drink, Rozalyn told herself it was the ale that caused her to surrender to the feel of his hard male strength. Nonetheless, her lips opened to his warm, compelling kiss, and her heart drummed so fiercely she knew her responses were not due to the brew. When Dominic touched her, she felt more than a shallow physical attraction. Love stirred in her and whispered across her soul. She had had no experience with love, but she recognized the feeling. What she felt for this powerful, uncompromising man was an emotion that defied description. It was wild and sweet, and she had no defense against it.

Logic flitted away on the breeze as her arms went around his neck, her fingers tunneling through the thick, wavy hair that curled about the collar of his buckskin shirt. She was lost to the taste and feel of him, and she could not breathe without drowning in the manly scent of him.

"God, woman, do you know how much I want you? Can you feel how much I need you?" Dominic breathed raggedly. His hand slid beneath her shirt to trace a path of fire to the peak of her breast. "So quickly have you become an obsession. I touch you and it turns me inside out."

Rozalyn knew exactly what he meant. She, too, was hounded by disturbing emotions and a maddening need to appease the hunger that consumed her.

"Then love me, Dominic," she moaned softly as his exploring hand trailed beneath the band of her breeches, intimately touching the velvety flesh of her thighs. "Prove to me that it is I alone you crave."

Dominic drew a deep, shuddering breath and peered into those spellbinding blue eyes. They mirrored the reflection of his own burning desire. He knew he was playing a dangerous game with his heart, knew he was allowing himself to be led deeper into a tangled web, but he could not have climbed down from the steed and walked away if his life depended on it.

His gaze drifted to a clump of trees to the south. The secluded canopy of the cottonwoods would grant them privacy. Then he swung from the saddle, still cradling Rozalyn in his arms. Although his nagging conscience was lecturing him on the hazards of becoming involved with this bewitching vixen, his footsteps took them into the dark paradise.

Beneath the low-hanging branches of the trees, Dominic set Rozalyn on her feet; and like a man cherishing a portrait that has long been stashed from sight, he drew the tattered shirt from her shoulders to reveal her ivory skin. She is a goddess, he thought as moonlight filtered through the trees to kiss her soft flesh. He let one tanned finger drift over her bare shoulder and then scaled the crest of a breast before his lips followed its enticing path, leaving fires smoldering on her quivering skin.

A sigh of longing escaped Rozalyn's lips when his tongue flicked each dusky peak, and she held his head to her as he worshipped her body with kisses and caresses.

Her breath came raggedly as her hands slid inside his doe-hide shirt to make contact with the hard wall of his chest.

As it is when mighty waves churn against the shore, an undertow of sensations swept Rozalyn into a sea of passion. His hands and lips moved like sensuous tides flooding over her skin, tantalizing each sensitive point, drowning her in their rapturous currents. She felt the coolness of the night curl about her as Dominic slid the baggy breeches from her hips to allow him access to every inch of her body. But the warmth of his tender touch dissolved the evening chill and Rozalyn melted like snow beneath the heat of a fire about to blaze out of control.

With the same dedicated concentration, Rozalyn then undressed Dominic, her eyes adoring the naked mass of muscle that rippled across his chest as she absently tossed aside his buckskin shirt. Her palms roved across the dark furring of hair that shadowed his lean belly before her nimble fingers freed the buttons on his breeches. Slowly, she drew them down his tapered hips until nothing prohibited a bold appraisal of the man who had stolen her innocence.

Rozalyn had not meant this night to evolve into a moment of passion. Indeed, she had gone in search of distraction, something to divert her thoughts and dim her memories of this tall, darkly handsome rogue. She had been willfully ignoring the tiny voice whispering that love had wrapped its gentle arms around her heart, but she could no longer lie to herself. Some women would have wanted time to consider what they felt, Rozalyn did not. Dominic was everything she desired in a man. He was a force that even her determined will could not handle. He was the challenge she would forever pursue. This awesome mass of brawn and muscle was the man of her dreams and she longed to assure him that her need was as fierce and consuming as his.

Boldly, she caressed every inch of his hair-roughened

flesh, seeking to intensify his desire until it raced
through his veins like the bubbly lava of a volcano. Her
wandering hands scaled his hips and then swept across
his muscled chest. They forged across the taut planes of
his body before descending to map his lean belly. Her
caresses ebbed and flowed, trickling across his thighs and
lightly brushing his ribs. Not once, but over and over
again, she allowed her hands to explore and entice until
she brought his passion to such a fervent pitch that
Dominic groaned in sweet agony.

She was a witch weaving a spell, and his heart thundered so furiously he swore his rib cage would crack
beneath its pressure. Like a man deprived of oxygen,
he was unable to draw a breath without gasping for air.
And when her quiet words echoed in the corners of his
mind, he found his wish had come true.

"I love you, Dominic," Rozalyn confessed, pressing
her body against his. As she clasped her hands behind his
neck and smiled into his shadowed face, she could feel
the heat of his desire pressing against her thigh. She
ached to become one with him, to give herself to him, to
share that splendrous moment that pursued and captured
time. "It is true. I do love you. . . ."

"As I love you," he whispered back to her. Dominic
drew her down with him to the thick carpet of grass,
entwining his body in hers. "Sweet angel, take me to
heaven. . . ."

Rozalyn reveled in his soft-spoken confession. At last,
she had found a man who wanted her as she was—wild
and free, aching to give her love and have it eagerly
returned. I am special to him, Rozalyn told herself as his
greedy lips captured one ripe bud and then the other. He
wants me, not my father's vast wealth, not the DuBois
name. Dominic loves me and I love him.

There was no place she would rather be than in the

never-ending circle of his arms. When she was with him all seemed right. This was where she belonged and this was where she would stay forever. She had waited for the man of her dreams to appear and now he was here, loving her, making her wildest fantasies reality.

With a cry of pleasure she accepted his hard, driving thrust, and he became the vital flame within her, her reason for being, her breath of life. Rozalyn wrapped her arms about him, feeling the corded muscles of his back flex and relax. Then they moved in perfect rhythm with the precious melody that strummed in her soul.

Dominic was lost to primitive needs as ancient as time itself for Rozalyn tore thought from his mind and left him a shuddering mass of raw emotion. Gentleness escaped him, and he crushed her soft, feminine body to his masculine form, groaning in the exquisite ecstasy of their union. His need for this wild, lovely witch with eyes brighter than the morning sky was a passion in itself. She tormented him at every step until he returned to her, refusing to release him no matter how frantically he fought against her hold on him.

Now he craved her luscious softness, and his mind spun senselessly as it did each time they touched or kissed. A strange sort of madness had claimed him when he'd glanced up to see this fetching misfit thundering toward him on her prancing bay stallion, and from that moment Dominic had been unable to control his desire to tame Rozalyn's wild heart. She was unlike any woman he had known—strong and willful. Her eyes sparkled with mischief, and when she smiled Dominic saw a new horizon. Yet she was a wildly passionate vixen, and he alone had freed her soul and sent it soaring.

Suddenly, fiery sensations engulfed him, and his body moved as if it possessed a will of its own. He was burning alive, and as rapturous fires devoured him, he felt he was flying into the sun, to be consumed by its brilliant heat.

And then a tremor shook the roots of his sanity and ricocheted through him. He clung to Rozalyn for what seemed an eternity, waiting for the fires of passion to cool, waiting for physical sensations to fade and deliver him back to reality. But, even as the flame of love became the embers of desire, Dominic was aware of an insatiable need smoldering in the coals. Although Rozalyn's brand of passion was fulfilling, Dominic realized that she lit fires that would never completely burn themselves out.

The many faces of this vivacious nymph swirled through his hazy thoughts as his body relaxed. He could see her, raven-hair flying, thundering down the street, her eyes livened by her impetuous spirit. Then he recalled how those intriguing blue pools had sparkled with mischief as she'd ground her boot heel into his foot. Another vision rose to overshadow that—an impish smile on a flawless face camouflaged beneath the brim of a peasant's cap. Then that faded into a woman's soft, velvety body, so beautifully formed he could not resist caressing it. Yes, Rozalyn's supple curves belonged to a goddess. She was a bewitching siren, she was what dreams are made of. And she was like a distant star placed high in the heavens, to be gazed upon from afar. Dominic had been granted precious moments, but he wondered if he would ever be satisfied now that he had known perfection. Those moments of ecstasy in her silken arms would never be enough. He was, like a bee, instinctively drawn to her nectar.

"Is it always like this?" Rozalyn questioned as her sooty lashes fluttered up to meet his pensive gaze.

One dark eyebrow lifted acutely and then slid back to its normal arch as a low skirl of laughter bubbled in his chest. He bent to kiss her dainty nose, but her innocent inquiry disturbed him for he was forced to admit to himself that it had never been like this.

"Only for us." The silky huskiness of his voice drifted across her flushed cheek. "Our passion for each other has created something unique, *amie*. Each time I touch you I wonder what new dimension of pleasure awaits me."

Rozalyn cocked her head to the side, sending her ebony hair spilling over her shoulder. "Do you always offer such generous compliments to the woman in your arms?" she queried, tracing the rugged lines that strayed from the corners of his eyes.

"I don't recall saying there have been other women." Dominic chuckled as he braced his forearms beside her shoulders.

"I am not so naïve as to think I am the first," she insisted, and then glanced away before she was entrapped in the emerald depths of his eyes. "I am still not certain that you would have denied Molly if I had not been sitting in the corner of the tavern."

"If I hadn't, I would be living in torment," Dominic sighed repentantly. "I would have been touching you, not her. I would have found no pleasure when my soul remained discontent."

It was all too easy to believe Dominic when Rozalyn was cradled in his strong arms. He had said he loved her and her soul was singing. She had waited for the right man to come along. She had held all other men at bay until Dominic had walked into her life, but she had been too skeptical too long not to question his fidelity. She had to know if his affection would stray when he saw a pretty face for when Rozalyn gave her heart it would be totally. She could not bear to be taken for granted, not after she'd lived with such a dispassionate father. She wanted to be loved, truly loved, for who she was. She wanted to belong, to be needed, not tolerated or ignored.

"And what of tomorrow, Dominic?" Rozalyn persisted. "Will you seek out another when I am not there to satisfy your craving? How many times can a man fall in and out of love?"

"Any man?" Dominic's index finger sketched her kiss-swollen lips. "I cannot speak for the entire male population, only for myself, and I can honestly say I have not been in love before this moment. I thought to tear you from my thoughts tonight, but I discovered the taproot ran too deep. I cannot forget you without sacrificing part of myself. Without you I would be only half a man."

A pleased smile blossomed on her face as she looped her arms about his shoulders, and her body moved provocatively against his, rekindling the eternal fire of desire.

"And because of you I have become a woman, one with needs only your love can fulfill. Teach me to return the pleasure of your touch so that you and I never fall out of love. . . ."

Her sensuous lips parted invitingly as her hands glided over his muscular hips, arousing his needs until he trembled with the wanting of her. She vowed to shower Dominic with love, never denying him the passion she yearned to give. This powerfully built man, with hair the color of midnight and eyes that sparkled like priceless emeralds, was her world. She could not name a moment when she had felt so whole and complete. Love is like touching heaven, Rozalyn mused as his mouth slanted across hers. The sweet sensation of his breath intermingling with hers stoked the fires of desire until they burst into flame.

Dominic wasn't certain what spell Rozalyn had cast upon him, but he felt swirling currents of passion course through his every nerve and muscle. She had but to touch him and he was aroused. Now, with caresses, she rediscovered his body, and the taste of her soft lips was sweeter than wine.

Again they sampled love's brew, losing themselves in heady pleasure. Man and woman, they ached to appease a primal craving. Dominic taught her to silently communicate her love, to convey emotions that mere words could not touch, and in the stillness of the night their love blazed anew, like a shooting star searing the heavens.

Chapter 8

Much later Rozalyn half-heartedly reached for her tattered garments and shrugged them on. When she tried to fasten the buttons of her shirt, Dominic helped her with the chore. He sighed heavily as he cupped her chin in his hand and lifted her lovely face to survey each soft, enchanting feature.

"I don't want to leave you," he murmured. His free hand slid around her waist to bring her body into intimate contact with his. "Leaving you last night drove me to drink. I hate to venture a guess as to what sort of crutch I will resort to tonight."

"Just so it isn't another woman," Rozalyn said saucily, and her blue eyes flared with the sparkle of mischief that delighted Dominic. "If I learn that you have returned to proposition Molly Perkins, I will have you staked out and left to the vultures."

"Spiteful wench," Dominic gasped in mock horror. "Is it not enough that I found myself surrounded by your pack of wolves? I wondered if you intended to see them extract a pound of my flesh."

"The thought did cross my mind momentarily." Rozalyn giggled as she ambled through the trees.

"What stopped you?" Dominic's voice was heavy with

136

curiosity. "I wouldn't have blamed you. If I had been watching you entice another man, I am not certain I would have been so forgiving."

Rozalyn turned back to study Dominic's awesome figure. He bore the stamp of rugged nobility and the sight of him in form-fitting buckskins made her heart beat faster. "I have a great deal of respect for your ability to defend yourself, even against impossible odds, so my conscience did not allow me to see any of my friends hurt because I was jealous," she admitted.

A wry smile grazed Dominic's lips as he swaggered toward her. He playfully scooped her up in his arms to plant a breath-stealing kiss on her lips. "Possessive minx," he chided. Then he laughed softly, nuzzling his face against the trim column of her throat. "Are you using me to satisfy your passions? Do you think to make me your slave?"

His teasing remark hit upon an exposed nerve, and the happy smile died on her lips. "Never that, Dominic. I have no wish to smother you, only to offer back the pleasure you give . . . and with such practiced expertise."

His footsteps halted at the outskirts of cottonwood trees, and he peered down into her face, his expression somber. "There can be no other woman now, Roz. Your love has erased the past, and I cannot see past the present. The thought of you in another man's arms, eagerly responding to his touch . . ." His voice trailed off as the vision of Jeffrey Corday came into his mind. He cringed at the thought of that spindly blond touching this captivating sprite. "You are mine, Roz, and no man will claim what is mine."

Rozalyn swore she was living a dream. His words warmed her heart and echoed in her soul. For the first time in her life she was content, completely at peace with herself. She no longer yearned to follow the restless wind. Her long wait for a man bold enough to earn her respect and gentle enough to win her love had been worthwhile. She had found him and she harbored no regrets. Loving Dominic was the easiest thing she had ever done. It was beautiful and right. No one could sever their strong bond of affection, she assured herself. She pitied those who had given their love to careless philanderers. Dominic was not like those men. He truly cared about her, and he was man enough to confess that love.

Their parting kiss kept Rozalyn warm even after he released her, and as she aimlessly wandered into the house, she very nearly collided with Tess who stood like a posted lookout at the back door.

"Where have you bin 'til all hours of the night, chile?" Tess demanded. "Ain't nothin' good happens after midnight, 'specially in the streets of St. Louis. There's witches and banshees prowlin' about at this hour. Did you meet up with any of them?"

"I had a perfectly enchanting evening," Rozalyn sighed as she floated up the back stairs. "I hope you enjoyed yours as well."

"I didn't enjoy nothin'." Tess sniffed irritably. "I've bin frettin' about you all evenin', wonderin' if some hooligan snatched you up off the street. I swear, chile, I'm gettin' too old to be lookin' after the likes of you. Yer gonna shove me into an early grave if I have to spend my time stewin' 'bout where you are and what yer doin'."

"That's nice," Rozalyn said absently. She was so absorbed in her own world that she was paying no attention.

Tess did a double take when Rozalyn sauntered down the hall, humming a soft tune. "What's gotten into that girl? The way she's been floating 'round on a cloud a person would think she was in love . . ." A wry smile rippled across the Negress' lips as she watched Rozalyn disappear from sight. "Glory be! She is in love. Well,

138

don't that beat all." Tess snickered as she closed her bedroom door. The possibility of planning a wedding in the very near future left her beaming with uncontained delight.

Tess stood back to appraise this vision in lavender, her discerning gaze ensuring that not a single wrinkle detracted from the loveliness of the garment. She had insisted upon helping Rozalyn dress for the dinner party, and she was pleased with the result. Rozalyn looked like a royal princess about to attend a ball. Tess could not remember seeing her young charge so radiant on any other occasion.

"Yer man must be somethin' special," she surmised as she circled around Rozalyn to view the creation from every angle. "I ain't seen you smile so much in years."

"He is," Rozalyn eagerly replied. She peered in the mirror to rearrange a renegade curl that had tumbled from the shiny ringlets pinned atop her head. "And I consider myself fortunate to have found him."

Tess chortled at the lovestruck expression on Rozalyn's flawless features. "Lawd, I never thought I'd live to see the day you found a man to suit you. Yore gran'mammy must be delighted that her—" The housekeeper bit her tongue before it outdistanced her brain.

"If Grand'mère's wish is to see me happy, then it has come to pass," Rozalyn replied, without cross-examining Tess about the comment she had left dangling in midair.

When the butler announced Dominic's arrival, Rozalyn hurried down the steps, Tess waddling along right behind her. The housekeeper was determined to have a close look at the rake who had so quickly taken hold of Rozalyn's heart, but she very nearly tripped over her own feet when Dominic emerged from the shadows to strike a pose at the bottom of the steps. Before her stood a

139

man who could make the Greek gods bow their heads in shame. He was every bit as handsome as Rozalyn was beautiful. Tess nodded in approval as her dark eyes flowed over the powerfully built gentleman.

Rozalyn was just as awestruck as the housekeeper. She had thought Dominic dashing in brown velvet, but his deep green waistcoat and matching silk vest accented the vivid color of his eyes. The fine fabric hugged his hard, muscular chest and clung to his thighs, and he wore a roguish smile that melted Rozalyn's heart. She found herself returning his contagious grin though she felt like a child gazing upon her idol. The mere sight of him aroused her and stirred sweet memories of a night that bordered on fantasy.

"My lady, you have again bewitched me with your beauty," Dominic growled seductively.

Lifting Rozalyn from the step, he held her in his arms. Then his gaze drifted to the plump Negress who was beaming at him, and he nodded a silent greeting as he set Roz on her feet. Dominic had been so distracted by this vision in lavender that he had failed to notice they had an audience.

"Tess had to see you in person," Rozalyn teased playfully. "I think she believed I'd conjured you up after I described you as tall, dark, and undeniably handsome."

"Off with you," Tess sputtered, flicking her wrist to shoo them out the door. "Yore gran'mammy is short on patience. She'll be pokin' her head out the door every few minutes, wonderin' what's keepin' the two of you."

As Rozalyn bounded down the steps toward the carriage, Dominic grasped her arm to detain her. When she glanced up questioningly, he answered her with a kiss warm enough to turn her into a pool of liquid desire.

"Mmmmm . . . I feared I would die for the want of that kiss. God, how long has it been? It seems like months." He groaned before his lips devoured hers once again.

When he finally granted Rozalyn a breath of air, she laughed light-heartedly and then turned toward the carriage. "You, sir, are outrageous. One would think you starved for affection."

"Am I not?" Dominic chortled as he quickened his pace to keep up with her strides. "If I had my wish, we would not have said adieu last night. I shamefully admit I squeezed the stuffing out of my pillow while I slept . . . it was a poor substitute for the feel of your soft, shapely body."

Rozalyn slipped her small hand into his and then smiled up into his handsome face. "Grand'mère's party cannot last until dawn. With any luck at all she will grant us a few moments of privacy."

"I doubt that." Dominic pouted like a child who had been deprived of a treat. "She will flaunt us like two prize canaries in a cage. I predict we will be put on display the moment we set foot in the house."

Rozalyn's gay laughter eased Dominic's sour mood, and when she smoothed the frown from his features with a feathery kiss, Dominic forgot the nagging feeling of apprehension that had plagued him throughout the day. He had been relieved that Aubrey DuBois had not yet returned from his warehouse on the wharf when he'd come to call on Rozalyn. There would be a better time to confront this adversary. But when? Dominic asked himself. He had to voice his grievances to the powerful furrier, but his preoccupation with Rozalyn had pushed that purpose to the corner of his mind. Patience, man, Dominic told himself. If he wasn't careful his intricate scheme would explode in his face. He had to proceed one step at a time. Soon he would confront Aubrey, but for the moment, he would enjoy the free-spirited pixie who occupied his thoughts.

When Dominic and Rozalyn stepped into the carriage, Mosley popped the reins over the horse's back, urging the steed into a trot. A sly smile lifted his lips for he'd witnessed Dominic's possessive kiss on the front steps of the mansion. Mosley could almost feel Chadwell's twenty-dollar gold piece weighting down his pocket. Dominic is hooked, Mosley assured himself. This gorgeous creature with shiny raven hair and bright blue eyes certainly had his master in a tailspin. Chadwell would be eating his words.

While the groom was gloating, Dominic was making use of the few moments of privacy. One kiss led to another, and Dominic would have sworn the carriage had sprouted wings for they seemed to have flown to the Rabelais mansion. Reluctantly, he broke the arousing kiss and dragged himself away from Rozalyn. But when he stepped from the carriage, Mosley was peering down from his perch, a wide grin stretched across his face, and Dominic could not fathom what the old man found so amusing.

"You have certainly been behaving strangely tonight," Dominic remarked. The man seemed to be harboring some juicy secret. "I didn't realize that driving a carriage was so highly amusing."

Mosley shrugged noncommittally as he climbed down from his perch. Dominic would have pursued his investigation if Rozalyn had not emerged from the carriage to distract him. Her bright smile could have illuminated the night sky, and it nearly blinded Dominic. As he propelled her toward the mansion, Mosley took a long draw on his pipe and then ambled toward the stables. A soft peal of laughter echoed in the darkness as Mosley disappeared into the barn to join the other grooms who were waiting to drive Madame Rabelais' guests home when the party drew to a close. Dominic doesn't stand a chance against Rozalyn's charms, Mosley mused as he sank down into a chair. And he was prepared to bet another ten-dollar gold piece against anyone foolhardy enough to take the wager.

Chapter 9

Lenore clasped her hands in delight when Rozalyn and Dominic appeared in the foyer. A perfect match, she said to herself. She had prayed for this moment and it had finally come.

When Rozalyn focused her attention on her ailing grandmother, she could not believe the drastic change in Lenore's appearance. There was lively color in her cheeks and her eyes twinkled with happiness. The beldame's face was no longer chalky. Indeed, she looked ten years younger than she had two days before! It seemed her expectation of Rozalyn's upcoming wedding had worked miracles. Lenore seemed to have drunk her fill at the fountain of youth.

A pensive frown puckered Rozalyn's brow for she wondered if there would truly be a wedding. Dominic had spoken of love, but he had not asked for her hand. Did he only presume that wedlock was inevitable since it was Lenore's intention to whisk them through a brief courtship? Marriage was what Rozalyn wanted, but what about Dominic?

Casting aside her worrisome thoughts, she approached her grandmother, giving the beldame a cheerful smile. Rozalyn was sitting on top of the world and nothing could spoil her festive mood. She was hopelessly in love, and she didn't care if all of St. Louis knew it.

"You needn't say a word," Lenore insisted as she accepted the kiss Rozalyn pressed to her left cheek. "I can see by the look on your face that all is well with you and Dominic." Her eyes circled back to the dashing rake who was garbed in rich green velvet, and for a moment she admired the awesomely built, strikingly attractive man Rozalyn had selected for her future husband. "Come here, young man, and pay your respects to this feeble old woman."

A wry smile caught one corner of Dominic's mouth as he strode forward to take up her hand and place a light kiss on her wrist. "You look charming this evening, madame," he complimented and winked subtly at Lenore. "Rozalyn has warned me not to let my eyes stray to other women tonight. I am not certain I will be able to keep my promise for I might be drawn into your enchanting spell. It is not difficult to understand how Roz inherited her beauty or to whom she owes her vivacious personality."

"Devil," Lenore teased, delighted with Dominic's playful attention. "I am much too old and decrepit to believe such nonsense. Now, have you set the date for your wedding? I would be heartbroken if I were to miss the occasion."

Sparkling green eyes drifted to Rozalyn. Then Dominic smiled tenderly as he wrapped an arm around her and drew her to his side. "Did you perchance invite a clergyman to this affair? I have already made it clear that yesterday would not have been soon enough to speak the vows."

When Dominic bent to press a kiss to Rozalyn's upturned lips, Lenore beamed. Silently, she applauded herself for having already considered what Dominic had suggested. This engagement party will serve a dual purpose, she thought, a cunning grin on her face. Nothing would make her happier than to hear Rozalyn and Dominic speak their vows this very night, and if everything went according to her scheme, Rozalyn would have a husband this very evening. But where the devil is Aubrey? Lenore wondered. She had sent him a message early that morning, stating that under no circumstances was he to miss his daughter's engagement party. If Aubrey did not arrive to give his daughter away at her surprise wedding, Lenore vowed she would find someone to stand in his stead. The inconsiderate lout.

"It just so happens I have invited a man of the cloth," Lenore announced, and her smile broaded when Rozalyn and Dominic gaped at her in disbelief. "The Reverend Fletcher says he will be only too happy to—"

"Rozalyn!" Lenore was cut off in midsentence when Mariette Jarmon swept from the ballroom to meet the man Lenore had been raving about for the past half-hour. Mariette's footsteps halted when she peered up into a pair of incredible green eyes. *Mon Dieu.* She had never been as envious of Rozalyn as she was at this moment. Rozalyn had landed herself a most dashing prize, but Mariette had lost two beaux to this wealthy beauty and she considered trying to steal this handsome catch away from Rozalyn DuBois. "I am most anxious to meet your fiancé," she purred as she sashayed forward, her violet eyes never straying from the attractive rake in green velvet. He was pleasing to the eye, and Mariette was already contemplating how it would feel to be held in his arms.

A twinge of jealousy sizzled through Rozalyn as she watched the curvaceous redhead ogle Dominic. Mariette was the type of woman who derived pleasure from causing trouble. She had always been an outrageous flirt and a tease, and Rozalyn had never particularly cared for her. Clamping a tight rein on her temper, Rozalyn forced a civil smile. She would view Dominic's reaction to this

145

seductive redhead. If he found Mariette intriguing, perhaps she would reconsider the hasty wedding.

"Mariette Jarmon, I would like you to meet Dominic Baudelair. He is—" Rozalyn was unable to finish her sentence before Mariette pounced.

"Dominic . . ." Mariette rolled his name off her sensuous lips in her soft husky voice. Then she strategically wedged herself between Rozalyn and her dashing beau. "I am so pleased to make your acquaintance, *monsieur*," she cooed as she batted her eyes at him.

Mariette's sticky-sweet smile was cloying to Rozalyn. The woman was so obvious she was disgusting.

"Come, Dominic, spare me just one dance. I want to know everything about the man who has stolen Rozalyn's heart."

Like a clinging vine slowly but surely wrapping itself around lattice, Mariette latched onto Dominic, and when she dragged him toward the ballroom, Rozalyn glared at her departing back. Then she turned quickly when she heard the beldame chortling behind her.

"Jealous, *chérie?*" Lenore queried as she arched a graying brow. "No need to be. Mariette is but a stuffy bag of silk and petticoats. I predict that Dominic will find her to be shallow company."

Rozalyn compressed her lips and frowned. Dominic was a man, wasn't he? And he had been tempted to seek out another wench the previous night. Who could say for certain that he didn't have a penchant for variety? He had claimed to love Rozalyn, but when tempted could he turn his back? And Mariette was tempting. . . . Her beauty attracted men and she had always been a mite promiscuous. She wouldn't think twice about dallying with an engaged man, not when she'd consorted with married ones!

"You do love him, don't you?" Lenore asked point-blank. Her bony fingers curled around Rozalyn's arm as she gave her granddaughter a sympathetic smile.

"*Oui, Grand'mère*, very much," Rozalyn confessed with a heavy sigh. "Mariette's flirtatious games never mattered until now."

"If you are concerned, why don't you march into the ballroom and steal Dominic back?" Lenore suggested. "There is no harm in allowing the man you love to know you care enough to protect your interest." The beldame snickered at the distraught expression on her granddaughter's exquisite features. "Dominic is worth fighting for. You know that as well as I do."

Like a cavalryman answering a command to charge, Rozalyn proudly drew herself up. She marched toward the ballroom and threaded her way through the crowd of guests who were studying the darkly handsome Dominic and the provocative redhead as they made their way around the floor.

Amusement danced in Dominic's eyes when he noticed the flash of temper in Rozalyn's blue eyes. Mariette had already propositioned him twice. If Rozalyn only knew the lurid suggestions that had flown from Mademoiselle Jarmon's pink lips . . . Dominic didn't want to think about what might happen in that case. Rozalyn already looked as if she were itching to sink her teeth into something, preferably Mariette.

"Ah, there is Rozalyn," Dominic announced as he forced Mariette back to a respectable distance.

Mariette's lips jutted out in an exaggerated pout when she spied the shapely brunette. As a wealthy heiress, Rozalyn had her pick of the crop, but this ruggedly handsome beau put all others to shame. How she envied Rozalyn's way with men. They flocked to her like kittens on the trail of fresh milk, but no man had met Rozalyn's expectations until this powerfully built rogue came along. Mariette wasn't blind. She knew Rozalyn cared deeply for Dominic, but the thought of causing Rozalyn distress delighted her. It would console her for all the times she'd gone home angry because her escort had spent more time dancing with Rozalyn than his own date.

"I hope you don't mind my intrusion," Rozalyn commented, an undertone of irritation in her voice. "After all, Dominic is my fiancé."

"But I do mind," Mariette purred. "I was having a perfectly marvelous time getting to know Nicki. He seems to have led such an exciting life."

Nicki? Rozalyn rolled her eyes in disgust. "Hasn't he though." She chided herself for resorting to sarcasm, but her temper was simmering. It was difficult to overcome her urge to snatch up the punch bowl and dump it on Mariette. Rozalyn had the feeling it would take such a drastic measure to cool Mariette's lust for her fiancé. She reflected that Mariette's scruples had been squashed flat because she spent so much time on her back.

However, using the same tactic Mariette had employed earlier, Rozalyn wormed her way between the pair. Then she practically led Dominic into the waltz in her attempt to put more distance between him and the sultry red-head.

"A mite obvious, weren't you?" Dominic's dark brow tilted mockingly as he gathered Rozalyn in his powerful arms. "Only last night when you warned off your unsavory friends, you praised my ability to defend myself. Didn't you think I could handle Mariette?"

"I did not doubt your ability to do so," Rozalyn assured him flatly. "Only your desire to resist temptation."

"You were jealous." Dominic laughed softly, his lips brushing over her temple.

Rozalyn's anger melted when he pulled her against him. "Extremely," she confessed.

"Put your fears to rest," he murmured, his voice like a velvety caress. Dominic bent Rozalyn backward, forcing

148

her to clutch his shoulders or risk falling flat on her back, and his eyes glowed with lambent hunger as his head moved deliberately toward hers. "I know what I want, *amie*. Nothing or no one is going to distract me."

The seductiveness of his tone and the alluring sparkle in his eyes left Rozalyn limp with pleasure. She didn't care that the guests were grinning at them. Dominic was creating a spectacle for St. Louis' most distinguished citizens, but Rozalyn was oblivious to that fact. She accepted his flaming kiss, and her heart ran away with her as his questing tongue probed into the dark recesses of her mouth. In that warm, sensuous moment, time slowed to a crawl. The entire ballroom and Lenore's guests faded into a foggy haze. Only the two of them existed, expressing their intense love for each other.

Rozalyn finally returned to her senses when a wave of applause rippled across the ballroom. She fought her craving to escape to the terrace and continue what they had only begun for when Dominic touched her, all thought evaporated. Now she knew only the wild yearning he so easily instilled in her.

Dominic drew a ragged breath as he pulled Rozalyn back into an upright position. Then he flashed the grinning bystanders a sheepish smile before turning his attention back to Rozalyn.

"It is most fortunate that you are followed by a slightly scandalous reputation, *chérie*," he chuckled as he whirled her around the dance floor. "Otherwise, we might be tossed out on our backsides for that public display of affection.

"Are you complaining?" Rozalyn moved closer to the fire that was burning her inside and out. "Could it be that you are having misgivings about playing this charade for Grand'mère?"

"Complain about a fiery kiss?" Dominic grinned roguishly. "Certainly not, *mademoiselle*," he protested.

"My only complaint is that I am forced to do the gentlemanly thing and keep my hands to myself. Were we alone, I assure you, nothing could save you from my zealous attention."

A tingle of excitement raced across her skin. Lord, how she adored his rakish smile and the sparkle in his emerald eyes. "Were we alone, I assure you that the very last thing on my mind would be being saved."

"Brazen gamin," he taunted with a low growl. "Don't entice me. With very little persuasion I will whisk you off into the night, forgetting that your grandmother has spent the last few days in frantic preparation for this grand ball."

Rozalyn's expression suddenly sobered, and her lashes fluttered up to critically survey his reaction to her upcoming question. "And what if Grand'mère does press the issue? What if she summons the clergyman and transforms this engagement party into a wedding ceremony?"

Dominic broke stride in the middle of the waltz, and his penetrating gaze bored into Rozalyn's for a long, silent moment. His conscience had already begun to bother him so he felt the need to be honest with her, to tell her what had brought him to St. Louis. The fact that Aubrey DuBois was her father complicated matters. An explanation, poorly handled, could be disastrous. Dominic wasn't certain there was ample time or that this was the proper place for a lengthy account of the events that had led them into this tangled web of deception, but he had not counted upon his maddening attraction to this lively spitfire. Nor had he anticipated that the dowager would hustle them through a whirlwind courtship to the threshold of wedlock. Dammit, it wasn't that simple!

His conflicting emotions were mirrored in his eyes and his lengthy silence caused Rozalyn's spirits to drop a notch. As doubt clouded her mind, she began to wonder if she had assumed too much. Dominic seemed reluctant to wed her. Rozalyn silently laughed at the irony of life. For the past three years she had been constantly hounded by men who would have leaped at the chance to wed her and her father's fortune. Now the tables were turned. Dominic had offered no binding commitment. He had only confessed that he loved her. Why had she taken him so seriously when she had been cynical of such professions in the past?

Perhaps she had allowed this affair to move too quickly. She must not let Lenore maneuver her into marriage, for it would break her heart to learn, too late, that Dominic had no intention of offering a lasting love.

Slipping from his encircling arms, Rozalyn strolled toward the refreshment table to seriously contemplate the matter. If it truly was marriage Dominic wanted, then he would have to suggest it. She had always been a bit unconventional, but she was not about to ask Dominic for his hand. Perhaps he desired only to be amorous until his fascination faded and he fell out of love. That prospect frightened Rozalyn. She knew she had found a man who matched her in spirit, but Dominic was much more worldly and experienced than she. His philosophy of love might be quite different from hers.

Silly fool, Rozalyn chided herself as she swallowed her pride along with a sip of punch. Guard your naïve heart or it could well be broken.

But, confound it, she didn't want to hide her emotions. She had been forced to keep them bottled in her dealings with her father. Indeed, she had spent nine painful years learning not to cry when she was aching inside because Aubrey ignored her. For once in her life she wanted to allow her emotions to flow freely. She had partially emerged from her cautious shell when she'd expressed her feelings for Dominic, but there were risks involved in loving him, risks Rozalyn considered worth taking.

"Rozalyn, we need to talk," Dominic insisted as he took the glass from her hand and set it aside.

"It can wait." Rozalyn forced a faint smile and tucked her emotions into a dark corner of her heart. She was not going to force Dominic into matrimony.

"No, it cannot," he contradicted as he propelled her toward the terrace door.

However, the orchestra struck up a lively tune, and Rozalyn was pried from his arms and herded into a circle of men who intended to share her delightful company before she consented to wed the man who had possessively kept her by his side. Dominic growled irritably at this untimely interruption. Just when he had mustered the nerve to tell her the truth, Rozalyn had been carted off to join in a folk dance.

But Rozalyn welcomed the interruption. She uttered no protest as she was passed from one pair of arms to another. This separation would allow Dominic to come to a decision. She had never wanted to be forced into marriage, and he would never be content if he was forced into it.

Heaving an exasperated sigh, Dominic rammed his hands into his trouser pockets. Then, deciding it best to rehearse his explanation in a quiet nook where he could hear himself think, he made his way to the foyer. What he had to confess to Rozalyn would not come easily. He could not risk a misunderstanding. With Roz's quicksilver temper, he could not expect her to calmly wait for him to untangle his tongue. Hell! He should have anticipated Lenore's manipulativeness. He knew how anxious the dowager was to see her granddaughter wed, and he was certain the spunky old woman had planned the entire scheme.

As a matter of fact . . . Dominic stopped dead in his tracks when he rounded the corner. Lenore, the supposed invalid, was dancing around her wheelchair as if it were a partner while a catchy tune drifted from the ballroom. Why, this conniving old woman had been feeding on Rozalyn's sympathy! Dominic snorted in disbelief. Lenore's sick spells and coughing spasms had been an act! No wonder she'd appeared ten years younger when they'd arrived. The dowager had undoubtedly wiped the chalky paste from her face and had erased a few painted wrinkles! *Mon Dieu*. Now the decrepit beldame was prancing around in her secluded corner as if she were dancing on air. Rozalyn didn't have the foggiest notion she had been manipulated into finding a beau. That scheming old witch had been wheezing and choking as if she were on her death bed when nothing could have been further from the truth. Of all the underhanded, deceitful . . .

When the front door creaked open, Lenore dived back into her chair and replaced her lap quilt before Dominic stepped into view. His eyes rolled in disbelief when Lenore's shoulders suddenly drooped, as if the weight of the world had been dumped upon them. Then, as if with extreme effort, the beldame rolled herself into the middle of the foyer, huffing and puffing and, of course, wheezing.

"It's about time you showed up for your only daughter's engagement ball." Lenore sniffed and then flung Aubrey a glare. "Here I am, practically in my grave and I am forced to see to the preparations. You couldn't tear yourself away from your precious work long enough to notice that Rozalyn was about to be married."

"I hope you will be hospitable enough to furnish refreshments during your lengthy sermon," Aubrey snorted as his weary steps brought him into the light.

Dominic flinched at the sight of the man he had been silently cursing for the past three months. He knew they would meet again, but he had not anticipated the irritation he now felt. Deciding to wait until Lenore had

153

raked her son-in-law over the coals before he pressed the issue of lower prices, Dominic eased around the corner to wait his turn.

When Aubrey aimed himself toward the study to pour himself a drink, Lenore rolled her chair forward to follow in his wake. "I expect you to give your blessing. to Rozalyn's marriage," she declared, her tone anticipating no argument. "Your daughter is very much in love, and the time has come for her to find a little happiness since you have cruelly deprived her of it these past years."

Aubrey sloshed his brandy into his glass before he pivoted around to face Lenore's condescending frown. "Rozalyn has never voiced any complaints about her life," he retorted. "But you, Lenore, have become a meddling old woman. The last thing I need is your interference in my life or Rozalyn's."

Sparks were flying from the dowager's eyes as she shook her doubled fist at Aubrey. "I happen to care deeply for that child. You killed Jacqueline with your lack of consideration, and I intend to see to it that Rozalyn is out from under your rule before you break her spirit as well. Her rambunctious antics are the direct result of your lack of interest in her. I want to see her wed to a man who will love her."

"If you have spent the day arming yourself for battle, you have wasted your time, Lenore," Aubrey told her placidly. "I have no intention of protesting Rozalyn's wedding. You have worked yourself into a snit, all for nothing."

Lenore sank back in her chair, relieved that she would not be forced to rave at Aubrey until he complied with her wishes. But she was vexed that the man showed neither elation nor displeasure over Rozalyn's engagement. It appeared that Aubrey didn't care one way or another. Lenore knew her son-in-law was callous, but she had expected him to display a smidgen of sentiment when faced with the possibility of losing his daughter.

"Would you care to meet your future son-in-law or can you spare the time?" Lenore inquired, her tone dripping with sarcasm.

"By all means," Aubrey's tone implied he could not have cared less.

Lenore flung him a glare that would have roasted an ordinary man, but to her dismay, her son-in-law deflected its heat by tipping up his glass and draining his drink. "How very considerate you are to devote a few minutes of your time to your daughter and her fiancé on the eve of their wedding," she snapped caustically. She spun her wheelchair around and propelled herself toward the ballroom. Pausing at the door, she twisted around to make her announcement before she summoned Dominic and Rozalyn. "I have arranged to have the ceremony tonight. I trust you will stay to give the bride away. That will probably be the most time you have spent with the child since her christening." On that bitter note, Lenore sailed out of the study, leaving Aubrey to gnash his teeth and mutter several disrespectful epithets.

Chapter 10

After overhearing the verbal battle between Lenore and Aubrey, Dominic was ready to make a quick exit. He was not about to approach DuBois after the man had been slashed to pieces for he had a long list of pecadilloes to bring to Aubrey's attention, not the least of which were the DuBois' sky-high prices at rendezvous. After thoughtful deliberation, Dominic decided it best to get the hell out of the house and send Mosley back with a humble apology. Mosley could explain that an emergency had arisen and that Dominic had been suddenly called away. Later, he would set matters straight with Rozalyn. Once they had come to terms, Dominic would approach Aubrey.

This mess could be untangled if it was handled logically, Dominic assured himself as he quietly tiptoed out into the hall. He was only fifteen feet from freedom. The front door was his salvation.

Aubrey stared blankly into the hall until a dark figure moved across his line of vision. The craggy features on the man's face seemed out of place above a green velvet waistcoat and a white silk shirt. It took Aubrey a moment to realize that the man was, indeed, out of place among Lenore's throng of guests.

"Hawk? Is that you?" Aubrey called after him. Hurriedly, he set aside his drink and went in pursuit.

Dominic cursed his rotten luck. He had almost made it to the front door without being detected. Resolutely, he turned back to greet DuBois who appeared in the foyer.

"What the devil are you doing here?" Aubrey asked incredulously. His wide eyes swam over Hawk's expensive garments. He had never seen this legendary half-breed in anything but buckskins. "I almost didn't recognize you."

Dominic sorely wished he hadn't. "I am visiting friends in St. Louis," he explained with a sick smile. "But something has just come up and the incident demands my immediate attention." God, he didn't want to be detained, not when Lenore was planning to see him wed in a matter of minutes. "Perhaps we can meet tomorrow for lunch. But I really must—"

"Is there a fire hereabouts?" Aubrey chuckled as he watched Dominic shift his weight from one foot to the other.

"No, but—"

"Then join me for one drink," Aubrey insisted. Clamping a hand around Dominic's arm, Aubrey hauled him toward the study before his companion could protest. "I would much prefer to visit with you than those stuffed shirts who have congregated in the ballroom. Perhaps we can leave together after I fulfill my obligation to my future son-in-law." He snorted disdainfully as he reached for the brandy snifter. "No doubt the man is some stuffy pillar of society."

"More likely a coward," Dominic muttered, half-aloud. If he could have contorted his body so he could have given himself a swift kick, he surely would have. He was up to his neck in trouble, and blurting out the truth at such an untimely moment could prove disastrous. "I really cannot spare the time." He tried to walk away but

Aubrey placed a glass in his hand.

"Have you met the grande dame of Rabelais?" Aubrey hoped to distract his fidgety companion.

"Uh . . . yes . . . as a matter of fact I have." Dominic glanced uneasily about him, and his eyes focused on the door as he brought his drink to his lips.

"Then surely you understand my need to leave," Aubrey grumbled. "The beldame has somehow managed to persuade my daughter to wed. Not that I object, you understand," he added with a careless shrug. "But it galls me that Lenore has placed herself in charge and orders me about as if I were her lowly servant."

"I sympathize with your plight, but—" Dominic could only manage to wedge in a few words before Aubrey broke in.

"I had hoped to purchase your furs last summer," the furrier said. "I wondered where you managed to sell your pelts."

Dominic ached to voice his displeasure with the last rendezvous, but he forced himself to respond to Aubrey's remark. "I found a buyer in St. Louis. He was far more generous." The temptation was overwhelming. Dominic had been silent much too long. "And speaking of the rendezvous, I have a few—"

"Well, I see you found each other," Lenore called out as Rozalyn rolled her back into the room. She was peeved that her search for Dominic had proven fruitless, but now her troubled frown evaporated.

Apprehension flitted across Rozalyn's delicate features, for the moment Lenore had informed her that Aubrey arrived, she had become tense. Her uneasiness ebbed when she saw both men in conversation. Perhaps her father's grudge against the Baudelairs had been forgotten. That must be so, or Aubrey would not be chatting with Dominic.

"Hawk and I have been talking business," Aubrey

explained as he bent his gaze on his mother-in-law. He nodded a silent greeting to Rozalyn and then turned his attention back to Dominic.

"Hawk?" A bemused frown clung to Lenore's brows as she glanced back and forth between Aubrey and Dominic. "It seems you are mistaken, Aubrey. This is Dominic Baudelair, Rozalyn's fiancé."

"Baudelair?" Aubrey's calm façade cracked like a shattered glass. "*Baudelair!*" The name exploded from his lips. "No wonder you changed your name to Hawk, you miserable bastard!" Aubrey roared.

The silence that followed Aubrey's booming attack was unnerving. Rozalyn peered incredulously at her father. Aubrey looked as if he were about to split at the seams. Never had he shown such emotion, not even when he'd lost Jacqueline. Aubrey's face flushed a furious red as he wheeled away and hurled his glass into the fireplace. His entire body was rigid with uncontained anger, and Rozalyn and Dominic stared at him as if he had gone stark raving mad.

"No one by the name of Baudelair will every marry my daughter!" he screeched, glaring with blatant hatred at the man he'd known only as Hawk.

"You promised me you would give them your blessing," Lenore spouted. "You are not going to back down on your word, Aubrey."

"I gave my consent before I learned this bastard's name." Aubrey scowled. He was glaring daggers at all three of them, as if they had conspired to deceive him. "There will be no marriage. By God, I forbid it!"

The threesome flinched as his thundering voice ricocheted off the walls and came at them from all directions. Rozalyn regained her composure and marched stiffly toward her father, her irritation rising sharply. Aubrey had ignored her most of her life, but he was now ordering her about. She decided that her father had lost the right to do so when he'd shut her out of his life.

"I have made my decision," she told him firmly. "If Dominic and I wish to wed, we shall do so. How dare you play the overprotective father after you have excluded me for so many years. You are being unreasonable, and you have yet to explain why you find the name Baudelair so distasteful."

"I do not have to explain myself," Aubrey hissed as his murderous gaze swung to Dominic.

Dominic frowned bemusedly. He didn't have the foggiest notion why his name had provoked such a drastic change in Aubrey's behavior.

"I refuse to give my blessing to this marriage. That is the beginning and end of it!" Aubrey spat out.

Lenore was so agitated that she forgot herself. Like steam rising from a boiling teakettle she sprang from her wheelchair, her charade forgotten as she turned narrowed eyes on Aubrey. Both father and daughter were dumbstruck when the frail, seemingly decrepit dowager launched herself toward them, and Lenore took advantage of their stunned silence and wagged her finger in Aubrey's peaked face.

"If you do not give your blessing, the wedding ceremony will go on without you," Lenore assured him. "Rozalyn does not need your permission. She is no longer a child. It will be a simple matter to find a substitute father among my guests. Heaven knows, she has been without one since the day she was born."

Aubrey was shaking like a leaf caught in a cyclone. "Sit down, old woman. I have endured your sermons too long. No matter how low your opinion of me is, I am still Rozalyn's father and I forbid this marriage!" His voice rose until he was all but shouting in Lenore's face.

Then Aubrey grabbed Rozalyn by the arm, and herded her toward the door. He was determined to escort his daughter home and to keep her there until Baudelair packed his belongings and returned to the mountains where he belonged. Baudelair! Aubrey could not believe what had happened. God, how he detested that name and all the tormenting memories associated with it.

But before Aubrey could storm through the door with Rozalyn in tow, Dominic blocked his path. The faintest hint of a smile bordered his lips as he met Aubrey's smoldering glare. "I believe you and I can solve this dilemma," he stated calmly and then darted a discreet glance to Rozalyn who was still trying to free herself from her father's painful grip. "I beg a private conversation."

"I have nothing more to say to you in public or private," Aubrey growled. "Now get the hell out of my way!"

As Aubrey charged ahead like a mad bull, Dominic agilely sidestepped, then caught Aubrey by the arm as he barreled by. DuBois squealed with pain as Dominic twisted his arm up his back, applying fierce pressure until Rozalyn was able to worm free.

"Take your hands off me, you bastard!" Aubrey hissed venomously.

Rozalyn backed toward the door and stared at her father as if she were seeing him for the first time. He had never displayed such rage. For the life of her, she could not fathom what ghost tormented him so. His eyes were glazed with a murderous hatred that made her blood run cold.

"Rozalyn, take your grandmother back to the ballroom," Dominic gritted out through clenched teeth, as he strained to contain the infuriated DuBois. "I have a few words to say to your father whether he wishes to hear them or not."

Nodding in compliance, Rozalyn hurried back to the wheelchair and gestured for Lenore to park herself in it. Lenore shrugged off Rozalyn's disapproving frown.

"I think it is best that the men settle their differences

161

in private," she concurred. She deliberately ignored Aubrey as she rolled past him.

"While they are debating the issue, you can explain how you managed such a miraculous recovery." Rozalyn frowned at her grandmother. "I am most anxious to hear what remedy you employed to relieve your fainting spells and coughing spasms."

When the women had exited, Dominic kicked the door shut with his boot heel. Deciding to cast diplomacy to the winds, he herded his struggling companion across the study and forcefully stuffed him into a chair. Once Aubrey had been planted in a seat, Dominic shoved the massive desk forward, pinning the man to the wall. Aubrey was not leaving that room until Dominic had presented his proposal and the two of them had come to terms.

"I don't know what grudge you hold against my family, and at the moment, I don't care. I returned to St. Louis for one purpose and one purpose only," Dominic declared, his voice revealing the pent-up anger that had plagued him since he'd descended from the Rockies the previous summer. "For the past six years you have been robbing hunters and trappers of their livelihood with your sky-high prices on supplies. Each year your prices are higher than the year before. You are single-handedly destroying what might be a profitable profession—trapping beaver and mink."

When Aubrey opened his mouth to interject a comment, Dominic gave the desk another shove, forcing the wind out of his nemesis. "You had your turn to rave, DuBois. Now it's mine. I will no longer permit highway robbery of hard-working trappers. Many of them have perished in the cruel terrain, battling Indians and wild beasts, but those who have survived deserve to be well paid for the hazards they face."

Dominic drew himself up in front of his captive

audience. "If you are prepared to be reasonable, so am I. If you agree to lower your prices and allow the trappers their rightful profit, I will gracefully bow out of this marriage you have so vehemently protested."

Aubrey's flaming blue eyes narrowed on the tall, muscular man who had backed him against the wall. "So that was the reason you planned to wed Rozalyn," he proclaimed, his voice acrid with anger. "You intended to use my daughter to get to me, didn't you, Baudelair?" He spat out the name as if it left a bitter taste in his mouth. "You thought I would approve of the wedding and cater to your wishes if you were my son-in-law. Well, it won't work either way. I will continue to run my business as I see fit. You are not going to dictate policy to me."

Aubrey's lips curled in a taunting sneer as his gaze traveled over Dominic's swarthy physique. "Did you charm my daughter with words of flattery, Baudelair? Poor naïve Rozalyn. She probably thinks you are actually in love with her." He snorted disdainfully. "Did you tell her the truth? Did you confess that you were attracted to her because you wanted favors from me? Did you admit to her that you were eager to wed her, only to gain an advantageous position in bartering? Did you shower her with lies or did you confess your real reason for coming to St. Louis?"

"I did not agree to marry her," Dominic replied. "That was Lenore's idea. But what is between your daughter and me is—"

Aubrey scoffed at those remarks, refusing to allow Dominic to finish. "I know you planned to use Rozalyn as your gambit. She was to be the bait for your cunning scheme, wasn't she? If you married her, you thought I'd be eager to keep peace with my new son-in-law, and if I rejected the wedding plans, you intended to bribe me into submission, isn't that it?" Aubrey laughed bitterly. "I would have expected such skullduggery from the Baude-

163

lairs. They use people like pawns in a chess game, calculating their moves, plotting and scheming to have their own way.

"Well, I will agree to nothing!" Aubrey's fist hit the desk. "I will not tolerate you as my son-in-law and I refuse to be bribed. I want you out of Rozalyn's life, out of my life!"

It was impossible to carry on a debate with Aubrey DuBois for he was in a rage. The man had garbled the entire incident, and Dominic was grateful that Rozalyn was not there to hear the truth twisted into a malicious lie.

We are at a stalemate, Dominic thought sourly. He knew Aubrey would never agree to a compromise, not for all the furs in the Rockies, but he was not going to budge from his position. Dominic itched to yank Aubrey out of his chair and shake some sense into him!

Tears rolled down Rozalyn's cheeks as she listened to the trenchant argument going on behind the closed door. She had not returned to the ballroom as Dominic had ordered. Instead, she had pressed her ear to the wall, determined to hear what both men had to say. The truth slashed into her like the sharpest of knives.

Rozalyn was overcome by emotions that rose from deep inside her and channeled through every part of her. She was trembling with humiliation and fury. God, how could I have been so blind? she screamed at herself. Her heart twisted in her chest and sobs of rejection quivered on her lips. She could barely contain her tormenting pain. No physical pain could compare to it. Her hurt splintered her soul. To love Dominic and to learn that he had deceived her was worse than sustaining a mortal wound.

Dominic had lied to her. Everything he had said had been calculated. While he'd been whispering sweet nothings in her ear, he'd been silently laughing at her, using her, just as all the other men had attempted to do. But this time it was not Aubrey's money her suitor coveted. No, he wanted favors from her father. He had murmured confessions of love only to win her loyalty. The cold, calculating bastard! He had set her up for the biggest fall she had ever taken, lifted her to the lofty heights of love and then sent her plunging to the depths of despair.

For the first time in her life, Rozalyn had expressed her emotions. She had laid her innocent heart at Dominic's feet and he had trampled on it. She had trusted him and he had betrayed her. God, why had she allowed herself to love such a deceitful scoundrel? She had thought Dominic was different. She had been certain that he returned her affection. But what he'd felt for her had been nothing but lust.

Now Rozalyn despised Dominic as passionately as she'd loved him. There is such a thin line between love and hate, Rozalyn thought bitterly. So quickly had her first love turned sour. But hate Dominic she did, with every beat of her breaking heart. She now despised his laughing emerald eyes and raven hair, but if she lived to be a hundred she would never forget that handsome face, his lying lips, his poison kiss.

Dominic had vowed he'd sought out Molly Perkins in an attempt to fight his growing attraction for Rozalyn, but that was another of his deceptive lies. He had gone to Molly because their night together had been nothing special to him. Like the wild, ruthless warriors of old, Dominic had wandered, intending to satisfy his cravings with other women. Then he'd been deceitful enough to swear he'd be jealous if she allowed another man to touch her as intimately as he had. Damn the man!

A sea of tears spilled from Rozalyn's eyes, flooding her flaming red cheeks. While she'd been falling hopelessly in love with that cunning blackguard, baring her heart,

Dominic had been gloating over the success of his scheme. No wonder he had hesitated when she'd quizzed him about the marriage Lenore had arranged. Dominic didn't love her. What he wanted from her had nothing to do with tender emotion. She had allowed him to take her virginity, but he'd seen her only as a conquest.

Dominic had used her! That thought echoed through her mind until Rozalyn wanted to scream, if only to drown out her bitter torment. She had thought Jeffrey Corday was one of the lowest forms of life, but she'd been badly mistaken. Dominic Baudelair was a snake. Lord, how she hated him and every memory of their time together. She prayed her father would reject his demands, for Dominic deserved no mercy after the way he had treated her, lying to her, using her for his selfish purpose. Never again will I trust a man, Rozalyn promised herself as she brushed away the tears streaming down her cheeks. Never again will I allow myself to believe in love. There is no such emotion. I should have realized that after living all these years with my father. Men are calculating creatures and I want nothing more to do with any of them. My mother died for the want of love, something Aubrey was incapable of giving. No man is, she thought cynically. They are all selfish beasts who take what they want from women and then discard them.

Another wave of tears threatened to destroy Rozalyn's crumbling composure and she felt an impulse to run. If she could have gotten herself in hand she would have stormed back into the study and told both men what she thought of them, but heart-wrenching sobs were dangerously close to overtaking her.

Lenore continued to press her ear against the wall, cursing her inability to catch Aubrey's words. "What the devil are they saying to each other?" she asked.

Rozalyn couldn't speak, not without bursting into tears. The urge to put as much distance as possible between herself and Dominic overwhelmed her. Her dream had been shattered and she had only one desire left now. She wanted to forget that Dominic Baudelair existed. In time I will forget, she vowed to herself. Yes, her heart would mend, but she was never going to forget how it felt to be used and betrayed. Dominic had taught her a valuable lesson—to open one's heart was to invite suffering and pain. And that pain was unbearable.

As Dominic's haunting vision materialized before her blurred eyes, Rozalyn burst toward the door. She could no longer contain her grief and humiliation. She had to find some place to hide before the dam of will power holding back her tears burst. She had to find a place to fall apart, to release her anguish and to gain control of her frazzled composure.

"Where are you going?" Lenore wanted to know as Rozalyn dashed toward the front door. "What did Aubrey and Dominic say to each other? Rozalyn?"

Rozalyn didn't hear her grandmother's rapid-fire questions. She was too overwrought. Her footsteps took her through the door and out into the night to find a sanctuary that would allow her to be alone with her tormented thoughts.

A frustrated sigh escaped Jeffrey Corday's lips as he paced back and forth in front of the Rabelais mansion. When the news of Rozalyn's engagement party reached the loan sharks' ears, they had gone in search of Jeffrey. The investors had been very unhappy to learn that Jeffrey was not the husband-to-be. Indeed, Corday had been informed that if he did not pay his heavy debts by the following morning he would be a cold corpse by evening. He was a desperate man. Although he had decided upon a plan of action, he hadn't quite worked out the minute details. His only hope was to kidnap St. Louis's wealthy debutante and hold her for ransom. Surely Aubrey DuBois would pay to see his daughter returned. At first he thought Aubrey would assume his daughter had been abducted by the thieves and thugs who roamed the streets . . . until Rozalyn returned to point an accusing finger at the true culprit. He would have to dispose of the feisty chit or Aubrey would tear him to pieces.

Jeffrey frowned pensively as his gaze lifted to the shafts of light shining from the window. How was he to snatch Rozalyn from the mansion without being recognized? Perhaps he could send a message, request a private word with Rozalyn. When she appeared he would . . .

His dilemma was solved when the door flew open and Rozalyn breezed down the steps, right into his waiting arms. Before she realized what had happened, Jeffrey had stuffed his handkerchief into her mouth and had imprisoned her in a bone-crushing grasp.

Another damned man! Rozalyn swore under her breath as Jeffrey wrestled her to the ground and tied her hands behind her back. God, how she loathed them all!

After Jeffrey tossed Rozalyn over his horse and strapped her in place, he disappeared for several minutes to deliver the ransom note. Rozalyn tried to free herself from the restraining ropes, but her attempts were futile. What does it matter? she asked herself as despair closed in on her. She was hurting and she was too raw inside to care what happened to her. At the moment, quick death would come as a blessing. As the bright lights of the Rabelais mansion vanished in the distance, Rozalyn cried silently. Nothing truly mattered now. She had learned the heart-breaking truth about Dominic. Damn him for causing her so much pain. She was slowly dying inside. Nothing had ever hurt her so deeply as being forsaken by Dominic, not even her father's constant dispassion. Being in love isn't heavenly, Rozalyn realized dismally. Love is hell and its bittersweet memories are eternal torture.

Chapter 11

Dominic eased one hip onto the edge of the desk and glared at Aubrey. He and DuBois had gone another round, Dominic offering compromising terms and the mulish furrier rejecting them. Aubrey had refused to enlighten Dominic about the reason for his hatred of him, yet he continued to curse the name of Baudelair. It was obvious that Aubrey thought himself betrayed by some member of Dominic's family, but by whom? Could it have been Dominic's grandfather, his father, or his aunt? She had moved to New Orleans long years ago. Dominic didn't have the slightest idea who could have been responsible for Aubrey's personal vendetta.

"You can hold me prisoner behind this desk from now until eternity, but I am not changing my mind," Aubrey growled.

"Then you leave me no choice," Dominic snapped back at Aubrey. His patience was running short, and he was prepared to take drastic measures. "I intend to assemble my own caravan for next summer's rendezvous. And I assure you, the trappers will flock to my trade store, not yours. They have had their fill of your exorbitant prices."

"You are not the first man to attempt to compete with

me," Aubrey sneered. "Your caravan will never reach Green River, not if I have anything to do with it."

The impatient rap at the door interrupted their argument and Dominic scowled in disgust. He had no intention of freeing Aubrey until they had reached a workable solution.

"Open this door!" Lenore demanded. "While the two of you are battling over rights to Rozalyn, someone has kidnapped her!"

"What?" Dominic wheeled toward the door, whipping it open to see Lenore holding a hastily scribbled ransom note.

After reading the demand, Dominic thrust the note at Aubrey who pushed the desk away and wedged himself free.

"How could anyone sneak into the house and snatch Rozalyn from a crowded ballroom?" he questioned incredulously.

"She was not in the ballroom," Lenore corrected. "She was eavesdropping on your conversation. Suddenly, she shot through the door as if she were being pursued by Satan himself. Whatever the two of you said must have upset her terribly." Her narrowed gaze riveted over first one astonished face and then the other. "I can only assume that someone was waiting outside to abduct her." She heaved an exasperated sigh and then shook her head. "I knew something like this would happen. Rozalyn has been cavorting with those hooligans who swarm the street. Now they have finally turned on her. I told her to beware of the company she has been keeping but she refused to listen."

Dominic groaned at the thought of Rozalyn eavesdropping on their conversation. He had ordered her out of the room to spare her feelings and to guard against misconceptions. But the curious little imp had undoubtedly plastered her ear to the wall, not missing a single word.

"Well, do you plan to pay the sum these kidnappers demand?" Aubrey smirked sarcastically. "Isn't this an ironic twist of fate? If you decide to pay to have your *fiancée* returned, it will cost you the financial investment for your caravan. And if Rozalyn is safely returned, she will have nothing to do with you after learning that you were only using her. No doubt, she will despise you as much as I do."

Blazing green eyes clashed with mocking blue ones, and it was all Dominic could do to keep from clamping his fingers around Aubrey's neck and shaking him. The man didn't care that his daughter had been abducted. All he wanted was revenge on Dominic. "You were putting words in my mouth, DuBois," he gritted out. "I said nothing against Roz. You twisted the truth until I almost didn't recognize it myself."

"Roz, is it?" Aubrey pounced on the shortened version of his daughter's name, his tone crackling with mockery. "It will be Mademoiselle DuBois to you from this day forward . . . if she allows you to speak to her at all."

"Since you have denounced the marriage, you pay the ransom," Dominic flung at the infuriating man, vindictiveness fanning into flame his already smoldering temper. "If you want Rozalyn back, then you pay the price. Perhaps it will convince her that you actually feel some small attachment for your own flesh and blood."

"I have no intention of sacrificing a penny," Aubrey retaliated spitefully. "Let her bereaved fiancé pay the price."

Dominic's patience snapped. With the quickness of a pouncing panther he grasped Aubrey by the lapels of his jacket and snatched him off the floor. Their faces were only inches apart, their eyes flashing barely contained fury. But before the two men could rip each other to shreds, Lenore vaulted from her wheelchair to demand their attention.

"It seems neither of you are concerned about Rozalyn's welfare. She could be lying dead in the dust, broken and abused, yet all the two of you think about is whatever it is that is gnawing at you. I don't know what this squabbling is all about, but I want it stopped this minute!" Her voice was becoming higher and wilder by the second. "I will be only too happy to pay the ransom. I seem to be the only one who truly cares what happens to that poor child." Her fuming gaze raked disgustedly over both men. "The two of you should be banding together to see that Rozalyn is safely returned. After she is, you can go for each other's throats. As a matter of fact, neither of you deserve her affection!"

Dominic shoved Aubrey away as if physical contact with the man repulsed him. Damn! He had been so furious with this heartless furrier that he could think of nothing else.

If Rozalyn loathes me; I deserve her wrath, he assured himself.

He dragged in the trailing reins of his temper and thoughtfully considered Rozalyn's predicament, and as he turned his thoughts to the abduction, he frowned pensively. Dominic could not agree with Lenore's speculation that ruffians were holding Rozalyn for ransom. Harvey Duncan and his unruly associates would never permit Rozalyn to fall prey to such a crime. No, it had to be someone else, someone in dire straits who thought to lay the blame on the obvious culprits. Jeffrey Corday! The name vibrated through Dominic's swirling thoughts. It had to be that skinny-legged milksop. None of Rozalyn's friends would lay a hand on her, not for all the gold coins in Aubrey's safe.

As Dominic spun on his heels and stalked toward the door, Aubrey walked toward his adversary to hurl another taunting jibe. "Have you decided to turn your back on Rozalyn and return to the mountains now that your conniving scheme has failed? If something happens to my daughter I will hold you personally responsible. I promise, you will never sell another fur pelt in St. Louis or at any market west of the Mississippi. And I further vow that no merchant will dare to sell you goods for your caravan, Baudelair. You are finished!" His derisive glare flooded over Dominic's powerful form, and then Aubrey scoffed at the man who dared make demands on him. "The legendary half-breed of the Rockies will become the laughingstock of hunters and trappers. No man challenges me and wins, especially not a Baudelair!"

Dominic grasped the doorknob until his knuckles turned white. Silently, he turned to glower at the red-faced man he was growing to despise more with each passing moment. "You are a disgusting excuse for a man, DuBois. Your only concern is for yourself and your precious fur empire. I pity Rozalyn. A life with you cannot be any life at all. You have been so poisoned by this grudge you bear against my family and your obsessive craving for power that you don't even give a damn about your own flesh and blood. If Rozalyn remains loyal to you it is only because she feels an obligation to her natural father, not because she respects you for the kind of man you are." Smoldering green eyes drilled into Aubrey's fuming face. "Maybe neither of us deserve her affection, but it was yours for the taking. Yet you turned your back on your own daughter just to feed this mysterious hatred that has left you a shell of a man."

"Get out of my sight, you loathsome vermin!" Aubrey howled, his voice rising until he was dangerously close to apoplexy. "If you have not packed your belongings and left St. Louis before the night ends, I will hunt you down and dispose of you myself."

Dominic stared at Aubrey, watching the man's composure crumble. The dam that contained his suppressed

173

emotions seemed about to burst, and Aubrey's entire body shook. His eyes held a demented expression resulting from some unexplained torment. It seemed the furrier could not bear to contain his soul-shattering pain for another moment.

"I once trusted the Baudelairs, and I was cruelly betrayed," Aubrey choked out, his voice crackling with hatred. "I hope their souls burn in hell, and yours along with them. If you think the price of trapping supplies is high now, wait until next summer, Baudelair. And don't you ever go near my daughter again. If she doesn't despise you by now, as I do, she will. I promise you that. Our feud with the Baudelairs has only begun!"

The man is a maniac, Dominic decided as he yanked open the door and stormed out. He could not fathom what Aubrey was ranting about and he did not intend to waste his sympathy on him. Dominic's foremost concern was Rozalyn. It was apparent that Aubrey was so bitter and furious he could not manage a sane thought. By the time DuBois calmed down, Rozalyn could be dead.

That realization hit Dominic like a hard slap in the face. If Jeffrey had kidnapped Rozalyn, he wouldn't dare let her live for Aubrey would crucify Corday when Rozalyn blurted out her abductor's name. Even Jeffrey, imbecile that he was, would have considered that possibility.

As Dominic quickened his step to fetch his groom and a mount, his mind buzzed with attempts to form a plan to free Rozalyn and to see that Aubrey received his just reward. He was not about to admit defeat to the powerful furrier, nor would he buckle beneath the man's vindictive threat. It was time Aubrey DuBois learned there was one man on God's earth who did not accept him as master. DuBois will not emerge the victor, Dominic promised himself. Aubrey's festering hatred had infected his life and had poisoned his dealings with his daughter and with the trappers. The man bore a grudge against the world and everyone in it. Dominic wuld have given his right arm to know why, but DuBois wouldn't explain so he decided there was only one way to deal with him—to make him comply with Dominic's demands. And that was exactly what Dominic was going to do—force Aubrey to comply. He would threaten him with that which Aubrey could never tolerate. DuBois would become a reasonable man because Dominic would allow him no other choice!

Calculating green eyes surveyed the dilapidated home that stood on the outskirts of St. Louis. Then Dominic frowned thoughtfully and swung from the saddle, handing the reins to Mosley.

"Do you want me to accompany you, sir?" Mosley inquired as he tapped the ashes from his pipe and prepared to dismount.

"This is a private fight," Dominic murmured absently as he peeled off his jacket and flung it over the pommel of the saddle.

Dominic silently stalked into the shadows and then circled around to the back of the two-story house. His gaze swung to the dim light that filtered through the drapes in the window above him before he scampered up the trunk of a tree, heading toward that beckoning glow. After he had inched his way along one overhanging branch, he reached out to grasp the narrow window ledge. His long body stretched across the distance between the branch and the towering ledge; then he found a foothold on the stones that jutted out from the structure.

A thankful sigh escaped his lips as he peered between the drapes to see Rozalyn bound, gagged, and tied to a chair. Since Jeffrey was nowhere in sight, Dominic pried open the window and eased himself into the room.

Rozalyn's head jerked up when she heard a faint sound, but her eyes burned hot blue flames when Dominic unfolded himself from the ledge and slid in the window. She had considered the possibility of being rescued, but if she could have selected her champion, it most certainly would not have been Dominic. The mere sight of him infuriated her, and the pain of betrayal slashed across her wounded heart like a double-edged sword.

Dominic approached Rozalyn cautiously, like a man wading into an alligator-infested swamp. Well aware that this hot-tempered spitfire would spout furiously if she was given the opportunity, Dominic left the gag in place and merely freed her from her chair. He was not about to untie Rozalyn and risk being clawed into bloody shreds.

As he propelled Rozalyn down the hall, she glowered over her shoulder at him and then jerked her arm from his grasp, assuring him that his touch was unwelcome. After they had made their way down the stairs, Dominic heard a faint rustling in the parlor. Pursuing the sound to its source, he craned his neck to peer into that room and saw Jeffrey polishing off the remainder of a drink. Corday then scooped up his jacket, intending to return for the ransom money.

The gloating smile playing on Jeffrey's thin lips evaporated when he glanced and saw Dominic's ominous form blocking the doorway. Sickening dread knotted in Jeffrey's belly and he frantically fumbled for the pistol he had stashed in his pocket. But in a heartbeat's time Dominic had pounced on him. As the pistol sailed out of his reach, Jeffrey watched it with dismay, and a frightened squawk burst from his lips when Dominic lunged at him again. Displaying his true colors, Jeffrey made a beeline for the door, but he yelped in surprise when an unforeseen obstacle entangled his storklike legs.

Rozalyn had seen her abductor barreling toward the

door—to freedom—and she had extended her leg, upending the uncoordinated lout and leaving him in a tangled heap at her feet. Jeffrey groaned miserably when he peered up to see Rozalyn emerge from the shadows in the hall. Then his pained gaze swung back to the man who looked as if he would delight in tearing him limb from limb. Terror ricocheted through every nerve and muscle in Jeffrey's body as he was hoisted into the air and flung across the parlor.

The cracks of breaking furniture intermingled with Jeffrey's pained whimperings as he fell and then rolled across the floor, his momentum finally halted by the wall. Judging by the agonizing pains that plagued him, he swore Dominic intended to make good his promise to break every bone in his body. His eyes fluttered up to see a pair of polished black boots. Then his blurred gaze lifted to survey hard, muscled thighs and a massive chest. Fiery eyes of emerald green bore down on Jeffrey, and he swore, then and there, he was a dead man.

But suddenly, the murderous expression that carved deep lines in Dominic's face evaporated, and was replaced by a menacing smile. "Although I would derive pleasure from disposing of you, I think I will leave that task to DuBois. He is already breathing the fire of dragons and you will become his scapegoat."

Jeffrey gulped despite the lump constricting his throat. He had been spared for the moment, but his dread of DuBois was almost as painful as immediate death. He knew Aubrey would show him no mercy. He was doomed.

While Dominic was delivering that sentence, Rozalyn was employing a letter opener to cut her hands free. That accomplished, she yanked the gag from her mouth and then stormed toward Dominic. Her face flushed with fury, she confronted the man she was beginning to love to hate. She grabbed Dominic's arm and turned him to face her.

"Perhaps you have graciously granted this scoundrel temporary pardon, but I will not! I am the one he abducted," Rozalyn reminded him hotly. "Jeffrey planned to kill me after he received the ransom money. I demand he pay penance . . . now!"

Since Dominic made no move to avenge her kidnapping, Rozalyn's fuming gaze circled the room for an appropriate weapon to use in her reprisal. Her eyes landed on the sword that hung above the mantel. Perhaps after she sliced Jeffrey in two equal pieces and then cut Dominic's hard heart from his chest she could overcome her anger. Or perhaps merely scaring the wits out of both of them would appease her need for vengeance, she mused as she stormed over to retrieve the sword. When she wheeled around to threaten the money-hungry Corday, Dominic snatched the weapon from her grasp and held it just out of reach.

"Calm down, Roz," he barked sharply. "Has no one told you to forgive is divine?" Damn, but she was in a fit of temper!

"I am not looking to acquire sainthood," she muttered, reaching up on tiptoe to retrieve the sword.

"Corday isn't worth killing," Dominic argued.

"Nor is he worth sparing," she parried, though still without the sword.

While Dominic and Rozalyn were debating over Jeffrey's future . . . or lack of it, Jeffrey attempted to escape, but Dominic caught his movement out of the corner of his eye. He grabbed Corday by the nape of his jacket, detaining him.

As Dominic hastily glanced around the room for a place to stash Jeffrey until he'd finished his debate with the vindictive witch who thirsted for blood—Jeffrey's as well as his own—he spied the coat rack upon the wall. Marching the struggling Jeffrey across the room, he hung Corday's tattered coat upon a sturdy hook, with Jeffrey in it; then he spun around to confront the flaming-eyed wildcat who hungered to make him a between-meal snack. Not that I blame her, Dominic said to himself. She is bitter and angry after overhearing Aubrey's accusations.

Damn, but she is beautiful, Dominic mused as his hawkish gaze flooded over her heaving breasts and flaming cheeks. And she was, even when she was angry— especially when she was angry. Rozalyn's eyes were snapping and her face was alive with splendid color. Now here is a force to be reckoned with, Dominic told himself. Jeffrey was no match for Dominic's overpowering strength, but Rozalyn was an entirely different matter. Hell hath no fury to match a spitfire's temper. Dominic sought to cool her anger at him, and quickly. Otherwise, there was no telling what this spirited woman might do. She had already threatened to take revenge on Jeffrey with his own sword.

"Rozalyn, I'm sorry," Dominic blurted out. "I had intended to explain the situation tonight, to make you understand. But we were interrupted and then . . ."

Rozalyn's head jerked up and her hard-won composure threatened to desert her. She didn't want to hear flimsy excuses. She had listened to scores of them from men like Jeffrey Corday. "There is no need to explain why you wanted to deceive me," she cut in. "Do you think it truly matters?" She was stung by the spiteful urge to deny her feelings for Dominic, to strike out and hurt him as she had been hurt. "I was using you, just as you were using me . . . from the beginning." Rozalyn took a deep breath, determined to continue without her voice cracking. "A pity, isn't it? We may never know which one of us was the bigger fool." She laughed bitterly, forcing herself to meet Dominic's probing gaze. "Perhaps it was I for being ensnared in Grand'mère's clever trap. Or maybe you for thinking you could maneuver my father, even when you

179

played both ends against the middle. It seems we were both using each other. We became each other's pawns, didn't we, Dominic? But it was only a game played to suit our separate purposes. We both emerged as losers. I, for one, am thankful the charade has come to an end. I had grown tired of pretending there was some deep affection between us."

Her words pierced Dominic's male pride like barbed arrows finding an intended mark. Why the hell was he apologizing when Rozalyn had openly admitted she felt nothing for him? "It does seem we were wasting our time on this worthless charade." He snorted derisively, and his mouth twisted into a mocking smile. Then his penetrating green eyes swarmed over her shapely figure, assuring her that he knew full well what lay beneath the frills and petticoats. "You certainly went to great lengths to convince me that you cared. And, of course, I was willing to accommodate you. I have never been one to deny myself pleasure, no matter what its source."

His insult struck Rozalyn like a slap across the cheek, and she retaliated instinctively. "You cannot know how difficult it was to submit. In actuality, I itched to tell you how much I despised you," she hurled at him, then caught her tears a split second before they spilled from her eyes. "You are a loathsome beast who took unfair advantage, and I am most grateful I will never have to see you again. The mere sight of you nauseates me!"

He winced in response to her spiteful words even as he cursed himself for confessing to love this hard-hearted vixen. She had been toying with him, charming him with her wiles, tempting him with her body. Damn her. He should have left her to Jeffrey!

"I find it inconceivable that any man would honestly admit to loving you. Jeffrey would have deserved a medal if he had found a way to marry you, even if he did so for your money. Life with you would be hell," Dominic flung at her. "You are temperamental and spoiled."

The nerve of this arrogant swine! How dare he speak to me in that condescending tone. He is no prize either, she thought huffily. "Do you think I would have married a man like you? If so, you are deluding yourself. I want nothing to do with you, and the sooner you disappear from my sight, the better. You are nothing but a womanizer, a philanderer. Your lusts couldn't be satisfied in a hundred boudoirs, much less one!" Rozalyn shouted at him. "I want to forget I ever knew you. As far as I am concerned last night didn't happen."

"I know," Hawk snorted derisively. "Unfortunately, I was there when it didn't."

His caustic rejoinder made her fume. "I hope my father manages to destroy you. Whatever grudge he has against the Baudelairs is now mine as well. If I never hear the name again it will be all too soon."

Dominic's temper had been strained once too often during the course of the evening. Finally forgetting logic, he decided Rozalyn was every bit as stubborn and spiteful as her father and he would not attempt to reason with her in her present mood.

Grumbling irritably, he stalked over to snatch up a piece of parchment, and quill in hand, he scratched out his own ransom note. After scribbling his name at the bottom of it, he marched back to Jeffrey, who was still dangling helplessly from the coat rack on the wall. Dominic pinned the letter on the lapel of Jeffrey's shredded jacket, and then he roughly scooped Rozalyn into his arms.

"Put me down this instant!" she shouted. "I am going nowhere with you."

But her struggle for freedom was futile. Dominic held her in a viselike grip until he had retrieved the rope and gag. Once he had replaced them, he tossed Rozalyn over his shoulder and strode toward the front door.

A muddled frown creased Mosley's brow as he watched Dominic approach him with long, swift strides. Mosley had expected Master Baudelair to emerge the victor, but he had not anticipated that the young lady would still be bound and gagged.

"Ride back to the Rabelais mansion and inform Aubrey that it was Jeffrey Corday who abducted his precious daughter," Dominic hastily ordered, setting his furious bundle in the saddle.

Mosley nodded agreeably and then vaulted onto his horse. "I will return home as soon as I deliver the message."

"Be quick about it." Dominic stepped into the stirrup and settled himself behind Rozalyn. "There is much to be done and time is short."

As Dominic gouged his heels into his steed's flanks and thundered off into the darkness, Rozalyn cursed the hard, lean body molded to hers. His closeness stirred memories she was desperately trying to put from her mind in order to survive this painful, one-sided love.

Blast it. Why hadn't Dominic released her and allowed her to go her own way? There was nothing left between them. They could never go back now that she knew he had only used her. Rozalyn wanted to erase the past week from her life and never think of it again. Her first taste of love had been hellish. She had sacrificed her heart for a few splendrous moments she would spend the rest of her life regretting. She had played with fire, and she had been badly burned. The scars of unrequited love would remain, but they would be hidden. No one would know how foolish she had been, but hereforth no man would touch her fragile emotions.

Aubrey DuBois silently seethed as he marched up the steps to Corday's home. He could not believe that fool

182

would dare hold Rozalyn for ransom. When he got his hands on him, Jeffrey would rue the day he was born.

A puzzled frown knitted Aubrey's brow when he entered the parlor and saw Corday hanging in midair. His angry gaze darted around the room, as he wondered what had become of his daughter. Mosley had burst into the house to inform him that Jeffrey was the one who had abducted Rozalyn, and Aubrey expected to find her in the man's clutches. When he glanced back at the unusual wall hanging, he spied the note attached to Jeffrey's shirt.

His eyes blazed as he read the letter Dominic had left for him.

Since you have stubbornly refused to comply with my demands to lower prices and have threatened my caravan, I have resorted to my only weapon of defense. I have taken Rozalyn hostage. As ransom, I demand reasonable prices at rendezvous. When we meet again at Green River, your daughter will be returned, provided you charge fair prices for the trappers' supplies. If not, you will never see Rozalyn again. This seems a small price to pay for compromise. I am sure you will oblige, knowing how you would detest the possibility of having a Baudelair as your son-in-law. If you refuse, I will, of course, name our first-born after you.

Until rendezvous,
Hawk

A bellow of pure rage erupted from Aubrey's lips. Crushing the letter he hurled it across the room. "That conniving bastard! I swear I'll see him hang for this! She cannot bear him a child! She cannot!"

Aubrey was so furious at the disastrous chain of events that he forgot about Jeffrey Corday and, his mind spinning with various schemes for revenge, he stormed from the house. Jeffrey made not a sound to call attention to himself. He would rather hang on his own coat rack than face Aubrey DuBois when the fur trader was in a fit of temper. If and when Jeffrey was rescued, he vowed to fetch his fastest steed and ride from St. Louis without ever looking back; for once Aubrey came to his senses, he would return.

Flouncing down on the carriage seat, Aubrey let loose with another enraged snarl. He knew he had little chance of catching the legendary mountain man. Hawk would be almost impossible to track when he was in his own element. But there was a man who possessed Hawk's resourcefulness. Aubrey had employed his services on several occasions. Ranes was harsh and ruthless—and he could be bought for a price.

Dominic's appearance and his interference in Aubrey's life had poured salt on an unhealed wound, and memories hounded DuBois as he ordered his groom to proceed to the wharf. He swore Satan himself had placed this curse on him. He had spent a lifetime trying to forget that bitterness and betrayal, but seeing Dominic had brought his memories to life. It seemed only yesterday that he . . . Aubrey refused to remember. With his jaw clenched and his eyes glazed with vengeance, he stared out the window. He wanted to think of nothing except the pleasure he would derive from seeing Dominic Baudelair pay for his unforgivable acts.

But, try as he might, Aubrey could not ignore the vision that emerged from the darkness. The memory was so vivid and tormenting that his insides were twisting into a tight knot. A muffled curse burst from his lips as he struggled to shake it off and focus his attention on the problem at hand. There will be no mercy for Dominic Baudelair, Aubrey vowed to himself. I will not waste an ounce of pity on the man who dared to abduct my daughter, and no man will force me into submission, especially not Baudelair!

After Dominic had hurriedly gathered his belongings, he gave last-minute instructions to the servants. Then, as he and Rozalyn rode off into the shadows, Mosley stretched out his hand, waiting for Chadwell to pay his bet. Grumbling, Chadwell dropped the ten-dollar gold piece into the coachman's hand.

Mosley's graying brow rose sharply as he stared at half the amount he'd anticipated. "The bet was double or nothing, remember?"

"Dominic may have left with that feisty chit, but he did not marry her," Chadwell muttered resentfully. "I am not handing over another coin until I know for certain that it is marriage Dominic has in mind."

"Stash another ten-dollar gold piece away for safe-keeping," Mosley advised before he pushed away from the wall and ambled toward his steed. "I'm still willing to bet Master Baudelair never frees himself from Rozalyn DuBois. If he could have left her in St. Louis and returned to the mountains alone, he would have. The man has met his match, and it is only a matter of time before he realizes it."

As Mosley rode off with the note Dominic had wanted delivered to Lenore, Chadwell stalked back into the house. Dominic marry that raven-haired hellion? Dominic marry at all? Chadwell snorted at the improbability. He had lost one coin to Mosley, but it would be returned. Rozalyn DuBois would come back to St. Louis one day, but she would come alone, Chadwell predicted. One could take Dominic Baudelair from the mountains, but one could not take the mountains from the man. Dominic was a vagabond, a wanderer never truly meant for civilization. He loved the Rockies and the adventurous life the mountains provided. It was only a matter of time before he realized the rugged terrain west of the Mississippi was no place for a woman, even one as free-spirited and resourceful as Rozalyn DuBois.

No, he would not lose another ten-dollar gold coin, Chadwell assured himself confidently. Dominic would eventually come to his senses, and he would be eager to send Rozalyn back where she belonged.

A soft chuckle drifted from Lenore's lips when she read the letter Dominic had sent to her. Carefully, she folded the parchment and tucked it in her sleeve. Things had worked out splendidly after all, she thought as she rose from her wheelchair to ascend the steps. Her pretended illness had led Rozalyn to a man who was very capable of handling such a willful sprite. For several hours that evening Lenore had feared her baiting had accomplished nothing, but after reading Dominic's note, she knew her dream would come true . . . eventually. Rozalyn would be in Dominic's care. And that is exactly where the child belongs, Lenore assured herself. Let Aubrey rant and rave. At least the man was showing some kind of emotion for the first time in more years than Lenore cared to count.

It had been wicked of her to deceive Rozalyn, she knew. But she'd felt she had to resort to rolling around in a wheelchair, painting her face chalky white, and stooping to violent coughing spasms. Manipulating Rozalyn had required drastic measures, and Lenore had employed them.

"If I could have found an alternative other than a deceitful one, I would have used it," Lenore murmured self-righteously. "But in this case the end justified the means."

A pleased smile bordered Lenore's lips as she eased herself into bed. Rozalyn had found a man who would protect her and care for her—love her. Rozalyn had met her match, and Lenore could not have been happier. The raven-haired rogue with the charismatic smile had taken Rozalyn with him, away from Aubrey. Lenore was not concerned because Dominic was carting her granddaughter off into the wilds. After all, she mused drowsily, Rozalyn always had been a bit too unconventional for civilization. The lovely hoyden would thrive in the wilderness.

Chapter 12

A thoughtful frown etched Dominic's craggy features as he surveyed the rolling hills of the Great Plains. He and Rozalyn had left civilization far behind and he could now breathe more easily. But his relief was short-lived, for when he glanced back over his shoulder blue eyes glared murderously at him.

Dominic had kept Rozalyn bound and gagged while he'd explained his intentions and described the ransom note he'd left for Aubrey. She had vehemently protested his plans, as he had expected, but with muffled complaints due to the gag. If he had allowed this spitfire to rave, she would have drawn a crowd before they'd escaped St. Louis.

For more than three days Dominic had tracked along the Platte River, refusing to untie Rozalyn, hoping her fury would ebb. His strategy proved successful. Rozalyn no longer shouted muffled curses at him. Each time they paused to eat she threw one of her tantrums, but Dominic hurriedly stuffed food at her and replaced the gag. Now Rozalyn was sulking, refusing to acknowledge that there was another human amongst the small caravan of pack horses that trailed along.

At least it has been a peaceful trip, Dominic mused,

veering into the tall cottonwoods that lined the river. He knew it was cruel and unjust to keep Rozalyn's hands tied to the pommel of the saddle, her feet to the stirrups; but he needed to reach his mountain cabin before harsh winter set in. He had no intention of being delayed in chasing this feisty minx through the wilderness when she attempted escape. And she would do just that, given the chance, Dominic reminded himself.

Rozalyn squirmed to find a more comfortable position in the saddle, then glared at the man who rode ahead of her, leading her farther away from civilization. No longer did she think of her abductor as Dominic Baudelair, but rather as Hawk. That was part of her desperate attempt to bury all memories of the handsome rogue who'd garbed himself in expensive silk and velvet. For her, Dominic had died the night they'd left St. Louis. The dashing, emerald-eyed rake who had stolen her heart and then betrayed her no longer existed. Now, she had to contend only with this powerfully built mountain man.

Her eyes took in Hawk's buckskin clothes, unwillingly admiring the way the deerhide garments clung to his muscular physique. The doeskin fringe that dangled from his clothing waved sensuously as he moved. A low-crowned, coonskin cap sat upon his raven head, and moccasins covered his feet and extended up to his knees. Around his tapered waist hung a wide leather belt. Attached to it was an encased butcher knife—Rozalyn would have dearly loved to get her hands on that—and strapped to Hawk's hips were two loaded pistols, either of which Rozalyn would have delighted in turning on the scoundrel who had kidnapped her. The broad leather strap stretched diagonally across his chest held other necessaries: a bullet-mold, a ball screw, an awl, a ramrod, and a bullet pouch. The sling on his saddle held a Hawken rifle, a handmade weapon produced by the Hawken brothers of St. Louis. The rifle was accurate up to two hundred yards and powerful enough to bring down a grizzly, or a buffalo.

Or an annoying half-breed, Rozalyn thought spitefully. At that moment, she would have had no reservations about snatching Hawk's prized rifle and testing its efficiency.

While Rozalyn was contemplating the various ways she could cut this ominous mountain man down to size, Hawk drew his steed to a halt. After swiveling around in his saddle, he stared pensively at Rozalyn. Her wild hair streamed about her shoulders in disarray, and her elegant gown looked the worse for wear after their long journey. Reasonably certain that there was no one within fifty miles, Hawk decided the time had come to remove Rozalyn's gag and garb her in appropriate clothing. The plunging neckline of her gown had been distracting and he intended to wrap Rozalyn's appetizing body in something less revealing. That would be a safety precaution, designed to protect Hawk from his lusty thoughts and Rozalyn from his unwelcome touch.

After pulling Rozalyn's steed up beside his, Hawk leaned out to remove the gag. He knew full well what her first words would be, even before she hurled them at him.

"I hate you!" Her voice echoed through the trees, sending the birds winging from the low-hanging branches.

"I knew you would say that." Hawk grunted. After swinging from his steed, he rummaged through his saddle bags. Once he had retrieved the garments he had brought for his fuming companion, he braved a glance in her direction. "I assure you that if I could have devised a better solution, I would have never dragged you out here with me. Unfortunately, taking you hostage was my only choice. We must both make the best of this intolerable situation."

Rozalyn made a face at Hawk and then muttered disrespectfully. For the life of her, she didn't know why she was polite enough to keep them to herself. Hawk did not deserve such courtesy. Earlier, she had vowed to burn off his ears with her curses, if and when he removed her gag.

After Hawk led the horses to the river to drink, he dragged Rozalyn from the saddle. Then, holding her by the arm, he thrust the buckskin garments at her. "These clothes will be more comfortable. Put them on," he ordered, his tone making it obvious he anticipated no argument.

But, holding true to form, Rozalyn thrust out a stubborn chin and turned up her nose at the buckskins. "I will wear my own clothes, thank you. I never accept gifts from men, especially those whom I despise."

So this is how it is going to be, Hawk thought. Rozalyn would spite him every step of the way, no matter how great or small his request. She had glared at him the previous day when they were caught in a thunderstorm, acting as if he were personally responsible for the inconvenience. She sniffed distastefully at their food and silently glowered at him when he forced her to sleep at his side.

Damn! It was time this belligerent minx learned to obey his commands. They were not flitting about in St. Louis, for God's sake! They were in the wild. Hawk had no intention of battling bobcats, unfriendly Blackfoot Indians, *and* this fiery chit. He would teach her to take orders if it was the last thing he ever did!

Hawk's fingers folded around the bodice of Rozalyn's gown. With one quick jerk, he ripped the dress to shreds, leaving her naked body exposed to his all-consuming gaze. "The choice is yours." He chuckled devilishly. "You can sit astride your horse like Lady Godiva or you can don the garments I have generously purchased for you."

Rozalyn clutched her tattered gown to her breasts, shielding herself somewhat from emerald eyes that danced with deviltry, and her face flushed a furious red as she glowered at the infuriating brute who had left her with no choice but to comply. Then her pent-up frustration erupted like flood waters bursting from a damn. Rozalyn flew at Hawk, itching to scratch out his eyes before she snatched his flintlock and turned it on him.

A surprised squawk bubbled from Hawk's lips when her nails scraped his cheek, and he caught both of her wrists before she could inflict another wound. But, as the torn gown fell away, the sight of her heaving breasts and creamy flesh distracted him. Her unclad body unleashed memories of another time and place. He relived the night they had made wild, sweet love, the night he had discovered unbounded pleasures in the circle of her silky arms.

Rozalyn saw the spark of desire flickering in his eyes. She, too, was tormented by the bittersweet dream she'd sworn was dead and buried. As his sinewy arms slid around her waist, drawing her against his hard, muscled length, their memories came to life. She could feel his bold manliness pressing against her thigh, feel the accelerated beat of his heart. It was futile to struggle against his overpowering strength, so she didn't.

There were subtle ways to prove to him and to herself that his touch no longer affected her. He could attempt to use her body for his lusty pleasures, but she would not respond to him. That would be a double victory. When Hawk realized she was no longer vulnerable to his caresses, he would release her.

Determined to test her theory, Rozalyn remained as still as a stone statue while his raven head deliberately drew nearer. His sensuous mouth slanted across her lips, which were frozen in a contemptuous frown.

Husky laughter rumbled in Hawk's massive chest when he planted what was to be a passionate kiss on unyielding lips. Although Rozalyn had intended to prove a point, Hawk considered her cool indifference a challenge. One dark eyebrow rose, and he withdrew to study the stubborn set of Rozalyn's jaw.

"Do you think your hatred for me can change the way our bodies sing when they touch?" he asked. His index finger trailed over her bare shoulder to circle the peak of her breast, teasing it to tautness. "Do not lie to yourself, Roz. Nothing can smother the spark of passion between us."

His caresses wandered over her body as if he hungered for her alone, but Rozalyn knew better than that. She willfully rejected the warm tide of pleasure that rippled across her skin when his exploring hands molded themselves to the curve of her hips. His touch was magical, but his kisses were poisonous. If she drank fully from his lips, her mind would become paralyzed and all would be lost. There was no cure for his spell. Abstinence was her only salvation.

"I have already told you that my response to your lovemaking was merely an act," she managed to say. "I only pretended to enjoy your touch, but I no longer have to pretend. Your caresses leave me cold, as if I had been exposed to Arctic winds."

The challenge was given and quickly accepted. Hawk swore she was lying. Rozalyn may have deceived him with her soft-spoken professions of love, but her body had responded willingly. She had yearned to caress him and she had done so. Perhaps she did loathe the sight of him as she claimed, but she had enjoyed their lovemaking and he was not about to deny himself the pleasure of touching her. They would spend long months together. If he held himself at bay, that would drive him stark raving mad. Having her so close without taking her in his arms and losing himself in the softness of her feminine flesh would be pure torture.

"Again the choice is yours, Roz," he murmured. His

hand began to flow across her hip to trace the silky smoothness of her thigh. "You can deny yourself the pleasure of passion if you wish, but I will not."

Before Rozalyn could protest, his mouth opened on hers, and his tongue traced her unresponsive lips until they parted beneath his warm, demanding kiss. Forbidden sensations trickled through Rozalyn's veins as Dominic's roaming hands discovered her sensitive points, though she chided herself for feeling anything but revulsion for this green-eyed devil. Hawk was crumbling every defense she'd sought to construct, doing it with persuasive gentleness.

Oh, why couldn't he be forceful with her! she thought. His fingertips swirled around each throbbing peak and then splayed across her abdomen. She could have hated him all the more if he had been rough and abusive, but she damned him and damned herself for responding.

Like tide waters rolling against a sandy shore and then ebbing into the sea from which they came, Hawk withdrew his hands. Emerald eyes that flamed with barely contained passion bore into Rozalyn's as Hawk unstrapped his belt and shed his buckskin shirt. The muscles of his chest flexed and relaxed as he cast his garments aside and then rose to full stature, a faint smile skittering across his lips when he took up Rozalyn's hand and laid it over his thudding heart.

"You remember how hot the flames of love can burn, don't you, Roz? The passion between us is not easily contained. Your hatred doesn't change the way I feel when you touch me. We may have our differences, but some things never change, things like my need for you, my craving for your kiss and caress."

The velvety huskiness of his voice, the compelling sparkle in his eyes, made her hands move involuntarily. As if they had wills of their own, her fingertips swam across a sea of hair-roughened flesh, and she could not keep her eyes from wandering over his granite shoulders, the taut tendons of his arms. Hawk was all male, hard, bronzed, and extremely attractive. Rozalyn hated to admit that she adored the feel of his rough flesh beneath her hand, that she thrilled to the way he stirred beneath her touch. She had always thought Dominic Baudelair handsome and charismatic, but he'd seemed slightly out of place in his fashionable velvet garments. Indeed, Rozalyn had considered him too much a man for the sophisticated fashions of aristocrats. Seeing him here in the wilderness, garbed in form-fitting buckskin she knew he was in his element. Hawk was a part of this vast, sprawling world beyond the Mississippi.

While her mind strayed she was falling into his seductive trap. Her hands were caressing the broad expanse of his chest, and her lips were brushing over his taut male nipples. Senses that had remained dormant for a week came awake, betraying her attempt not to feel, not to enjoy. This raven-haired devil could easily weave his spell about her if she did not guard her fragile heart that had just begun to mend.

Fool! He will only hurt you, her wounded pride said, just loudly enough to catch Rozalyn's attention before she was swept into arousing sensations. With the quickness of a striking cobra, she darted sideways and hurriedly scooped up Hawk's discarded clothes and his pistols. A stunned expression appeared on his craggy features when he found his own flintlock aimed at his chest.

Rozalyn's mouth curved upward in a devilish smile as she snatched up the horses' reins and then steadily backed away, leaving Hawk unarmed and unclad.

"Now it is your turn to portray Lady Godiva," Rozalyn taunted. Slowly she inched away, drawing the string of horses with her. Hawk deserved to be left naked like the beasts of the wild since he was one of them. His humiliation would be small consolation for the heart-wrenching pain he had put her through. "No doubt you will play your new role as effortlessly as you portrayed a doting lover."

"You would leave me here with no weapons of defense, no protection from inclement weather?" Hawk was incredulous.

Rozalyn's eyes flooded over his nude body. "It seems only fitting that the wolf who stalked about St. Louis in sheep's clothing should be exposed for what he is."

"How far do you think you will get in the wilderness without running into trouble?" Hawk took a bold step forward, but when Rozalyn cocked the hammer of the flintlock, he stopped in his tracks. "This is hardly St. Louis, minx. Unfriendly Indians and ruthless ruffians roam here. They will not grant you amnesty."

"I can take care of myself," Rozalyn insisted. Cautiously watching Hawk's every movement, she drew the buckskin shirt over her head and pushed it down over her hips. "You should be more concerned about your welfare."

As the buckskin shirt fell into place, Hawk noted the alluring picture Rozalyn presented. Lord, even the doehide garment could not disguise her beauty. The front of her shirt gaped to reveal the full swells of her breasts, and the long fringe on the garment's hem dangled sensuously upon her thighs. Hawk had hoped that attire would be less distracting than her provocative gown, but Mother Nature had been overly generous with Rozalyn. It was impossible to conceal her beauty, whether she was at her best or worst. How could he keep his lusty thoughts from running rampant when he looked at her? And worse, how could the rough-edged hunters who roamed the plains control themselves when they caught sight of this alluring minx?

He winced apprehensively when he noticed where

Rozalyn's backward strides were about to lead her. "Have a care, nymph." Hawk inclined his raven head toward the hazard that lay a few feet behind her. "You will be up to your lovely neck in trouble if you don't watch where you step," he warned her.

Rozalyn flung Hawk a withering glance, annoyed by his attempt to distract her. She knew he was baiting her. If she dared to turn her head, he would pounce on her. "Don't expect me to fall for that trick," she declared sarcastically.

Broad shoulders lifted and then dropped in a lackadaisical shrug. "Ah, well, it was worth a try. But I should have known you were too clever to—"

His remark was cut off by Rozalyn's surprised squawk. Her foot had settled into ground that was not solid. Quicksand! She screamed in panic as she felt the slushy murk curl around her legs, frantically flapping her arms, as if she could sprout wings and fly to freedom. But feathered fowl she was not! The weight of the clothing, belts, and pistols she was carrying sent her deeper into the voracious sand, which pulled her downward.

Rozalyn had let go of the lead horse's reins when she'd been taken by surprise, and, startled, the animal had bolted to the side, leaving her with no means to drag herself from disaster. Now panic gripped her as quicksand oozed about her waist, and her wild eyes flew to the naked mountain man who was grinning with sadistic glee.

"Get me out of here!" Rozalyn screeched furiously. She was angry with herself for not heeding Hawk's warning and agitated with him for not being more persistent. Damn him! He was thoroughly enjoying the sight of her floundering in quicksand.

Hawk swaggered toward Rozalyn and carefully leaned out to relieve her of his clothes and supplies. When she stretched out her arm to grip his hand, he quickly withdrew it. Calmly, he stepped into his breeches. Then he simply stood and watched the quicksand mold itself to her shapely body.

Rozalyn sputtered in outrage. Hawk had every intention of letting her suffocate in the sand! He was going to stand there, watching in wicked satisfaction while she vanished from sight. The hard-hearted scoundrel! He was loving every minute of this.

"My father will never agree to your terms if you do not deliver me to the rendezvous," Rozalyn reminded him coldly, as the damp sand crept across her ribs.

"I have always prided myself on being resourceful," Hawk boasted. Then he flashed Rozalyn a haughty smile. "I'll think of something."

"Dammit, Hawk!" she fumed. "Give me your hand!"

He laughed. "Gladly . . . if only I could devise a way to detach it from the end of my arm."

Rozalyn was becoming more infuriated by the second. How dare he tease her when she was about to meet her maker. Did this mountain man have not one smidgen of compassion?

"If I save you from imminent death, will you promise to behave yourself in the future?" Hawk asked.

She put out her defiant chin, the only part of her anatomy that wasn't covered with quicksand, and the look she gave was tantamount to a spiteful curse that condemned his miserable soul to hell.

Hawk had no difficulty decoding her murderous glare. Chuckling, he turned his back on the stubborn vixen who was up to her neck in trouble. "Very well, you have made your choice. Being a gentleman, I will respect your decision."

She could not believe her eyes when he strode over to regather the scattered horses. "Murderer!" she shouted at him.

"Sticks and stones . . ." Hawk taunted wickedly. "I will not come to your rescue until you promise not to attempt another escape. You have already proven you cannot handle yourself in the wild, but I must commend you on your versatility. Not only can you dive headlong into disaster, you can back into it as well."

Rozalyn breathed a defeated sigh as the quicksand towed her farther into its dark depths. "I promise," she choked out begrudgingly. She wondered if those were to be her last words, for Hawk seemed to be in no rush to retrieve her.

After he had tethered the horses to a nearby tree he ambled back to the pool of quicksand. Bracing his legs, he crouched down to extend a helping hand, but just before Rozalyn could entwine her fingers in his, Hawk retracted his arm and grinned mischievously.

"There is another stipulation I neglected to make. . . ."

Rozalyn was infuriated by his roguish grin. She knew full well what price he expected in return for his chivalry, if one could call it that. The lout! He wanted her to surrender to his lust after he had saved her life.

"You conniving bastard," she spat at him and then hastily closed her mouth before she swallowed quicksand.

The teasing smile that dangled on one side of Hawk's mouth evaporated. He squatted down on his haunches to meet Rozalyn's exasperated glower. "I am sure you believe that to be true—and perhaps it is. But that doesn't change what lies smoldering between us. I want you, Roz—and without a fight," he said simply.

Rozalyn would have burst into frustrated tears if she had not been so determined not to let this invincible mountain man see her cry. Straining her neck above the murk, she nodded her compliance. "Without a fight," she agreed submissively.

His firm hand folded around hers, dragging her from the bottomless pool of quicksand that had very nearly swallowed her up, and Rozalyn breathed a sigh of relief when his strong, competent arms went around her. Hawk held her until her legs no longer wobbled beneath her.

Then his warm green eyes swam over her shivering skin, as he steered her away from the deadly quicksand and lifted her into his arms. When he had peeled off her soiled shirt and cast his breeches aside, he carried Rozalyn into the river to cleanse her.

His hands flowed over her skin, washing away the clinging sand, and Rozalyn died a thousand deaths as he provocatively massaged her body. She knew he had broken her heart the last time she'd dared to play this dangerous game, but being held in this man's arms would always rekindle her desire. It would always be like this with Hawk. When he made love to her, her soul sang.

The fresh clean scent of him invaded her nostrils, reviving memories of their lovemaking and creating a need Rozalyn could not ignore. As her wandering finger-tips trailed across his shoulder, her sense of touch evoked currents of pleasure, and when her lips tasted his bronzed skin, her quiet sigh intermingled with the chattering of the birds. Hawk filled her senses. In that serene moment all was forgotten, and he became her world. It was as if they were the only two people on earth. Even the sun hid its head behind the western horizon to grant them complete privacy.

Rozalyn was transported back in time, back to the splendrous world of tender emotion. She could not fight her memories of the past when they mingled with the present. Even though surrendering to passion would only break her heart again, she could not deny him, not when it meant denying herself the pleasures that awaited her.

Staring at Rozalyn with deliberate concentration, Hawk slid an arm beneath her knees. Allowing the water to cradle her, he set her adrift while his hungry kisses flowed over the trim column of her neck. Meanwhile his fingers meandered over her thighs and then traced the shapely curve of her hips. He allowed his hands and lips to wander where they would, but he soon became painfully aware that he was afire, though he was standing chest deep in water. His aching need for this lovely nymph consumed him, and he could not contain a sigh of pleasure as his lips whispered over her silky skin, tracing each curve and swell of her exquisite body.

Lord, he loved to caress her satiny flesh, and he found her soft, full lips more intoxicating than wine. Hawk would have been content to spend the remainder of the night making love to this glorious angel. It didn't matter that she despised him. He needed her, yearned to ease the tormenting craving that had hounded since he'd dragged her from civilization. He had brought this free spirit into his world, a world that had been complete and satisfying until she'd come into his life. Now Rozalyn had turned his world upside down and nothing made sense anymore, nothing except touching her, taking her with him on the most intimate of journeys.

A shuddering sigh tumbled from Rozalyn's lips as Hawk's practiced hands glided over every inch of her body. He was fueling a fire that all the water in the Platte couldn't cool. His touch satisfied some of her needs, but it also created new ones. She swore the hunger he'd provoked would devour her before it was satisfied.

She could profess to despise him for what he had done, but that didn't prevent her from responding to him. This bold mountain man with dancing green eyes and jet black hair was the devil's own temptation. Rozalyn was helpless to defy him, and her traitorous body arched toward his seeking hands. She craved far more. She longed to feel his hard, muscular body pressed against her.

When Hawk lifted her back into his arms and carried her to shore, she voiced no protest. She had fought Hawk once, but all her efforts had been wasted. Now it seemed inevitable when she was with him. She still loved the man she had tried to hate.

Eyes that flickered with blatant desire raked over Rozalyn's naked flesh, and Hawk's devouring gaze did not waver as he set her on her feet. "I can never seem to get enough of you," he breathed raggedly. "You have become an obsession, one so fierce and uncontrollable that I . . ."

Suddenly Hawk lost all interest in conversation. His lips were too eager to engage in something far more arousing. As he drew Rozalyn down onto the thick carpet of grass that lined the river, his hands curled around her waist to lift her above him, then his lips feathered over the peaks of her breasts. Again, his caresses roamed and aroused. They glided over every inch of her satiny skin until her body moved instinctively toward his. His hands and lips did delicious things to her, maddening things.

As her soft, yielding body molded itself to his, Hawk groaned in pleasure. Rozalyn had come to him, even when she'd vowed she would not. Nothing had changed. All thought escaped him when her sweet lips melted upon his, her tongue darting into his mouth and deepening a kiss in which their breaths intermingled. Her slim fingers tunneled into his hair, tangling in the thick raven strands, and her body insinuated itself provocatively onto his. Hawk moaned from the delicious torment. Her touch, her kiss, the feel of her burning into him drove him to the verge of insanity. It was easy to lose himself in the sensations she was weaving about him, easy to yield to the primitive urges that flooded over him.

Rozalyn was all too aware of him, of the brawny columns of his long legs, the hard contours of his hips. Hawk was masculinity personified. He could make his will her own. She wanted him as a starving traveler wants nourishment. The sensations that riveted through her bordered on desperation. Rozalyn moved closer to the flame, eager to surrender all, just to appease the over-whelming need that made her entire body tremble uncontrollably.

Unable to hold himself at bay a moment longer, Hawk moved toward her, responding to her feminine softness. His hands splayed across her hips, holding her to him as he drove into her, his open mouth covering hers and muffling her cry of pleasure. And they were one, sharing the savage urgency of their embrace. As passion engulfed them, their bodies burned in its sweet, violent fire. She met his deep thrusts and clung fiercely to him as he moved against her, filling her with sensations that were wild and satisfying. Their dark world came alive with golden flames whose curling fingers rose higher to weave a blazing spell about them.

Rozalyn was prepared to sacrifice her last breath for release from the maddening desire that possessed her as Hawk took her higher and higher into the flames. Her flesh was ablaze but her soul was still reaching upward to touch the lofty crest that towered beyond passion's inferno. For one long moment Rozalyn felt she was dangling in midair, trapped between desire's raging flames and rapture's satisfying warmth. And then she let go, unable to battle the fierce emotions that had taken over her mind and body. She feared she would tumble back into the outstretched arms of the flames, but suddenly her soul soared, like an eagle testing its wings and gliding along on the wind. Time stood still as she circled and dived in lofty flight. I have been here before, she thought to herself. But each time was different somehow, wilder, sweeter. . . . And then the wind beneath her wings stilled and she was drifting downward, back into the hazy sea of reality. She lay limp and drowsy in Hawk's encircling arms, her cheeks flushed with the blush of contentment, her breath whispering softly against his sturdy shoulder.

Had it been a dream or had she truly transcended the physical limitations of her body? Rozalyn wasn't certain. Slowly, her long lashes swept up to see a pair of emerald green eyes thoughtfully studying her. A tender smile grazed his lips when he combed his fingers through her tangled tendrils which were extended on the grass. Rozalyn reached up to trace the strong line of his jaw and quietly returned his smile. It was not a dream, she decided. Hawk's lovemaking left her with the illusion that he had performed magic, but her sensations were real. He could make her respond, even when she would have preferred not to yield to his skillful caresses.

"You may always despise me, Roz, but even that doesn't matter when I hold you like this," he rasped, his voice husky in the aftermath of passionate lovemaking. "It has always been like this between us and it always will be." Hawk bent to drop a kiss onto her kiss-swollen lips and then withdrew to stare into her shimmering blue eyes. "Promise me you won't try to escape me. The wilderness can be harsh and cruel to those who have not learned to respect it. There are dangers lurking in every shadow, ones you can't possibly imagine. Whatever else you believe about me, I don't want to see you hurt."

Rozalyn caught herself the split second before she read more into his softly spoken words than he'd intended. His main concern was delivering her to her father, nothing more. If she got into trouble, he would be inconvenienced. That is what concerns him most, she told herself. Like the menagerie of supplies strapped to his belt and to his pack horses, she was another possession, something required to fulfill his purpose. You have been a fool once. Spare yourself the heartache of believing in a man who sees you only as a means to an end, she told herself.

Squirming away, Rozalyn sank down in the grass and peered across the river, watching the silver waves roll across its surface. She was not going to fall prey to her foolish heart this time. A time would come when she could escape him, and she would flee without looking back. The dangers that awaited in the shadows could be no more deadly than having one's soul bared and bleeding.

"It seems you and I are stuck with each other . . . temporarily," she conceded. "I may be your captive, but I cannot and will not become your whore. I complied with your terms to ensure my safety . . . only that." She lied without batting an eye, praying that Hawk would not test her resistance to his magic spell during the time they were together.

He propped himself up on an elbow and reached over to trail his index finger over her bare arm, but she shrank away as if scorched by his touch. Her frosty tone and her open refusal of his caress spoiled the moment. He retaliated without thinking.

"I have not lived in the wilderness all these years in celibacy," he said sharply. "You are not the only woman this side of the Mississippi. Indeed, I have known several who would be eager to exchange places with you."

Rozalyn vaulted to her feet and glared at him. "Then search out your harlots and bed every one of them," she snapped. "As a matter of fact, I shall be eternally grateful to be spared your attention. Indeed, I would rather confront a grizzly bear."

As Rozalyn dragged her pallet from the pack horse and made up her bed, Hawk slammed his fist onto the ground, cursing his impulsive rejoinder, knowing it would surely come back to haunt him.

After properly berating himself for his stupidity, he stepped into his buckskins, then set about making his bed, which he slept in alone. For several minutes he lay staring up at the ceiling of stars, mulling over several comments that might ease Rozalyn's irritation with him.

But he thought better of voicing an apology. A stone wall would soften sooner than this stubborn chit. Rozalyn was mad as hell and his only recourse was to let her steam and stew. Once she had simmered down he would reopen the subject, using considerably more diplomacy than he'd employed this time. They were not going to spend every night sleeping on separate pallets, Hawk vowed. Perhaps the only way to get along with Rozalyn was to give her her way—but not on this matter! Hawk was only willing to concede for the moment. If he were not allowed to touch her during the long months they spent in each other's company, he would not be able to keep a clear head and thus protect them from the dangers of the wilderness.

There are subtle tactics for getting one's way, Hawk reminded himself as he drew the quilt over his shoulder. He was going to devote his spare time to devising some.

Chapter 13

After two days of strained silence, Rozalyn's temper was rising. Hawk continued to sport the smug smile that irked her each time she glanced in his direction. Although Hawk had been polite and considerate, considering the circumstances, she was determined not to be wooed back into his arms. She had sworn there would be no more passionate encounters and she had meant it. She had very little else left; she was not about to relinquish her self-respect.

Flouncing onto the ground after a long day of traveling, Rozalyn turned a cold shoulder to her companion as she choked down her meager ration of pemmican. To her, it tasted a great deal like sour grapes. When she dared to glance in Hawk's direction, he was studying her with calculating green eyes, and plastered on his face was that infuriating grin she was beginning to detest.

"What could you possibly find so amusing for hours on end?" Rozalyn asked challengingly.

He lifted one shoulder and then let it drop while he chewed on his meager meal. "You," he replied pleasantly enough. "You are waging civilized warfare, minx. If the daggers you've been glaring at me were real, I would be the recipient of so many stab wounds, water would run through me like a sieve."

Rozalyn reacquainted him with her knife-hurling glare. "Believe me, Hawk, were I to get my hands on a weapon of any kind, there would be nothing civilized about the tortures I have in mind for you. Indeed, I'm not certain your head on a silver platter would satisfy me, not after what you've put me through."

Hawk heaved an exasperated sigh. He had been pursuing a new tactic—giving Rozalyn no further cause to despise him—but even his cheerful, accommodating demeanor didn't faze her. It seemed she had her heart set on hating him, and she appeared to be thriving on working at it.

"Are you so intolerant of every man who falls from your good graces, your highness?" Hawk snorted, deciding to throw diplomacy to the winds since it had gotten him nowhere with this foul-tempered witch who continued to breathe fire at him.

When Hawk threw down the gauntlet Rozalyn quickly snatched it up. Her eyes burned into him like hot blue blazes. "What the hell do you expect me to do? Thank you for kidnapping me? Praise you for whisking me from civilization and dragging me off to only God knows where?" Her agitated gaze flickered down her torso and she slapped away the ant that had been foolish enough to take an overland route across her leg. "You ripped my only gown to shreds and forced me to dress like your younger brother. You feed me tasteless rations that would make a starving wolf turn up his nose. And you—" Rozalyn had glanced over to see that Hawk was paying no attention at all. He was looking right past her, as if she weren't even there. That did it! "Dammit, would you at least look at me while I'm speaking to you? I am not your horse. I am a woman who has been sorely put upon. I cannot endure much more of this existence." Still, he did not do her the courtesy of glancing in her direction. Rozalyn was at her wit's end. "Confound it, Hawk, why don't you just shoot me and get this over?"

When Hawk snatched the pistol from his belt and aimed it at her, Rozalyn's mouth dropped open and her eyes bulged from their sockets. For God's sake, she was only trying to make a point! She hadn't expected him to take her literally. Rozalyn swore she had viewed her last sunset when the flintlock exploded and a bullet roared past her shoulder. Although her ears were ringing, she heard a pained growl from close behind her. With sickening dread, she swiveled around to see a large bobcat keel off the ledge behind her and land in a heap at her side.

A terrified scream was trapped in her throat when the cat attempted to rise, and instinctively, Rozalyn vaulted to her feet and flew into Hawk's arms, knocking him off balance.

With a pained grunt, Hawk landed on his back, Rozalyn on top of him. Pushing himself up on one elbow, he snatched up his other pistol, then peered around the shapely bundle of buckskin in his lap to make certain the wounded cat would not launch a second attack. When the beast sank back and lay motionless on the grass, he arched a taunting eyebrow.

"Now, what was it you were saying? Have you suddenly decided I'm not so offensive after all?" Flashing her a roguish grin, he combed his fingers through her unruly hair, tilting her pale face to his. "Now that you have me where you want me, perhaps you might disguise your passionate craving for me behind an appreciative kiss. After all, *chérie,* I did just save your—"

Indignant, Rozalyn jerked back as if she had been bitten by a bobcat. Then she flung herself from the arms of the contemptible rogue who saved her life one minute only to mock her the next. She wobbled away from Hawk on shaky legs, determined to get a grip on herself after her near brush with disaster. Damnation, she had run to Hawk as naturally as she drew a breath, but the last place she wanted to be was in his powerful arms. She was vividly aware of how vulnerable she became when he touched her. She again vowed there would be no more touching. It always led to intimacy between them, and she and Hawk had taken their last tumble in the grass.

When Rozalyn reached the pack horses, she rummaged through the saddlebags until she located the brandy Hawk kept stashed from sight. Her shaky hands folded around the flask, and she pulled the cork to take a drink. Although she was searching for newfound courage after the hair-raising incident, the liquor set her throat afire and she almost choked on it. Desperately, she tried to catch her breath but it simply wouldn't come.

Chuckling, Hawk swaggered over to whack her on the back. "Really, *mademoiselle*, I thought you were too sophisticated to guzzle brandy like a backwoodsman."

His taunt only stoked the fires of her anger. Flinging Hawk a challenging glare, Rozalyn tipped the flask and choked down another fiery gulp. Then, fighting to keep from sputtering, she thrust the liquor at her nemesis.

"If you are going to force me to dress like a heathen, I might as well behave like one," she snapped. Her voice was not as strong as she had hoped. Instead of railing at Hawk she was croaking like a sick bullfrog.

Hawk laughed. Then he took a sip of brandy before holding out the flask to his companion, whose hair cascaded about her like a silken cape. "By all means have another drink. Far be it from me to tell you what to do. But don't blame me if you wind up with a headache. This brandy will knock you for a loop, little brother," he teased, a grating smile on his face.

Rozalyn grabbed the bottle. "I can hold my liquor as well as you can so don't lecture me on temperance. As a matter of fact, the less you say to me the better. I would prefer to converse with yonder steed."

While Rozalyn downed another long swallow, Hawk bowed exaggeratedly before her, fighting like the devil to keep from laughing. "As you wish, *chérie*. If you prefer the horse's companionship to mine, then discuss your dire situation with him. No doubt, he will be a more attentive listener than I."

Turning up her dainty nose, Rozalyn moved around to confront the beast of burden's face. In that position she took another swallow of brandy. The fire had burned itself out now, but her nose and lips were becoming numb. She really didn't care. The brandy had taken the edge off her temper, and a false sense of security washed over her as she continued to freely sip from the flask.

"Do you know what a miserable excuse for a man your master is?" she asked the chestnut steed, her voice slurring noticeably. Rozalyn's hazy gaze careened toward Hawk who had plopped down on his pallet to finish his unappetizing meal. "Well, I'll tell you. Hawk is a heathen, a brute."

When the steed snorted, seemingly in agreement, Rozalyn beamed in satisfaction and took another drink. "Even you know a horse's—"

"Your language is not befitting a lady," Hawk cut in, flinging her a disapproving frown. "I have not stooped to name calling and I would appreciate it if you didn't slander my good name.

"I am not talking to you," Rozalyn insisted, an ornery smile turning down the corners of her mouth. "I was speaking to the horse and it is my firm belief that he will carry no tales." The horse pricked up his ears and flared his nostrils at the scent of the brandy now held beneath his muzzle. Rozalyn hiccupped, grinned sheepishly, and then continued, "S'cuse me. Now where was I? Ah yes, your disgusting master . . ."

For more than an hour Hawk sat silently, listening to

211

Rozalyn ridicule him in her conversation with the pack horse. At length, Rozalyn's voice began to drag and she had difficulty keeping her train of thought. Finally she found it necessary to plant herself on the ground to avoid falling down. Hawk bit back a grin. The little imp was drunk. He had never seen this side of Rozalyn, and he could not help but chuckle at the comical expressions passing across her face.

When Rozalyn rose clumsily to retrieve more brandy, Hawk came to attention. However, her weaving footsteps caused her to collide broadside with the pack horse before he could reach her. The animal sidestepped skittishly, and Rozalyn was thrown backward. Her agility had been drowned in brandy so she landed in a heap.

A miserable groan escaped from her lips when she attempted to get her bearings and climb to her feet. The world was spinning furiously about her and she was no longer certain which way was up. Had night fallen or had the liquor blinded her?

Before Rozalyn could determine the answer to that question, she found herself hoisted from the ground and set upon her feet. But her buckling knees refused to bear her weight and she would have collapsed if Hawk had not slid a supporting arm around her.

"Fetch another bottle," she requested slurrishly. And then, holding the drained flask up to the moonlight, she smiled a silly smile. "This one seems to have a hole in it. All the brandy has leaked out."

Hawk rolled his eyes heavenward. "I think you have had enough for one night. You are not going to appreciate the headache that will greet you at sunrise. If you drink another bottle of brandy, you may not wake at all," he lectured.

His preaching slid off her like water from a duck's back. Heady sensations had her reeling and she didn't have a care. Nothing Hawk could say would upset her;

she was sitting on top of the world. Or was she beneath it? Rozalyn couldn't tell.

"I can tolerate another drink," she assured him. "As you can plainly see I am in full command of my . . ." Rozalyn frowned when the thought she had wanted to put to tongue flitted away with the evening breeze.

"Your senses," Hawk prompted, steering her toward her pallet.

Rozalyn reversed direction to aim herself toward the saddlebags, weaving unsteadily "Ex . . . actly," she murmured sluggishly and then grumbled when her fingers seemed all thumbs. It had suddenly become impossible to unfasten the lacings on the leather bag. "I could use your assistance, Falcon."

"The name is Hawk," he corrected disdainfully.

Her head swiveled around, and she wondered which of the two mountain men she saw had driven her to drink. "I knew that," she declared over her thick tongue. "Why couldn't you have taken a normal name when you crossed the Mississippi? Chester or Sam." Rozalyn hiccuped again and then frowned when her once-deft fingers fumbled over the lacings. "But *Hawk?* Heavens, one would think you were a feather-winged fowl who alights on tree branches. Can you?"

The ludicrous question and her ridiculous expression set Hawk to chortling. This time he made no attempt to muffle his mirth. His long strides took him to Rozalyn's side and with one lithe movement he scooped her into his arms.

"Of course I can fly," he declared. Then he steadied his inebriated nymph's head before it rolled off his shoulder. "But not as high as you are soaring at the moment."

When Hawk had deposited Rozalyn on her pallet, he returned to fish a brandy bottle from the saddlebags, still chuckling at the lingering vision of an uninhibited minx with glassy eyes and wild raven hair. Lord, she would regret her overindulgence the following morning. How well he remembered the night he had attempted to put this distracting witch from his mind by drowning his troubles in a bottle. He had gained nothing but a throbbing headache for his efforts. Since that night Hawk had limited himself to one or two drinks. Once he had taken his limit, he returned the flask to the saddlebags.

A muddled frown plowed his brow when he returned to the pallet where he had deposited Rozalyn. She had vanished into thin air! Sweet Jesus, all he needed was to track that intoxicated bundle of trouble through the wilderness in the dark. Had she decided to flee from him in her condition? No doubt, the liquor has armed her with bravura, he thought sourly.

"Dammit, Rozalyn, where are you?" Hawk called, his keen eyes scanning the shadows. "Rozalyn!" His booming voice resounded about him, but Rozalyn did not respond.

Hawk flinched and lunged for the rifle that lay beside his bedroll. Bracing it against his shoulder, he aimed the weapon toward the sound that had startled him. When several leaves drifted down from the overhanging branches of a tree he lifted his eyes to see an oversized bird perched above him.

Cursing Rozalyn's feather-brained antics Hawk set the gun aside and glared up at her. "What the sweet loving hell do you think you're doing? Come down from there before you break your foolish neck!"

His sharp tone had no effect on her, for Rozalyn was thoroughly convinced she could fly. Fluttering along the branch, she prepared to spread her wings and soar.

"Watch your step!" Hawk shrieked when she over-extended herself. "Dammit, woman, are you out of your mind?"

But Rozalyn was past hearing, and Hawk's heart leaped when her foot slid from the limb. As far as she was concerned anything was possible while she was floating on a sea of brandy. She had but to stretch out in flight and she would be airborne. Testing that theory, Rozalyn raised her arms to take to the air.

"Good God!" Hawk snorted in disbelief. He had stalked toward the tree trunk to retrieve the daring minx, but the moment he realized what she intended to do, he darted beneath her.

Before Rozalyn made a crash landing beside the fallen bobcat, Hawk snatched her in midair and then gave her a sound shaking.

"Damnation, you could have killed yourself," he growled furiously.

Rozalyn's head snapped backward and then rolled lifelessly on her shoulders as her body became limp in Hawk's trembling arms. Grumbling over the disastrous chain of events that had led to this moment, Hawk strode back to tuck Rozalyn beneath her quilts.

"Isn't it enough that she hates me?" he said to the heavens. "Must she drink herself senseless each night to avoid me?" When no divine answer appeared in the night sky, Hawk heaved a frustrated sigh, then sank down beside the sleeping bundle of mischief. When his anger dwindled, a sentimental smile rippled across his lips, and he reached out to brush her tangled ebony mane away from her face so he might trace the sensuous curve of her lips.

"Sleep well, sweet princess," he murmured before he bent to press a light kiss to her unresponsive lips.

After reloading both pistols and placing them beside his pallet, Hawk stretched out to grant himself a few hours of sleep. But when he closed his eyes, he pictured Rozalyn conversing with the pack horse, then flapping her arms as if she were about to loft herself into the air. A muffled chuckle rumbled in his chest, and he wondered if Rozalyn would remember her antics when she woke from her brandy-induced sleep.

An agonizing groan tumbled from Rozalyn when she dared to open her eyes the following morning. The bright light was blinding and she quickly blocked it with her arm. The abrupt movement set her head to spinning, and her stomach lurched as if she were riding out a storm at sea.

"Good morning, sleeping beauty." Hawk mercilessly watched Rozalyn turn green around the gills. "Would you care to join me in a cup of coffee before we break camp?"

When Hawk's cheerful voice ricocheted through her head, Rozalyn pushed herself into an upright position—carefully. She feared at any moment she would lose the previous night's supper. Her head was pounding in rhythm with her heart and her insides were on fire! But she was not about to let Hawk know how greatly she was suffering for he would harass her for the entire day.

Forcing a feeble smile, she accepted the steaming mug and cautiously took a sip. "Thank you," she rasped.

"A bit under the weather, I see." Hawk chuckled as her trembling hands lifted the cup to her bluish lips.

"I feel fine," Rozalyn insisted grouchily.

"Odd, you don"t look it," Hawk observed. Then he offered her a slice of pemmican.

Rozalyn wasn't sure she could face another stick of dried beef, but she managed to choke down her breakfast, only to keep Hawk from mocking her.

"I don't suppose you recall what happened last night," Hawk commented between bites.

Warily, Rozalyn glanced in his direction to find him grinning from ear to ear. Had something happened? She could only remember talking to the pack horse in order to avoid conversing with Hawk, but she was not about to let on that she had no recollection of her actions.

"Of course, I know what happened," she assured him, striving for a bland tone.

"Good, then would you mind telling me why you tried to fly from yonder tree?" Hawk questioned. Noting the shocked expression on her pallid features, Hawk bit back a chuckle. She didn't have a clue as to what she had done. "It seemed a bit unconventional and daring, even for you."

Rozalyn composed herself as best she could and then clambered to her feet. "I was simply experimenting with flight," she said as coolly as she could.

Hawk digested her response, not believing her for a minute. No sane person would take a headlong dive from a tree without a pair of wings, not even Rozalyn. Experiment indeed! "Why don't you just confess that you drank yourself into a stupor and very nearly killed yourself in the process?" He smirked.

Wheeling around, Rozalyn nailed him to the tree with her glare. Hawk was testing her temper and she could not tolerate his badgering, not in her present condition. God, she felt awful. Never again would she indulge in brandy. Besides, she couldn't even remember whether she had enjoyed herself.

"What I did last night was none of your concern. If you do not approve of my behavior, it makes little difference to me. I can think of worse pranks than attempting to fly," she muttered, stalking toward her mount.

"Such as brazenly offering yourself to me while you were swimming in brandy?" Hawk suggested, grinning rakishly. "Perhaps you intend to shrug off what happened between us, but it was a night I will long remember. . . ."

Rozalyn broke stride, and her mouth gaped as she pivoted around to face his ornery smile. My God, had she

217

seduced the very man who had broken her heart, the man who was using her as a ploy to barter with her father? True, she had heavily indulged in brandy, but she hadn't completely lost her mind . . . had she? Rozalyn inwardly groaned at the thought of giving Hawk another weapon to use against her. Had she thrown herself at him like a shameless hussy, coaxing him to make love to her? Had she told that infuriating brute that she actually felt something for him?

After considering a sarcastic rejoinder, Rozalyn compressed her lips and decided it best not to rise to the taunt. She wasn't certain whether Hawk was teasing her or mocking her with the truth. Anything she said might make matters worse. Raising a proud chin, Rozalyn marched to her steed.

It was wicked of him to tease her so, Hawk decided. But he was giving Rozalyn exactly what she deserved for tongue lashing him during her conversation with the pack horse. Let her steam and stew. Let her wonder if she had offered herself to him in a moment of madness. That would teach her to drown her inhibitions in a bottle of brandy. She should fret after her careless stunt of attempting to fly from a cottonwood tree. When Rozalyn had taken that fall it had stripped ten years off Hawk's life. He had very nearly suffered a heart seizure, wondering if he would reach her in time. But the most disgruntling fact was, had the situation been reversed, Rozalyn would have stood aside to allow him to break his neck. At least he had cared enough to rescue her from impending doom. She would never return the favor. Indeed, she would applaud his tomfoolery and wish him harm.

Grappling with that thought, Hawk pulled himself into the saddle for the trek. "I lied," he confessed after an hour of watching Rozalyn squirm on her perch. "Even while you were behaving in a most unladylike manner you made no attempt to seduce me."

Inwardly breathing a sigh of relief, Rozalyn straightened in her seat. "That was a rotten trick, Hawk. I am humiliated enough after carrying on like a lush. You needn't have added insult to injury by proclaiming that I tried to fly naked into your arms to appease some unexplainable craving brought on by the brandy."

"You did not approach me in a fit of passion," Hawk informed her curtly. "Though I would not have rejected you if you had. But as far as attempting to fly from a tree is concerned, you did that . . . and most unsuccessfully. Next time you insist upon resorting to such perilous antics, I suggest you use a net. Had I not reached you in the nick of time, you would have had reservations on a flight to your final destination." Hawk grunted disdainfully and cast her a pointed glance. "To heaven or hell, I cannot say, but I would be happy to speculate upon it."

"Strange, I thought this was hell and you were Lucifer." Rozalyn sniffed and looked at him scornfully.

The faintest hint of a smile bordered Hawk's lips before he nudged his steed into a trot. "For you, I suppose it is since you see me as such a vengeful dragon. But I have often heard it said that one gets what one deserves."

Rozalyn pulled a face at Hawk's departing back, but nothing seemed to melt the dragon's scales. Oh, how she would love to put that arrogant, bull-headed varmint in his place! He was delighting in making her miserable. And no doubt, he had split his sides laughing at her ridiculous behavior the previous night. Rozalyn swore she would never go near another bottle of brandy as long as she lived. She could make a fool of herself without the aid of liquor. Besides, the brandy had not helped her forget the man who haunted her, she thought dismally. As soon as the fog of whiskey parted she looked back on the past and she remembered how deeply Hawk had hurt her. Nothing

219

could make her forget how agonizing that was.

The day would come when she and Hawk went their separate ways, and when they did, Rozalyn promised herself she would never give the frustrating rogue another thought. Somehow she would find a way to escape him, to return to the world from which she had come. Then she would begin to live again. But she wasn't going to fall in love again. Doing so had very nearly torn out her heart.

As the sun filtered through the canopy of trees that lined the North Platte River, Hawk came awake with a start. The sound of human voices filtered into his drowsy thoughts, making him curse in annoyance. For more than a week he and Rozalyn had tracked northwest, following the river. They had veered around a scouting party of Osages without being noticed, but that had been their only contact with any form of human life. Hawk had become lax, for he was reasonably sure he had not been followed from St. Louis. But he was wrong, he thought as his keen gaze circled their surroundings.

He crouched in the heavy brush and then cautiously poked his head up to locate the source of the voices. A low growl of disgust erupted from his lips when he spied three men who were making their way along the river in a canoe. His narrowed gaze focused on the burly white man who sat between two Blackfoot Indians. Jarvis Ranes, or Half-Head as he was called by the trappers who roamed the Rockies, was paddling upriver. Hawk's blood ran cold as his eyes took in the white man's scarred face and the left side of his head where part of his scalp was missing. Aubrey had sent the most ruthless excuse for a man in pursuit of Rozalyn. The fool, Hawk thought sourly. Half-Head might bring Rozalyn back in one piece, but not without leaving brutal scars that even the discerning eye could not detect. The bloodthirsty mountain man who befriended members of the hostile Blackfoot tribe would make Rozalyn wish she were dead.

Hawk had heard tales about Half-Head's cruel use of women, and he had seen the results of Half-Head's mistreatment of women from the Crow tribe. Thinking of Rozalyn being forced to succumb to Half-Head's lusts turned Hawk's stomach.

He held his breath, hoping the threesome would continue upriver without realizing their prey were tucked safely in the thick brush that lined the stream. As the canoe glided through the water, he ducked behind a gnarled tree stump and waited for the danger to pass.

The sounds that had awakened Hawk had also dragged Rozalyn from sleep. She rolled to her feet, her heart alive with the hope of rescue, and her eyes darted to Hawk who was crouched in the bushes. Then she darted into the clearing to call for help. In her mind, anyone's company had to be better than Hawk's and she thought when she explained her dilemma and offered a sizable purse for her safe return to St. Louis, she would have nothing to fear.

The movement behind him caught Hawk's attention, and he snarled in disgust when he saw Rozalyn scampering toward the departing men. Hawk pounced like a tiger upon his prey, but Rozalyn's cry for assistance came forth before he could clamp a hand around her mouth. When Hawk forced her to the ground, knocking the wind out of her, Rozalyn gasped for breath. She could not voice another word, but it didn't matter. The threesome had heard her muffled yelp and had changed direction to seek out the sound.

Rozalyn was yanked to her feet so quickly her head spun, and before she could locate her tongue and make use of it, Hawk tossed her onto the back of her horse. As the steed galloped away, Hawk catapulted onto its back and tugged on the rope to force the pack horses to follow.

"You little fool," he breathed down Rozalyn's neck. "Your cry may lead to your own death as well as mine. If you knew who your father sent to retrieve you, I doubt you would find my company so distasteful."

"Anyone's company has to be better than yours," Rozalyn muttered, but when Hawk's arm fastened about her, she relinquished her attempt to jump to freedom.

"Not Half-Head's." Hawk snorted derisively. "The man makes me seem a saint."

"I cannot imagine that." Rozalyn's tone was caustic.

"Believe it," he barked sharply. "Half-Head lives with the Blackfoot Indians who are constantly at war with the whites and every other tribe in Wyoming territory. He kills his own kind to prove to the Blackfoot that he is their blood brother. And when Half-Head has a craving for women he has no objection to resorting to rape. In fact, he prefers it that way . . . with every woman."

Hawk let his comment flutter off into the breeze as they thundered through the maze of trees that lined the river. Rozalyn felt a shiver of revulsion dart down her spine. Perhaps she should be more discriminating in the future when she sought assistance. But she began to wonder if Hawk was purposely frightening her to prevent her from escaping. She wouldn't put it past him. How could she know for certain that this Half-Head was such a vile brute? And where had Hawk dreamed up such an odd name? Rozalyn had not seen the men's faces. She had only heard their voices. For all she knew President Jackson might have been coming to rescue her from her abductor's clutches.

After Hawk pushed the horses until they labored, he slowed them to a trot. He didn't dare stop moving, not when Half-Head was in hot pursuit. Although the enemy was afoot, Hawk was taking no chances. He could never let his guard down when that frightful beast was stalking him. His gaze drifted back over his shoulder. No doubt, Half-Head knew who had kidnapped Rozalyn. The burly brute would delight in settling his score with Hawk, and he would gladly accept money after having his way with Rozalyn. Damnation, Hawk muttered under his breath. Aubrey had sent the most ruthless henchman he could find to avenge Rozalyn's abduction. If DuBois cared anything at all about his daughter's safety he would have looked elsewhere for assistance, but he hungered to see Hawk dead and that obsession had overshadowed his concern for his only daughter.

Hawk's apprehension delighted Rozalyn. She had never seen him so cautious. Spitefully, she wished she could be the one to instill such anxiety in him. That would provide some consolation for the pain he had inflicted on her, the agony she had endured by remaining in his company when she was still so vulnerable.

"So you are afraid of this Half-Head fellow," Rozalyn prodded.

"I respect his abilities," Hawk answered. "Half-Head and I had a scuffle that he swore he would not soon forget."

"A number of people seem to have grudges against you," Rozalyn taunted. "It does make one wonder where the fault lies when so many enemies long to loose a bullet with your name on it." A thoughtful frown knitted her brow. "How did this Half-Head come by his name?"

"His given name is Jarvis Ranes," Hawk explained, casting another apprehensive glance over his shoulder. "But he came by that name when he lost half his scalp in battle."

"I suppose you are the one who raised half his scalp and caused him to become known by such an uncomplimentary nickname." Although Rozalyn was merely taunting Hawk, a wary frown appeared on her features when he did not immediately respond to her remark. She peered over her shoulder to survey the chiseled expression carved on his bronzed face, and she knew at once that she had hit upon an exposed nerve. The deadly gleam in his eyes told her all she wanted to know. "It was you, wasn't it, Hawk?" she choked out.

"If I had not been interrupted by his two Blackfoot friends I would have lifted all that murdering bastard's scalp." There was venom in Hawk's voice, and it made Rozalyn shudder uncontrollably. "Half-Head brutally killed two of my friends for the fur pelts they had collected. And what he did to my friend's squaw is not a tale fit for your ears. I would have seen Half-Head lying in a pool of his own blood if time had permitted."

Rozalyn wanted to hear no more. Her eyes darted fearfully about her. At any moment she expected to see two savages and their ominous leader leap from the shadows. She voiced no complaint when Hawk insisted that it was far too dangerous to slow their pace or take time to rest. Perhaps being with him was not the worse of two evils, Rozalyn told herself. The grisly picture he painted of Half-Head was vivid enough to create nightmares, and she didn't want to close her eyes for fear of being haunted by her overactive imagination.

It was long past midnight of the second day before Hawk reined the horses to a halt and rummaged through the saddlebags for the dried beef that was to serve as their meager meal. Rozalyn was almost too weary to eat. But when he thrust the stick of tough beef at her and ordered her to chew on it, she complied. Nor did she protest when he dragged only one fur quilt from the pack horse to serve as their bed. That particular night she would fall asleep on Hawk's shoulder, content to lie in the protective circle of his arms. There would be no campfire to provide warmth, only the heat of their bodies molded together inside a quilt cocoon.

Hawk's dark eyebrows lifted in surprise when Rozalyn snuggled up against him and laid her head on his shoulder. "I wondered if I would have to bind and gag you to force you to sleep this close to me." Hawk laughed softly.

The feel of his hard warmth was as cozy as any camp-fire, and Rozalyn was too exhausted by their hectic pace to rise to his taunt. "There are a great many things about you that I do not appreciate"—she sighed tiredly and her slender arm curled about his neck—"but I must admit that you make a most comfortable pallet."

As her supple body moved against him, he was aroused, but he controlled the overwhelming urge to take her honeyed mouth. This was not the time to lose his head, not with the gruesome threesome tracking them. Sleeping alone while Rozalyn was so close at hand had been a torture worse than death, but this was nine kinds of hell! Rozalyn was sprawled over him, her knee intimately situated between his thighs, her soft feminine scent warping what was left of his senses. She was so temptingly close, yet she might as well have been twenty yards away for all the good her nearness would do him now!

How the devil was he to sleep with Half-Head sniffing out his tracks and this alluring minx using him as her pillow? The answer to those discomforting questions buzzed through his mind until the sun raised its head. Hawk did not sleep at all. He merely lay on the ground like a stiff corpse, not daring to move for fear of arousing his male needs. To make matters worse, his eyes kept popping open each time he heard a sound, ensuring they had no unwelcome visitors creeping up on them.

Rozalyn moaned drowsily as Hawk scooped her up in his arms and set her upon her mount. After he swung into his own saddle, he gestured toward the northwest, touching his heels to the black stallion's flanks to start the pack train in that direction. A concerned frown creased Rozalyn's brow when she eased up beside Hawk. Dark circles surrounded his eyes and he looked very tired, as if he hadn't slept a wink during the night.

Rozalyn couldn't fathom how he could push himself without some much-needed rest. Her own muscles screamed each time she moved. She would have done almost anything for a feather bed and a brass tub—anything except facing the man Hawk had described as the devil himself.

The more she contemplated the man Hawk had described, the more prone she was to believe that he had not exaggerated. If this awesome mountain man feared another human, even a little, that man had to be a monster. Rozalyn was in no hurry to make Half-Head's acquaintance and she sorely regretted her blunder. If she had kept silent, they would not be fleeing like hunted animals.

"Hawk?" Rozalyn cast a sideways glance at her weary companion. "I'm sorry. . . ." Her apology was soft and sincere.

His broad shoulders lifted and dropped carelessly. "It is no matter. Half-Head would have discovered us sooner or later. At least now I know who your father has sent to dispose of me."

"Do you know why Papa hates your family so?" she inquired.

"No," he said simply. "But I hope to find out." A lopsided smile rippled across his lips. "At least I am not left to wonder why you have so little use for me. Your father accused me of scheming, but what you and I—"

Rozalyn cut him off. "It is all in the past." She was still nursing her wounds and she could not bear to hear Hawk's excuses. She didn't want to go through agony again. Once had been enough.

Hawk could tell by the stubborn set of her jaw that the subject had been closed so he let the matter drop. Besides, it would have led to an argument and he didn't need to be sidetracked just now.

Chapter 14

By the end of their fifth day of flight, Hawk was completely exhausted. He had pushed himself relentlessly and he was reasonably certain that the time he had put between them and Half-Head would grant him a few hours' rest.

Rozalyn leaned back against a tree to study Hawk as he stripped off his fringed shirt and knelt by the river to wash. She admired the broad expanse of his back, the muscles that rippled over his arms and shoulders. Dammit, why did she still find this rough-edged mountain man so attractive despite what he'd put her through? And why did she sympathize with his weariness when he had brought this upon himself?

Turning away from the arousing sight of Hawk's bronzed skin and masculine contours, Rozalyn breathed a discouraged sigh. It seemed her penance for running wild in the past few years was to find herself in the company of the one man she couldn't have. Perhaps if she were more of a woman she could capture this lion of a man. Maybe if she learned to control her flighty temper Hawk would have had more respect for her. Oh, why couldn't she stop wanting what she knew she could never have? Hawk was a shiftless mountain man. He didn't need a woman to love and care for him. You must forget him if you hope to salvage your sanity when you emerge from this ordeal, she told herself, Think of something else!

Taking her own advice she turned her thoughts to food . . . or to the available substitute for it. After rummaging through the supplies, she found a few dried rations to munch on, but she was restless and her eyes circled the surroundings. She wondered how close Half-Head was.

Rozalyn was startled when Hawk's shadow fell over her. She thought she had been paying close attention to all that transpired, but obviously she had not developed her senses. She did not have the ears of a wolf or the eyes of an eagle. Hawk did. He seemed to have an uncanny knack for anticipating disaster before it was upon him. The day he had spotted the bobcat that had been tracking them Rozalyn had heard nothing but the chirping of birds. If she had been alone, she knew she would have become the bobcat's evening meal.

"If you would like to bathe in the stream, I'll stand watch," Hawk offered tiredly.

Nodding agreeably, Rozalyn set aside her tasteless rations and ambled toward the river. She didn't care that Hawk was watching her. The thought of bathing and easing her aching muscles was foremost in her mind. Let him gawk. That was all he could do. Hawk had his hands full in keeping one step ahead of her father's henchman. He wouldn't dare force himself on her with such trouble nipping at his heels. Perhaps Hawk would find himself wanting her, but he deserved to be uncomfortable. Even such discomfort did not compare to the ache that nagged at her mending heart.

Hawk's eyes turned a deeper shade of green when Rozalyn stepped from her buckskin breeches and peeled off her shirt, and when the water molded itself to her body, he groaned inwardly, wishing instead his arms were encircling her. His courteous suggestion had been a mistake, he realized dismally. The sight of Rozalyn's ivory skin, sparkling with tiny water droplets, was hard on his blood pressure. In the waning sunlight her shapely silhouette was like an alluring vision, a dream that lay just beyond reality. Although his body was weary, his craving for this gorgeous naiad was insatiable. He had only to gaze upon her and his obsession with her flooded his mind.

Lord, the woman would drive him to an early grave. Hawk plopped down on a fallen log and propped himself upon his Hawken rifle. If he didn't die from wanting this minx, he would die at the hands of Aubrey's henchman . . . because of her. Damnation! Carting Rozalyn off to the wilds had been a foolish deed. Now she was so entangled in his thoughts that he wondered if he could ever rout her without tearing out his heart. She had burrowed deeply into his life, and he could not even view a sunset or a sunrise without also watching its mellow colors caress the exquisite features of Rozalyn's face.

Perhaps he should have left her for Half-Head and his merciless braves, Hawk thought sourly. Then his hungry gaze focused on Rozalyn, and he watched her glide across the river like a graceful swan. Dammit, having her with him was turning him inside out. If he had sacrificed this priceless gem to Half-Head, at least he might emerge from this nightmare in one piece. Keeping her with him was like furnishing his own private room in hell. He spent his waking hours craving her, even while they fled from that murdering scoundrel, Half-Head. And if that dreadful threesome caught up with them before they reached the precipices of the Rockies, Rozalyn would probably applaud the attack and encourage Half-Head to make mincemeat of her abductor. Hawk believed that Rozalyn hated him. They had played a risky game with each other's hearts, and he sorely regretted his part in it.

For a while, he had actually believed that this cynical enchantress had softened toward him. He had been an arrogant fool. Rozalyn had been laughing at him all the while. He had made her body burn with desire, but he had not been able to tame her wild heart. The blue-eyed imp had remained free as a bird when pursued by the most dashing bachelors in St. Louis. If they hadn't won her affection, how the hell did he think he could accomplish that feat in the span of a week? Hawk berated his arrogance. He must have the intelligence of a pine tree to think he could curl this rebellious beauty around his finger.

Another agonized groan rattled in Hawk's chest when Rozalyn emerged from the stream. Water ebbed from her bare shoulders and from the provocative peaks of her breasts. Hawk watched in pained torment as the river surrendered up this vision of incomparable loveliness. Beads of water, sparkling like diamonds, danced on her flawless skin, and he felt a wild urge to quench his thirst by kissing her moist flesh. Her body was perfection, her breasts full, her waist trim, her legs long and shapely. God, no man should be forced to endure such a cruel form of torture, Hawk thought as his devouring gaze flooded over the enchantress he longed to caress.

But Rozalyn had informed him in no uncertain terms that she expected him to seek his pleasure elsewhere, that she had no intention of accommodating him. He was miserable, where once he had been happy and carefree, flitting from one maid to another, until this raven-haired minx with lively blue eyes blew into his life and tilted his world sideways. Hawk could endure no more of the tempting sight of her. He turned his back before his failing will power abandoned him entirely. This was no time for distractions and Rozalyn was that and more!

When Hawk threw one leg over the log and presented

his back to her, Rozalyn frowned in disappointment. She had hoped to tempt him, to torment him, to make him regret the way he had used her to get at her father. But obviously he was no longer interested in her. She had been an easy conquest, and now he had tired of her. Disheartened, she shrugged on her buckskins and ambled toward the horses, hurt because she'd been unable to attract him. God help her, she wanted this green-eyed devil who had already forsaken the love she had freely offered. He doesn't have to love me, Rozalyn told herself. She had learned to accept the fact that Hawk had no place in his life for love, but for him to ignore her, as her father always had, was almost too much to bear. If she couldn't win Hawk's heart, was it asking too much to want his respect, his friendship? But she wasn't helping matters by taunting him with her body. That was a spiteful thing to do. Maybe Hawk had been right about her. Perhaps she was too temperamental and spoiled to deserve any man's affection. But could she give more than her heart? She had confessed her true feeling for Dominic Baudelair a lifetime ago. Then she had been at ease with him. She had been herself, but obviously Dominic had not been impressed.

When Hawk heard Rozalyn's footsteps behind him, he glanced back to punish his senses once again. God, he had been an idiot to think buckskins could conceal this vixen's shapely physique. The garments clung to her damp skin, hugging each curve and swell as he ached to do, and lustrous strands of ebony swirled about her face and flowed down her back like a dark, shiny waterfall. How he longed to run his fingers through those silky strands, to inhale the fresh scent of her.

Rozalyn could not decode the expression in Hawk's glazed eyes, but it disturbed her to see his powerful shoulders slump dejectedly. She had never seen this mountain lion look defeated, not once in their brief, unusual acquaintance. Hawk had always appeared invincible, strong, and determined, as if he had no qualms about taking on whatever trouble came his way. But now he seemed listless. There was no recklessness in his smile, no fiery sparkle in his eyes.

After extracting one of the flintlocks from his belt, Hawk thrust the weapon at Rozalyn. "Keep this with you. I have no doubt that you can use it as efficiently as I can."

Her jaw sagged and she stared incredulously at him. Hawk was offering her a pistol after he had kept her bound and gagged, after he had left her unarmed for fear she would turn his own weapon on him. Why?

"Is something wrong?" she queried.

Hawk cast Rozalyn a withering glance, careful not to allow his eyes to linger overly long on the titillating cleavage that lay exposed between the loose laces of her shirt. How could she ask such a preposterous question? What is right? he asked himself tiredly.

"Only everything," he grumbled. "My life expectancy has been shortened considerably since you and I crossed paths. Your father and Half-Head thirst for my blood. You would see me chopped into bite-size pieces and fed to a pack of wolves." His breath came out in a rush. "I am contemplating turning my pistol on myself and ending the suspense of wondering how it will end."

When Rozalyn offered him back the flintlock, Hawk laughed bitterly at her insinuation. "*Merci*. You are too generous. It's nice to know you can be so compassionate. I'm sure you would delight in watching me dispose of myself before someone else has the opportunity."

Rozalyn wasn't at all certain Hawk needed compassion. He didn't need to wallow in self-pity when he faced a man who was itching to dispose of him. On the other hand, anger would sustain him until they were safe. With that in mind, she faced Hawk, determined to add fuel to his dim flame.

"Do you truly expect sympathy?" She sniffed caustically and then smiled to herself when Hawk came to immediate attention. "You have made me your pawn in a dangerous game. Do not expect me to praise you for it. If you decide to kill yourself, I will be left to defend myself against a man you have described as a vicious beast. My future appears as grim as yours, Hawk. Believe me, I have enjoyed better days. But I do not intend to lie down and surrender just because trouble lurks in the shadows. If I followed that policy, I would have thrown myself off a cliff long ago."

The faintest hint of a smile pursed Hawk's lips as he watched Rozalyn tuck the flintlock in her belt, straighten her shirt, and flounce toward the horses. He had needed a lecture and Rozalyn had given him one. Hawk would have thanked her for those much-needed insults, but then she would have known that he'd realized he had been subtly maneuvered. Let her gloat, he told himself. He rose and ambled up behind Rozalyn. She needed to feed her spirits, just as he did.

"If Half-Head does catch up with us and . . ." Hawk paused to consider the worst and then he carefully chose his words. "If something happens to me, save the pistol for your own defense. You will have only time for one shot. Take deadly aim on the white man and remember he has as many lives as a cat. Make your shot count for you may not have the chance to reload."

Rozalyn swallowed hard, silently chiding herself for making the foolish mistake of calling to the merciless bounty hunter. Several times during the past week she had spitefully wished harm to befall Hawk, but it was to be by her own hand, not by the hand of a half-crazed, half-scalped maniac. Revenge was her right. That big brute, Half-Head, would not deprive her of it, she promised herself.

An exasperated sigh escaped her lips, and restlessly, she strode over to busy herself by unstrapping the pallets from the pack horses. Had she become so vindictive that she would actually enjoy seeing Hawk die a painful death? She had been humiliated by his rejection, but was she so vain and heartless she wanted his life sacrificed to satisfy her taste for revenge? Was she as harsh and vengeful as her father? If so, it was no wonder Hawk had never fallen in love with her. Who would want a spoiled, selfish, spiteful woman as a wife? What had she done to deserve Hawk's devotion? How could he respect her when she had complained every step of the way, spiting him and making their journey as intolerable as possible. Rozalyn had even mocked him for furnishing her with rations unfit for human consumption. She had ridiculed him for forcing her to sleep on the cold, hard ground. Sweet merciful heavens! She had even accused him of brewing a thunderstorm to drench her! Was it surprising that he had little use for her?

"Roz?"

Hawk's low voice filtered into her troubled contemplations, and she turned back to see him fling an arm over his horse's back for support. An apologetic smile flitted across his lips and then vanished when his eyes bored into hers.

"I'm sorry I dragged you into this mess. If I had it to do over again, I would have left you safely tucked away in St. Louis." His silent footsteps brought him forward until he stood gazing down into Rozalyn's lovely face. Gently, he reached out to comb the unruly ebony strands away from her shoulders. "I know I deserve your wrath, but when this ordeal is over, I hope we can begin agai . . . without pretense. It might be different, much different."

As he bent to offer a repentant kiss, Hawk's warm breath whispered across her lips, and Rozalyn's wounded heart responded, despite her attempt to feel nothing. She had despised Hawk and the bittersweet memories he had created. But the heartache of one-sided love was fading, to be replaced by feelings of warmth and admiration. At least Hawk was not throwing her stupidity in her face, even when she justly deserved it. Rozalyn was beginning to get over hating this raven-haired rogue who had turned her wrong-side out, exposing her carefully guarded emotions. But she still wondered if she would ever get over loving him. He had stirred so many emotions, touched so many parts of her, arousing anger and resentment but also passion too fierce and over-whelming to forget. Rozalyn feared the sweet memories he'd created would never die, no matter how deeply she buried them. She could pretend he meant nothing to her. She could hurl cutting remarks at him to ease her wounded pride, but she couldn't keep herself from loving this resourceful woodsman who had become all things to her. Time could ease the hurting, but it could not erase the love. To forget Hawk, Rozalyn would have to stop breathing, and even in death she wondered if her restless soul would still be plagued with torturous memories of what might have been.

A turmoil of emotions erupted deep inside her, and Rozalyn reached out to trace the rugged lines of Hawk's face. There was a strange sort of peacefulness between them now. Their anger had faded, giving way to a silent understanding. Rozalyn was stung by the insane impulse to press her lips to his, to mold her body to the sinewy length of him. She wanted to forget everything that had any semblance to reality, even if Hawk mocked her because she'd vowed never to go near him.

"Make it like it was for that short time in space," she murmured. Her body moved instinctively toward him until she was flush against him. "Kiss me, Hawk. Make me forget where I am and why."

Flaming green eyes focused intently on her quivering lips, and ever so slowly his head came toward hers. Rozalyn died with pleasure at his gentle touch. Then his full lips rolled over hers, caressing, savoring, creating a need that unfurled in every part of her being. As his arms slid about her waist, cradling her against his hard chest, Rozalyn swore she would melt into a pool of liquid desire if it were not for his supporting embrace. The musky fragrane of him clung to her, intoxicated her, as did his kiss. The world was tilting sideways. She wound her arms around his neck to press her body even closer, feeling the fire kindle, knowing it would burn out of control, not caring if it did.

Sweet agony pulsed through her when his kiss became more demanding, and she held him even closer. Fire consumed her, and she became part of the blaze. When Hawk's roaming hand wandered over her and then tunneled beneath her buckskin shirt to knead her breast, Rozalyn voiced no protest. Indeed, she welcomed the sensations he aroused. She craved his touch, even when she'd sworn she would never again grant him privileges with her body.

"God, woman, the feel of you drives me mad," Hawk rasped, his voice heavily laden with desire. And when her adventurous hand dipped beneath the band of his breeches, he sucked in his breath. "Don't do that. I won't be able to think at all."

But Rozalyn could not help herself. She ached to feel his hard flesh, hungered to map the muscular contours that tensed and relaxed beneath her inquiring touch. "You need not think?" she whispered as she nibbled at the pulsations along his neck. "Just hold me close for a time. I—"

When a hissing arrow sailed past her ear, Rozalyn screamed. It lodged in Hawk's shoulder and terror filled Rozalyn's eyes. Wheeling around, she saw two Blackfoot warriors and their hideous leader spring from the under-brush. How had these men managed to catch up with them? she wondered bewilderedly. Hawk had kept a fast pace, pausing only when she ... Rozalyn groaned, knowing her presence must have slowed Hawk's flight. If he hadn't been dragging her along with him, he would have had no difficulty in eluding Half-Head and his renegade friends.

Feeling personally responsible for this ambush, Rozalyn looked back at Hawk who had dived for his rifle without taking the time to yank the arrow from his shoulder. As he rolled to his feet, his rifle exploded and one attacking brave fell before he could launch the hatchet he was preparing to hurl. Before Hawk could grasp his pistol, the other savage was upon him and Hawk was forced to the ground. He growled like a wounded panther when the arrow was rammed deeper into his bleeding shoulder, but the pain only served to infuriate him.

Rozalyn detected the deadly gleam in Hawk's eyes, that same savage flicker she had noticed the night he had lunged at Jeffrey and had then left the scrawny blond in a crumpled heap. She had seen that ominous sparkle again when Harvey and his men had surrounded Hawk. But now Hawk's enemies hungered for more than coins. The muscular savage was fierce competition, and he was as adept in battle as Hawk was. Powerful bodies strained as the pair rolled through the grass in an attempt to gain the advantageous position.

The moment Hawk managed to knock the knife from his opponent's hand the huge white man was upon him. Half-Head sneered maliciously, and slammed the butt of his rifle against Hawk's wounded shoulder, causing more blood to stain the buckskin shirt. Hawk hissed as searing pain shot through his chest, but he was only distracted for a moment. Agilely, he spun away from Half-Head's fist, and positioning the brave between them, he made the warrior take the brunt of the blow.

The color seeped from Rozalyn's features when she saw the venomous snarl that etched Half-Head's ghastly face. A jagged scar stretched from his left eye, across his temple, and around the bald side of his head. His face bore evidence of more than one battle, and Rozalyn cringed at the sight of him, knowing his ugly face would reappear in her nightmares.

Rozalyn shivered as Hawk faced this ghastly giant. Half-Head stood six-foot-six and must have weighed at least two hundred and forty pounds. How could Hawk fight both men? He was wounded and one of his enemies was huge and bloodthirsty.

Although Rozalyn kept her pistol aimed and ready, she was unable to get a clear shot at either of Hawk's assailants, and she would not risk hitting Hawk. Watching the bloody battle was frustrating. She felt utterly useless. Frantically, she tried to think of a way to even the odds without getting Hawk killed in the process.

Half-Head kept Hawk at arm's length, allowing the Blackfoot warrior to charge into him like a battering ram and then pellet his defenseless prey with one punishing blow after another. Finally Rozalyn vaulted onto her horse and thundered between the men, knocking the brave to the ground and dazing him momentarily. When she reined the steed around to make another run, Half-Head cursed a blue streak. He had not expected interference from the woman. He cursed again when Hawk squirmed free. Then his murderous glare riveted over Rozalyn who was gouging the steed in the flanks and charging at him.

Although Half-Head dived to safety, Hawk's fist had struck his face and, as he got to his feet, Hawk's second well-aimed blow sent him stumbling backward. Half-Head twisted around to crawl beneath the steed's belly, avoiding Hawk's next attack. When the frightened horse reared, Rozalyn clung to the saddle, but it stumbled, so she leaped to safety. Her gaze darted to the stunned Blackfoot warrior who was staggering to his feet to lend Half-Head a helping hand. Frantically, Rozalyn grabbed the discarded rifle and clubbed the brave over the head.

When the warrior wilted into a senseless heap, Rozalyn breathed a sigh of relief, but it was short-lived. Her eyes landed on the twosome battling each other so ferociously she would have sworn two grizzlies were fighting for supremacy. Hawk's once handsome face was bruised, swollen, and battered. Half-Head, ugly ordinarily, presented an even more gruesome sight with one eye swollen shut and blood trickling from the corner of a mouth that was twisted in a murderous snarl.

When Hawk sidestepped an oncoming fist and then kicked Half-Head in the groin, Rozalyn flinched. The half-scalped brute came uncoiled like a vicious rattlesnake about to sink his fangs in an intended victim. And he did! Rozalyn swore the barbarous beast would chew Hawk's arm off at the elbow. Half-Head was like a madman, swearing, pouncing, and retreating, pouncing again.

Hawk's loss of blood and his fierce battle against difficult odds were beginning to drain his strength. His movement was not as agile as it had been and his blows lacked the force required to bring Half-Head to his knees.

Rozalyn could not follow Hawk's instructions to save one bullet for her own defense. At the moment, he seemed more in need of assistance than she. Clutching the long-barreled flintlock in shaky hands, she took careful aim. When Half-Head leaped on Hawk, his powerful fingers clamping around his foe's neck and choking the life from him, she discharged the pistol. With a pained grunt, Half-Head collapsed on top of Hawk, clutching the wound in his side.

It took the last of Hawk's strength to shove Half-Head away. Panting in attempt to catch his breath, he then crawled from him on all fours. Sickening dread drained Rozalyn of color. When she raced over to pull Hawk into an upright position, she found the entire right side of his shirt was stained with blood, and the shaft of the arrow had broken off beneath his flesh. Hawk's face had paled beneath his ruddy tan, but he struggled to keep his feet, though the world was careening about him. Breathing was an effort and standing was virtually impossible. If Rozalyn had not offered him assistance, he swore he would have been sprawled beside Half-Head.

"Get the horses," Hawk commanded. Latching onto the trunk of a nearby tree, he cradled his right arm against his bruised ribs.

Rozalyn nodded mutely and hurried off to gather their belongings. When she led the string of horses back to Hawk, her breath froze in her throat. Half-Head's outstretched arm was reaching toward the dagger that lay in the grass. His dark eyes flickered maliciously as he propped up on an elbow and hurled the knife at Hawk.

"Hawk!" Rozalyn screamed at the top of her lungs.

His gaze swung around and he ducked away from the dagger that sailed through the air to pin his left shirt sleeve to the tree. A wicked smile raised Hawk's puffed lips on one side. Then he yanked the knife free and stalked toward Half-Head, the dagger poised in his left hand.

"When last we met, I left my task half-finished," he said. He stalked steadily toward his wounded prey, his eyes glittering menacingly. "I will see that your head-stone bears your new nickname."

"No!" Rozalyn charged at Hawk to snatch the dagger from his hand. She had seen enough blood for one day and she doubted she had the stomach to watch this murderous beast lose the other half of his scalp.

Despite Hawk's reservations about allowing a man like Half-Head to live, he permitted Rozalyn to herd him toward the horses, and, with considerable effort, he swung into the saddle.

"If you survive your wounds, we will end our feud at another time, Half-Head," Hawk told him coldly.

"Will you still be hiding behind a woman's skirt?" Pushing himself into a half-sitting position, the monstrous Ranes gave Hawk a scornful glance.

"Will you fight your battle alone or will you surround yourself with a Blackfoot war party?" Hawk countered, his tone as taunting as Half-Head's had been. His gaze drifted to the unconscious brave who had not moved a muscle since Roz had pounded him into the ground with the butt of the rifle.

Before the two men got into a shouting match, Rozalyn snatched up the pack horses' reins and she slapped Hawk's steed on the rump, sending him trotting off through the trees. Then her eyes drifted back to the grisly-looking mountain man, whose disgusting leer made her shiver repulsively. His sordid thoughts were obvious, and his words gave credence to his lurid stare.

"You may elude me for a time, woman, but I will come for you. Do not doubt it." Half-Head chuckled roguishly, and his lips curled in a suggestive smile. "I will prove to you that I am more of a man than Hawk, the kind who can tame a woman like you."

Gouging her steed, she followed after Hawk, but Half-Head's vow continued to ring in her ears until she eased her horse up beside Hawk. Her relieved smile vanished when she met Hawk's icy glare.

"I should have killed him," Hawk muttered. He sucked in his breath when the horse's canter jarred his aching body.

"One man is dead, another is seriously wounded, and

the third has been stripped of his senses." Rozalyn grumbled. "I should think that would satisfy your thirst for blood."

"Half-Head will follow us," Hawk growled. "It was a mistake to let him live."

"I'm sure he feels the same way about you," Rozalyn assured Hawk tartly. "As a matter of fact, I'm wondering why I permitted either of you to . . ." Her voice trailed off as she watched the last of the color drain from his peaked face, and she gasped when Hawk buckled over in the saddle, his head resting against the stallion's neck. "Hawk?"

He could hear her calling him, her voice echoing as if she were at the opposite end of a long tunnel, but he could not find the strength to utter a word. Darkness circled him like a vulture waiting to swoop down on its prey, and he gave way to the black abyss that closed in on him. Gratefully, he surrendered to the deafening silence that blocked out his pain.

Rozalyn heaved an exasperated sigh. Blast it! The man was ranting about disposing of his foe one moment and the next instant he was crumpled over his saddle. Did she dare stop to tend Hawk's wounds? She knew Half-Head would be tracking them as soon as he could walk. Perhaps Hawk was right. Letting that vicious scavenger live was an invitation to more trouble. But dammit, she could not stand there and watch Hawk lift Half-Head's scalp any more than she could allow Half-Head to strangle Hawk.

Her thoughtful gaze circled the surroundings, seeking a secluded spot in which to hide Hawk until he recovered from his wounds. Her eyes settled on the bluffs that towered on the opposite bank of the river. Rozalyn guided the horses into the water, hoping their course would be difficult to track if she followed the North Platte until she could find a suitable place to make the climb onto the precipices.

It was almost two hours before she located a winding path that led up the cliff. During that time Hawk had roused only once, and her growing concern for him had caused her to quicken her pace. Rozalyn breathed a grateful sigh when she spied a cave among the fallen boulders. Nature had provided a corral for the horses and sanctuary for two weary travelers.

With a great effort Rozalyn dragged Hawk's bulky body from the saddle. He stirred long enough to drape his arm around her shoulders and to make the walk to the mouth of the cave. Once inside it, he wilted like a delicate flower that had been too long in the sun. Rozalyn wore herself out hauling his lifeless body farther into the cavern.

Heaving an exhausted sigh, she trudged back outside to tend the horses and fetch water to cleanse Hawk's wounds. She grimaced as she drew his blood-stained shirt over his head so she could inspect his wound, but summoning her composure, she poured whiskey on the knife and on Hawk's jagged flesh. In the wake of a hasty prayer, she performed primitive surgery. Then, having removed the splintered arrow shaft from his shoulder, she bandaged the wound and wrapped his right arm tightly against his ribs.

When she had completed her task she raked trembling fingers through her tangled hair and sank down cross-legged beside Hawk. A tender smile overshadowed her worried frown as she bent to press a kiss to his swollen lips. Peering into his ashen face evoked warm, protective emotions she would have preferred not to feel.

If she had any sense at all she would take the supplies and flee. Hawk was in no condition to pursue her and Half-Head was nursing his own injuries. But she couldn't leave Hawk like this. He needed her as he never had before. Rozalyn brushed his tousled raven hair over his forehead; then her fingertips wandered down his cheek to settle on the dark matting of hair on his chest. She could feel his heart thudding faintly against the palm of her hand. He seemed so vulnerable.

My, but she had come full circle, loving, hating, and then loving him again. Rozalyn swore she never wanted to see this green-eyed devil again but here she was, playing nursemaid to the very man who had broken her heart.

This is all Lenore's fault, she thought sourly. Grand'mère staged her sickness to force my hand.

One deceit had led to another and Rozalyn had been caught in the middle. If Lenore hadn't pushed her granddaughter into a hasty courtship none of this would have happened.

Sagging back against the musty wall of the cave, Rozalyn dragged the Hawken rifle up onto her lap, determined to stand watch over her unconscious patient. When her eyes flitted back to Hawk, a small voice whispered in her soul: You will never get over loving this man, Rozalyn. He may never care deeply for you, but that won't keep you from chasing an impossible dream.

Chapter 15

Hawk groaned miserably as he shifted on his pallet. Every bone and muscle screamed when he moved. Even his eyelids ached when he tried to open his eyes. His fuzzy gaze settled on the vision that hovered above him.

"Roz? I didn't think you would be here when I awoke," Hawk rasped. Then he grimaced when a sharp pain stabbed at his shoulder.

"I might not have been if I could have found your compass," she teased. Masking her concern, she pressed a damp cloth to his fevered brow.

Gritting his teeth, Hawk propped himself up on his left forearm and peered at his surroundings. "How long have I been asleep?" he asked.

"Three days," Rozalyn said calmly.

"Three days?" Hawk echoed. Then he collapsed on his back, clutching his tender ribs. In a softer tone he continued, "Have you seen any sign of Half-Head?"

"No, I doubt that he is any more capable of moving than you are. If he tries, he will risk having his insides fall out. Hawk?" Rozalyn's mouth dropped open when the mulish man pushed himself into an upright position and struggled to his hands and knees. "What the sweet loving hell do you think you're doing?"

"I intend to stay one step ahead of your father's henchman," he hissed as searing pain shot through his arm.

"You will be too busy killing yourself to notice whether Half-Head is sneaking up on you," Rozalyn scolded.

Hawk seemed as determined to leave as Rozalyn was to have him stay put. She crouched before him and then settled herself on his lap, forcing him to lift her weight as well as his own if he attempted to rise from his pallet. He was going nowhere, even if she had to use her feminine wiles to make sure of it.

One dark eyebrow shot straight up when Rozalyn grasped the hem of her shirt and lifted the garment over her head. The sight of her naked flesh and the provocative smile playing on her lips provoked a suspicious frown. "If I had demanded that you strip, you would have slapped my face," he grumbled, his eyes roaming over her ivory skin.

Rozalyn slid her arms around his shoulders, careful not to brush against his tender wound, and an impish smile pursed her lips as she leaned against him, her breasts brushing wantonly against his chest. "I am always more agreeable when the idea is my own," she murmured. Her warm kisses feathered along the taut tendon on his neck. "I require a certain fee for nursing you back to life."

Hawk knew damned well she wanted to keep him tucked in the cave until she decided that he was healthy enough to travel. But it was her method that waylaid him. He had never been able to refuse this desirable nymph, nor could he now. His good arm slid about her waist to caress her hips, and desire crowded the pain of his wound to a far corner of his mind. Perhaps it wouldn't hurt to delay their journey a few hours, he decided.

Rozalyn had only intended to distract Hawk until he realized he was too weary to leave his pallet, but when the spark of passion leaped between them her body caught fire and began to burn. As her wayward hands flowed over his hair-roughened flesh, Hawk swore she possessed the power to heal. Her caresses massaged away the ache in his muscles and spun his nerves into tangled twine. Then her soft lips skittered across his laboring chest, leaving him relaxed and pliant beneath their arousing touch.

Rozalyn urged him onto his back, and she curled up beside him, her hands and lips continuing to work their subtle magic. Lord, how she loved touching this powerful mass of brawn and muscle. She marveled at his potential strength now in repose. Hawk was a lion. Although weak and wounded, he was still awesome. Lovingly, her fingertips trailed over his muscular thighs, sketching their hard contours, deriving pleasure from merely touching him, watching him, inhaling the manly scent of him.

"I know your purpose, vixen," Hawk assured her, his voice husky with desire. "You plan to take advantage of me in my weakened condition." His lips glided across her velvety skin, finding the rosy peak of her breast, and his hand followed to gently knead the soft mound that was pressed to his cheek. "Do you intend to drain the last of my strength so I will be unable to move from my spot?"

A faint smile pursed Rozalyn's lips. Then her seeking hand trailed beneath the band of his breeches to travel over the hard muscles of his hip. "You are very perceptive, mountain man," she whispered as she twisted away, letting her moist kisses roam across his ribs. "You are the one who taught me the meaning of passion and you are going nowhere until you have appeased the craving you have instilled in me. If you think you are strong enough to ride, then you are strong enough to make love to me."

"In this dark, musty cave?" Hawk chortled at the brazen minx who had stripped him of his breeches, leaving his entire body susceptible to her tantalizing kisses and caresses.

"Would you prefer to go outside?" A teasing grin lifted one corner of her mouth. She rose and slowly pushed the buckskin breeches from her hips. Then she shook out her hair, sending a waterfall of ebony tendrils spilling over her shoulders.

Hawk groaned in torment. His all-consuming gaze drank in her exquisite body, lingering on the dark curls that partially concealed the swells of her breasts; then his eyes wandered lower, to sketch the trim curve of her waist and the slope of her hips. Rozalyn was so breath-takingly lovely that Hawk could not drag his gaze from her. He knew she was only toying with him, taunting him. She feared he could provide no protection if they ventured into the wild while he was still recuperating from his injury so she was offering her delicious body as a temptation to keep him from making the rugged journey before he'd fully regained his strength. And although Hawk knew she was prepared to give her body to him without offering her heart, he could not resist the temptation. Rozalyn was a wild, beautiful bird who thrived on freedom. A man could never truly make her his captive, but Hawk was prepared to settle for whatever she was offering, if it were only for a moment. In time she would return to the world from which she had come and he would remain in the wilderness where he belonged. But for now . . .

"Come here, woman," he growled huskily.

Their eyes met, and Rozalyn knelt before Hawk, he could see flames of passion in her eyes. She leaned forward, her breasts brushing wantonly against the solid wall of his chest. It was the slightest breath of a touch, a whisper of warm flesh. Then her hands ascended to cup his face, and her soft lips barely skimmed his mouth, gently offering pleasure before slowly withdrawing.

Her tender seduction blocked out memory and logic.

Hawk could no longer think. His brain had ceased to function the moment her satiny skin had come into contact with his flesh, making him sharply aware of the contrast between his well-muscled body and her softness. Only Rozalyn felt so good in his arms.

Her touch was deliberate, stirring him with the faintest strokes, and his pain became sheer pleasure. Hawk was oblivious to all except his maddening need. His hand tunneled through her tangled hair to tip her head back, and his kiss lost its gentleness as passion raged within him. The probing insistence of his tongue forced her lips apart; he molded her body closer, and closer still. His mouth explored and Rozalyn eagerly responded. His hand caressed and she moaned in soft surrender.

As they lay side by side, their bodies touching, their hearts beating as one, the raging fire between them became the vital flame of love. Rozalyn took him to her, reveling in the sweet splendor of possessing, of being possessed. She was vividly aware of the sinewed columns of his body straining against hers. Hawk was masculinity in its raw, pure state and she drew strength from him, feeding on the churning emotions that engulfed her.

She answered his hard, demanding thrusts, her body moving in perfect rhythm with his. He was taking her higher, allowing her to glimpse the glorious horizon that awaited them on the far side of the sun. She was soaring on golden wings, flying beyond the perimeters of reality, caught in a current of ecstasy that lifted her and then flung her to dizzying heights of pleasure.

Suddenly the sun exploded, and her emotions diverged in a thousand different directions. Her need for this reckless mountain man was maddening—a craving that defied reason, a fierce, compulsive hunger. The rapture of his lovemaking was wild, sweet torment, and Rozalyn clung to him as incredible sensations converged within her, driving her onward to that timeless moment of sublime ecstasy.

When the soul-shattering sensation came, time stood still, and for what seemed forever Rozalyn was shaken by wave upon wave of ineffable pleasure. Her nails dug into the rippling muscles of Hawk's back. She was afraid to let go, afraid to learn this had all been a fantastic dream. Slowly the sensations ebbed, taking her strength with them. A tremulous sigh escaped her lips as she cuddled against Hawk's warm body. No words passed between them. There was no need for speech. Their sweet, companionable silence said it all.

For a time they slept, a peaceful, relaxed sleep filled with contented dreams. When Hawk's lashes fluttered up, he smiled at the shapely beauty beside him. Stunned by her loveliness, he reached out to comb his fingers through her ebony strands. This tempting sprite had shown Hawk many faces, but the one he viewed now tugged at his heart. Her flawless features were soft in repose, her skin, like satin, brushed lightly against his.

She deserves better than this, he scolded himself. How could he have snatched her from her secure world and forced her into the wilderness? Troubled by his thoughts, Hawk inched away to pull on his breeches.

Once Hawk had staggered to his feet and donned his shirt, he nudged Rozalyn awake. Her eyes drifted up to see the awesome mountain man poised before her. Where had he gotten the strength to rise was beyond her. She would have been content to sleep until dawn, but Hawk was dressed and she was immediately aware of his intention.

"Can't we delay until morning?" She accepted the clothing Hawk thrust at her, but not without frowning her disappointment. "I still contend that you are not healthy enough to travel."

"I have to be," Hawk muttered, turning away before Rozalyn could protest the idiocy of his plan.

Rozalyn's breath came out in a rush. Grumbling, she climbed to her feet and reluctantly followed in Hawk's wake. He was not strong enough to ride, for heaven's sake! If the ride didn't kill him the infection would. All the protests she intended to voice when she marched outside died on her lips.

Hawk flung his left arm over the saddle, preparing to swing onto his horse. "Thank you for saving my life, *wanyecha*," he murmured. When he graced her with a boyish smile that cut deep lines through his bronzed features, Rozalyn melted in her moccasins. "If I felt I had the choice, I would be content to spend the night in your arms. But I cannot breathe easily until we put more distance between ourselves and Half-Head." His smile faded and a hauntingly rueful expression appeared in his eyes. "I know you gave yourself to me because you thought it would keep me here for a time. But even passion cannot disguise the fact that you would truly prefer not to be housed in such close quarters with your worst enemy."

"Better you than Half-Head." Rozalyn picked up the horse's reins and then turned back to Hawk who was struggling into the saddle. "You are not my worst enemy, Hawk," she told him quietly. "If I could be granted one wish it would be that the two of us become friends."

"Friends?" Hawk chuckled, but carefully. Laughter jarred his wound. Again the smile evaporated from his ashen lips. "This thing between us can be only fire or ice, Roz," he told her soberly. "There is no room for any emotion in between. We hurt each other and we grow cold and insensitive for a time, but when we dare to touch it ignites a blaze that neither of us can control." Hawk touched his heels to the stallion's ribs, urging him toward the rocky path. "Friendship? Ah . . . if only it were that simple. . . ."

A disheartened frown etched Rozalyn's features while

251

she stared at Hawk's departing back. Did he dislike her so much, except when he was satisfying his lusts? Why could he not look upon her as his friend? The man could use at least one since he seemed to be surrounded by enemies. Heaving a discouraged sigh, Rozalyn followed Hawk along the winding path that led down from the bluffs. Her gaze swung back to the cavern where they had made wild, sweet love. She must leave those tender memories behind, just as Hawk had; she was a fool for falling in love with him again. Hawk offered her passion, nothing more. How many more of these lectures would she have to deliver to herself before she accepted the truth? she wondered, then she realized they would become a daily ritual. The strong affection she felt for this powerfully built mountain man would be with her forever—and Hawk didn't want forever. Although she knew in her heart that they had no future together, Rozalyn could not stop wanting what she knew she could never have.

Chapter 16

Relief flooded over Hawk's pallid features when he saw the silhouette of Fort William on the western horizon. The log stockade established four years earlier for trade with the Indians, was located near the junction of the North Platte and Laramie Rivers. Around it, rich, lush grass, thick groves of cottonwood trees, and sparkling water made a peaceful picture in the waning sunlight. While inside, the fort contained living quarters for weary travelers, warehouses, and trading posts. Never had Hawk been so anxious to reach this sanctuary.

His eyes drifted to the enticing beauty who rode silently at his side, and a sense of pride swelled within him as he remembered how Rozalyn had handled herself in the face of catastrophe. He had put her through hell, but she had emerged with no more than a scratch. A lesser woman would have perished, but not Rozalyn. After her frightening trials, she deserved to be in the care of those who were able to keep a watchful eye on her.

Hawk had pushed himself to near collapse, but he was certain Half-Head was still forging his way north. Hawk's only chance was to leave Rozalyn in capable hands while he led Aubrey's ruthless henchman in circles. Then Half-Head would find himself ambushed. The bastard deserves no better, Hawk told himself bitterly.

A wry smile skittered across Hawk's lips when he spied a trading party of Sioux emerging from the stockade. It was Rozalyn's misfortune to glance in Hawk's direction at that moment. She frowned warily when she noticed the calculating look in his eyes. It spelled trouble. Rozalyn would have given anything to have been able to read his mind.

Her gaze narrowed on the small group of Indians who moved toward them. Each brave was dressed in bright, colorful garments and was heavily strapped with symbolic weapons. Their paint ponies were adorned with bells, feathers, and ribbons that the Indians had gotten at the fort in exchange for furs and blankets. The Sioux had painted their faces and chests with yellow-moss pigment and ashes before attending the trade ceremony. Why all this pomp and circumstance? Rozalyn wondered. And why was Hawk grinning at the decorated braves who approached them in their proud, aloof manner?

When Hawk began to speak a foreign tongue, Rozalyn peered bewilderedly at him. Bravely, she darted a glance at the warriors, who were studying her as if she were a piece of merchandise they were considering purchasing. One brave circled around her, scrutinizing her from all angles. Then he reached out to lift a tangled strand of her hair, making Roz flinch uncomfortably.

"What is going on here?" Rozalyn wanted to know.

"Quiet," Hawk ordered, without taking his eyes off the chief. "Chief Zitkatanka and I are bartering."

Rozalyn breathed an exasperated sigh and impatiently followed Hawk's conversation with the Sioux chief, though she didn't know what they were discussing so seriously.

"*Wiwasteka,*" the chief acknowledged as he surveyed Rozalyn with piercing black eyes.

Hawk nodded agreeably. "*Wastewayakapiwin.*"

A faint smile skipped across Zitkatanka's weather-beaten face. Then he turned his attention to the three braves who were clustered about him and gave an order.

Suddenly the Sioux braves swarmed around Rozalyn, uprooting her from her perch and placing her in front of one of them. She screeched in indignation, and her wild blue eyes flew to Hawk who was grinning like the ornery weasel he was.

"What have you done?" Rozalyn shrieked at him. Unsuccessfully she tried to free herself. The brave appeared to have no intention of allowing her to escape from his bone-crushing grasp.

"I have traded you for the right to hunt and trap in the Sioux nation this winter," Hawk casually informed her, only to be assaulted by a string of curses. "Chief Zitkatanka promises to hold you in high esteem, and he also says you are a very beautiful prize."

"You refused to give me to Half-Head and yet you eagerly trade me to the Sioux?" Roz hissed as she was led away. "I have heard what Indians do to captive white women. Damn you, Hawk!"

"I thought you would be pleased with the arrangements since you have no fond attachment to me or Half-Head." He chuckled, massaging his aching shoulder. "Besides, what better place to stash you for safekeeping than with the Sioux? Half-Head won't go near their camp; the Sioux and Blackfoot are mortal enemies."

As the Indians carted Rozalyn away, kicking and screaming at the top of her lungs, the smile vanished from Hawk's lips. Wearily, he slumped in his saddle, his body crying out for much needed rest. But he could not stop, not just yet. He had to ensure that Half-Head had no chance of finding Rozalyn. She had dared to turn her pistol on Half-Head and he was merciless and vengeful. Hawk knew full well what would happen if Half-Head got his hands on that fiery beauty. The thought made him shudder uncontrollably, and he quickly cast the ghastly picture from his mind, turning his thoughts to his purpose.

Hawk had made arrangements with Chief Zitkatanka, promising to deliver fur pelts for trade if the Sioux would keep watch over Rozalyn until he had settled his score with Half-Head. His gaze shifted to the stockade and he nudged his steed into a trot. At least he could enjoy a decent meal and one night's sleep before he planted tracks north, Hawk decided. Come the morrow, he would find the perfect spot to meet the murdering scoundrel who pursued him. Hawk intended to confront Half-Head once again, but he would not risk Rozalyn's life. She would be safe with the Sioux chief while he disposed of Half-Head.

The Sioux village, set amid the stately aspens and pines of the foothills, had not enjoyed a quiet moment since Chief Zitkantaka had brought Rozalyn back with him from Fort William. Rozalyn had made several attempts to escape from her wigwam, and the chief had been forced to post guards. By the end of the fourth day Zitkatanka was at his wit's end. He had generously offered Hawk's woman clothing worn by Sioux squaws, feasts of friendship, and a fine pony to ride during her stay. But Rozalyn had thrown one tantrum after another. Nothing could subdue her, except the sleeping potion the shaman had spoon-fed her the previous night. That was the first peaceful night in the camp since Roz had arrived.

Now Zitkatanka's face fell when he stepped into Rozalyn's tepee. It looked as if a cyclone had blown through it, upending the neat stack of buffalo hide quilts and eating utensils. Rozalyn stood in the middle of her wigwam, her feet apart, her eyes blazing with fury, and her wild hair tumbling about her shoulders. Never had the chief seen such a blatant display of anger in a woman!

"Take me back to Hawk this instant!" She shouted at the chief as if he were hard of hearing. She had awakened from her sleep-drugged dreams, infuriated that the medicine man and his assistant had held her down and forced her to swallow a foul-tasting sedative. "I will not remain here! Not another minute. Do you hear me?"

"*Wakishaha* . . ." The chief mused aloud, his narrowed gaze surveying the damages. This fiery-tempered woman never strayed from her purpose. She was determined to have her way or make life miserable for those who thought to subdue her.

Zitkatanka had given his word to Hawk, but he was not certain how long his people would tolerate this belligerent white woman in their midst. There was already talk that she was possessed by demon spirits. Zitkatanka had tried to explain to them that Roz was Hawk's woman and that he himself knew her to be wild and unruly, but even he had expected nothing like this! Hawk was a blood brother of the Sioux, a man of honor. Zitkatanka greatly respected the half-breed, but his friendship was being sorely tested.

"Take me to Hawk!" Rozalyn gritted out, silently swearing she would make Hawk pay dearly for forcing her on the Sioux.

How dare he treat her like some domestic animal, bartering and trading her at whim. First he had used her to bargain with Aubrey. Now he had traded her to the Sioux for hunting privileges. Would she ever learn not to trust the conniving weasel? Hawk had claimed that she would be safer with the Sioux than with him, but Rozalyn knew he was only anxious to have her out from underfoot until the following summer.

Zitkatanka stared into Rozalyn's blazing blue eyes for a long, thoughtful moment. He owed Hawk a favor, it was true. But this woman was only manageable when she rode

257

at Hawk's side. Although, he could not speak English, Zitkatanka knew what Rozalyn demanded. There are times when words are unnecessary to convey messages, and this was one of them. Rozalyn had expressed her displeasure by shouting and leaving her wigwam in a shambles.

Finally, Zitkatanka nodded in compliance. *"Chanyata."* He stepped over to draw open the flap of the tepee. After gesturing to the west, he addressed Rozalyn with a faint smile. *"Wiwasteka."*

The tension drained from Rozalyn's body when she realized the aging chief had decided to grant her wish. She followed him outside and peered at the tall pines that towered to the west, just below the snow-capped peaks. When she fell into step behind Zitkatanka, Rozalyn noticed the wary expressions on the faces of those who had gathered about them. She had made a bad impression on the Sioux. No doubt, she would not be welcome if she ever returned.

But dammit, Hawk was not going to order her about, she told herself determinedly. She would not sit idly by while he traded her for favors and deceitfully claimed to have her best interest at heart. He didn't want her with him, but that was no reason to pawn her off on the Sioux nation!

When Rozalyn rode off with Chief Zitkatanka and three braves as escort, she mentally prepared the lecture she intended to give that scoundrel Hawk. She would damned well let him know exactly what she thought of his tactics. He had uprooted her from St. Louis, and he was not going to conveniently tuck her out of sight when the mood suited him. When she got her hands on him, she'd pound some sense into him, she promised herself.

After easing back on the cot, Hawk smiled up at the

Indian maiden who had graciously offered him her room and a massage for his tender shoulder. Chumani was more than willing to offer more. Indeed, there had been times when Hawk had come to Fort William with visions of this lovely Crow maiden dancing in his head. Chumani had been sold by the tribesmen to a white trapper two years earlier, but the man had perished in a snowslide while hunting in the mountains, so she had returned to Fort William to trade the fur pelts they had collected. Then she had remained at the stockade instead of returning to her people to be traded to yet another man.

Although Chumani was eager and willing to please him, Hawk had informed her that he had taken another woman and that he was tied to her, even though she lived among the Sioux. For the life of him, Hawk didn't know why he had confessed even the smallest amount of sentiment for that blue-eyed witch. Nor could he fathom why a woman who had once aroused him no longer appealed to him.

Chumani had quietly displayed her disappointment, but she had not become loud and vocal. That was not the way of this Indian squaw. Hawk knew full well if the situation had been reversed and it was Rozalyn he faced, she would have loudly protested. Why did he have an obsessive need for that fiery vixen when he could have Chumani who obeyed his demands without complaint?

Heaving a weary sigh, Hawk closed his eyes and relaxed beneath Chumani's gentle touch. He had spent the better part of a week setting traps to ensnare Half-Head, watching, awaiting an opportunity to strike. But the white man had never shown his grizzly face. Could Half-Head have perished from his wound? Where was the miserable brute?

"Are you feeling better, Maishu?" Chumani questioned, calling Hawk by the name the Crow had given him.

"Much. . . ." Hawk breathed. "You have a gentle touch, Chumani."

A rueful smile rippled across her lips. Lovingly, she continued to massage Hawk's shoulder; then she applied a fresh poultice to the mending wound. "This woman of yours . . . she must possess great powers to win your loyalty, Maishu." Carefully, she eased herself down by his side, continuing to speak to him in the Crow dialect. "There was a time when you and I were very close. I had hoped one day we—"

"I owe the woman my life." Hawk broke in before Chumani stirred up too many memories. He had a tender place in his heart for this Crow maiden he had known since childhood, but everything had changed now. Hawk's life was entangled with Rozalyn's, and only time could sort out the mess he had made of things. "I cannot easily forget my debt."

"I wish I were the one who had such a strong hold on your heart, Maishu," she murmured. She leaned toward him, her dark eyes intently focused on his sensuous lips. "I have missed you these past months. . . ."

Her soft body brushed against Hawk's bare chest, and her lips opened in silent invitation. But it was not the same, Hawk thought miserably. There was no fire in her kiss, no breathless urgency compelling him to pull this shapely maiden into his arms. Hawk cursed himself a hundred times in that moment, for he knew only the blue-eyed spitfire made him burn with desire. Damn her! She had taken his freedom. Hawk could no longer touch another woman without comparing her to Rozalyn.

The feisty witch had cast a spell on him. He had once enjoyed the charms of many woman, but the feel of Chumani's skin and her feminine scent no longer tempted him. He wished he had not returned to the fort. He should have stayed in the wilderness, away from any female who might remind him that it was Rozalyn he wanted.

When the creaking of the door made Hawk and Chumani draw apart, Hawk cursed the intruders, not for interrupting their embrace, but simply because of who they were. There stood Rozalyn, her eyes blue fires. She looked as hostile as a Blackfoot war party. Behind her, Chief Zitkatanka was grinning at Hawk's uncomfortable predicament.

"So this is the real reason you traded me to the Sioux," Rozalyn hissed venomously.

Try as she might, she could not overcome her jealousy. She had spent the past week wondering if Hawk had met up with Half-Head and if the lout was still alive. But here he was, at the fort, camped in the room of an Indian woman, holding her in the very arms that had held Rozalyn not so long ago.

Hawk overlooked Rozalyn's stormy remark to fling an annoyed comment at Zitkatanka. "I thought you were my friend. You promised to keep the woman until I came to retrieve her," he snapped.

"If you were truly a friend of the Sioux you would not have forced this woman upon our people," the chief countered. "She has been shouting her anger since we took her from you."

"The great chief of the Sioux cannot control this mere wisp of a woman?" Hawk eased upright on the cot, his mouth twisting in a mocking smile. "Could it be that your trophies from battle were stolen from a worthier brave? How is it that you cannot keep one white woman in your midst without meeting with trouble when you have led your warriors into battle against fierce enemies and emerged the victor?"

The insult stung like the barb of an arrow, wounding the chief's male pride. He puffed up indignantly, his dark eyes glistening with anger. "This is no ordinary woman. She does not behave like a squaw and she is very determined to have her way. But her way is not that of our people. She is trouble—yours. . . ." Zitkatanka pointed a tanned finger at Hawk. "I did not bring this woman to this land. It was your doing. Soon, my people will journey to our winter village. I wish to gather our belongings on the travois before this woman tears our camp apart." His dark eyes narrowed on Hawk and he paused a moment before delivering his ultimatum. "If Hawk-that-Soars wishes to trap beaver in the Sioux nation he will take charge of his woman and let the red man live in peace."

Rozalyn wanted to scream out her frustration, but she somehow managed to keep silent while Hawk and Zitkatanka argued in the Sioux dialect. How she wished she could speak the Indian tongue. Nothing would please her more than to shout curses at Hawk in that language. Her gaze drifted to the shapely Indian maiden who was garbed in a beaded doehide dress. The expression on her young face assured Rozalyn that Hawk had stolen her heart as well. But why should that come as a surprise, she asked herself bitterly. Hawk had a unique way about him, a masculine charisma that no woman could resist. Except for me, Rozalyn told herself proudly. This was the last time she would ever lay eyes on Hawk. The man had hurt her too many times, in too many ways. The only way to salvage her sanity was to put a world between them.

Tilting a proud chin, Rozalyn marched up to Chumani and forced the semblance of a smile. "Perhaps you cannot understand my words, but I will speak them just the same. You can have your lover translate since he is well versed in many languages." Her eyes took on a mutinous gleam when they momentarily swung to the bare-chested Hawk. "Since you seem to greatly prize this"—Rozalyn searched her vocabulary for a single word to describe a conniving, two-timing, insensitive brute, but a succinct description of Hawk escaped her—

"this man . . . if one can call him that," she added in a reasonably civil tone, "he is yours for the taking. What little respect I once had for him has vanished." A sugar-coated smile grazed her lips when her gaze focused on Chumani. "And you can tell your lover to go straight to hell. I never want to see him again."

Chumani had picked up a few words of English during her stay at the fort, but she could not keep up with Rozalyn's rapid-fire remarks. Although she returned Rozalyn's sticky smile, she didn't have the foggiest notion what the white woman was babbling about.

"Dammit, Roz, what you think was going on here, wasn't," Hawk protested. "Chumani was only tending my wound."

Rozalyn refused to speak directly to Hawk or even to acknowledge his presence. As a matter of fact, she would have preferred him to drop off the edge of the earth. She continued to speak to Chumani, who didn't have the faintest idea what she was saying.

"Tell the miserable bastard that I was unaware his lying lips had sustained an injury. My eyes did not deceive me. When I opened the door, the two of you were kissing. Since Hawk has made his bed here, he can damned well sleep in it. I want no more association with him. And you can also tell him that he was right about one thing—there can be nothing but fire and ice between us, not friendship. He has spoiled any chance of that."

Hawk's temper got the best of him. The Sioux chief had refused to provide protection for the troublesome witch who refused to look at him when she spoke. Roughly, he grabbed Rozalyn by the arm, spinning her around to meet his perturbed glare. "You seem to forget that you are my hostage, minx. You will go where I tell you, when I tell you. Must I remind you that you gave me your word that you would cause no trouble until I deliver you to the summer rendezvous?"

Rozalyn glowered at the hand that held her captive; then she focused her menacing stare on a pair of smoldering green eyes. "Kindly give me back my arm. If you have need of one, why not take Chumani's? She seems eager to offer that and anything else that might pleasure you." Rozalyn's tone was very sarcastic. "As far as my word is concerned, I feel no obligation to you or to the Sioux chief. My word is only as binding as your loyalty." Snapping blue eyes pinned Hawk against the adobe wall. "Your loyalty is no deeper than the benefit you can derive for yourself." With that, Rozalyn jerked her arm free and stormed toward the door.

"What do you intend to do? Set out alone for St. Louis? Half-Head might still be running loose. I would hate to venture a guess about how you would fare with him." Hawk snorted. "The truth is, you need me as much as I need you."

Rozalyn pivoted about, and her eyes raked over Hawk disdainfully. "I have decided to find myself a scout who can protect me from the hazards of the wild. That shouldn't be too difficult. The stockade is swarming with hunters and trappers. I am certain one of them will accommodate me in *any* manner I so choose."

A devilish smile crept to the corners of Hawk's lips. "It won't be the same, *chérie*. You will find yourself comparing your future lover to me. His kiss and caress will only serve to help you recall how it was between us."

Rozalyn fought an urge to shake the stuffing out of him for voicing that arrogant remark. Did he think he was the only man on earth who could stir her? The conceited ogre. Oh, why had she sought Hawk's help in her dealings with Lenore? If she had selected another man, she would still be at home.

"We shall just see about that," Rozalyn parried spitefully. "I intend to try your philosophy. I will sleep with every man in the stockade until I find one who suits me and you will quickly be forgotten."

When Rozalyn stalked off, the Sioux braves moved aside to let her pass, but they quickly closed in around the door when Hawk charged after her. A muddled frown plowed Hawk's brow when he confronted Zitkatanka who refused to move from the exit. Why the devil was the Sioux chief protecting that fire-breathing witch? Not ten minutes ago, the chief had sworn the woman was worth her weight in trouble.

"I do not think it wise to approach your woman until she has gained control of her temper," Zitkatanka advised. A wry smile worked its way across his lips. "She wreaked havoc in our camp. In her present mood, I fear you and this trading post will fare no better."

Hawk could not argue with the chief's sound logic, but neither could he turn Rozalyn loose in a stockade brimming with men. The thought that she might escape annoyed him, but the thought of her surrendering to another man turned him wrong side out. Dammit, why couldn't that stubborn wench listen to reason? He hadn't invited Chumani to kiss him! But Rozalyn would never believe that. She was so stubborn and defiant that he could declare the sky was blue and she would deny it.

"Whatever else the woman is, she is my responsibility," Hawk grumbled as he bodily removed the Sioux chief from his path. "I have to find her."

Zitkatanka grasped Hawk's arm to detain him, a slow smile drifting onto his weather-beaten features. "You have also fought bravely in battle, Hawk-that-Soars. But I do not think even you can control the woman with blue fire flickering in her eyes." He inclined his head toward the gentle Crow maiden who had never raised her voice to a man and who would never dare to do so. "The other woman is obedient. She would make you a good wife. But this one is as free and wild as an eagle. Force cannot tame the woman with sky-blue eyes. Take heed to my warning

265

and do not chase impossible dreams."

Although Hawk knew the wise chief was right, that didn't change the way of things. He couldn't allow Rozalyn to escape him, not if he hoped to deal with Aubrey DuBois. Rozalyn was Hawk's only weapon. Muttering under his breath, he elbowed his way through the congregated Sioux warriors, and his keen gaze circled the adobe huts that lined the stockade, searching for some sign of the woman who had kept his life in constant turmoil.

Chapter 17

After storming out of Chumani's shack, Rozalyn marched across the compound to approach a group of trappers. She requested a volunteer to take her back to St. Louis, and although some of the men leered at her, she firmly stood her ground. Jonas Adler offered to serve as her guide, so Rozalyn followed him to his shack to discuss the details of their journey.

When Jonas closed the door and shoved the wooden bolt against the lock, Rozalyn frowned warily. She was in no mood for a tête-à-tête after her confrontation with Hawk. She was too raw inside to turn to another man when it was Hawk she wanted.

But he doesn't want you, Rozalyn reminded herself harshly. She had found Hawk with another woman—twice. First, Molly Perkins and now the lovely Indian maid, Chumani. Why had she allowed herself to believe that, in time, Hawk might feel some emotional attachment to her? It was obvious that he preferred to take his pleasure wherever he found it. Rozalyn had only been convenient for a time. Hawk was a man with animal lusts and indiscriminate tastes. He could never refuse the temptation of a woman, any woman.

Rozalyn's contemplative musings were interrupted

when Jonas strolled up in front of her. He was sporting a rakish grin that left her with the uneasy feeling that he expected some physical form of payment for becoming her escort to St. Louis. Isn't that just like a man? she thought cynically.

"What's your name, pretty lady?" Jonas inquired, his all-consuming gaze flooding over her curvaceous figure and hovering overly long on the full swells of her breasts. "If we are to spend the next few weeks together, I think we should be on a first-name basis."

"Rozalyn." She took a step back, causing Jonas to chuckle at her obvious mistrust of his intentions.

"If you don't mind my asking, Rozalyn, what are you doing so far from home?"

Rozalyn thoughtfully chewed on her bottom lip, wondering whether to tell the truth or concoct a lie. She was mindful of the catastrophe that had befallen her the last time she'd allowed her tongue to outdistance her brain. While she was contemplating her reply, the door rattled beneath a fierce, impatient knock.

"Roz, open this door!" Hawk commanded gruffly.

"Go away," she shouted back at him. "I never want to lay eyes on you again."

Hawk's response was as loud and angry as hers. "I have something to say and I am not leaving until I have said it!" he thundered.

"Go tell it to someone who cares. I'm sure Chumani will hang on your every word!" Rozalyn all but screamed.

"She is a long-time friend."

"At least you have one to your credit."

A wary frown was now on Jonas' brow. "Who the hell is that?"

"Rozalyn, I am dangerously close to losing my temper," Hawk warned.

"Then why don't you run along and retrieve it before it completely escapes you." She sniffed. Although she

268

had heard the faintly dangerous undertone of Hawk's voice, she didn't care how furious he became. She could never make him as angry as he had made her. "Please be on your way. I am not alone. I am entertaining a gentleman at the moment, and I have no wish to be disturbed."

"*Open this door!*" Hawk bellowed, emphasizing each word.

"Only when hell freezes ov—"

Rozalyn flinched when the door crashed against the wall, the lock broken to bits, the leather hinges sagging. The scant moonlight framed Hawk's ominous figure which cast a long, threatening shadow. The furious gleam in his eyes would have made a panther cower, but it did not intimidate Rozalyn. She was just as angry as Hawk was, even more so. After all, she was the woman scorned, and hell had no fury . . .

Like a noble knight coming to a damsel's defense, Jonas sheltered Rozalyn's body with his own. "Now hold on, Hawk." Jonas flung up a hand to forestall the fuming intruder who barreled into the room. "The lady and I were discussing business."

"Like hell you were," Hawk growled mockingly. His glistening green eyes cut into Jonas like an eagle's sharp talons. "Take my advice, Adler. Leave while you can still walk away on your own strength."

"I don't want to fight you," Jonas managed to say in a civil tone. "The lady has shown her preference so why don't you accept that and leave us alone." It was difficult to remain calm when Hawk's flaming green eyes were boring right through him. Jonas knew of Hawk's reputation as a fighter, and he was not looking for a brawl, not with Hawk. "If you will walk quietly away, we will forget the incident happened."

"The lady belongs to me," Hawk gritted out, glaring around Jonas's broad shoulders to give Rozalyn the evil eye.

Jonas swiveled his head around to cast a quizzical glance at the dark-haired beauty. "Did you come to the fort with Hawk?"

"No."

"Yes." Hawk contradicted her. "All the way from St. Louis." When Jonas' gaze swung back around, a sly smile rippled across Hawk's lips. "The lady and I have become very well acquainted during our long journey together."

The implication hung heavily in the air. Jonas had no difficulty deciphering what Hawk meant. He also knew better than to battle with the man when he had his mind set on something. Rozalyn, breathtaking as she was, could not be worth having his body rearranged by the awesome mountaineer breathing down his neck. Jonas decided it best to bow out while he was physically able to do so.

"Sorry, miss." Jonas veered around Hawk, leaving Rozalyn with no protection from her nemesis. "Hawk is a friend of mine. In this country a man needs as many friends as he can get."

When Jonas pulled the wobbly door shut behind him, Rozalyn glared at the haughty smirk plastered on Hawk's handsome features. How she detested that arrogant smile. Her temper, which had been sorely put upon several times in the course of the evening, exploded.

"How dare you boast of your conquest!" Rozalyn railed.

But words did not wound this big brute, and fuming glares bounced off him. Rozalyn was furious, so furious that she had an urge to throw something. She ached to strike out and hurt him, just as she had been hurt. Snatching up the porcelain pitcher from the crude commode, she hurled it at Hawk. He grunted uncomfortably when the makeshift weapon slammed into his belly, and before he could recover from the first assault or wipe the water from his eyes, a flying night stand collided with his shin.

Frantically, Rozalyn's eyes darted around the room, searching for another weapon to hurl. The only object within reach was the cot. She upended it, but before she could shove it at Hawk, he lunged at her. Roughly he caught her to him, and she went into a frenzy. God, how she detested being restrained. Lately someone was always holding her down or tying her up. As his lean fingers dug into her waist Rozalyn reacted instinctively, desperately fighting for her freedom.

Hawk swore he had latched on to an enraged wildcat. Rozalyn fought him with every ounce of strength she possessed, clawing at his face, pounding on his chest, leveling blows to his tender shoulder. When he finally managed to restrain her, he jerked her full length against him, restricting all movement.

The feel of his heart thudding against her shoulder, of his muscled torso crushing into her, played havoc with her sanity. Rozalyn was on the verge of hysteria. She hated herself for allowing Hawk to upset her so.

"Let me go! I detest your touch," she choked out, finding it virtually impossible to fight back her tears. She wanted to be anywhere except in the confining circle of Hawk's arms. She despised him for suppressing her with his superior strength.

"I am not releasing you until you calm down." Hawk clamped his arms more tightly about her when she writhed for freedom.

"And I will not calm down until you let me go!" Rozalyn hissed back at him.

Again tears threatened. Hawk's manhandling was the last straw, and suddenly she was sobbing, frustration causing her to shudder uncontrollably. Rozalyn didn't want Hawk to see her cry, but she couldn't help herself.

When she succumbed to tears, Hawk's fierce grip

eased and he cradled her in his sinewy arms, his hands gently massaging away her tension. Kissing away her tears, he murmured soft words of compassion. And Rozalyn cried all the more, sobbing like an abandoned child, releasing the pent-up anger that had claimed her.

"I did leave you with the Sioux for your own protection," Hawk whispered against the trim column of her throat. "I tried to set a trap for Half-Head, but he didn't come. When I returned to the fort Chumani offered herself to me, but I refused her. Do you hear me, Roz? I did not touch her. Nor did I invite her kiss." He sighed heavily and then cupped Rozalyn's tear-stained face in his hands. A faint smile brimmed his lips when he felt Rozalyn's rigid body relax against his. "I did not invite the kiss," he repeated. "I was waiting for this. . . ."

His lips took hers, devouring yet savoring the sweet taste of her. Rozalyn wanted to believe his quiet words, but she didn't dare. A lifetime ago she had trusted him and he had betrayed her. Time had not erased the pain of lost love and she was afraid to surrender to emotion again, afraid of experiencing the same anguishing hurt and disillusionment. Her attraction to him was purely physical, she tried to tell herself. One day, when this ordeal was over, she would forget the way it was between them, forget the power Hawk held over her body.

Hawk was possessed by the same gnawing hunger that overwhelmed him each time he dared to touch this shapely nymph. He must be mad to crave a woman who detested him so. Why couldn't he and Rozalyn just enjoy each other as they had that first night in St. Louis?

Why rehash the past? Hawk asked himelf. He and Rozalyn could never go back. There was too much distrust, there were too many conflicts now. They were both too stubborn and headstrong to compromise, and perhaps the dream they had once shared had been born of pretense. They had been actors in a play, living their roles. They had become infatuated too soon and they had allowed themselves to be swept up in a fantasy. Hawk told himself these things, but that didn't stop him from wanting Rozalyn, madly, passionately.

Even while Hawk was mentally listing all the reasons why they were wrong for each other, why they could never come to terms, he was holding her in his arms. He craved the honeyed taste of her lips, the sweet fragrance that was so much a part of her. He ached for this blue-eyed witch who could weave spells about him, make him forget reality.

Rozalyn could feel the tension draining from her body. She cursed herself for yielding to Hawk's embrace, but she could not bring herself to reject him. His touch was magic. It always had been. Now he was consoling her in his own way, and Rozalyn needed his strength. She needed to become whole and strong again, so she could face the trials ahead of her.

Her arms slid around his shoulders, and her head rested against his bare chest. For a long, quiet moment they held each other. It was a silent apology of sorts. Rozalyn was ashamed of herself for throwing a tantrum and Hawk berated himself for not having more clearly explained his reasons for sending Rozalyn to Chief Zitkatanka. She would not have been in such a fit of temper if he hadn't taunted her about trading her for hunting rights. Why was it so difficult to be honest with her? What was he afraid of? Of course, Rozalyn had told him she detested him so many times that he had come to expect condemnation from her. But wasn't he man enough to admit that he was guilty of employing the same tactic? Perhaps he and Rozalyn simply brought out the worst in each other. Perhaps they could never enjoy a compatible existence. They were too much alike although in some respects they were very different.

"I made a spectacle of myself at the Sioux camp."
Rozalyn muffled a sniff. "I'm sure the chief thinks I am
possessed by demon spirits."

Hawk chuckled softly. "I think Zitkatanka admires
your spirit . . . but he prefers to do so from a safe
distance." His fingers absently combed through the
tangled tresses that streamed over Rozalyn's shoulders.
"I am as much to blame for your behavior as you are. If I
had told you I wished to keep you safe from Half-Head
instead of leading you to believe I had bartered you,
perhaps—"

"I still would have protested," Rozalyn finished for
him. Slipping from Hawk's encircling arms, she turned
her back on him and wiped away the last of her tears.
"You were right about me, Hawk. I am spoiled and set in
my ways. I don't appreciate being ordered about, and I
am not accustomed to taking commands without
question. My father expected nothing of me, nor I of him.
I have long been in control of my life, just as you have. It
is not easy to change." A demure smile touched her lips
as she slowly turned back to face Hawk. "It is true, you
know. Chumani would not cause you as much trouble.
She is shy, retiring, and submissive. I can never be any of
those things. I have grown up like an untended wild
flower. And as much as you may disapprove of the way I
am, I cannot—will not—change," she softly amended.
Raising beseeching blue eyes, Rozalyn met Hawk's
solemn expression. "Please let me go. Let's end this
constant feud for dominance. You and I have brought
each other nothing but trouble. Let Jonas take me back to
St. Louis. I will pay him well for the time he cannot trap
in the mountains."

"No," Hawk said flatly. "Your father owes the
trappers a long-standing debt. You are all I have to
bargain with."

"Is that all I mean to you? Do you see me as no more

than a gambit?" Rozalyn tilted her chin and summoned her composure. "Look again, Hawk. I am not a possession to be bartered and sold for your purpose. I have feelings and you have trampled all over them."

"I once told you that you meant far more to me than a pawn to be played to my advantage, but you rejected me," Hawk muttered sourly. "Don't press me for a confession. I'll not make that same mistake again."

"I rejected you?" Rozalyn echoed incredulously. "That is not at all what happened and you damned well know it. You were playing a game with me, using me, maneuvering me for your purpose. Do you expect me to thank you for that?"

"Should I thank you?" Hawk parried, his voice carrying an undertone of sarcasm. "Perhaps I should refresh your memory, *chérie*. I apologized for what happened with your father and you said it made little difference because you had professed love just to keep me dangling from a string to suit your purpose."

"I only said those things because I was hurt by your use of me to gain favors from my father," she argued defensively. "When I said I loved you I—" Rozalyn slammed her jaw shut before her tongue outdistanced her brain.

"Hawk's expression became stone sober. "Are you admitting that you did love me?" he asked point-blank.

Rozalyn had vowed never to speak those words again, not unless she knew beyond a shadow of a doubt that Hawk felt some deep affection for her. She still didn't have the faintest idea where she stood with this reckless mountain man, and she was too proud and stubborn to bare her heart again. It was too soon to risk having her mending heart broken again.

"I thought I was . . . in the beginning." Rozalyn carefully chose her words. Presenting her back to him, she stared at the opposite wall. She was afraid to look

Hawk squarely in the eye, afraid he could decode her emotions. "But what I feel most of all now is bitterness and betrayal. I can never love a man I cannot trust, and I would never know when you might turn on me."

"Those are my sentiments exactly." Hawk laughed without humor. "You saved my life once. I cannot imagine why, for you have repeatedly threatened to do me bodily harm." Hawk raked his fingers through his tousled hair and then let his arm drop loosely at his side. "And don't ask me why I have this fierce instinct to protect you from Half-Head, an instinct that runs deeper than my own need for survival."

Heaving a sigh, Rozalyn pivoted to face him. A rueful smile grazed her lips as her index finger traced the stubble on Hawk's jaw. "Does it mean so much to have my father deal fairly with your friends?"

Her gentle touch turned Hawk to mush. He felt like a growling panther being soothed and stroked into purring with satisfaction. His reaction to this quick-tempered vixen truly baffled him. How could he be so furious with her one minute and so content the next? She had managed to drive him mad somewhere between St. Louis and Fort William, and she still had him swinging back and forth, on an emotional pendulum, between passion and fury. He wondered if he would be capable of rational thought, after they had gone their separate ways. He had grown accustomed to contrasting sensations, to the fine line between love and hate, madness and sanity. When Rozalyn finally walked out of his life how would he function? Where would he find such a challenge? The threat of constant danger in the wild did not lure him as strongly as this blue-eyed temptress.

Hawk had awakened each day during the past two months, wondering when and how he and Rozalyn would clash, trying to determine how to deal with her. When she was gone, how could he greet the dawn sky that reminded him of her blue eyes? How could he face the sunset when it reminded him of the warmth of her smile? Finally, Hawk pushed aside his troubled contemplations and circled back to her question.

His lean fingers folded around her hand, bringing it to his lips. "I made a vow, Roz. I promised my fellow trappers better treatment at the summer rendezvous. It is a vow I cannot break. Too many lives have been lost for too little. One day soon I hope you will understand why your father's dealings are so important to me."

His strong loyalty to the trappers who faced the hazards of the wild touched Rozalyn's heart. She wished Hawk felt that same strong loyalty to her, but she was glad she was beginning to comprehend how much he loved the life he led. This vast and often perilous wilderness was a part of him. It was in his blood. How could she hope to compete with his love of it. Could she burrow into a heart that belonged to towering mountains and fertile meadows?

I can't, Rozalyn realized sadly. She could remain at Hawk's side, taking the passion he offered, learning to respect her competition; but she could not take the mountains from this awesome man who was half-wild, half-civilized. Resigning herself to the bleak truth, she expelled a heavy-hearted sigh. Her lot in life was to love this rogue with the dancing green eyes and shiny raven hair. She would go on loving him from a distance, knowing she could never have him all to herself, but that was like trying to grasp a handful of moonbeams.

Perhaps it was best to share her life with Hawk until it was time for them to part. And when they went their own ways, she could only hope that a warm memory of her would linger in his heart. Perhaps, now and then, he would remember her. Maybe he would smile quietly to himself as he recalled how fiercely they had fought and how wildly they had loved.

Her lashes fluttered up, and misty blue eyes sketched his craggy features, adoring the unique way smile lines splayed across his face. "Then I shall help you keep your vow to your friends," Rozalyn promised softly. "I will become your pawn if you can afford my price."

When her silky arms slid around his neck, Hawk looked pleasantly startled. Then a cautious smile slid across his lips. "We have bargained before, minx. I am still uncertain which of us emerged the winner. What must I pay for your devotion to my cause?"

"In return I request your loyalty," Rozalyn informed him huskily. Her body moved suggestively against his hard, male contours, kindling the old familiar flame Hawk was hard-pressed to ignore.

"My loyalty?" One dark brow rose to a quizzical angle. "I'm not certain I understand your meaning."

"Don't you?" Her throaty voice made his skin prickle. "Perhaps it is best if I show you what I mean," she said as her breasts taunted his bare chest. "When another woman behaves like this"—her inviting lips feathered across his, dragging a tormented groan from his throat—"do not respond to her in this manner." Her open mouth slanted across his lips, and her darting tongue intruded to tease and arouse. Slowly, she withdraw, but only far enough to increase Hawk's craving for her.

"And if some other woman should assault you in this manner"—her bold caresses trickled down the thick matting of hair on his chest and then weaved across the corded muscles of his thigh—"do not answer her invitation like this. . . ." Her hand folded over his, leading his fingertips to the front of her gaping shirt to mold flesh against flesh.

Hawk's knees buckled beneath him. The feel of her satiny skin beneath his palms fed his hunger for her and left him breathing in ragged spurts. Her inventive techniques were arousing his passion.

"And if this wicked witch dares to do this"—a roguish grin crossed Hawk's lips, and he grasped the hem of her buckskin shirt, drawing it over her head, baring her full breasts to his hawkish gaze—"I suppose it would never do for me to touch her like this. . . ."

His hot, greedy kisses spilled over the slope of her shoulder to trace a path of fire to the taut peak of her breast while his skillful hands ventured along her ribs. Caresses, as light as the skimming touch of a butterfly, fluttered across her skin, sensitizing each nerve ending.

"Most definitely not." Rozalyn, too, breathed erratically now.

"And this wouldn't do either, I suppose," Hawk murmured against the valley of her breasts as his adventurous hands hovered over the leather laces of her breeches.

"Nor this . . ." Her lips moved provocatively against his, pressing his bold manhood against her and suggesting an intimacy that made Hawk's heartbeat quicken.

"I thought not," Hawk groaned, his voice tormented. He was quickly losing interest in this tempting game. After all, he could endure only a limited amount of such teasing before his primal needs took command of his body.

He glanced toward the upended cot and then thoughtfully studied the plush fur rug set before the small hearth. An inviting flame glowed in the fireplace, one Hawk could not resist. His good arm slid beneath Rozalyn's knees, and swiftly, he carried her across the demolished room and set her on her feet. The golden light caressed her flesh while his flaming green eyes devoured the exquisite sight of her.

And Rozalyn studied him in the flickering fire light as he stripped from his breeches. Again he reminded her of a sleek black panther, a solid mass of brawn and muscle. The hard terrain of his body aroused her, tempted her to

279

touch what her eyes beheld, and she could not resist running a dainty finger over the lean muscles of his belly or the sinewy columns of his thighs.

"I want no other woman to know you by touch, Hawk." Rozalyn's voice was soft, but insistent. "During the months we spend together I ask that we share passion only with each other. That is all I request of you. I will demand nothing more and I will expect nothing less. If you can accept me on my terms, I will make no attempt to escape you."

Hawk's husky laughter drifted about them, tickling Rozalyn's senses and urging her closer to his hard, masculine strength. He hooked his arm around her waist when she involuntarily swayed toward him, lifting her petite body from the planked floor as he peered into her spellbinding blue eyes. "You have made me an offer I cannot refuse. A truce then, temptress . . . on your own terms. Shall we seal our vow with a kiss?"

He did not allow Rozalyn the opportunity to accept or reject his suggestion. His sensuous lips swooped down on hers with such savage urgency that she could not draw a breath, could only surrender to his crushing embrace. His kiss carried enough heat to inflame the night. Her body, alive with rapturous sensations, quivered with anticipation.

When Hawk pressed her to the fur rug, his practiced hands began to move over her, eliciting eager responses. Long, lean fingers glided up and down her thighs, drifted over the shapely curves of her hips. Like a river meandering along its course, his caresses flowed across her belly, then rose in leisurely fashion to encircle the throbbing peaks of her breasts. Rozalyn sighed with pleasure when his lips retraced their tantalizing path across the inviting contours of her body. Over and over again his kisses and caresses aroused and massaged, making desire unfurl in every part of her being. But

280

Rozalyn hungered to return the sweet torment.

Perhaps she could not compete with the majestic mountains and their perilous beauty. And she was unlike the submissive Indian maiden who had once shared Hawk's bed, but she could prove to him that she could stir him in her own way. She would not say that he had captured her heart, but she could silently show Hawk that she worshipped the feel of his muscular body, that she treasured their intimate moments of giving and sharing.

When Rozalyn propped herself beside him, Hawk watched her glistening hair tumble over her shoulders and whisper across his chest. The flickering light captured her perfect features, casting bewitching shadows on her ivory skin as her gentle hands splayed across his chest and then descended to map the hard muscles that curled around his ribs. Ever so slowly, her caresses glided across his abdomen, and he caught his breath when her fingertips traced the corded muscles of his inner thigh. Then her touch receded, skipping across his hair-roughened flesh to curl around each male nipple.

Hawk swore he would die of pleasure when her moist lips followed the titillating trail she had blazed with her provocative caresses. He couldn't breathe. His mind had turned to mush, his body to clay. She was molding him into her own creation, leaving him a quivering mass of muscle that flexed and relaxed each time her fingertips grazed his pliant flesh.

A muffled groan tumbled from Hawk's lips. Her skillful touch was driving him insane. Rozalyn knew how to please and arouse him, to make him quake with maddening hunger. A gnawing arose in the pit of his belly, and it channeled through every part of his body. Adeptly, he twisted away from Rozalyn's tempting touch. Then his sleek, hard body moved over hers, his muscles taut as he braced himself above her.

Rozalyn's lashes fluttered up to meet the fire that blazed in his emerald eyes. Their glow took her breath away, and the savage nobility in his rugged features made her feel like the defenseless prey of a mountain lion. His gaze pierced her soul, freeing deep-seated feelings that had been safely tucked away.

"Roz . . . You touch me and I cannot control the fierce passions that rage within me." His voice was rough and ragged, his gaze so intense that she could feel the heat of it upon her skin. "You think me a beast, a heathen?" His raven head came deliberately toward hers, his eyes focused on the sensuous curve of her lips, as if he were mesmerized by the sight of them. "I am that," Hawk confessed huskily. His eyes took on a pained expression when he noticed the red blotches on her face where his stubbled beard had brushed abrasively against her tender skin. "I am half-man, half-savage. Even when I garb myself in the fancy trappings of a gentleman I cannot be like your sophisticated dandies. I wanted you, even in the beginning, and I was never gentleman enough to deny myself. The fire between us has always lured me into its flames. I cannot help what I am and I cannot help wanting you. Love me, Roz." His voice echoed with barely restrained desire. "I need you as a starving man craves nourishment. . . ."

His muscled body settled intimately upon hers, and Rozalyn eagerly accepted him and his kiss, which bespoke his undeniable hunger. As his solid strength became hers and she, in turn, became a living, breathing part of him, sensations erupted in them with the suddenness of a thunderstorm, sweeping them up into the whirlwind of passion.

His sinewy arms folded about her, molding her closer, as his tense body drove into hers, creating a hypnotic rhythm that took them into the eye of the storm. There was no longer a breath of gentleness in his embrace, only a fierce, maddening need to appease the hunger she had instilled in him. But Rozalyn did not crave tenderness. She responded to the wild abandon of his lovemaking, her hips arching to meet his hard thrusts.

She had a mystical power over this awesome mountain man, a power more potent than force or strength. Her touch could arouse his savage passions and when he came to her there was no holding back. He gave all of himself to her, as she gave to him, and their fiery lovemaking melted their icy anger and transformed it into a passionate flame.

If she could not have Hawk forever, at least she had touched the raw emotions that lay beneath his tough exterior. Perhaps he could never love her, but he could not forget the intense heat of their lovemaking. There was black magic between them; it forged their bodies and souls into one being.

Hawk groaned in exquisite pleasure as his body surged against hers. The violent storm between them had tossed them far from reality, and they were now drifting on a sea of splendrous sensations. When Hawk reached that moment of sublime contentment, his spent body shuddered against Rozalyn's yielding contours. Then he inhaled a ragged breath, his senses still filled with the arousing scent of her. The heady pleasure of their passion made him smile quietly to himself. If this be a dream, he never wished to wake.

His hands absently combed through her lustrous tendrils which glowed in the fire light, and reluctantly he slid down beside her. While he stared pensively at the hearth, Rozalyn rolled on to her stomach to watch the curling fingers of the fire skip across the burning log.

"What is she like, Hawk?" Rozalyn didn't know what possessed her to pose such a probing question, especially at this moment, but the words were out before she could bite them back.

283

"Who?" A puzzled frown creased Hawk's brow. He couldn't think past that very moment.

"Chumani," Rozalyn murmured. "She is very pretty."

"That she is," Hawk agreed softly. A wry smile slid across his lips when he shot Rozalyn a sideways glance. Then he eased her onto her back, his body hovering only inches from hers. "And Jonas? I suppose a woman could find him attractive."

"She could," Rozalyn concurred. Her wandering hand flowed over the bulging muscles of his arm. "If she weren't comparing him to you."

"Did he kiss you?" Hawk had to know. That possibility had plagued him since he'd learned Jonas had escorted Rozalyn to his cabin. "Did you let him—"

Rozalyn pressed her index finger to his lips to shush him, and her eyes sparkled like sunbeams twinkling in the early morning sky when she graced him with a smile. "You don't want to know." She tossed back the same phrase he had once given her when she had asked a prying question.

But Hawk did not respond in the same way she had. He damned well wanted to know what had gone on behind the closed door and her answer could not come soon enough to suit him. "You are not leaving this cabin until you tell me exactly what you and Jonas were doing. I know you weren't talking because I was listening!"

"I am not divulging any intimate secrets," Rozalyn assured him with a mischievous smile. The possibility of Hawk being even the slightest bit jealous delighted her.

"Ornery minx," Hawk grumbled, but he could not suppress the grin that surfaced in response to the impish expression that was plastered on her perfect features. "Did he touch you like this?" Hawk decided to employ Rozalyn's playful tactics. His inquiring hand roved over the soft swells of her breasts. "Did his kiss kindle a fire that threatened to burn out of control?"

As his warm lips skipped lightly over hers, Rozalyn responded to his arousing embrace, but not to his probing question.

"Tell me, damn you," Hawk growled in frustration, his arms tightening to crush her feminine body against his own hard contours.

"The right approach might persuade me to divulge my sordid secrets," she purred suggestively. "Perhaps after you make love to me again . . ."

Hawk peered incredulously at her willing smile. "Now?" My God, their lovemaking had been so thorough and devastating that Hawk seriously doubted he could find the energy to move, much less indulge in a repeat performance.

Rozalyn giggled at the startled expression on his chiseled features. "If you haven't the strength, perhaps I should summon Jonas. He is not nearly as old as you are and he seemed willing enough to accommodate me earlier."

"Old?" Hawk hooted like a disturbed owl. "I do not consider myself old!" His voice was acrid with indignation.

"But you are not as young as Jonas. He cannot be more than three years my senior. A very compatible match, I should think," Rozalyn teased. "Sleeping with another man might prove to be a very worthwhile experiment. I have always been one to test theories rather than accepting them as truth."

"He is not man enough for a high-spirited woman like you," Hawk assured her tartly.

"And you are?" Rozalyn put the question to him, then frowned dubiously.

"I am," he insisted, a wide grin stretching across his lips to reveal pearly white teeth. "And I will prove it if you insist."

"I do," Rozalyn murmured, her arms sliding over the muscled planes of his back.

Hawk came to her then, intent on proving his prowess. But within a moment he realized he had only proved his insatiable need for this lively beauty. He was caught up in a volcanic upheaval of sensations, sensations as potent and as engulfing as before. Time ceased to exist. He was consumed by exciting feelings that spilled over him like smoldering lava. And long after the flame of passion had cooled, the fire of desire still flickered within him. Although Hawk's hunger had been appeased, he knew the flame within him merely waited to burst into a raging blaze.

"Nothing . . ." Rozalyn murmured drowsily. Releasing a contented sigh she cuddled against Hawk's masculine warmth, satisfied to remain in the unending circle of his arms.

A curious frown knitted Hawk's brow. Had he missed part of her comment while he was lost to the cloudy haze of pleasure that had fogged his mind?

Rozalyn stretched like a contented feline basking in the summer sun. "Jonas and I did nothing. There wasn't time," she confessed.

"And if there had been time?" Hawk prodded.

A sleepy smile melted on her kiss-swollen lips. "Truly, I had no wish to make comparisons, for fear of what I might discover."

Her quiet words pleased him. Rozalyn had not exactly announced that she cared for him, but at least her attitude had mellowed slightly. Hawk could hope for little else where Rozalyn was concerned. He had given her no reason to trust him, to care for him. Indeed, he had taunted her unmercifully on most occasions.

He was afraid to allow this feisty hoyden to get close to him. Coward, whispered the tiny voice in his soul. That is true, Hawk admitted. Facing a disturbed grizzly or a starving mountain lion did not stir as many unsettling emotions in him as confronting this raven-haired vixen.

Hawk approached his enemies with fierce determination, but when it came to this affair of the heart he had displayed his true color—canary yellow. He, quite simply, did not know how to handle Rozalyn. She was unlike any other woman he had known, certainly unlike the gentle, obedient Chumani who never raised her voice or heaved makeshift weapons when she was moved to anger. Rozalyn was a misfit. She didn't know her place in a man's world. She didn't have a place in this wilderness, yet she was too unconventional for civilization. Just where the hell did a woman like Rozalyn DuBois belong? Hawk heaved a weary sigh. This serious contemplation had given him a five-foot-two inch headache. He feared he knew the answer to that disturbing question, but he was too tired to deal with it just now. He would sleep on it and then ponder it during their long ride into the Wind River Mountains, he decided.

And in the meantime, he would sleep with this distracting beauty by his side. A contented smile crept across Hawk's lips as he molded his body to Rozalyn's soft curves. Ah, this is heaven, he mused drowsily. Rozalyn had tamed the restlessness that had once claimed his soul. He was content where he lay. If there was never to be another night like this one, he would remember the way the flickering fire light caressed her shapely body, the way her satiny skin felt upon his lips, the way his hands wandered across the tantalizing curves and swells of her nymph's body. He would smile and recall how they had made love before they had ascended into the Mountains of the Wind.

Part II

In all thy humors, whether grave or mellow,
Thour't such a touchy, testy, pleasant fellow,
Hast so much wit and mirth and spleen about thee,
There is no living with thee, nor without thee.

—*Addison*

Chapter 18

The spellbinding beauty of the Wind River Mountains
kept Rozalyn mesmerized. To the northwest, were rocky
summits, bathed in shades of pastels and encircled by
halos of puffy white clouds. Below, lining the plush
mountain meadows were clumps of spruce, aspen, and
pines. Tumbling over the broken boulders that had
toppled from the towering peaks was a clear mountain
stream that looked so inviting, Rozalyn had to fight the
urge to veer down the treacherous ledges to stand beside
its turbulent waters. She longed to peel off her moccasins
and wade into the slower-moving rapids, to let fine mist
spray across her face. But she knew the water would be
like ice since she and Hawk had been forced to wear their
heavy, buffalo-hide coats to ward off the chill.

They had departed from Fort William in late October,
and now the mountain air was heavy with the threat of
snow. It seemed they had ridden forever, but there was
no sign of the cabin Hawk had promised her at their
journey's end. A curious frown knitted Rozalyn's brow
when her gaze swung from the white-capped peaks to the
mountain man who rode ahead of her.

"Just where is this cabin?" she asked, her impatience
evident.

Hawk twisted in the saddle to flash her a grin that thawed her chill. He looked magnificent when he sat so tall in the saddle. His bulky buffalo-skin jacket made him appear even more impressive than he already was. No simple task, Rozalyn thought to herself. She had always considered it impossible to improve on his perfection, but the fringe and the small, colorful beads that adorned his coat gave him a wild, reckless appearance that made her heart flutter.

When Hawk gestured toward the towering summits that lay to the north, Rozalyn caught the look of pride on his craggy features. "The cabin sits upon snowy slopes, beyond the rivers of the wind. And to the west, shrouded in spirits of the past, lies a splendrous valley where the never-ending waterfall whispers. . . ." A faraway look appeared in his eyes, and he seemed to be glancing back through the window of time. He was—to years past when he was a young lad living among the Crows. He had followed this route with the great chief, viewing the awesome splendors of nature, and now he could almost hear Arakashe telling him the tragic legend. Strange, Hawk had not thought of that Crow legend in years. Why had the words spilled so easily from his tongue?

Rozalyn studied Hawk for a long moment, impatiently waiting for him to continue. When he didn't, she prodded him. "Hawk? Is something wrong?"

When her quiet words filtered into his pensive deliberations, Hawk focused his attention on Rozalyn. "I was just recalling the legend my grandfather once told me, when I was a child. I cannot fathom why it suddenly popped to mind."

Rozalyn pricked up her ears and straightened in the saddle. She had often heard that Indians were a superstitious lot and that mountain men were prone to believe the savages' explanations of that which they did not understand. Did Hawk believe the wild tales he had heard as a child?

"Tell me the story your grandfather passed on to you," she insisted as she edged her steed up beside Hawk's.

He chuckled at the lively curiosity in her blue eyes. "There are dozens of legends that rule each Indian nation, *amie*. Is it so important that I tell you this particular one? Will any of them satisfy you?" For some inexplicable reason, Hawk didn't wish to reveal the haunting tale of tragic love. Something about it unnerved him although, for the life of him, he wasn't quite certain why.

"I wish to hear all of them," Rozalyn demanded enthusiastically.

Hawk leaned out to press a kiss to her cold, but responsive lips. The fleeting touch warmed him and stirred memories that overshadowed all other recollections. "Perhaps we should create our own legend in the mountains of the wind and let the breeze whisper our tale to all forthcoming travelers who pass through this wilderness."

A becoming blush stained Rozalyn's cheeks as she remembered the nights they had spent beside the campfire, loving away the icy chill that settled upon the mountains. "I'm not certain I want to hear such stories repeated in any language," she murmured demurely.

When Rozalyn nudged her stead to take the lead along the narrow path, Hawk's throaty laughter drifted about her and then sânk into the canyon below them. "Are you ashamed of them?"

Rozalyn did not reply. Instead she fired a question at him in the hope of dropping the sensitive subject. "Will you tell me the legends of these mountains or must I find someone else to accommodate me?"

His astute gaze studied the shapely lass who rode ahead of him. Rozalyn didn't have the foggiest idea where she was going, but that didn't faze her. Her destination was not as important to her as the adventures she encountered getting there. What a delightful companion she was, sighing over the majestic scenery, playfully arousing him to passion each night, and taunting and teasing him as they wound their way higher into the ravines and jagged peaks.

"If it is a legend you desire, *chérie amie,* then a legend you shall have," he promised. After sorting through a myriad of tales, Hawk inhaled deeply and then let the words trip off the end of his tongue. "Among the Indians that roam the mountains, superstition is strong and those who discount it are frowned upon. What you hear you do not dare to question. That is a code of the wilderness."

"*Bien entendu,*" Rozalyn muttered impatiently, certain she was not going to believe a word of the nonsense Hawk was about to relate.

"There are great spirits ruling the people with red skin. These spirits dwell in the shining mountains. The wind that whistles along the peaks of Wind River and whispers through the meadows of Yellowstone carries the chants and warnings of these powerful spirits. At the headwaters of the Yellowstone River reside the spirits of the spring. In the land beyond, there are hot mineral springs that bubble more than fifty feet in the air, creating a hissing noise that echoes the voices of the magic spirits. These great springs are so hot that meat can be quickly cooked in them. Nearby, waterfalls sparkle and leap and thunder over the rocks that cut through the magic canyon. The river tumbles over the rock terraces, forming pools where a man can enjoy a delightful bath in the warm, spirit waters of this paradise.

"On the far side of the valley is an acid spring that gushes upward, spills over the treacherous rapids, and tumbles into the river. And below its gushing waterfall is a sacred cave where the shaman of the Crow collects vermilion, the blood-red pigment used for war paint and dye. Below the boiling springs the water overflows into a small, deep pool where the bubbling-hot water sits upon the cold springs that also feed the river. It is said that a man can lower bait through the simmering waters into the icy depths of the pool. When he catches one of the fish that inhabit the cooler depths, he passes it through the steaming waters and has his meal cooked on its way out of the magical pool."

Hawk grinned outrageously, and Rozalyn rolled her eyes in disbelief. "That is a mite far-fetched." She sniffed. "I have heard references to Colter's Hell, where eternal fires heat underground rivers and send them spurting up into the air like a vocano of water. You don't honestly believe the fantastic reports of explorers who have been alone too long in the wilderness, do you?"

One shoulder lifted in a nonchalant shrug and Hawk broke into a wry smile. "I told you it is not wise to discount the beliefs of those who inhabit these magic mountains. Nor is it advisable to disclaim the existence of Morningstar, the great father spirit of the Crow. One day your cynicism might come back to haunt you." His low, soft chuckle warned Rozalyn to beware of voicing her suspicions, as if the wind might pick up her words and carry them to the great spirit. "In these mountains, the Crow believe that the wild animals and birds that pass through the land of fiery rivers and icy springs possess mystical powers which have been granted to them by Morningstar. When a party of Crow cross the region, the medicine man always offers food and bright, polished stones to each magical spring his people encounter. The spirits of the springs will not curse the red man's journey or cause him defeat in battle if they are given offerings to appease them."

Hawk reined his steed to a halt and gestured down the rugged slopes to a strange-looking monument that stood in the middle of the meadow below them. It was an eerie arrangement of animal and human skulls placed in a circle around a towering shrine of elk horns. The pyramid rose like a lone tree, gracing the valley with its mystical presence.

"It is here that the Indians shout petitions to their gods. They believe that contributing an elk or antelope horn to the pyramid will ensure success in hunting. Those who fail to make an offering, and have perished because of it, are left here to add credence to the Indian belief in the supernatural," Hawk explained.

An odd tingle shot down Rozalyn's spine when she stared down at the sacred pyramid. This is all superstitious nonsense, she told herself. Offerings to the spirits? Mountain springs of fire and ice? Did Hawk truly expect her to believe such preposterous tales?

And yet, as they wound their way through the majestic mountain passes, listening to the murmur of the waterfalls, viewing the breathtaking beauty that greeted them at twilight and dawn, Rozalyn realized the spell of these mountains. And she was equally awestruck by the raven-haired man who tracked his way through the sprawling wilderness. Rozalyn found herself depending on Hawk as she had no other person. Each night when they made camp he was there to offer warmth and passion, and at sunrise her eyes would sweep open to see his muscular frame silhouetted against the colorful mountain summits. He would turn to greet her with a heart-stopping smile as radiant as the sun. It made her warm and giddy inside, though frosty mountain air crept over her exposed skin.

Their arguments had become the exception rather than the rule, for Rozalyn had come to respect Hawk's resourceful capabilities in the mountains. Despite some remaining resistance, she found herself looking up to him. He moved with masculine grace, spoke with authority; and he had developed a sixth sense that warned him of danger long before it approached. He was wise beyond his years when it came to knowing how to survive in the rugged terrain through which they were traveling. His excellent marksmanship kept them in fresh meat, even though Rozalyn had stopped complaining about choking down the pemmican cakes they often depended upon for nourishment.

When game was plentiful Hawk would hunt and Rozalyn would be one step behind him, studying him with pride. Their laughter rang through the meadows while they picked wild cherries and chokeberries, playfully feeding each other nature's fruits. And all the while, Rozalyn was falling deeper in love with the man she'd sworn not to succumb to a second time. But she could not help herself. Hawk was always there to lay a protective arm about her shoulder, to stand watch over her. He filled up her days and nights, leaving her with no other memories except those that evolved around him and the rugged country that was so much a part of him.

One evening, just before dusk, Hawk had cast Rozalyn a dubious glance before going off to hunt fresh game for their evening meal. Rozalyn had insisted that she remain in camp instead of following her usual custom of accompanying him. She had much on her mind and she wanted to be completely alone with her troubled thoughts. With each passing day, her attachment had deepened for a man who whispered words of wanting and needing in moments of passion, but who said nothing about lasting love. This disturbed her greatly. Hawk treated her with respect, so much so that she found herself thinking he actually did care for her. Yet, she knew she was only a convenience, someone who could appease his lusts and share his warmth. Would he surrender her to Aubrey without regret when summer came? Rozalyn's heart twisted in her chest when she visualized their parting.

She could see herself standing there, her eyes swimming with barely contained tears, her heart withering in her chest. She would be loving him, wanting him, knowing she had been first and foremost a bargaining tool to use against her father. How could she say goodbye to this raven-haired rogue with eyes the color of emeralds? How could she return to St. Louis and leave her soul in these mystical mountains?

An agonizing groan escaped Rozalyn's lips. It was answered by an unexpected growl from the thick brush that crowded the lower rim of the canyon. Hesitantly, she glanced over her shoulder and horror filled her eyes. There, on the ledge above her was a bear cub—and its mother. Two pair of coal black eyes focused intently on her. Rozalyn was on her feet before she realized what she was doing. Frantically, she grabbed the pistol Hawk had left for her, and her heart catapulted into her throat as she took aim at the mammoth beast that had moved ahead to protect the cub. When another warning growl echoed through the canyon, Rozalyn reacted instinctively. The pistol exploded, but the shot only served to enrage the grizzly.

Rozalyn tried to still her pounding heart when seven hundred pounds of disturbed grizzly reared up on its hind legs to its seven foot height, but a frightened shriek erupted from her lips when the grizzly growled and hunkered down on all fours to pursue her. Her eyes darted from side to side as she tried to decide what to do. She didn't dare take to the open valley in search of Hawk so she scrambled up the rocks, searching for a tiny niche that would protect her from imminent disaster. The bear's third ferocious growl made Rozalyn cry out so loudly that even Morningstar, the spirit of the mountains, could not help but hear her. Nonetheless, praying hard and fast, Rozalyn wedged herself between two boulders as the grizzly lumbered toward her. When the angry beast pounced upon the rocks and swatted at her with its powerful paw, Rozalyn shrank away, certain she would lose her head if the monstrous bear's paw connected with its target.

She couldn't breathe for her heart was lodged in her throat, and her life was passing before her eyes. The grizzly pushed up into an upright position, wrapping its powerful legs around the boulders, and breathed down her neck. Rozalyn screamed again. Then, like a frightened rabbit, she darted from the opposite end of the boulder, hoping to locate a safer sanctuary that might allow her to wait out the grizzly. If she could tuck herself into a narrow crevice, perhaps the bear would tire of its game and leave her in peace.

Relief washed over her hunted features when she spied a broken slope that formed a natural cave with an opening only large enough for her to crawl inside. It wasn't nearly wide enough to house a seven-hundred-pound bear. Rozalyn hastily glanced back at her pursuer while she dashed madly across the ledge, praying she could reach the cave before the grizzly sprang on her, but as she did so, her moccasined foot slipped on the loose pebbles, flinging her off balance. She cried out as she fell, scraping against the jagged boulders that lay at the base of the canyon wall.

"Roz . . ." Hawk's booming voice echoed through the valley, and the color drained from his ruddy features when he saw Rozalyn plummet over the rocks to land in a broken heap. As the huge grizzly bounded from the ledge to pursue her victim, Hawk braced the Hawken rifle against his shoulder and took careful aim. He could hear his heart thundering in his ears, drowning out Rozalyn's whimperings.

He must drop the grizzly before she cut Rozalyn to shreds, and the distance between them would sorely test the accuracy of the rifle. There would be time for only one shot. It would take too long to reload so he must hit his mark on the first attempt. Steadying the rifle, Hawk peered down the long barrel and gently pulled the trigger. The crack of the Hawken vibrated around the walls of the canyon and Hawk sagged in relief when the grizzly tumbled over the rocks. Although the shot had not killed her, she had been sufficiently dazed. The grizzly wobbled up on all fours, hearing the call of her cub from the elevated ledge.

As soon as the bear retreated to join her cub, Hawk raced across the meadow to inspect Rozalyn's injuries. "Oh, God," he groaned, as he scrambled up the rocks to her lifeless form. Her arms were flung outward, and her hands dangled limply over the boulders that had stopped her fall. She was lying on her back, her eyes shut, her face scraped and bruised. Her left leg was twisted up behind her as if someone had carelessly tossed a rag doll aside, and it had landed in a contorted position.

Scolding himself for leaving her alone, Hawk carefully scooped her into his arms. Then, guarding his steps, he edged down the side of the cliff toward the camp. Rozalyn had not moved a muscle or shown the slightest sign of life. Apprehensively, Hawk bent over her, laying his cheek to her breast. He feared she might not have survived the fall, and a choked sigh rattled in his chest when he felt the faint beat of her heart against the side of his face.

After laying her on the pallet, Hawk glanced up at the ledge to ensure that the grizzly had retreated to her cave high above the precipices that jutted out over the valley. Then he turned back to Rozalyn and his pain was evident on his craggy features.

Damnation, if only he hadn't dragged her into this treacherous terrain . . . if he hadn't left her to fend for herself while he went in search of game. . . . Blast it, Rozalyn had not yet developed a sixth sense. She couldn't feel the approach of danger.

Setting aside his regrets, Hawk inspected her inert body for signs of broken bones. He berated himself again when he saw that her left ankle was swollen and the back of her head had been slashed by the jagged rocks. Dammit, she could have been killed! Even now, she could perish from the fall she had taken.

This is no place for a woman, he told himself. He had taken leave of his senses when he'd carted her into the perilous wilderness. Rozalyn hadn't known the first thing about survival in the mountains. He had taught her the basic necessities, but they weren't enough to protect her.

While Hawk held a cloth to the wound on the back of Rozalyn's head, and as he cradled her protectively in his arms, her eyes fluttered open. Her vision was hazy, her thoughts clouded; but she sighed contentedly when she saw Hawk's face hovering above her.

"Hawk, I . . ." She licked her swollen lips, desperately trying to formulate thoughts she could not seem to put to tongue. The silent darkness was calling to her. . . .

"Roz?" Hawk laid his head to her breast, fearing the worst. But the vital flame, dim though it was, still burned within her. Gently, he eased her back to the pallet and covered her with quilts to preserve her warmth.

When he'd made Rozalyn as comfortable as the situation permitted, Hawk sank down beside her. His keen gaze swept the now-quiet valley, his eyes shifting to the north. He wished he and Rozalyn were safely tucked in his cabin, and a rueful smile pursed his lips when his gaze circled back to Rozalyn's pale face. Lovingly, he reached out to trail a tanned finger over her bruised cheek.

"Can you forgive me for all this, *ma chérie amie?* You have always invited trouble, but this time I have led you into it." He looked toward the heavens, thinking if this request was answered he would never request another favor. Then, he prayed that Rozalyn would live and that she would not be permanently injured by her fall.

The deep circles under Hawk's eyes revealed the strain he'd endured the past two days. Rozalyn had roused to consciousness several times during the journey to his cabin, but her words had made no sense at all. When Hawk finally drew her limp body from the back of his horse and then eased her onto his soft bed, Rozalyn sank into another restless sleep.

Assured that she was resting as comfortably as possible, Hawk went outside to unload the supplies and care for the horses. As he glanced up from his task, he glimpsed a man approaching in the distance, and a faint smile grazed his lips.

"Where have you been so long, Hawk?" Bear-Claw called when he drew nearer. Then the burly mountain man swung down from his steed and ambled toward Hawk, cradling his rifle in his arms. "Twice I have come to share your company, only to find your empty cabin."

"The fall has been a busy season," Hawk said evasively, returning to his chores.

"You have been trapping?" Bear-Claw chuckled softly, his pale eyes dancing with amusement. "Do you think to outdo last year's heaping stack of pelts? You take life too seriously, Hawk. The mountains provide life itself. Why must you be so eager to find profit in them?"

Hawk eyed the older mountain man for a long, thoughtful moment. Bear-Claw was a long-time hermit of the Rockies, a man who seldom mingled with others. Never had he descended from the mountains to attend the festive rendezvous. The shaggy-haired hunter was content to live off the land, and he did not hunger for the luxuries of civilization. It wasn't that he didn't approve of sophistication, Bear-Claw was simply satisifed with his lot.

"Did you come to lecture me or to share my company, Bear-Claw?" Hawk asked point-blank.

Bear-Claw's laughter wafted away in the crisp mountain breeze. "Would you be insulted if I came to do a bit of both?" The old man rubbed his backside and then cast his companion a beseeching glance. "Will you offer a soft seat to a weary traveler? The nag's rump makes an uncomfortable seat for these brittle old bones."

Without waiting for a formal invitation, Bear-Claw aimed himself toward the log cabin he had helped Hawk build several years earlier.

"I have been to St. Louis to sell my furs and I brought a woman back with me," Hawk blurted out before Bear-Claw could reach the door.

The abrupt comment stopped the old mountain man in his tracks, and his head swiveled around to peer incredulously at Hawk. "You took a woman . . . a white woman?" he croaked in astonishment. "What devil possessed you to traipse all the way to St. Louis without informing me first?"

"Because you complained about the journey five years ago and I had already made up my mind to go." Slowly, Hawk walked up beside Bear-Claw, bracing himself for a lengthy sermon.

"Made up your mind to go?" Bear-Claw prodded, his thick brows forming a suspicious frown.

"I was determined to confront Aubrey DuBois and to ensure reasonable prices for the trappers at next summer's rendezvous."

Bear-Claw shook his head and grumbled in disgust. "You might as well have slammed your head against a rock wall." He snorted derisively. "DuBois is a stubborn, bitter man. You wasted your time going to see him."

"I was determined to make the effort on behalf of

the other trappers," Hawk insisted. Then he peered curiously at the old man. "Do you have any idea why Aubrey—"

Anticipating the question, Bear-Claw cut in. "I knew him when he first came into the mountains, when he was a young man full of dreams." His rugged features were clouded by another frown. "We were even friends once, before his hatred poisoned him, before he turned against the mountains and all those who inhabit them."

"What caused his bitterness?" Hawk pressed.

He was most anxious to know why Aubrey had flown into a rage when he had learned Hawk's true name. Bear-Claw held the key to Aubrey's secretive past, and Hawk was willing to bet the hermit knew exactly what had caused the feud between DuBois and Baudelairs. But for some reason the old man was reluctant to enlighten him. Again Hawk posed the probing question.

Again Bear-Claw openly avoided it, countering with an inquiry of his own. "Who is this woman you brought back with you? I hope to hell she can cook. Is she pretty? Lord, it has been a long time since I've laid eyes on a white woman."

"Her name is Rozalyn DuBois," Hawk informed the mountain man, carefully awaiting his companion's reaction.

"What?" Bear-Claw hooted in disbelief, and his wide eyes swung to Hawk. "You married Aubrey DuBois' daughter. Sweet mercy! I never believed Aubrey would be so forgiving!"

"No . . . I didn't exactly marry her." Hawk stumbled over his words like a tongue-tied idiot. There was no delicate way to explain his rash action. Hawk feared Bear-Claw would be questioning his comrade's sanity, or lack of it, by the time he fumbled his way through an explanation.

"Well, what exactly did you do?" Bear-Claw gave

Hawk the evil eye. "I can hardly wait to hear the mangled workings of your mind. It is beyond me why Aubrey would allow one of his clan in the mountains, especially when she is accompanied by a Baudelair."

"DuBois didn't allow it. The man despises me for some unknown reason, which you apparently know and I do not. The truth of the matter is I kidnapped the lady," Hawk announced, bracing himself for another loud crow of disbelief. When it had come and gone, Hawk hurried to explain "DuBois refused to grant the trappers lower prices on their supplies, and he threatened to attack my caravan if I dared to compete against him at rendezvous. Kidnapping his daughter and ransoming her for lower prices was the only way to counter his malicious threats."

Bear-Claw's shaggy brown mane whipped about his face in disarray as he shook his head. "I taught you everything you needed to know about surviving in the mountains. I nursed your wounds when you met with disaster. But had I known you were so short on common sense, I would hae given you up for a lost cause long ago."

"I knew exactly what I was doing!" Hawk replied self-righteously. "I have in my custody the one thing DuBois will not tolerate handing over to me—because my name is Baudelair. Now, are you going to tell me why this furrier despises me or must I ask other trappers who have been in these mountains for a long time?"

Again, Bear-Claw evaded the question, and his thoughtful gaze sought the closed door. "Rozalyn? Did you say Aubrey's daughter was named Rozalyn?" A deep skirl of laughter rumbled in his chest. "That is irony in its purest form."

A frown distorted Hawk's craggy features. "You find her name amusing?" Damn, one or the other of us is crazed, he thought sourly, Bear-Claw for voicing such strange remarks or myself for dragging Rozalyn with me into the wilderness. "It seems your long hibernation in the mountains has eroded your brain, either that or you are plagued with a distorted sense of humor." His tone carried an undertone of mockery, his eyes a sparkle of impatience. "I want to know what started this mysterious feud."

Bear-Claw's mirth evaporated and his expression sobered. Then his gaze shifted from the door to Hawk's annoyed frown. "Does she know about me? Have you told your woman that I once knew her father . . . in the beginning . . . before he became the trapper's back-stabbing foe?"

"She knows nothing. I have not yet introduced her to any of the trappers who roam these mountains." Hawk peered bemusedly at Bear-Claw. My, but he was behaving strangely.

"I wish to keep it that way." His eyes bored into Hawk's, anticipating no argument. "The less Rozalyn knows about the man she calls her father, the better. She is his one link with the tormenting past, a living symbol of all the bitterness DuBois would have buried. But if he truly wanted to forget, why did he select that particular name for his child?" Bear-Claw mused aloud. A speculative frown creased his bushy brows. "I wonder if Aubrey considered giving her that name the best way to deal with his torment. Or perhaps he could not truly forget, would not let himself forget, what happened."

Hawk was about to fire another impatient question when the shabby hermit poked his head inside the cabin to look at the sleeping beauty nestled beneath the thick fur quilts. A rueful smile touched Bear-Claw's parched lips when he spied Rozalyn's delicate features and dark lustrous mane spilling over her pillow.

"Did you feed her a potion so she would sleep away the winter?" Bear-Claw smirked. "I wouldn't be surprised after hearing how you've spent the past few months." Quietly, he closed the door and then plopped down on the bench outside the cabin. "While you're unloading the remainder of your supplies you can explain everything that has transpired since last we met."

"I will be happy to . . . as soon as you tell me why Aubrey DuBois has such a bitter hatred for the Baudelair clan," Hawk parried, his narrowed gaze holding Bear-Claw hostage.

Bear-Claw's eyes took on a faraway look. Then, heaving a sigh, he nodded in compliance. "It's too late to undo the damage you have unwittingly done. But, yes, I will tell you why you have ignited DuBois' wrath, and why he thinks the Baudelairs have wronged him. I pity you, Hawk. Aubrey will never forgive and forget. I fear you have disturbed a sleeping lion."

One of many, Hawk thought resentfully. Eventually he must contend with Aubrey, and there was Half-Head to consider. Hawk wondered if it would be a matter of time before that murdering white man came to finish what he had begun on the banks of the North Platte. Then his apprehension mounted as Bear-Claw unfolded the painful events of the past. Now DuBois' behavior made sense to Hawk. No wonder the man had flown into a sputtering rage. Bear-Claw's rendition of the incident that had embittered Aubrey assured Hawk that he and Rozalyn could have no future together, even if they wanted one, and despair closed in on him. He cursed himself for abducting this blue-eyed minx. Had he known of the tragic feud between the Baudelairs and DuBois, he never would have gone near Rozalyn. But he had, and the cross he was now forced to bear was as great as the one Aubrey labored under.

Chapter 19

A quiet, groggy moan echoed in the darkness as Rozalyn roused sluggishly, and her heavily lidded eyes circled the unfamiliar confines of the cabin. The rustic lodge was fifteen feet long, and its primitive walls were made of logs packed with mud and moss to prevent the drafty mountain wind from seeping inside. The split-log floor was randomly strewn with thick fur rugs to ward off the cool dampness; the ceiling above her was no more than a clapboard roof held together with wooden pins. Although the shack was crude there was a certain raw beauty to it.

Rozalyn's hazy gaze settled on the fireplace and the blackened stone hearth. Silhouetted by the flames was the awesome form of a man in buckskins. Although his back was to her, she knew who her companion was, and she was most thankful he was the first living creature she saw upon awakening. Through her tormented dreams one thread of sanity had been a constant. She had continued to see Hawk's ruggedly handsome face. He had been there, just beyond the darkness, calling to her.

"Hawk?" Her throaty voice drifted across the room, and Rozalyn managed a groggy smile when he swiveled around in his chair to peer at her. But suddenly a startled gasp burst from and her and she shrank away from the unfamiliar mountain man who rose and approached her. What had Hawk done to her now? Dumped her in a total stranger's lap while she recovered from her injuries? Damn the man. He hadn't shown her the smallest amount of consideration.

"Where is Hawk and where am I?" Rozalyn asked.

A broad grin split Bear-Claw's lips as his keen gaze swept over her shapely form. "Hawk brought you to his cabin after you were injured." His silent footsteps brought him to the edge of the cot, where he towered over his wary patient. The lovely young woman looked out of place on a crude bed made of split logs and softened only by a mattress stuffed with grass and leaves, but her exquisitely delicate face made Bear-Claw smile again. He knew why Hawk had been unable to leave this fetching young lass behind. She was a rare beauty.

"Since Hawk was most anxious to set his beaver traps I offered to stay here with you while you were on the mend." His weathered hand brushed across her brow to ensure that her fever had ebbed. "My name is Bear-Claw. I have known Hawk since he was a skinny-legged pigeon fluttering around the forests. In fact, I can even boast that I taught the young stripling to be self-sufficient in these mountains. When I first began to instruct him, he couldn't shoot a lick. And what he did with a butcher knife was downright disgraceful. Couldn't skin a hide clean to save his life." Bear-Claw chuckled to himself. "But time has been good to Hawk. He learned quickly and has become proficient with a rifle and a knife. Although I proudly claim to have taught him to survive, and most successfully, I do not, however, take the blame for his foolishness. That, he must have acquired all by himself."

Her companion seemed friendly enough—he'd very nearly talked her ears off in these few moments—still, Rozalyn eyed the bulky creature with extreme caution.

Bear-Claw was the image of a mountain man, she noted. Around his neck dangled a necklace of claws, similar to those of the monstrous grizzly that had swatted at her head. No doubt, this was how the crusty pioneer had acquired his nickname. Coarse, bushy hair framed his weather-beaten features and dangled loosely about his broad shoulders, and his skin, due to constant exposure to the elements, was almost as dark as an Indian's. That and his sinewy physique gave him a rough, hardy appearance. His clothes were similar to Hawk's, but they were adorned with even more beads and polished bones. Although Bear-Claw looked as old as father time, Rozalyn doubted the man could have been so agile if he were as ancient as he appeared.

Since Rozalyn was hesitant to speak, Bear-Claw rattled on in his usual, long-winded manner. "I cooked you some rabbit stew to warm your insides. Though it isn't my specialty, I have received a good many compliments from wayward travelers who have gone long days without nourishment. I don't imagine it compares to the delicacies you are accustomed to eating, but it will sustain you just the same. Shall I fetch you a bowl?"

"*Merci*," Rozalyn murmured, forcing a meager smile.

When Bear-Claw spun about and strode back to the kettle that hung over the hearth, she eased into an upright position. Stars swam before her eyes and the room tilted sideways, then threatened to slip out from under her. Deciding it best to remain abed until she had regained her equilibrium, Rozalyn wilted back to the cot.

When Bear-Claw saw the raven-haired beauty sink back onto the fluffy mattress, he snickered softly. "Still a mite groggy, I suspect. 'Tis no matter, *mam'selle*. I've got no aversion to spoon-feeding my patient." When the mountain man had parked himself on a chair beside the bed, he dipped up some broth and offered it to his reluctant companion. "It isn't poison," he assured her with a gentle smile that melted the coarseness of his features. "If Hawk didn't trust me to nurse you he wouldn't have left you in my care. I know I'm not much to look at, but you need not fear for your safety. I never did take to manhandling women and I have no respect for those who do."

When Bear-Claw graced her with his compassionate grin, Rozalyn relaxed a bit. Propping herself upon an elbow, she accepted the steamy broth. "It is very good," she complimented, and then opened her mouth to accept the next heaping spoonful Bear-Claw had waiting for her.

"Didn't I tell you?" Bear-Claw beamed in satisfaction. "Wait until you sample my johnny-cakes and corn pone. The very aroma of them will set your mouth to watering, missy."

While Rozalyn quietly sipped her porridge, Bear-Claw rambled on, skipping from one unrelated topic to another. The longer he talked, the less apprehensive Rozalyn became about sharing a cabin with the aging hunter. Slowly, she warmed to him, deciding that the mountain man was a mite windy but harmless.

Now she knew where Hawk had heard his tall tales. Bear-Claw rattled off one story after another until drowsiness overcame her. Rozalyn eased back onto the bed and snuggled beneath the warm fur covering. Peacefully, she slept while Bear-Claw kept constant vigil over her.

The longer he sat silently studying the blue-eyed beauty the more attached to her he became. It was easy to understand why Hawk had impulsively dragged this lovely creature of civilization back into the wilderness with him. Just peering into Rozalyn's bewitching features gave a man a warm feeling. Although Rozalyn could not remain here in the wilds forever, she could provide Hawk with memories to last a lifetime.

A quiet sigh tumbled from Bear-Claw's lips. It was a

shame Hawk had not consulted him before venturing from the mountains. Hawk could have spared him the agony he'd feel upon surrendering this exquisite beauty to Aubrey. Although Hawk had discovered how it could be between a man and a woman, he must face the inevitable pain of losing this lovely creature. Bear-Claw found himself wondering if perhaps Hawk wouldn't have been better off with his freedom than living with the despair of knowing there was no future for him with Aubrey DuBois' daughter.

"Of all the women in the world, why did Hawk have to get himself involved with this one?" Bear-Claw grumbled while he climbed the ladder to the loft where his pallet awaited him.

Bear-Claw had never bothered to tell Hawk about the feud between DuBois and the Beaudelairs because he saw no need. Aubrey had dealt with Hawk at rendezvous, but he had never known the trapper's true name. That wasn't unusual. Almost every man who ventured into the mountains took a new name and a new identity. Bear-Claw hadn't thought it wise to stir up the painful past if it wasn't necessary, and things had been going well until Hawk had made the mistake of traveling to St. Louis. That was where the trouble had started. If Hawk had stayed put, Aubrey would have been none the wiser and the young woman would not have found herself caught in the crossfire of an undying feud.

Heaving a disgruntled sigh, Bear-Claw wriggled beneath the fur robe. A clash between Aubrey and Hawk was inevitable. DuBois would never permit his daughter to be linked with a Beaudelair, not after all that had happened years ago. Hawk would have to accept harsh reality. Bear-Claw supposed that was one of the reasons the younger man had decided to spend a few weeks alone in the wilderness. He'd needed time to come to terms with the truth and to accept his fate. How many weeks would it take for Hawk to relinquish his obsession for this enticing beauty? And God forbid, what would happen if Hawk couldn't give Rozalyn up as he had promised to do in his ransom note to Aubrey?

Confound it. If Hawk had listened to Bear-Claw's advice, he'd have been satisfied to live the life he'd made for himself in the mountains. But no, the lad was overeager, hot-blooded. He had an uncommon need to see progress and change. My God, Bear-Claw grunted sourly, I wouldn't be surprised to learn that Hawk had invited homesteaders to journey into this wilderness to set up housekeeping! It was getting so a man couldn't live in harmony with nature without having neighbors breathing down his neck. Hawk lived twenty miles from Bear-Claw's crude cabin and that was close enough. A man needs his space, Bear-Claw mused. The closer he came to people, the more entangled his life became. Bear-Claw had seen enough tragedy and heartache, he wanted no part of it. He, too, was plagued by old, unhealed wounds, and they were much easier to tolerate when there was nothing or no one around to remind him of life as it had once been.

For almost a full week Rozalyn enjoyed Bear-Claw's company. The dizziness had ebbed and her tender left ankle had begun to mend, thanks to the hermit's natural remedy. Although Rozalyn had no complaint about the meals Bear-Claw prepared for her or the long hours they spent conversing on a myriad of subjects, she was developing a severe case of cabin fever. She longed for activity, something to distract her from wondering when Hawk would return and whether he had missed her. Was he plagued by the same, discomforting loneliness that tormented her?

"I would like to ask a favor," Rozalyn begged as she

313

sipped a mug of Bear-Claw's own concoction—a brewed tea. Although it varied greatly from the drink Rozalyn had sampled in civilization, she had acquired a taste for the potion.

"Anything," Bear-Claw generously offered. Then he leaned close to flash her a wry smile. "Anything except divulging my recipe for johnnycakes, that is."

Rozalyn giggled at his teasing grin. "I wouldn't dare attempt to copy your special recipe. It is something else I request of you." Her lashes fluttered up to study his ruddy face. "Teach me to survive in the wild, just as you once taught Hawk. I feel inadequate in these mountains."

Bear-Claw frowned pensively for a moment, grappling with her request. Finally, he nodded agreeably. "That is a great deal to learn in so little time, but we will make an effort."

So Rozalyn's introduction to survival in the wild began. Bear-Claw patiently taught her to skin the game he brought in for their meals, and he gave her lessons on food preparation and storage, as well as instructions on sewing buckskin garments. Sewing was a skill Rozalyn had heretofore overlooked. Indeed, Bear-Claw was eager to share his knowledge until Rozalyn insisted that he teach her to become accurate with his rifle.

After he watched Rozalyn take aim with the flintlock and consistently hit the targets he had set for her, he agreed to allow her to clutch his prized weapon. "Brace your legs and hold the rifle firmly against your shoulder," he instructed. "Hold it steady, and with authority. No, no, girl. I didn't say choke it!" Yanking the weapon away, he showed Rozalyn the proper way to cradle the rifle.

Rozalyn did as she was told, or so she thought. But she was too interested in taking aim over the long barrel and impressing Bear-Claw with her marksmanship. Before the mountain man could add another word of caution,

Rozalyn squeezed the trigger. A surprised squawk erupted from her lips when the rifle kicked like a mule, slamming against her shoulder and knocking her completely off balance. While she lay sprawled on the ground, Bear-Claw calmly strode over to retrieve his weapon.

"You didn't steady the rifle firmly against your shoulder. I noticed that right away. You are a mite impatient, flatlander . . . but you'll learn."

When Bear-Claw ambled away, Rozalyn scraped herself up off the ground and then followed after him. His footsteps took him to the river, where he intended to proceed with the next facet of her education. Announcing that it was time to learn the proper procedure for setting a beaver trap, Bear-Claw waded into the cold mountain stream. Reluctantly, Rozalyn, too, eased into the icy water, grimacing when chills ran up and down her spine.

Having found a natural dam in the rivulet, Bear-Claw cocked the trap. "Put this contraption into the water, just deep enough for the width of one hand to move between the surface and the trap trigger."

Carefully, the mountain man drew the attached chain to its full length and then secured it by driving a sharpened stick into the river bed. Motioning for Rozalyn to accompany him, he waded to the bank to locate a willow twig. "Next you must peel the stick and dip it in the bait." He stuffed the twig into the end of the antelope horn that dangled from his belt. "This is what we trappers call medicine," he explained with a wry grin. "It is a secretion taken from a dead beaver." After handing Rozalyn the twig, he gestured back to the river. "Take the stick bait and carefully place it above the submerged trap. The scent of the bait lures the beaver to spring the trap on his paw. The trap will drown the beaver before he can free himself by gnawing off his snared paw."

Rozalyn made the mistake of jerking straight up when Bear-Claw described the cruel trapping method and the tormented captive's painful means of escape. Her abrupt movement caused her to lose her footing on the mossy rocks. She yelped in surprise as she went splashing into the icy stream. Muffling a chuckle, Bear-Claw lumbered into the water to offer her a helping hand.

As the mountain man assisted her to shore, an embarrassed smile crept across her lips. "You must think me a clumsy oaf."

"No, just a mite green," Bear-Claw corrected. "But you'll learn."

By the end of week one, Rozalyn had heard that familiar phrase so often that she wanted to scream. She swore she would never accomplish even the simplest task without bungling it. Her first experience in building a temporary lodge was disastrous. She painstakingly stretched animal skins over several flexible saplings, but their tops were not tightly secured so the bent trees broke loose, flinging the skinned tarp to the ground several feet away.

"I know," Rozalyn grumbled disgustedly, stalking over to retrieve the tanned skins. "I'll learn . . . eventually. I only pray that I will live long enough to get the hang of this."

Bear-Claw plopped down on a fallen log and cast his annoyed companion a teasing grin. "I didn't say this was going to be easy," he'd reminded her with a soft snicker. "You must practice the task time and time again until you get it right."

Although he did his damnedest to prevent it, a skirl of laughter bubbled in his chest. He remembered the previous night when he had shown Rozalyn how to prepare a bed of coals to warm her when sleeping in the wilds. She had neglected to scoop enough dirt into the hold to sufficiently cover the smoldering coals, and when she'd squirmed down onto her cozy nest, her blanket caught fire, nearly roasting her like a duck. Bear-Claw had doused her with water before she'd been set ablaze.

"Would you care to try your hand at making another warm bed?" he asked.

Rozalyn frowned at the grinning mountain man. "My backside was sufficiently scorched last night," she assured him grouchily. "I don't think I will undertake that task again for a few more days. Since I cannot endure much more heat, I intend to avoid sleeping over fires until the burns have healed."

When Rozalyn finally managed to complete their overnight lodge, Bear-Claw scooped up the stack of skinned beaver hides. Patiently, he taught her how to scrape the skin, stretch it over a willow hoop, and then set it out to dry. Rozalyn was extremely proud of herself for completing the task without chopping off her fingers in the process.

She was slowly learning the techniques required for surviving in the wild. Although she was not yet proficient in them, she knew the basic necessities, and the weeks of constant instruction had distracted her so she did not spend all her time wondering when Hawk would return.

Bear-Claw reminded her of Harvey Duncan. He could spin the liveliest yarns, thereby preoccupying her on the long night when her thoughts inevitably turned to Hawk. She was now totally at ease in the mountain man's presence, and his companionship made her days without Hawk less difficult to bear.

Nodding in approval after tasting the beaver-tail soup and hoecake Rozalyn had prepared for their noon meal, Bear-Claw complimented her efforts. "You have become a full-fledged mountaineer."

A proud smile blossomed on Rozalyn's lips. *"Merci, monsieur."* Gracefully, she curtsied before him. "I had a most competent instructor."

When Bear-Claw glanced past her to stare out the window, her eyes followed his gaze and then her heart almost stopped beating. A lone rider was approaching the cabin. Impulsively, she vaulted to her feet and dashed through the door to greet the man who had long filled her dreams.

A wide smile stretched Hawk's lips when he saw Rozalyn running toward him. Her blue eyes were dancing with the lively sparkle he had not been able to forget the past three weeks, and her shiny raven hair trailed wildly behind her as she closed the distance between them. His hungry gaze swam over her flawless features and her curvaceous figure now clad in form-fitting buckskins. God, how he had missed this gorgeous creature whose smile was as radiant as the summer sun.

Hawk grunted uncomfortably when Rozalyn leaped at him, her arms curling tightly about his neck. The feel of her body instantly aroused him, and her feminine scent warped his senses. He stood there, a rifle in one hand, the horse's reins in the other, and Rozalyn draped about his neck like a clinging vine, determinedly fighting the urge to rid himself of horse and weapon, and then squeeze the stuffing out of this lovely minx.

A dark eyebrow rose sharply when Rozalyn kissed him with enough heat to set the forest ablaze. "Your overzealous greeting might lead a man to believe you had actually missed him." He chuckled softly.

Blushing up to the roots of her raven hair, she unwrapped her arms from Hawk's neck and suddenly became cool and aloof as she snatched the reins from his hand and sauntered off to hobble his weary steed. "How could I miss you when you left me in such capable hands? Bear-Claw proved to be most entertaining company. Time has flown by while I have been living with him.

318

How long have you been gone?" Feigning an innocent smile, she glanced back at the awesome man with tousled raven hair and laughing green eyes. "A week? Surely no more than that."

Hawk's handsome face fell. "Three weeks and three days . . . exactly," he grumbled, his disposition soured by Rozalyn's comments. His narrowed gaze pelleted over the older mountain man who had strutted from the cabin and propped himself against a supporting post. "And what, exactly, have the two of you been doing in my absence?"

Bear-Claw's smile became broader, if that was possible. "It would be simpler to list the things we haven't done, wouldn't it, Roz?"

"If you have overlooked any facet of my education, I cannot imagine what it might be. You have been very thorough," she declared, her expression brimming with fondness and respect as she looked upon the bulky mountain man.

Hawk did not appreciate their all-too-cheerful banter, nor did he appreciate the insinuation Bear-Claw had left dangling in the crisp mountain air. When Rozalyn disappeared inside the cabin to set another place at the table, Hawk glared at the gloating mountaineer.

"It seems you have developed a strong attachment for the lady," he growled accusingly.

Bear-Claw sauntered off the stoop to unfasten the pile of pelts from Hawk's steed. "Roz is a rare gem," he acknowledged. "I have not known such pleasure in years. It makes me wonder why I've wasted decades living like a hermit."

Hawk didn't like the sound of that either. His lean fingers clamped into Bear-Claw's arm and he roughly spun the man to meet his perturbed glower. "I trusted you above all others. I thought I could depend on you. How could you—"

"Put your fears to rest." Bear-Claw chuckled, then

319

unclasped Hawk's tanned fingers from his forearm. "Roz asked me to teach her to survive in the wild and I did but comply. Must I remind you that I am old enough to be the girl's father?" Amusement faded from his weathered features as his troubled gaze fastened on the closed door. "I have become her friend, nothing more. She is your woman, Hawk. What she feels for you is strong, too strong, I'm afraid."

"Did she say that?" Hawk's level gaze bored into Bear-Claw.

"She didn't have to," the mountaineer responded with a heavy sigh. "I saw the look in her eyes while she watched you approach, and I also saw the expression on your face when she flew into your arms. You have become far too attached to Aubrey DuBois' daughter. She is the one woman you cannot have."

Hawk's frustrated gaze swung to the closed door. "Dammit, Bear-Claw, what am I going to do?" he asked, his voice wavering.

Bear-Claw's big hand folded around Hawk's slumped shoulder in a gesture of consolation, and for a long, quiet moment they both stood staring at the cabin. "You will do what you must do," he predicted softly. "You might not have realized that in the beginning, but you know it now. When the time comes, you will have to let Rozalyn go."

Nodding mutely, Hawk ambled toward the cabin. While they took their meal, he could not drag his eyes off Rozalyn. The cool mountain air had heightened the color in her cheeks, and her eyes glowed with pleasure each time he peered into them. Hawk fought the overwhelming urge to abruptly order Bear-Claw from the cabin so he could be alone with this tempting beauty. He had spent three agonizing weeks anticipating his return, but being home had turned out to be a torment.

Rozalyn felt the heat of Hawk's gaze upon her, and she knew the lambent hunger in his eyes was reflecting her own, barely restrained emotions. Although Rozalyn had been grateful for Bear-Claw's constant company, she wished he were a hundred miles away when Hawk's hand slipped under the table to map the curve of her hip. And her heart stampeded around in her chest like a runaway stallion when his caress glided over her thigh, taunting, arousing, driving her mad with a craving that beaver stew and hoecake could never appease. Fire spread across her quivering skin as his roaming hand dipped beneath the band of her breeches to make tantalizing contact with her satiny flesh.

It was impossible to carry on a normal conversation when Hawk was caressing her. He had always been proficient at seducing her in front of an audience. Lenore had not suspected his bold touch, and now Bear-Claw rattled on, relating Rozalyn's misadventures in the wilderness, while Hawk turned her inside out with his titillating caresses.

When Bear-Claw insisted that he and Hawk spend the afternoon hunting game for a homecoming feast, Rozalyn's heart sank. She couldn't bear to have her raven-haired mountain man out of her sight. But, masking her disappointment, she forced a cheerful smile and followed both men to the door. When Bear-Claw stepped off the stoop to fetch the horses, Hawk reversed direction, however. His long, graceful strides brought him back to Rozalyn, and his flaming green eyes were burning so intensely that she trembled.

Hawk's callused hands folded about her face, tilting it to his and his voice was raspy with desire as he spoke. "Tonight . . . when Bear-Claw falls asleep. . . ." His words sizzled across her skin like lightning streaking a night sky. "You may not have missed me these past few weeks, but I have most certainly missed touching you, holding you. Later I intend to show you how much."

His mouth descended upon her parted lips, gently at first. But as the flame of passion engulfed him, his kiss deepened. Rozalyn would have gladly surrendered her last breath for a dozen more kisses like the one she was receiving. Wild feelings coursed her, cresting waves of sensation that curled all the way down to her toes. Instinctively, her body moved closer to the hard, muscular warmth of him as his questing tongue probed, his lips devoured, and his sinewy arms enfolded her, crushing her to him as if he never meant to let her go.

When Bear-Claw loudly cleared his throat to gain their attention, Hawk reluctantly stepped away, and stared silently at Rozalyn, a promise in his eyes. Without a word, he turned and walked away, leaving her to brace herself against the door casing.

When the two men disappeared from sight and the wind began to whistle around the cabin, Rozalyn stepped back inside. Sighing heavily, she stood at the window and stared pensively into the distance, seeing nothing but a pair of sparkling emerald eyes and a rakish grin.

"It is as always, *mon ami*," she whispered ruefully. "You are always so close, and yet so very far away."

A distraction, Rozalyn told herself. I must find something to preoccupy me until Hawk returns. Deciding to cook one of Bear-Claw's recipes to impress Hawk, Rozalyn rummaged through the supplies in search of the necessary ingredients. Once she had built a blazing fire in the hearth, she poured the batter into the pan that dangled above the flames.

The creak of the door made her turn, smiling a greeting. "My, but the two of you are back sooner than I—"

Fear streaked through her when unwelcome intruders burst into the cabin, but a callused hand muffled what would have been a cry of alarm. Rozalyn fought wildly to escape as her captors' unrelenting arms dragged her into the cold.

Chapter 20

Huge snowflakes flitted down from the gray sky, leaving the mountain meadow dusted with a light blanket of peaceful white. Hawk's eyes lifted to study the intricate crystals as they drifted gracefully about him. This was the first snowfall of winter. Soon, the world would be cloaked in white. He found himself whimsically wishing for a heavy blizzard that would keep him and Rozalyn confined to the cabin for days on end. He could envision the two of them cuddled together beneath the fur quilts, staring into the flames leaping in the hearth, and making wild, sweet love while the wind and snow wailed outside their door.

"Daydreaming again?" Bear-Claw snickered, and pausing to prop himself on his rifle, the elder mountain man surveyed his restless companion with a mocking grin. "You are itching to get back to the cabin, aren't you, Hawk? What visions are dancing in your head, or dare I ask?"

Hawk's emerald gaze strayed south, past the thick clump of aspens and pines that stood between them and the cabin. "My visions have nothing to do with hunting," he admitted absently.

"I wondered how long you could endure the separation." When an antelope appeared in the clearing ahead of them, Bear-Claw brought his rifle to his shoulder to take aim. "One last shot," he promised. "If I don't fell my prey, I won't pursue it."

The crack of the rifle splintered the frosty air and the unsuspecting animal dropped where it stood. A proud smile pursed Bear-Claw's lips as he glanced over at Hawk. Half-heartedly, Hawk returned the grin and then followed the old man as he claimed his game.

Bear-Claw was content to live out his life in this majestic and treacherous terrain. The old mountain man lived off the land, taking only what was necessary to survive. He had no inclination to venture back to civilization, even occasionally. Hawk had shared Bear-Claw's attitude until Rozalyn had happened along. Now he wondered if he could ever go back to long, lonely months of isolation. Rozalyn's presence would linger within the confines of his cabin and upon the snow-crested slopes for years to come, he predicted dismally. With each passing day he was more convinced it had been a disastrous mistake to bring her into his world. She had touched too many emotions and had become an integral part of his environment. Routing her from his thoughts would be more difficult than tearing off an arm.

Hawk impatiently waited for Bear-Claw to skin the carcass, but since the hermit was taking more time than he could bear, he gave him a helping hand, then all but trotted through the thicket with the carcass slung around his broad shoulders. Bear-Claw chuckled in amusement for it was obvious what Hawk had on his mind. If he could sprout wings, he would fly to the cabin, Bear-Claw decided. He had dragged Hawk into the forest out of pure orneriness, just to test the young stag's patience, but Hawk was short on patience. His thoughts were not on a homecoming feast. Indeed, the man would gladly skip supper if he could have his raven-haired nymph for dessert.

The wry smile Bear-Claw was sporting evaporated when they dismounted from their horses and stared up the hill at the cabin. Something was amiss, he could sense it. And Hawk could, too. Bear-Claw could tell by the look on the younger man's face that he anticipated trouble.

Smoke rolled from the partially opened door, causing Hawk to curse himself for leaving Rozalyn alone. Dropping the fresh carcass, he dashed toward the cabin, shouting her name.

Breathlessly, Bear-Claw leaped onto the stoop and then grimaced when Hawk's furious bellow shook the log walls of the cabin. He stepped inside to see Hawk clutching the arrow that had been left as a reminder of another time and place.

"Blackfoot?" Bear-Claw asked in disbelief. "What were they doing here? They rarely come to the high country."

"It was Half-Head and his marauding savage," Hawk gritted out between clenched teeth. His smoldering green eyes focused on Bear-Claw's concerned face. "If he harms a hair on her head, I swear I'll show him a torture he'll wish he never knew existed."

"How could that murderous brute know you were keeping a woman?" Bear-Claw mused aloud.

"DuBois hired him to dispose of me and retrieve Rozalyn," Hawk explained, grasping the smoking pan of johnnycakes and removing them from the fire. Snatching up his pistol, a rifle, and a hatchet, Hawk stalked back outside, his keen gaze circling the area. "I knew he would come, but like a fool, I left Rozalyn unattended."

"Aubrey DuBois sent that miserable excuse for a man to fetch his daughter?" Bear-Claw snorted in disbelief. "My God, does he care nothing for the girl?"

"Very little it seems." Hawk swung into the saddle, then peered somberly at Bear-Claw. "DuBois is more concerned with disposing of me than seeing Roz safely returned. I swear he is a madman, poisoned with bitterness and vengeance."

"It would seem so," Bear-Claw muttered disdainfully. "Had I known he would have so little concern for the girl I would have snatched her from him myself."

Hawk did not bother to comment. He gouged his stallion, sending the beast thundering off in the direction he assumed Half-Head had taken if he was heading to the Blackfoot winter camp in the western valley of the Wind River Range. All his thoughts were on Rozalyn, and the dreadful picture that leaped into his mind made Hawk's blood turn to ice. He pictured Half-Head's ruthless smile, and he could not help but wonder if the lustful barbarian had ravished Rozalyn before kidnapping her. Damn the bastard to hell, Hawk swore under his breath.

"Where are you taking me?" Rozalyn demanded to know.

A satanic smile, the kind Hawk had envisioned, stretched across Half-Head's thin lips. "To the Blackfoot camp," he informed her. "Yer lover won't dare show his face there, not unless he wants to risk having his scalp lifted. The Blackfoot don't get along with anybody, except me."

Ignoring the hideous man's leering smile, Rozalyn tilted her chin courageously. "I will double whatever price my father paid you if you will let me go," she bargained.

"It ain't enough," Half-Head scoffed, his dark eyes raking Roz with blatant hunger. "I got unfinished business with Hawk . . . and you. You owe me somethin' for takin' a shot at me, woman, and you'll pay dearly when I git you to camp. I'll teach you to be my obedient squaw."

326

Rozalyn inwardly cringed at the venom in his voice, and she wished her hands were free so she could claw the disgusting leer off Half-Head's ugly face. It was a pity the brute did not wear a full beard to disguise his bland, course features, but Bear-Claw had informed Rozalyn that no Indian tribe would have anything to do with white men who wore mustaches and beards. The Indians detested facial hair, and they wanted no association with trappers who camouflaged their faces with thick beards.

"If you think Hawk will fall for whatever trap you intend to set for him, you are a bigger fool than I thought," Rozalyn taunted, deliberately setting aside her wandering thoughts. "You cannot win against him, even if you surround yourself with Blackfoot warriors. Hawk will come, and you will lose the rest of your scalp."

Half-Head's hand slammed against her cheek, and the blow made her reel. If she had not been tied to the saddle she knew she would have toppled from her perch. Flinging the abusive Half-Head a mutinous glare, Roz licked her swollen lip, tasting her own blood and spitefully wishing to slash that brute's hide to see if a man with a heart carved from solid rock could bleed.

"You will soon learn that I am more of a man than Hawk," Half-Head hissed menacingly. "When I take you, you will have no thought of another man. I promise you that!"

Rozalyn had the sinking feeling the vicious brute was right. Her thoughts would be brimming with hatred for him so she would be unable to think of anything else. Deciding it best not to provoke Half-Head further, she held her tongue, however. Soon, he would receive his just reward. When Half-Head had demanded to know what had become of Hawk, Roz had informed her captor that he had gone to trap more beaver. Let the bastard think Hawk would be several days behind him, and that he would come alone to avenge her abduction. When

Hawk sprang upon them, Half-Head would be taken unaware.

Discreetly, her gaze shifted from Half-Head to the arrogant Blackfoot warrior who rode beside her. The Indian appeared just as unapproachable as the ruttish white man. It would do little good to attempt to sway the brave, she decided. The man could not possess an ounce of decency or sense if he had befriended this half-scalped fiend.

Twice Rozalyn managed to slow their pace through the mountain passes by nudging her steed and galloping off in the wrong direction. Half-Head had been forced to retrieve her. Each delay had cost Rozalyn several painful slaps, but she endured Half-Head's manhandling silently, knowing that assistance would come and the abusive brute would pay.

When Half-Head led them down a narrow ravine, Rozalyn glanced up to see Hawk crouched on the bluff above them. Her heart thudded furiously when Hawk's eyes focused on hers momentarily. She could see the rage stamped on his rugged features, feel the tension radiating from his powerful body. He reminded her of a fierce mountain lion poised to pounce, his face twisted as if he were about to snarl.

A low, threatening growl that rivaled a panther's for ferocity actually did echo through the ravine. Half-Head swore under his breath when he glanced up to see his enemy springing at him, he glared angrily at Rozalyn, silently accusing her of lying to him. But before Half-Head could snatch his pistol from his belt, Hawk was upon him, knocking him from the saddle and into the snow. When the Blackfoot brave grasped his dagger and started to hurl it into Hawk's back, Bear-Claw appeared on the cliff. The warrior's arm halted in midair when he heard the click of a hammer, and he peered up to see the long-barreled rifle aimed at his chest.

"I wouldn't do that if I were you,"Bear-Claw advised. The expression on his weathered face assured the warrior that Bear-Claw would enjoy putting a bullet through him.

Rozalyn watched in anguish as the two men tumbled over the jagged rocks. When Half-Head's fist connected with Hawk's midsection, she squeezed her eyes shut. But she quickly opened them and saw, to her relief, that Hawk had answered the powerful blow and that Half-Head was staggering backward. Sneering at his foe, Half-Head leaped on Hawk, and again the two men rolled across the broken boulders. Even the blanket of snow did not soften their fall and Rozalyn grimaced imagining how painful it must be to tumble over the sharp-edged rocks. The one who managed to walk away from the battle would undoubtedly be marred by cuts and bruises.

Each combatant strained to prevail, but it seemed they had come to a stalemate, neither able to gain an advantage. Adrenalin spurted through both men, giving their powerful bodies superhuman strength. Hawk was as determined to seek revenge as Half-Head was, and nothing short of a rockslide could interrupt their fierce battle. Suddenly, Hawk crouched, yanking Half-Head off balance, and hurling him into a forward somersault. Then, like a striking snake, he pounced on his dazed victim, using his muscular legs to inflict a painful blow to Half-Head's groin. When the hideous brute fell back to his knees, hugging himself and growling in agonized fury, Hawk's heel caught him in the chin, snapping his bowed head backward.

Rozalyn breathed a thankful sigh, certain the brawl was over. But to her dismay, Half-Head snatched up his knife, and, a vicious sneer curling his lips, he vaulted to his feet, jabbing the razor-sharp blade at his mortal enemy. Hawk dodged the assault and clutched his own knife, prepared to match blade with blade. Then both men circled, like two warring beasts about to enter into another phase of battle. They retreated and advanced, each waiting to catch the other off guard. For what seemed a breathless eternity they measured each other with calculating gazes, striking, recoiling, and then lunging again. Half-Head finally made the fatal mistake of overextending himself in an attack. After agilely side-stepping the assault, Hawk wheeled around and buried his dagger in his enemy's heaving chest.

When Half-Head let loose with a furious growl, Rozalyn turned her head, sickened by the bloody sight. She expected Hawk to further humiliate his fallen foe by relieving Half-Head of what was left of his scalp, but to her relief, Hawk strode toward her. When he noticed the discolorations on her face, he snarled vindictively and pivoted back toward Half-Head, vowing to finish what he had begun three years earlier.

"No more, please . . ." Rozalyn choked out.

Her words were muffled by the sound of the Blackfoot brave's horse thundering through the ravine. Hawk spun around to watch the warrior's retreat, then he glared at Bear-Claw.

"Why did you allow him to escape?" he muttered.

"Why do you think I brought you with me, if not to even the odds. You are losing your touch, old man. There was a time when no one could have escaped you if it was not your want."

A sheepish smile spread across Bear-Claw's lips as he stared down at his disgruntled companion. "I was so distressed about Rozalyn being abducted from the cabin that I forgot to reload my rifle after I shot the antelope. If that Blackfoot had called my bluff you would have been in a helluva lot of trouble."

"My thanks for at least looking convincing," Hawk snorted gruffly. But his expression became tender when he looked at Rozalyn's bruised face. "Did he . . . ?" Hawk couldn't bring himself to ask the question that haunted him. He wasn't sure he could bear hearing the grizzly details of her captivity.

"Shouldn't we be getting back to the cabin?" Bear-Claw interjected, noticing the strained silence between Hawk and his woman. "I'll fetch our horses while you tend to the lady."

Hawk hurriedly untied Rozalyn's hands and feet before swinging up behind her in the saddle. The feel of his hard body stirred a myriad of warm memories in her, and Rozalyn slumped back against Hawk, content to be safe in the circle of his arms. There was no place she would rather be.

"Remind me to express my gratitude for the rescue when we have returned to the cabin." She sighed contentedly. "Half-Head promised to compensate me for insulting him once we reached the Blackfoot camp. I am eternally thankful I was not forced to endure more than his beating. . . ." Her voice trailed off and she shuddered involuntarily when her gaze drifted to the fallen brute. Rozalyn didn't want to imagine how repulsive Half-Head's treatment of her would have been. She could think of no greater torture than being forced to surrender to him.

Hawk sagged in relief, and then he drew Rozalyn even closer against him. He would have been unable to forgive himself if this enchanting minx had suffered Half-Head's degrading assault. Rozalyn belonged to him, and the fact that Half-Head had struck her infuriated him. If Rozalyn had not protested, Hawk would have derived satisfaction from sending Half-Head to his maker with not one strand of hair on his head.

However, he deliberately cast aside his vengeful thoughts. Rozalyn already thought him to be half-savage. He need not confirm her low opinion by allowing her to witness him lifting a scalp from a fallen enemy. Still, it seemed unjust not to repay Half-Head for all the scalps he

331

had taken during his miserable, murdering life.

The feel of Rozalyn's womanly body brought Hawk's thoughts back to the present. She was safe. That was the important thing. The devil could deal with Half-Head.

"I am anticipating your display of gratitude, *chèrie amie*," he murmured, nuzzling the trim column of her neck and inhaling the delicious scent of her.

A tingle of delight ricocheted through Rozalyn. She could imagine the two of them nestled together beneath the quilts, sharing. . . . But her spirits sank when she remembered that she and Hawk would not be alone in the cabin. Bear-Claw could not set out for his own shack late at night, especially with a blizzard impending. Despair closed in on Rozalyn as they journeyed through the snowy passes. Going home might have been . . .

Home? Rozalyn frowned. She no longer had a home. She was a vagabond. She did not truly belong in these rugged mountains, nor could she ever again be content in St. Louis. What would become of her once Hawk delivered her to her father? Rozalyn didn't want to ponder that depressing question. She and Hawk would go their separate ways soon enough. But for a lifetime she would remember how it had been between them. She would never forget this awesome mountain man with coal black hair and eyes of emerald green. Together, they had fought their way cross-country, but, oh, the pleasures they had discovered when they'd made love. . . .

Chapter 21

An apologetic smile hovered on Bear-Claw's lips when he glanced at Rozalyn. "Sorry about your johnnycakes. We didn't return in time to rescue them."

Her shoulder lifted in a careless shrug. "It is no matter. I'm sure they wouldn't have been as tasty as yours," she murmured absently.

While Hawk and Bear-Claw set to work preparing the carcass for roasting, Rozalyn stirred up another batch with a less than enthusiastic effort. Each time she paced in front of the window, her gaze locked with Hawk's. She could see the impatient hunger in his emerald eyes, feel the intense heat that radiated from them. But Bear-Claw remained an obstacle to privacy.

When the evening had lengthened, Hawk was prowling about the cabin like a caged predator, Rozalyn was wringing her hands, and Bear-Claw was beaming like a weasel who has feasted on a plump chicken. He was greatly amused by the young mountain man's discomfort.

"I suppose we should retire," Bear-Claw finally announced, stifling a yawn. "It has been a full, rich day. Hawk?" His gaze lifted to the loft above Rozalyn's cot, his ornery grin intact. "Shall we allow the lady privacy while she prepares for bed?"

333

Hawk would have preferred that Bear-Claw grant him and Rozalyn privacy, but he knew the old man wasn't about to budge from the cabin. His gaze settled on Rozalyn for a moment before he reluctantly followed Bear-Claw to the ladder that led to the loft.

He hadn't intended to snuggle up to Bear-Claw's broad back that night! In fact, the very thought of spending his sleeping hours in a crowded loft with that ornery mountain goat turned Hawk's disposition as sour as a lemon. Grumbling a good night to Rozalyn, Hawk peeled off his shirt and eased beneath the quilts, only to hear Bear-Claw cackling like a nesting hen.

"Quiet, old man," Hawk grumbled, nudging Bear-Claw farther away. "And don't press your luck. You know I am not at all pleased with the sleeping arrangements. Be advised that the slightest badgering from you could provoke me into shuffling you out of your cozy nest to share the shed with the horses."

Bear-Claw was not intimidated by the threat. With a forceful tug he pulled on his share of the fur quilt, leaving the right side of Hawk's tense body bare. "Ungrateful oaf," he snorted, burrowing deeper into the cozy warmth of the bed. "But for me, you would have been a dead man this afternoon. That Blackfoot had every intention of burying his hatchet in your back."

"You were a lot of help," Hawk sniffed, his voice dripping with sarcasm. "What kind of fool ventures into battle with an unloaded rifle? I'm beginning to wonder if my purpose would have been better served if you had taken my enemy's side."

"Go to sleep," Bear-Claw ordered gruffly, giving the quilt another tug when Hawk threatened to pull it away. "You are only pouting because you have to sleep above rather than below. The sooner you learn to keep your hands off that woman the better. You know there can be no future for the two of you. Do you think to send her home with your child to further infuriate her father?"

That possibility stripped Hawk of argument. He had been thinking only of his insatiable craving for his blue-eyed enchantress. Now he wondered if they had already created a child? He didn't want to consider the repercussions. He just wanted Rozalyn in his arms, responding ardently to his kisses and caresses. Dammit, what had happened to the simple life he had known, the good, free life in which he had had to answer to no one but himself?

Grappling with these distressing thoughts, Hawk flounced about, seeking a more comfortable position. But he was unable to find one becuase he was too aware of the shapely nymph who lay abed below. The hours crept by at a snail's pace, and although Hawk begged for sleep, it didn't come. He had dreamed of this night for three torturous weeks. Finally Hawk lost the battle of self-conquest. Carefully, he inched away from Bear-Claw and swung a leg over the loft, his bare foot groping for the rung of the ladder.

But he expelled the breath he had been holding when Bear-Claw propped himself up on an elbow, a mischievous grin on his weathered features. Even in the darkness Hawk could see the ornery mountain goat beaming at him.

"Just where do you think you're going in the middle of the night?"

"As if the varmint doesn't know," Hawk muttered under his breath.

Bear-Claw patted the empty space beside him. "Settle yourself in your nest, Hawk. You aren't going to lay a hand on that girl, not while I'm sleeping under the same roof."

"That can quickly be remedied," Hawk growled spitefully. "The way you're behaving, one would think you were her father." Begrudgingly, he plopped down on the spot he had just vacated.

Refusing to respond to that comment, Bear-Claw flung the quilt over Hawk's puffed chest. "Go to sleep for Christ's sake. Think about something besides your lust for Roz. You are already in so deep, it's going to tear out your heart to let her go."

Mulling over Bear-Claw's remark, Hawk squeezed his eyes shut, and tried to clear his mind. But how does one think of nothing when one is aching to appease an obsessive craving that has preoccupied him for twenty-four days?

While Hawk battled the beast within him, Rozalyn lay on her back, staring at the loft above her. She had heard Hawk and Bear-Claw arguing, and she suspected that the old mountaineer would not tolerate their dallying in the darkness, right under his nose. And just why is that? she wondered. She knew Bear-Claw had become as fond of her as she had become of him. Was he playing the protective father? Unlikely, for Bear-Claw must have known she and Hawk had been intimate during the months they had spent together. How could any woman resist a man like Hawk? Rozalyn had only known him a day before she'd surrendered to him.

Heaving a heavy sigh, she shifted onto her side and willed her eyes to close. Perhaps it was best that she and Hawk kept their distance, the quiet voice of reason said. What future could they have? They could share the winter, but when the summer came, they would be forced to part. Oh, what's the use? Rozalyn thought miserably. She hugged her pillow, knowing it was a pitiful substitute for what she craved. But it was all she had, all she would ever have when Hawk traded her back to her father.

To Rozalyn's dismay, when she woke the wind was whispering down the gullies and a gloomy gray sky was spitting snow. Within an hour the wind was whistling and then it was screaming as it swept across the towering precipices. Bear-Claw turned away from the drafty window, announcing that he couldn't depart during a blizzard. Parking himself in a chair and whittling on a twig, he waited for Rozalyn to prepare their breakfast.

The mere thought that Bear-Claw could be an uninvited guest for many days soured Hawk's testy disposition. Like a pouting child who has not been granted his way, Hawk paced the confines of the cabin, praying the inclement weather would ease before the day was out. Reluctantly, he plopped onto the chair across from Bear-Claw and glared at the intruder.

Ignoring Hawk's blatantly hostile stare Bear-Claw eased back onto his seat. "Did I ever tell you about the time I happened onto glass mountain?"

Hawk rolled his bloodshot eyes, evidence that he had not slept a wink, and chugged his coffee. "At least a dozen times," he grumbled grouchily. "And every time you spin that yarn it becomes more unbelievable."

"But Rozalyn hasn't heard it," Bear-Claw parried, undaunted by Hawk's gruff attempt to silence him. "I was out hunting one spring when I spotted a magnificent antelope grazing in the distance. I crept closer to take careful aim and when I fired, the animal never moved. I knew I couldn't have missed at that range, but neither could I explain why I hadn't wounded my game." After taking a small sip of coffee, Bear-Claw continued with his tall tale. "When I moved closer, the antelope showed no sign of catching my scent. He continued to graze as if he were alone in the meadow. I knelt to steady myself and then fired again. But again nothing happened. It was the strangest thing I'd ever seen. By then I was getting frustrated. I checked my rifle to be sure it wasn't misfiring, but there was nothing wrong with it. After my fourth shot with the same baffling results I was getting

337

mad as hell. Had I been drinking I would have sworn I was imagining things, but I was stone sober."

Rozalyn paused from her chore to cast a bemused glance at Bear-Claw. She had heard dozens of the old man's fantastic stories, but this one was the most outrageous of all. "And how did you solve such a dilemma?" she asked. "Was the antelope a mirage?"

Bear-Claw gave his shaggy head a negative shake. "It was no mirage and I wasn't hallucinating. Since I was determined to solve the mystery I grabbed the butt of my rifle and stalked toward my prey, planning to club him over the head, if need be. But lo and behold, I crashed right into an invisible wall. After investigating, I found it to be a transparent mountain that had the effect of a telescope. Why, that antelope was miles away! It was no wonder my rifle didn't faze him."

"Miles," Hawk crowed in disbelief. "The last time I heard that tale it was three shots and half a mile."

"Are you saying I'm exaggerating?" Bear-Claw challenged, proudly drawing himself up in his chair.

"That is exactly what I'm saying," Hawk snorted as he propped his elbows on the table to glare at the old mountain man.

Before the two men came to blows over the authenticity of the far-fetched tale, Rozalyn shoved their plates beneath their noses.

"At least this won't be difficult to swallow." Hawk sniffed sarcastically.

"I don't take kindly to your calling me a liar," Bear-Claw grumbled, taking fork in hand.

"More coffee?" Rozalyn interjected, laying her hand on Bear-Claw's shoulder to soothe him before he rose to Hawk's taunt.

The older mountain man retracted his claws and lifted his empty cup. "Please." His twinkling eyes settled on the comely beauty who hovered beside him. "Sit down, lass. I think I've neglected to tell you about the time I was attacked by a pack of hungry wolves up in the Yellowstone. I thought I had seen my last sunrise when . . ."

Hawk inwardly groaned as Bear-Claw began to weave another wild tale. He was afraid he and Rozalyn would not enjoy a moment's peace until spring thaw. Bear-Claw would undoubtedly be stranded with them for the duration of the winter. If so, he knew he would become stark raving mad.

And so it went for three endless days while the ferocious winter storm raged outside the mountain cabin. Hawk became like a man walking on needles and pins. His self-restraint had been jabbed and pricked until it resembled a sieve. He would have given most anything to have the meddling mountain man out from underfoot. And Rozalyn fared no better than Hawk. The days and nights of being so close and yet so far away made her tense and edgy. Each time she brushed past Hawk, caught his male scent and felt the hard warmth of his body tormentingly close to hers, she wanted to scream out her frustration, to run into Hawk's arms and end the agony of wanting.

But while Hawk and Rozalyn prayed for the storm to cease, Bear-Claw was grinning in wicked satisfaction. Hawk was now certain the old coot intended to plant himself in the cabin for the winter; he did not believe Bear-Claw would return to the isolation of his own shack. The hermit had become a permanent fixture in Hawk's cabin and had seemingly relinquished his claim that a man could enjoy living alone in the mountains.

Finally, after an entire week had passed, Bear-Claw announced that he needed to return to his cabin. Rozalyn was elated, and she muffled a chuckle as she watched Hawk practically drag Bear-Claw toward the door and into the snowdrift that rose in front of the shack. When the mountain man wormed away and reversed direction to say adieu to Rozalyn, Hawk's mood turned pitch black once again.

Ignoring the annoyed growl behind him, Bear-Claw focused his full attention on Rozalyn's lovely face. Suddenly his own expression became woebegone. "My cabin isn't going to be the same anymore. I had almost forgotten the pleasure of companionship . . . and the beauty of women. You are particularly beautiful." His index finger sketched the delicate line of her jaw and the creamy curve of her cheek before he bent to brush a light kiss to her brow. "Take care of yourself, flatlander. Meeting you has brought a certain warmth back into my heart. I wouldn't want anything to happen to you."

Rozalyn nodded mutely, allowing a smile to graze her lips. Then she moved toward Bear-Claw to return his farewell embrace. "You are a true friend. I am indebted to you for taking me under your wing and teaching me the ways of the mountains. Hawk and I will anticipate your return visit."

"As long as you wait a month . . . or even two," Hawk grumbled, half-aloud.

Paying no heed to Hawk's sarcastic rejoinder, Bear-Claw gave Rozalyn a loving squeeze. "You are going to be a difficult woman to forget. . . ." He sighed and then reluctantly withdrew to pivot away. "Come. Help me saddle my horse, Hawk. No doubt the critter is no more anxious to make this journey than I."

Hawk was only too happy to accommodate his old friend if it would accelerate his departure. When he threw the saddle on the steed's back and tightened the girth, he glanced back over his shoulder to find Bear-Claw staring somberly at him.

"You have been more than a month without Roz, and now you have been living with her only as a friend." Bear-Claw's voice was low and deliberate; his narrowed eyes drilled into the younger man's. "It is best for all involved if you continue on this straight and narrow course for the remainder of the winter."

Hawk rose to his full stature, and he gazed at the rustic cabin from which a thin curl of smoke drifted to mingle with the gray clouds that hung so close to the mountain peaks. "I don't think I can," he breathed defeatedly. "The sight of her leaves me with a craving that I fear nothing can appease."

"And if you don't restrain yourself you will live to regret it . . . if you're lucky." Bear-Claw's hand folded over Hawk's slumped shoulder, demanding his undivided attention. "I myself am living proof of what torture forbidden love can wreak. Why do you think I have lived like a hermit? Because I've spent the past few decades trying not to remember what I cannot seem to forget." His rueful gaze swung to the cabin on the hill, and a remorseful smile quivered on his parched lips. "I know what you are feeling for that girl, Hawk. I have been there. I didn't want to fall in love either. God, I fought it with every part of my being. But the longer I stayed with her, the more impossible it became to exercise self-restraint. I knew she wasn't mine to keep, should not have been mine, but we were young and reckless then. We thought love could conquer all."

Bear-Claw laughed bitterly as memories cut into his soul so sharply his bittersweet love affair might have happened only yesterday. Pulling himself into the saddle, he then stared long and hard at his young friend. "I have told you the reason Aubrey cannot forget his past, why he loathes the name of Beaudelair, and of my own connection to this complicated affair. If you are wise, you will profit by the mistakes of others. You can see what torment I have been forced to endure. I exist in a solitary fashion, make very little contact with civilization, and avoid all that might remind me of the past.

Whatever choice you make, you must be prepared to live with it, Hawk. You know inevitably the snow thaws and summer blossoms in these mountains. A foolish man blunders blindly ahead without preparing himself for the moment of impending doom. But it will come to you, just as it did to me. If you do not choose to deny yourself, then you damned well better make plans to deal with the pain that will most surely follow. You will spend the rest of your days wondering how you can live with memories that will most surely follow you to your grave if you fall in love with a woman you cannot have."

Bear-Claw's probing gaze and pointed words stabbed Hawk like a knife. He knew the old mountain man spoke from experience, but even as he listened to Bear-Claw's depressing sermon, he kept picturing a devastatingly attractive sprite with hair as dark as midnight and eyes that burned with a blue flame. Could he honestly get through winter wanting her as he did? Rozalyn made him feel every inch a man when he lay in her arms, and the mere thought of the passionate hours they'd spent set off uncontrollable sensations.

Somber green eyes fastened on the weather-beaten face above him. "Were the days and nights you spent with your woman worth the pain, the years of aching loneliness?" Hawk asked point-blank. "Could you have denied yourself the love you felt for her? Wasn't it worth the price you paid? If you had not surrendered to love, wouldn't you have spent the rest of your life wondering how it *might* have been if you had dared to follow your heart? Can you truthfully say that love, brief though it might have been, was not better than decades of emptiness?"

After peering down into Hawk's sincere gaze, Bear-Claw stared back through the window of time, past the bitter years of regret to that sweet, perfect time, that surpassed anything he had known since. For a long, pensive moment he was lost to blissful memories of an oval face that radiated with an angelic smile. He well knew why Hawk was having such difficulty keeping his distance from that blue-eyed beauty. Indeed, some things in this world were impossible to resist, no matter what the consequences.

"Even now, after all these years, I would be a liar if I said I could have walked away from her when her eyes bid me to stay," Bear-Claw confessed with a melancholy smile. Then he focused a concerned stare on Hawk. "But can you blame me for not wanting to see you and Rozalyn hurt when I know how it feels to suffer?"

"Can you blame me for wanting to share the winter with her, even when I know it is all I can ever have?" Hawk countered, his eyes misting with an emotion Bear-Claw had never before seen in them. "I have never wanted anything in life as much as I want her. I left her with you for three weeks, trying to forget, to convince myself that our separation was for the best. But the ever-present thought of her was the cause of and the cure for my torment. I tried to leave her with you for the winter, but my footsteps led me back to this cabin."

"It is that bad, is it?" Bear-Claw managed a soft chuckle.

"It is that bad," Hawk confessed, his eyes already drawn to the cabin and to the bewitching enchantress who awaited him.

"Then it seems you have made your choice and there is naught else to do but to learn to live with your decision. I pray you will have an easier time burying your memories, but I fear doing so will be more difficult than you can imagine." Bear-Claw reined his steed around and aimed himself toward his home. "I wish you and Roz happiness that will last a lifetime, even if it must be found in one season in the mountains."

As Bear-Claw blazed path through the drifted snow,

Hawk watched him depart, then, heaving a sigh, he wheeled toward the cabin. The mountain man's parting words dogged him at each footstep. He wanted Rozalyn with every fiber of his being, yet he knew she would be taken from him. Aubrey would never permit Hawk to keep what he had come to crave. Knowing that, Hawk realized he should keep his distance, but not touching Rozalyn would be torture. God! Why had he carted her off with him in the first place?

Chapter 22

When Hawk pushed open the front door, his mental tug of war evaporated in the golden firelight, for before the hearth lay a vision so tempting it stole his breath away. Bare, silky arms protruded from luxurious fur quilts, and long tendrils of raven hair spilled over them. Rozalyn's welcoming smile melted his heart and it was all Hawk could do to keep from tearing off his bulky coat and dashing into her arms.

She awaited his return, no longer able to deny her need for the man who had taught her soul to sing. Pride be damned, she had told herself while she'd spread the tempting pallet before the fire. She wanted Hawk and she was tired of keeping a tight rein on her emotions. It no longer mattered that she would lose him when summer came. She could think only of the present and of their sweet memories. Even if they had no future, she wanted to enjoy this winter and the rapture she would find in his arms. Now was enough.

It had to be enough, she reminded herself.

Slowly, she drew away the fur quilt, revealing her bare flesh to Hawk's all-consuming gaze. Then she rose from the inviting pallet before the hearth and moved toward him, her eyes locking with his. Her heart was in her hands, and her love glistened in the sapphire pools fixed on his flaming green eyes.

"I have been waiting for you," she murmured as she unfastened his coat and eased it away from his broad shoulders. His buckskin shirt soon lay atop the discarded jacket, as did his breeches. Then her hands wandered over the expanse of his chest, and she felt his heart stampeding against her palm. When she lifted her gaze to study his craggy features, she saw a need in his eyes that matched her own mindless craving. "I have missed you . . . truly." Her fingertips tunneled into his crisp raven hair and curled about his neck to bring his head down to hers. "Make love to me, Hawk. I need you so. . . ."

When her sensuous lips parted invitingly, Hawk died a thousand times before his eager mouth found hers. He was like a man who'd been stranded in a blizzard without food or drink, a man who had a maddening craving for nourishment. He tasted her, savored her fervent response. Then his arms enfolded her, molding her slender body to his hard contours, as he released the pent-up passion that had tormented him for more than four weeks.

"God, woman, I thought I would die of wanting you," he whispered raggedly. His warm breath skimmed her cheek, while his hands rediscovered every inch of her. Hawk was trembling, so eager was he to lose himself in her sweet fragrance and her tantalizing body.

A provocative smile bordered Rozalyn's lips, and taking his hand, she backed away, leading him toward the fire. "Come, my handsome adventurer, show me how much you missed me. In turn, I will show you how very much I have longed for your company."

While Hawk obediently followed behind her, his eyes devouring her, he asked himself if this was the same feisty beauty he had met in St. Louis. Rozalyn had mellowed. Her spirit was still evident, that fascinating zest for life, but she was different somehow. Her stubborn refusal to admit there was something magic between them was gone. Now she confessed her need for their passionate lovemaking. Could it be that she finally realized . . .

All thought deserted Hawk when Rozalyn stretched before the hearth like a contented feline basking in the heat of the sun, and his body went rigid with an indescribable hunger. Like a powerful grizzly dropping down on all fours, he crouched beside her. His hands mapped the satiny curves of her hips, then glided over the taut peaks of her breasts. He groaned as his lips whispered across her quivering flesh, caressing, worshipping the feel of her. Ah, touching her was heaven.

Rozalyn felt that she was melting into the luxurious furs when he caressed her so tenderly, as if he were cherishing this moment. She did not wonder at his feelings. She just wanted him, yearned to become his possession. His hands and lips were weaving a spell that was filling her with ineffable pleasure, preparing her for the ecstatic moments to come. Her body arched toward his as she reveled in the rapture of his touch, sighing softly as streams of sweet agony spilled over her.

While he pleasured her, Rozalyn's fingertips splayed over his shoulders and the muscular terrain of his back. Then her adventurous hands tracked along his hips in a whisper of a touch that made Hawk's powerful body thaw like melting snow. When she came upon her knees to take possession of his lips, Hawk moaned beneath her fiery kiss. She had set his world ablaze and flames were spreading through him, engulfing every part of his being. Hands as gentle as a summer breeze feathered across his hair-roughened flesh, leaving not one inch of his body untouched by her tender caresses. Her moist lips trickled over his shoulders and her inquiring hands never remained still for a moment. They tempted and taunted, receding and then drawing him closer . . . and closer still.

Hawk could no longer deny the fire burning in him. His breath came in ragged spurts; his heart beat in frantic rhythm. When Rozalyn lay against him and slid her leg intimately between his thighs, a groan of tormented pleasure burst from his lips. This brazen temptress had used her wiles to seduce him and he now ached to ease the craving she had aroused. Like a lithe jungle cat, he eased back onto the fur pallet, drawing Rozalyn down beside him. His breath caught in his throat when a waterfall of glowing ebony tumbled across the plush quilt, to be highlighted by the dancing flames in the hearth. Hawk marveled at the soft texture of her skin in the glistening light. And in the depths of her blue eyes he saw raw emotion which held him spellbound. The moment was like something out of a dream, the same dream that had visited him each night for four agonizing weeks. And now that his vision had come true, Hawk didn't care if he ever roused from this rapturous fantasy.

His arm glided about her trim waist, and as he twisted to settle himself upon her pliant body, his kisses rained upon her flushed cheek. "Take me to paradise, Roz. I can no longer endure the hell of wanting you. I need you. . . ."

His husky words vibrated on her skin before his firm mouth parted her lips to drink deeply of a kiss that bespoke undeniable hunger and impatient need. Rozalyn responded fully to his ardent embrace, loving him so completely that she held nothing back. Her sigh of longing was answered when his lean, masculine body blended into hers. As she felt the sweet urgency of his manhood, she marveled at the sensations that flooded over her when he was within her. Heaven was living and dying in his arms, giving and sharing passionate pleasure.

Hawk clutched her tightly to him, his need so overwhelming that he could not control his emotions, which erupted, spilling over him and threatening to strip him of his sanity. Then his body moved instinctively into hers setting a sensuous rhythm that deepened their intimacy, and his questing tongue probed the dark recesses of her mouth. Their breaths mingled while their bodies became one.

It seemed their universe was aflame, the heat of their union igniting their nerves and muscles, inflaming their very souls. Hawk was a living breathing part of a fire that blazed hotter than a thousand suns. He knew no flame burned brighter than this all-consuming blaze. What had once seemed inconceivable became reality. The long weeks of craving had been worthwhile. He had discovered the essence of life, a euphoric pleasure.

And then, the split second before he feared he would sacrifice his last breath to the pleasure he had found, his soul took flight, soaring wild and free, gliding on the uplifting currents that fed passion's flame. He knew the ecstasy that awaited him, but knowing what lay on the far side of reality did not prepare him for the indescribable sensations that claimed him, numbing him to all that had come before this rapturous moment. His body shuddered in response to the soul-shattering emotions that gripped him, and for a time the world stopped spinning. Hawk couldn't draw a breath or still the furious beat of his heart. He could only cling to Rozalyn, riding out the tumultuous waves that tumbled over him, disorienting him.

Rozalyn felt his lean fingers digging into her flesh, but his fierce grip did not pain her. She was lost to passion's sweet release. In the wake of desire's stormfire, she found ultimate fulfillment. It was like a gentle rain trickling down upon the dancing flames, making them ebb and then sizzle into smoldering coals.

The only sound that reached her ears was the crackling of the logs in the hearth. The only thing she saw was Hawk's ruggedly handsome face which hovered above her. Her eyes locked with his fathomless green pools, and in them Rozalyn saw her world.

The faintest hint of a smile settled on Hawk's features as his index finger trailed across her kiss-swollen lips. The confession on the tip of his tongue tumbled free before he could give it a thought. "I love you, Roz." He felt her relaxed body go rigid beneath his, and for a moment he regretted his words. "I have never said that to any other woman—except one. That was a lifetime ago when I met a young beauty with incredible spirit and an adventurous heart, but she didn't believe me when I spoke from my heart. She thought I was only using her, as if she meant nothing to me." His lips feathered across Rozalyn's, melting her tension. "What I felt for her then has blossomed into something far more engulfing than love, yet I know not what other name to attach to it."

Rozalyn was afraid to believe his hushed words. She had waited an eternity to hear them and now she feared she had only imagined them. Remembered pain came rushing back to fill her with doubt. She recalled how hurt she had been when Hawk had been bargaining with Aubrey. She had told herself over and over again that she could live with a one-sided love, that she would expect no more of Hawk than the passion he could give. Now his confession aroused conflicting emotions. She desperately wanted to believe him, but the voice of reason bade her to beware.

"You needn't speak of more than passion, Hawk. It is enough," she quietly assured him, battling for composure.

His hand curled beneath her chin, forcing her to meet his level gaze. "No, it isn't enough," he contradicted. "Not any more. Desire and passion cannot touch what I feel for you. Perhaps you do not return my deep affection, but I can no longer hide what I feel. It is tearing me to pieces to keep it bottled up inside me. I love you and I want to say it each time emotion overflows from my heart. Believe me, Roz. I make no false claim. I have no motive for voicing my affection other than to satisfy a need to do so."

Rozalyn stared up at him, and the naked emotion in his beguiling green eyes dissolved her fears. She lifted a hand and then traced the strong line of his jaw. "And I can no longer disguise what I have felt for you since the day we met. That first night . . . so long ago . . . I didn't want to believe love could truly be staring me in the face. But it was," she whispered. "I realized you were the man I had conjured up in my dreams, the faceless image that had finally emerged from the shadows. I couldn't get over loving you, even when I thought I had been betrayed. And I love you now, though I know my soul will wither and die when summer comes. But I accept whatever terms I am allowed. I want today and all the tomorrows that await me in your arms."

"Even when you know we can't have forever?" Hawk queried softly. "Can you still love me as if we had an eternity when you are well aware the time will come when we will be forced to say goodbye?"

Rozalyn nodded slightly, and a rueful smile pursed her lips. Lovingly she ran her fingers through his tousled hair. "I will do what I must to be granted what time we can have, but I won't stop loving you when summer comes. My father may take me away, but he cannot strip me of my memories. I will look back on this winter in the mountains and I will remember."

Hawk eased onto his side, turning Rozalyn so that her shapely body was molded familiarly to him, and entwining her fingers in his, he gazed into the dancing flames, watching them skip across the glowing logs. "Then we will make these months ours . . . until it's time for you to go," he promised huskily. "I prefer to love you, even though I know I will be forced to give you up. It is preferable to spending the winter fighting churning emotions. I have battled myself far too long as it is."

Rozalyn twisted to face him, looping her arms over his muscular shoulders. "We shall make the most of our time together. We have the winter and the spring. They will be the most beautiful of seasons, and in years to come, I will look back and remember the glorious time when the world was ours."

Her parted lips whispered over his, kindling a flame that could never burn itself out, and then she moved suggestively against him, sensitizing every part of his being. "Do you know the moment I first fell in love with you?"

Hawk laughed softly, striving to keep his mind on her words rather than the arousing way her hips arched to his. "No, minx. It's a wonder to me that I impressed you when the rest of your beaux met with defeat."

Rozalyn ignored his remark, and her hand absently trailed along the sinewed columns of his legs. She didn't want to think of men who had not stirred her to deep emotion. "It was when you dared to seduce me right under Grand'mère's nose."

"And I knew I would never forget the mischievous imp who offered me a kiss that carried a bit," he chortled. "I proclaimed you were the light and love of my life—and it was no lie I gave." A ragged sigh bubbled from his chest as he nuzzled against the silky flesh of her shoulder. "I do love you, Roz. I knew I had met my match. The torment of believing you hated me for betraying you was agony to bear."

His quiet words softened her, and she regretted the harsh, biting remarks she had made to soothe her injured pride. "Hawk? If I ask something of you, will you answer me honestly?" Rozalyn knew she had no right to request this of him but she was aching to know.

He leaned back to peer into her quizzical blue eyes. "What is it, *chère amie?*"

"When winter comes again . . . and I have gone away . . ." Roz tried to express her thoughts in a delicate manner so Hawk would not be annoyed by her prying question. "When you long for a woman . . ."

His tanned finger glided across her lips, quieting her and a tender smile grazed his lips. "This is our hideaway . . . yours and mine. The memories that linger here will remain always. Hear this and believe it, sweet nymph. This cabin will stand as a monument to the love we share. It will be all I have left. And no matter how far away you are, part of you will remain here with me."

Hawk hadn't said that another woman wouldn't satisfy his passions, but at least he had said their love mattered to him. He was a man who had been attracted to many women. She could not expect his fidelity in years to come, but the thought of another woman sleeping in his arms tore her heart in two.

"While you are flitting about St. Louis with a procession of men trailing after you, vying for your attention, will you allow—"

It was Rozalyn's turn to press her finger to his lips to silence his question. She realized it would be impossible to cling to an emotion that couldn't last forever or to make promises neither of them might not be able to keep in the years to come. "I was wrong to question you, to expect you to predict your future. Nor can I foretell mine. I suppose we must both do what we must to survive." Her voice trembled, and her eyes swam with tears. "But for now, love me for all the tomorrows we cannot share together."

Ever so gently, Hawk pressed her onto her back, his kisses and caresses silently communicating the pleasure he discovered when he touched her. His breath whispered over the satiny slope of her shoulder, his lips brushing the throbbing peaks of her breasts as his hands reverently mapped the soft planes of her body, coaxing, arousing, spreading an invisible coverlet of rapture over her skin. His tongue flicked; his lips possessed. His caresses weaved intricate patterns across her belly before his hands receded to circle each dusky peak. His skillful touch was like that of a harpist stroking the strings, making her body sing with exquisite pleasure.

It was sweet agony. Rozalyn knew she could never forget the green-eyed rogue with hair as black as midnight. How could she submit to another man after she'd enjoyed Hawk's lovemaking? Their love had had its own unique design, one that could never be duplicated. No, she could not love again when the very essence of her would remain locked in this secluded mountain cabin. That despairing thought made her impulsively clutch Hawk to her.

When he came to her, catching her cry of rapture in his mouth, taking her into space, Rozalyn surrendered her soul to him, and, momentarily, the tormenting thoughts that had crept from the shadows of her mind were forgotten. This was her reason for being, giving and sharing her love. Like a butterfly emerging from its cocoon, the love would have short life, but its flight was spectacular. On velvet wings it skimmed the earth and then gracefully drifted aloft on a current of wind, dipping, diving, sailing as if its flight would continue forever. . . .

And so it was to be, through the winter and the rebirth of spring. The harsh cold of the high mountains did not dampen the beauty of their ill-fated love, which grew more precious and meaningful with each passing month, spinning a silken bond that blocked out their grim future. This was their time for loving, and it was magnificent, like the sun sparkling on the blanket of snow that cloaked the majestic Mountains of the Wind.

Chapter 23

A muddled frown captured Hawk's brow when he stepped onto the stoop and saw Rozalyn lying in the snow, moving her arms and legs in exaggerated sweeping motions. "What the devil are you doing?" he asked, then laughed incredulously.

Rozalyn raised her head and grinned impishly. "I'm making angels in the snow," she informed him, then bounded to her feet to display her efforts. Gesturing about her, Rozalyn indicated several celestial imprints in the fluffy snow.

Hawk chuckled at her playfulness. It was one of the many things he adored about his free-spirited enchantress. Because of it, when she was with him, there was never a dull moment, and Rozalyn had seemed even more lively the past few months. Hawk basked in the warmth of her love; then, shaking his head at her silliness, he strode off the porch. But when he attempted to pull her into his arms, she fell backward to create another angel in the snow.

He frowned disappointedly as Rozalyn peered up at him with dancing blue eyes. "Don't you want to help me? Surely imprints of angels will ward off the evil spirits the Indians believe to be lurking in the mountains."

"I'm a grown man." Hawk sniffed distastefully. "I have better things to do than make childish snowprints."

"Oh?" One perfectly arched eyebrow lifted as she regarded his haughty stance. "Like what, for instance, *monsieur?*"

A grin of roguish anticipation spread across Hawk's chean-shaven face, and he strode closer, his dark shadow eventually falling over the playful nymph who was frolicking in the snow. "Things that separate boys from men. Why would I wish to make angels when I could be making love!" Rozalyn's light-hearted laughter rang through the crisp air as Hawk straddled her, pressing her deeper into the snow. "Mmmm . . . this is more to my liking," he growled seductively. Pinning her arms above her head, he nibbled at her frosty lips, making them melt beneath his. "These are the things a man does while boys are off playing. . . ."

Rozalyn squirmed beneath Hawk, her movements arousing him rather than discouraging him. "Where is your youthful spirit?" she taunted. "You will grow old before your time if you do not allow yourself the simple pleasures in life."

"My youthful spirit is here," Hawk murmured as he settled himself full length upon her. "She has been my companion these past few months, my constant source of amusement and pleasure."

"And you are squashing her flat," Rozalyn giggled. "Unhand me, sir. I came to frolick in the snow, not to be buried in it."

Reluctantly, Hawk pulled himself up on his knees, only to have Rozalyn vault to her feet. With a bubble of laughter, she gave him an abrupt shove that sent him sprawling and evoked a startled squawk. Her giddy laughter danced on the breeze as she bounded away, leaving Hawk staring up at the early morning sun. Rolling to his feet, he raced after her in fast pursuit, swearing to get even with her for her prank.

Rozalyn yelped when she found herself scooped from the ground and hurled into a tall drift, and before she could fight her way through the snow, Hawk lunged at her. The chill of being half-buried in snow evaporated when his body molded itself to hers. Her damp lashes fluttered up to view the boyish grin that cut deep lines into his swarthy features. Lord, how she loved him. They had laughed and loved away the winter in this secluded paradise, and just when she swore she couldn't fall any deeper in love with Hawk, he graced her with one of his charismatic smiles and she was even more lost to him. Suddenly realizing that within a few months, she'd never witness another of his radiant grins made her soul bleed.

The playfulness vanished from her features. This was to be their last day at the cabin. Hawk had announced that they were traveling to Fort Cass and then on to Yellowstone to trap beaver in the spring. A desperate urgency to recapture the pleasure they had shared overwhelmed Rozalyn, and her arms slid around his waist. Drawing him closer, she kissed him heatedly.

Hawk sensed her need, saw in her eyes a frantic hint of fear. "Don't look at me as if it were over, as if this dream were about to come to an end," he said huskily. "This wonderland is still ours, Roz. We have the spring. I will show you sights that exceed your wildest imagination and I will take you in my arms each night when darkness casts its mystical shadow on the mountains."

"Do you promise, Hawk?" Her eyes were wide, like those of a young child anticipating an adventure that will live forever in memory. "Will we have other gloriously loving moments?"

"Scores of them," he assured her before his mouth swooped down on hers, stealing her breath and chasing away her fears.

As Rozalyn responded to his fiery kiss, the familiar

weight of his sleek body forged into hers. The fire he kindled within her flared and sent her blood to simmering.

"When we camp for the night, remind me to finish were we left off," Hawk murmured, his voice heavy with passion. Reluctantly, he withdrew, suddenly finding the winter chill hadn't been so noticeable when he was wrapped in Rozalyn's arms. "Damned if you don't have the uncanny knack of making me forget my purpose, minx." Hastily, he brushed off the snow that clung to her buckskin clad body.

Her adoring eyes took in the dashing mountain man in the long buffalo-hide coat. "You are a fine one to speak of distraction," she teased, following his path through the heavy snow. "I was innocently forming angels in the snow to scare off evil spirits when I was bodily attacked by one."

Like a sparrow hawk swooping down on its prey, Hawk jerked Rozalyn into his arms and then planted her on the back of her horse. "A devil, am I?" he snapped in mock irritation.

"The devil himself," Roz declared.

Hawk's hand leisurely glided over her thigh to caress her hip and then tunneled beneath her coat to make arousing contact with her bare flesh. Then a wicked grin rippled across his lips, displaying pearly white teeth. "Tonight . . . when we are huddled around the campfire, I will hear you beg for my so-called attack, *chérie*," he prophesied in a seductively low voice.

Rozalyn felt herself grow warm and giddy inside as his roving hands wandered possessively over her. Her eyes remained upon him as he drew away and then swung into his saddle to sit straight and proud upon his steed. He looked like a god. The wild nobility in his dark features touched her soul and warmed her heart, and the confident way he carried himself stirred her emotions, bringing tears to her eyes as she followed him down the mountain. She turned in the saddle to get one last glimpse of the rustic cabin in the Mountains of the Wind. She was leaving a multitude of sweet memories behind. In her mind's eyes she could see them cuddled close by the fire, talking quietly together or sewing clothes from the animal skins they had hunted and cleaned. Hawk had taught her Indian games, and they had played them on leisurely days when weather permitted. He had told her of his life among the Crow and he'd spoken of the beliefs of his mother's people, holding her spellbound with his tales. They had roamed the mountains in search of game, had endured a ground blizzard in a small lean-to beneath a canopy of pines, had played cards during the long evenings, and had made wild sweet love during the nights.

Hawk had touched her every emotion, and Rozalyn had learned to read his many moods. She knew when he was restless, wanting to wander, and when he craved no more than her silent presence beside him or the feel of her body molded to his. And Hawk had come to know when she needed to be left alone and when she longed to feel secure and protected in his embrace. They had grown together, learned the true meaning of love and companionship, and they rarely spoke of the upcoming summer. They had preferred to exist in their fairyland, living as if there were no tomorrow. Although the mountains were filled with danger, they also brought them contented peace. Rozalyn was no longer trying to change her destiny. She knew her father would insist that she return with him to St. Louis, and knowing that, she had seen to it that every hour she spent with Hawk was a cherished treasure.

As they made their way down the snow-clogged ravines, she kept glancing back over her shoulder at the cabin, and she was dying a little inside. She knew she would never pass this way again and that tormenting thought was crushing her, leaving her no hope.

Muffling a sniff and managing a meager smile, Rozalyn raised her face to Hawk's when he grasped her hand. His eyes drifted back in the direction her gaze had taken and he sighed heavily.

"The memories are sweet, *amie,* the best. . . ." His pensive stare measured the towering aspens and pines that reached toward the clear morning sky. "But we have half a lifetime yet to live in the meadows of Yellowstone." His head came toward hers as he stretched across to press a light kiss to her responsive lips. "Don't leave me, Roz. Don't withdraw into the past, not yet. That time is coming soon enough."

Mustering her courage, Rozalyn forced a wider smile, drawing upon his strenth, his ability to face the future without dwelling on the past. "Tell me about Fort Cass. Is it like Fort William?"

Nudging his steed, Hawk led the way down the snow-covered slopes. "It is similar in some ways," he acknowledged, thankful Rozalyn had changed the subject. He didn't want to think about what they were leaving behind. His secluded cabin would become a sepulcher of forbidden memories all too soon. "The stockade was established in 1832. It is set on the meadow where the Big Horn River empties into the Yellowstone. The trading post was built to barter with the Crow." A wry smile pursed his lips when he glanced over at Rozalyn. Hawk drank in her natural beauty, which was evident despite her manly garb. One look into her flawless face and no one would be able to resist this gorgeous creature. "I expect you will meet some of my unruly friends when we reach the fort. We will rest there before setting our spring traps in the Yellowstone."

"In the land of the magic springs? Where spirits dwell in the warm, steamy baths?" Rozalyn taunted. "I suppose my ear will be bent with more fantastic stories of glass mountains, boiling rivers, and talking beavers that befriend lonely trappers."

Hawk chuckled at the skepticism in her voice. "No doubt you will. You know how superstitious we mountain men are."

"And lusty," Rozalyn added with a mischievous grin. "Will I be in need of a large stick to fight off these mountain dragons?"

That thought soured Hawk's disposition. He could well imagine the reception that awaited Rozalyn when his rambunctious comrades laid eyes on a white woman, especially one as bewitching as she. Making a mental note, Hawk vowed to ensure that Rozalyn was well armed, in case she was swarmed by overzealous trappers at the fort.

"Do not be surprised if such an event should occur," he warned. "My friends appreciate a beautiful woman and I cannot always hold myself responsible for their actions. But I have no doubt that you will be able to fend for yourself. You never had difficulty keeping me at a safe distance when we first met."

I never had difficulty holding a man at bay until you came along, Rozalyn silently amended. If his idea of being stifled was to be denied pleasure for a day after making a lady's acquaintance, Rozalyn hated to venture a guess at the assaults she might anticipate from Hawk's rough-edged comrades. Sweet merciful heavens, she would need a suit of armor. As another thought crossed her mind, Rozalyn focused narrowed eyes on the handsome trapper who rode by her side.

"What will you be doing while I am fighting off this swarm of men who have had very little association with white women in recent years? I suppose there is another Indian maiden waiting, at Fort Cass, to massage your weary muscles."

"Do I detect a hint of jealousy?" A roguish grin caught one corner of his mouth, curving it upward.

"Do I have a reason to be jealous?" she asked point-blank.

Hawk reined his steed to an abrupt halt. With one quick move he uprooted Rozalyn from her mount and transplated her onto his lap. The passionate kiss he proceeded to bestow on her left her body tingling with pleasure. "Does that answer your question?"

Rozalyn hastily drew in air when Hawk granted her a breath. Then she composed herself and looped her arms over his shoulders, flashing him an impish grin. "I fear I wasn't paying close attention, would you mind repeating that?"

Hawk returned her contagious smile. "Not at all." Lord, he loved to watch the sunlight sparkle in her blue eyes, to feel her petite body brushing suggestively against his. He could lose himself in the tantalizing fragrance that was so much a part of her. "For you, *amie*, anything. . . ."

His arms tightened, seeking an intimacy that was impossible with their hindering garments, and his lips grazed hers in a gentle whisper of a kiss before they settled firmly upon hers. A need as ancient as time accosted him when his mouth slanted over Rozalyn's, impelling his wandering hand to slip beneath her jacket and trace the band of her breeches, then swirl across her hips.

Suddenly Rozalyn couldn't remember where they were or why. Her body had forgotten it had a brain. She was ardently responding, eager for his touch. Nothing had changed between them. The fire of passion burned just as brightly as it had on those nights in his cabin, as intensely as it had that first night so long ago. Time had not diminished their flame. It blazed anew each time they lost themselves in the circle of each other's arms.

Hawk was yanked back to reality when his overloaded steed stumbled in a deep snowbank, and a squawk of surprise tumbled from Rozalyn's lips when she found herself sailing through the air. As she landed atop Hawk's belly, he expelled a pained grunt and then flashed his horse a disgruntled frown.

"I think it best to ride single until we descend to the meadows," he advised as he hoisted Rozalyn to her feet. "My mount doesn't seem to appreciate our dallying on his back while he is having difficulty navigating through these snow drifts."

A becoming blush stained her cheeks because she felt a mite foolish, but when Hawk pulled her into his arms, she lost all track of time and place.

A moment she stood there, knee deep in snow, before Hawk scooped her up and slung her over his shoulder, playfully swatting her derrière. "We are making miserable time," he grumbled. "At this pace we won't reach the fort for a month."

When he had set Rozalyn back on her own horse, she flung him a wry smile. "You cannot blame the delay on me. I was sitting on my steed, minding my own business," she reminded him saucily.

Hawk's dancing green eyes raked her concealed figure as if she were poised before him without a stitch of clothing. "The fault still lies with you," he insisted. "If you weren't so distracting I wouldn't have difficulty keeping my hands off you."

"My fault?" she repeated increduously. My, but he could twist logic until it made no sense at all. "I did nothing to entice you or distract you," she protested self-righteously.

He gave her a long, provocative look that assured her he liked what he saw and would have no aversion to doing more than gazing at her if they were elsewhere. "Your being here is enticement enough," he growled seductively, and then he let loose with a wolfish cry.

As Hawk eased his steed down the snow-blanketed slope, a pleased smile rippled across Rozalyn's lips. Lord, his rakish grin and the suggestive tilt of his eyebrows had sent a tingle along her spine. A longing sigh tripped from her lips as she studied Hawk's departing back. No matter how long she lived, she would never forget his hawkish stares and devilish grins. But those were only two of the things that would warm her memories, she mused pensively. For years to come she would remember their first meeting, their first splendrous night. In the beginning, Hawk had refused to consider her a friend as well as a lover. But time and the trials they'd undergone had drawn them closer. They had shared more than passion. Their blossoming love had bound their minds as well as their hearts, and as they had come to know each other's moods, they had confided their innermost thoughts. And yet . . . A troubled frown knitted Rozalyn's brow. Beneath Hawk's playful raillery and amorous assaults, she sensed that he was withholding something.

At times he seemed miles away, as if he were grappling with some disturbing vision. When she had questioned him, he had shrugged off his deliberations and had quickly pursued another subject. Rozalyn wanted no secrets between them, not even one, but Hawk seemed to prefer to keep this one dilemma to himself. Was he pondering the future? Was he planning his confrontation with Aubrey? Or was he harboring some past pain?

Rozalyn's meandering thoughts scattered when they descended from the snowy summits to find that spring indeed graced the mountain meadows. Across the sprawling pastures a herd of bison grazed on the tender new sprigs of grass, and the chatter of birds filled the air, serenading them as they made their way toward the junction of the Bighorn and Yellowstone Rivers.

The spectacular scenery momentarily made Rozalyn

forget their days were numbered. This was a breathtaking paradise. She spent her nights in the rapturous circle of Hawk's arms and viewed the grandeur of nature while they tracked their way north. Although Hawk had spotted a hunting party of Blackfoot, they had managed to take cover in the thick underbrush before being discovered. That had been their only near-brush with calamity since they'd left the cabin. Rozalyn was most grateful that they had emerged unscathed for Bear-Claw had told her stories about the ruthless Blackfoot tribe that prowled the wilderness.

One evening while they crouched before the campfire, she peered off into the distance and sighed contentedly. She sat comfortably between Hawk's muscled legs, her head resting against his sturdy shoulder. Hawk, who had propped himself against the mound of saddles and supplies, was enjoying the peaceful serenity as he hugged Rozalyn. He followed her gaze past the snow-capped precipices that glowed like silver in the full moonlight. The tranquil setting had a soothing effect on him until an unsettling thought darted through his mind and he flinched involuntarily. He had traversed this unclaimed territory at least a dozen times in the past, but the journey had never been as pleasurable as it was with Rozalyn by his side. How in God's name would he be able to follow this trail again without remembering? Each sight would recall Rozalyn's shapely silhouette. Her memory would linger, not only in his cabin, but also in every valley and atop every pastel-colored summit.

How could he endure the next journey alone after he had shared this one with her? And even worse, how could he possibly convince Aubrey to allow Rozalyn to remain in the mountains after what Bear-Claw had told him about the man's bitter past? These dismal questions dampened Hawk's spirit for he believed Aubrey would go on hating him because of something that had occurred more than thirty years ago, something over which Hawk had no control. If the passage of time hadn't eased Aubrey's resentment, how could Hawk hope to mellow him? Nonetheless, he continued to ponder several solutions. They all had flaws, but he was certain there was some possibility he had overlooked.

"A penny for your thoughts," Rozalyn murmured, studying the faraway expression that had settled on his ruggedly handsome features.

A tender smile grazed Hawk's lips when he glanced down into her spellbinding blue eyes. "I was just thinking how empty life will be without you."

Rozalyn wished to heaven she hadn't pried since she was trying very hard not to think about the dreadful day she would be taken from Hawk's life. She trembled uncontrollably, then twisted to face him, her body arching to fit itself intimately to his.

"Hold me close. Make the world go away. It seems so cruel and unfair—"

With a muffled groan his firm lips swooped down on hers, plundering her mouth with a fierce, impatient hunger that he made no attempt to control. The world faded from Rozalyn's mind when she surrendered to the erotic feel of his hands and lips. Then his hard body entwined with hers, blocking out all thought. Over and over again Hawk murmured of his love, his insatiable need, and Rozalyn, with breathless kisses, told of her deep feelings for him. Together they soared like a shooting star that leaves a fiery path across the night sky, burning brighter until, with one final blaze of glory, their souls forged at the perimeters of the universe.

Hawk's thudding heart shriveled in his chest when he glanced down to see tears misting Rozalyn's eyes. Moonbeams cascaded down her ebony hair which was spread across the thick carpet of grass, and he could not help but resent Aubrey DuBois, not only because of his unfair treatment of the trappers, but because he would soon seize the one thing more precious and dear to Hawk than life. Sweet Jesus, why had he traded Rozalyn for reasonable prices for supplies, he asked himself acrimoniously. The very fact that he had used her thus would make it impossible to keep her when the bargaining was done.

Think man, he growled to himself. But his mind was too numb with passion's pleasure to devise a scheme to defeat Aubrey . . . if indeed there was one. The hopelessness of their ill-fated love descended upon him like a rockslide. He might well become a hero to the trappers if he managed to get them a profitable margin, but he had made his own life hell by using Rozalyn to get his way. All the money to be gained from beaver pelts couldn't fill the vacuum that would envelop Hawk when he had to trade Rozalyn back to Aubrey. Dammit, the man has no true concern for his daughter, Hawk thought sourly. Confounded it, there is nothing fair about the whole business!

Chapter 24

Pensive blue eyes appraised the crude fort set at the fork of the Yellowstone and Bighorn Rivers, and a knot of apprehension coiled in the pit of Rozalyn's stomach as she wondered what awaited her. Apart from the fort were dozens of wigwams that housed the Crow who had ventured from their winter camp to trade for supplies and flashy trinkets. And inside the log walls were a horde of barbaric ruffians who had not laid eyes on a white woman in years. Rozalyn swallowed hard. Would she find herself battling men who had as many arms as a wheel had spokes? Or would these men Hawk considered his friends respect his claim on her?

Rozalyn wasn't certain whether she would prefer to take her chances with the so-called savages or be swarmed by the rough-edged lechers inside the stockade. If Hawk had asked her, she would have said she preferred that they make camp alone, leaving both heathens and mountain men to their own kind.

When the stockade gate swung open to grant them entrance, Rozalyn's gaze circled the many faces that stared at the new arrivals. With an effort she forced a smile when several burly men swarmed around them before they could dismount.

"Well, glory be!" Two-Dogs hooted when he recognized Hawk. Then he ogled the young woman in buckskins. After he had thoroughly assessed the curvaceous beauty with long, flowing hair, he refocused his eyes on Hawk. "I heard you was dead. But then, maybe you are at that. Why else would you be travelin' with this angel?"

Hawk grinned down at the heavyset mountaineer whose wide smile exposed the lack of several teeth. "How goes the trapping Two-Dogs? Or have you been hibernating like the grizzlies this winter?"

Two-Dogs snickered at Hawk's taunt, but his gaze strayed back to the enticing beauty whose appearance gave new meaning to doehide garments. Two-Dogs had seen his share of appropriate clothing for the wilderness, but none of it had looked as appealing as Rozalyn's.

"I've done my share of trappin'," Two-Dogs finally got around to saying. "But I lost part of my pelts and some possibles when a party of Shoshone snuck up on me."

"Shoshone?" Hawk raised a dark eyebrow. "Since when have they pestered white trappers? I thought they were reasonably friendly."

"Mostly they are, but sometimes they like to practice what they do for a livin'—sneak up on people. And they were damned good at it." A sheepish grin caught the corner of his mouth as he dragged the coonskin cap farther down on his forehead. "S'cuse me, ma'am. I forgot m'self."

"Rozalyn, this is Two-Dogs." Hawk hastily introduced the trapper. "And that"—he extended an arm toward a tall, lean, stubbled-faced man who was drooling over Rozalyn from a distance. "This grizzly character is called Ol' Fuzzy."

Rozalyn had no difficulty realizing how the young man had acquired his nickname. His head was capped with thick red hair that curled so tightly it hugged his temples and forehead.

"And this poor excuse of a man is Trapper." Hawk indicated the stout mountaineer with sparkling green eyes. "And beneath that ungodly homemade cap is Wolf-Paw."

Hawk gestured toward the short, wiry older man who wore a most unusual hat, no doubt of his own design. The crown of the cap was a wolf's head, and the animal's gray hair formed ear flaps that extended to the collar of his wolf-skin coat. Rozalyn wondered if Two-Heads would have been a more appropriate name for the crusty mountain man until she noted the heavy strand of claws that encircled his neck.

"I'm pleased to meet all of you," she murmured, even though she was being devoured by four pairs of unblinking eyes that sought to peer through her buckskin clothes to determine exactly what lay beneath them.

A muddled frown appeared on Hawk's brow when Trapper suddenly pivoted about and marched toward the gate. "Where are you off to in such a rush?"

"To bathe," Trapper threw over his shoulder. "I ain't got no notion to offend the lady."

"Bathe?" Two-Dogs and Wolf-Paw hooted simultaneously. "You ain't bin near water since the time you fell in the river, tryin' to snare a fish."

Trapper puffed up indignantly. "I got no aversion to bathin'," he protested. "But I had no cause to wash when I was livin' with you and the rest of these uncivilized hooligans."

Hawk watched in amazement as all four men strode through the gate to take to the river like a raft of ducks. "It seems your presence has already caused a stir," he remarked, flashing Roz a wry smile. "You should be flattered that these backward trappers have made such personal sacrifices to impress you."

"It leave me to wonder if one can wash away one's upbringing," Rozalyn mused aloud. "After the blatant stares I received, I can only pray the river can cleanse their off-color thoughts."

A low skirl of laughter bubbled from Hawk's chest. "They were a mite obvious, weren't they?" Agilely, he hopped to the ground and then pulled Rozalyn from her saddle. "They aren't so bad, once you get to know them. Granted, they are starved for affection, but you might be surprised to find these men have better manners than the so-called gentlemen you have met in St. Louis."

"I suppose they couldn't be any worse than Jeffrey Corday," Rozalyn muttered.

"They are hardly in that skinny-legged milk sop's class." Hawk snorted. Then he gave her a beseeching smile. "Don't begrudge these men their fawning over you. They mean no harm. They are my friends."

Rozalyn had never been able to resist the charismatic smile that made Hawk's face even more dashing. "Very well," she said agreeably. "I will be cordial, but if one of them—"

"If one of them offends you, I will personally see to it that he is properly punished," Hawk finished for her. After pressing a fleeting kiss to her puckered brow, Hawk gestured toward one of the rustic cabins that lined the inner walls of the fort. "Our accommodations, *mademoiselle*. When I have shown you to our quarters I will inform Benjamin Phillips of our arrival."

When Hawk disappeared inside a large cabin set apart from the smaller shacks, Rozalyn entered after him. It was similar to the one in which they had slept at Fort William. In one corner were a bed and crude night stand. Near the fireplace stood a small table and chairs. Although the accommodations were a far cry from the elaborate furnishings of her St. Louis mansion, Rozalyn wasn't complaining, not when she and Hawk would be spending their nights cradled in thick fur quilts. Her contemplative deliberations were interrupted when Hawk again eased open the door and strode inside, carrying an armload of supplies.

"Benjamin Phillips, the keeper of the fort, better known as the Prince of Yellowstone, has invited us to dine with him," Hawk announced after setting aside his menagerie of goods. When he had drawn a large pouch from the pile, he presented it to Rozalyn. "For you, *amie.*"

A muddled frown clouded her brow as she accepted the gift, but a gasp burst from her when she unfolded a gown of sapphire blue. It was adorned with so much lace that she knew it must have cost a fortune.

"Where did you . . . Why?" The question flew from her lips while her wide astonished eyes focused on Hawk's broad grin.

"I bought it for you while I was in St. Louis . . . after I found myself falling in love with you," he explained. His callused hand brushed across the plush velvet, silently admiring the rich fabric. "It might be the only time I am allowed to see you in it." His husky voice trailed off and Hawk found himself wishing he hadn't put that depressing thought to tongue.

Determined not to give way to her sinking spirits, Rozalyn tossed him a saucy smile. "You prefer to see me in it, as opposed to *out* of it?" One delicately arched eyebrow lifted at a provocative angle. "Monsieur Baudelair, you sorely disappoint me."

Hawk's arm slid about her waist, and a roguish smile flitted across his lips. "*Ma belle coccinelle*, I have always maintained that you were overdressed when you were wearing more than a smile." His velvety voice sent chills across her skin. "But if you were to take a meal with my friends while you were wearing not a stitch, I fear they could not be held responsible for their actions, nor could I.

Any man has only a certain degree of self-restraint."

It became increasingly difficult to concentrate on his hushed words when his adventurous hands were mapping the curves of her body and his moist lips were skimming the column of her neck. But then, Hawk was also having difficulty in following a train of thought while he was so preoccupied. The feel of her yielding flesh transformed his playfulness into desire.

His mouth settled on her opened lips as he pulled her full length against him, both of them aching with a need more potent than the craving for food and drink. Rozalyn's runaway heart tumbled against her ribs like an acrobat performing aerial maneuvers while his lips traced a path of fire to the laces of her buckskin shirt. But just when Hawk would have peeled off that hindering garment to reveal Rozalyn's natural beauty, a rap at the door interrupted him.

"Who is it?" Hawk called, his voice thick with unappeased desire.

"Well, who the hell do you think it is?" Trapper snorted. Hawk immediately recognized the gravely voice. "There ain't nothing out here 'cept Indians and mountaineers. Open up. I brought somethin' for the lady."

When Hawk whipped open the door to fling Trapper a withering glance, his face froze. The stubble-faced, tattered Trapper was now freshly shaven and freshly clothed, and he exuded a sticky sweet fragrance that Hawk presumed to be cologne . . . or at least a substitute for it. Trapper's rugged features had been scrubbed until they shined and his hair had been washed and slicked back in a fashion Hawk had never seen displayed by the mountain man.

"Trapper?" he squeaked in disbelief.

"Well, o' course," the man grunted haughtily, pushing his way around the human obstacle—Hawk—to have a closer look at Rozalyn. Drawing a recently plucked bouquet of wild flowers from behind his back Trapper bowed and then presented them to her. "For you, ma'am." His smile revealed his pleasure in viewing such a lovely young beauty. "I'll admit it's bin some time since I seen a white woman, but I don't recollect layin' eyes on one as fetchin' as you."

Rozalyn could not be insulted by the honest admiration in the man's eyes, and a radiant smile blossomed on her lips. "Thank you for the lovely flowers and the compliment."

Hawk watched the scene with a mixture of pride and displeasure. He had the uneasy feeling that their stay at Fort Cass would be nothing short of frustrating if his comrades persisted in hovering about Rozalyn. That fear became reality when the other three trappers filed into the cabin, bearing more gifts—handsome jewelry and enough spring flowers to smother a bumblebee. The dramatic change in the men's appearances baffled Hawk. If there had been a red carpet hereabout, he wouldn't have been the least bit surprised in seeing it rolled out for the princess of Fort Cass. And to make matters worse, he was now the most disheveled-looking man in the group.

His usually good disposition turned sour. He had anticipated that his friends would swarm about Rozalyn, but he had not expected to be shuffled back into a corner like an outcast weed. Elbowing his way through the crowd of drooling admirers, Hawk herded them toward the door.

"If you gentlemen will excuse us, Roz and I would like to bathe and change before dinner." He gestured his tousled head toward the small tub set in the small niche. "Why don't you make yourselves useful and draw a bath for the lady."

"You ain't gonna stay in here with her while she

bathes, are you?" Two-Dogs howled. "That wouldn't be proper. Even I got enough couth to know that."

"Why shouldn't I?" Hawk's challenging gaze riveted over his four friends. "The lady happens to be my wife." He didn't know what had possessed him to tell that lie, but it had flown from his lips before he'd been able to bite back the impulsive comment.

Rozalyn looked every bit as shocked by the remark as the trappers. She didn't understand why Hawk had said that. They weren't married and never could be.

"What?" Fuzzy squawked incredulously. "Yore married? To this perty lady? Ain't there no justice in this world?"

Rozalyn giggled at the way Hawk puffed up like an indignant toad as four pairs of envious eyes raked him from head to toe, silently assuring him that this lovely wild flower could do far better than a mountain man who needed a few rough edges shaved off.

"She could have done worse," Hawk snapped, an unpleasant edge to his voice.

"He isn't so bad, really," Rozalyn defended, fighting to keep a straight face.

"It ain't so much that he's bad or good," Trapper sniffed, eying Hawk with open suspicion and more than a hint of envy. "It's just that I heard him swear to high heaven that he wasn't never gonna tie the knot. Next, I suppose he'll be tellin' us that he's gonna give up the good life and traipse back to civilization and start garbin' hisself in the confinin' trappin's of gentlemen."

"No, I haven't completely lost my senses," Hawk muttered, wishing he had kept his mouth shut in the first place.

"You mean yer gonna keep this lady up here in the high country? Yer gonna drag her around like a squaw?" Wolf-Paw crowed. "She ain't used to this way of life, for Christ's sake! You musta lost part of yer senses or you wouldn't consider such a crazy idea."

"Out!" Hawk's arm shot toward the door, but his comrades didn't budge. They just stood their gaping at Hawk as if he had sprouted another head. Hastily, Hawk propelled the congregation toward the door. "Go fetch the water. I haven't the time or the inclination to answer your prying questions."

When the door slammed in their faces, Hawk pivoted back around to Rozalyn. Upon seeing the impish grin on her face, he grumbled, "Well, dammit, I had to tell them something to curb their lusts," he defended.

"But wedlock?" Rozalyn teased unmercifully. "Even they were skeptical of such an announcement, knowing you are a dedicated bachelor. You could have told them any number of incredible tales and they would have been more prone to believe you."

"It was the only excuse that came to mind," he declared crabbily. "Not that you cared. They were obviously out to impress you, and you seemed to be enjoying their amorous attention."

Rozalyn inhaled the delicate blossoms in the bouquets and then shrugged nonchalantly. "At first I was apprehensive, but these mountain men, rough around the edges though they may be, have shown themselves to be as pleasant and considerate as Harvey Duncan and his friends."

Hawk rolled his eyes as he recalled how Harvey and his hooligans had swarmed around Rozalyn. No doubt, the trappers would follow suit. He was prepared to fling her a sarcastic rejoinder when the door rattled beneath an impatient rap. How the foursome had managed to heat water and tote buckets back to the cabin in such a short time baffled Hawk. But there they were, parading into the room to pour the bath water into the small tub. Their task completed, they bowed before Rozalyn and then marched out leaving Hawk to breathe a sigh of relief. But his sigh lodged in his throat when Rozalyn shed her buckskins, revealing her ivory skin to his all-consuming gaze. Lord, he groaned to himself. Would he ever be unaffected by the sight of her body, ever be able to look upon her without feeling the instant rise of desire? Even after all the time they had spent together, his craving hadn't lessened. Hawk wanted Rozalyn as he always had—wildly and irrationally.

A sigh of pure pleasure tumbled from Roz's lips as she eased into the tub. Weeks of traveling had prohibited the luxury of a bath and the icy mountain streams made it impossible to relax for one would suffer frostbite. After lathering her arms and legs, she scrubbed away the grime, completely absorbed in the simple satisfaction of soaking in a tub.

While she frolicked in her confining bath, Hawk parked himself on the bed, with a glass of brandy for comfort. Why had he been so protective of this ravishing beauty? he asked himself. He loved Rozalyn and she loved him. Wasn't that enough? Did he have to behave like a jealous husband in the presence of his friends? For heaven's sake, Hawk grumbled to himself, Roz was no frail, defenseless woman. She could give what she got and always had. She didn't need someone fluttering over her.

And how the devil was he going to explain his way out of his lie when Aubrey Dubois appeared at rendezvous to whisk Roz away. Damnation, why hadn't he told his friends that Rozalyn had been lost in the wilderness or that she had come to assist the missionaries who flocked into the area to save the savage souls? Lord, anything would have been better than what he'd told the trappers.

The more Hawk pondered his comment, the more annoyed he became—and the more he drank. Bear-Claw was right, he thought miserably. He should never have allowed himself to grow so attached to Roz, not when he knew he would be forced to give her up. For years to come, he would endure the taunts of his friends. Well, he had asked for this, hadn't he? He was the one who had carted Rozalyn into the wilderness, falling deeper in love with her with each passing day. He was the one who had confessed his love when he'd known it was futile to allow his emotions free rein. But he would not have relinquished any of the time he had spent with Rozalyn. She had brightened his days with laughter and inflamed his nights with indescribable passion. Life had never been so wondrous as it was when he gazed into the fathomless pools of blue that flickered with living fire. He had never been so happy, Hawk reminded himself. This deep a love came only once in a lifetime, and not even that often to scores of unfortunate souls. How could he begrudge the months they had spent in paradise when so many of his friends didn't know and would never comprehend the meaning of the word? But dammit, what could he anticipate from the rest of his life after Aubrey snatched away his sun, moon, and stars?

Hawk swallowed that depressing question with a gulp of whiskey. Damn, there were days when thinking of life without Rozalyn got the best of him and this was one of them. His confrontation with the other trappers only served to remind him that Rozalyn would collect a crowd of available bachelors wherever she went. And perhaps one day another man would come along to make her forget the passion she had shared with Hawk one winter in Wyoming Territory. Hawk clung fiercely to his bottle, as if it held the key to his salvation. Only when he was numbed by liquor could he forget what would be missing for the rest of his life.

"Well, what do you think of your generous purchase?" Rozalyn pirouetted before him, allowing him to view the extravagant gown he'd given her from all angles.

Hawk very nearly melted into his brandy bottle when he glanced up at her. He had known the moment he'd spied the gown in a boutique that it was made for this shapely sprite. But, as was usually the case, alterations were needed. The trim-fitting waist hugged her midsection, but the bodice could have been a mite fuller, Hawk thought drearily. The rich velvet stretched tightly beneath the generous curve of her bosom, pushing her creamy breasts upward until they were dangerously close to spilling forth over the material. The décolleté of white lace rimming her exposed flesh was enough to set a normal man on fire. Hawk hated to think how his love-starved comrades would react when they laid eyes on her. Sweet mercy, they would be breathing down her neck like a pack of wolves about to devour a dove. Nonetheless, Rozalyn looked absolutely breathtaking in her finery with her dark hair fastened atop of her head.

"As always, you are stunning," Hawk slurred, his tone less than enthusiastic as he raised his half-empty bottle in toast.

A bemused frown knitted Rozalyn's brow as she watched Hawk hoist himself from the bed and weave unsteadily toward the tub. After he had stripped from his buckskins and stepped into his lukewarm bath, a light tap at the door had him scowling once again. Rozalyn eased open the door to peer at an unfamiliar face. The man was dressed in a tailored jacket, and his blond, immaculately trimmed hair framed a square face. Although he was not particularly handsome, his stylish clothes and refined manner demanded her respect.

"There is no question that you are Rozalyn," he declared, his hazel eyes assessing her sapphire gown and, even more closely, the form beneath it. With sophisticated flair, he struck a pose and then bowed before her. "I am Benjamin Phillips, my dear," he said, offering her his extended arm. "I have come to escort you to dinner. The pleasure of your company will long be remembered in the humble outpost on the edge of civilization."

"Close the damned door," Hawk grunted sourly. "The draft could well be the death of me."

Benjamin's face fell when he craned his neck to see Hawk hunkered down in the small tub, long bare legs crowding his broad shoulders. His jaw sagging, he swung back to the dazzling young lady who did not seem the least bit offended by the naked Hawk's splashing.

Noting Benjamin's astonished expression, Rozalyn countered with a calm smile. "My husband has not yet completed his toilet, *monsieur*. Perhaps we should—"

"Your hus . ." Benjamin strangled on the word. He could not imagine a man like Hawk entangled in wedlock. He, too, had heard the man boast that he'd have unlimited freedom to wander and to dally with every available female until his dying day. Not that he could find any complaint with the enticing beauty Hawk had selected for his spouse, Benjamin mused. But Hawk . . . Benjamin couldn't believe it.

"What is so blasted shocking about that?" Hawk hooted. Huffily, he propped himself in as dignified a position as he could manage when crammed into a small tub with his long legs bent up about his shoulders. "Virtually thousands of people have entered into the institution of marriage."

"But never in my wildest dream did I expect you to be one of them," Benjamin snorted. After composing himself, he gave Rozalyn an apologetic smile. "Although I can see for myelf what prompted you to eat crow, Hawk, I am still bewildered by your announcement."

Hawk's dripping arm indicated the door. "Will the two of you kindly grant me some privacy? I will join you in your quarters as soon as I am finished." Grumpily, Hawk snatched up the sponge and lathered himself. "The way you and the rest of the men have been behaving, I doubt my lovely wife will be neglected while I am soaking."

"On that you can depend," Benjamin insisted, a rakish grin spreading across his tanned face.

"Do I look worried?" Hawk sniffed sarcastically. "Now will you please shut the blasted door and leave me in peace?"

Rozalyn suppressed an amused giggle as Benjamin propelled her across the square to his quarters. My, but Hawk's disposition had turned sour enough to curdle milk. She recalled he'd said that he would be a jealous lover, but she had not anticipated such a blatant display of hostility. Still, the fact that he cared enough to let the jealous green monster torment him was flattering. Although Hawk had confessed his love for her, Rozalyn had never overcome her apprehension that another winter's snow would bury his memories of their time together. She'd felt the challenges of the mountains and the availability of a lovely Indian maiden would make his memories dim, and she didn't wish to be forgotten. It was bad enough that they would soon be parted, but being replaced in his affections was a disquieting fear that constantly nagged at her. And I will be forgotten, she told herself. Hawk was too much man to live out his life in celibacy, but that didn't stop Rozalyn from silently wishing he could.

Her rambling thoughts evaporated when Benjamin steered her into his elaborately furnished quarters. His appurtenances were not the crude, hurriedly assembled objects that lined the walls of their simple abode. Plush, stuffed chairs, imported from the East, stood in every corner, and fine French brandy had been stocked in the delicately carved cabinet that stood near the large oak table. Tapestries depicting the magnificent creatures of nature hung upon the walls. On the white linen tablecloth fine China and silverware rested. Indeed, the refinement and sophistication of civilization had been brought to this niche in the wild. It is as Hawk said, she mused, her eyes circling the elegant quarters. The Prince of Yellowstone surrounds himself with luxuries one might find in St. Louis.

"It is possible to take a man from culture, but one cannot take culture from the man," Benjamin boasted as he made an exaggerated bow. "Although I am compelled to dwell amid these majestic mountains, I still demand the finer things in life, unlike some of my unsophisticated friends." His gaze shifted to the procession of clean-shaven trappers who had come to take their evening meal with the lady—without being invited.

Before Benjamin could utter a protest, Rozalyn was snatched from his side and whisked to the far end of the table. Once she had been seated, the trappers surrounded their fairy princess like four hovering bodyguards, and when Hawk entered the dining room, Benjamin had plopped into his chair and was brooding while the other four men were being quite social.

Heaving an exasperated sigh, Phillips thrust a drink into Hawk's hand and then gulped down his own. "I didn't invite those heathens to join us," he grumbled.

Hawk leisurely sipped his brandy and then gestured his head toward the opposite end of the table. "Beauty and her beasts." He smirked caustically. "It appears that you and I must be satisfied with our own company. I feared Rozalyn would cause a stir, but I did not anticipate that neither of us would be allowed to get a word in edgewise." Easing back in his seat, Hawk's gaze circled back to the administrator of the fort. "So tell me, what news has passed through here during the winter? Has the American Fur Trading Company gained ground against our notorious entrepreneur?"

Benjamin nodded affirmatively as he, too, settled back in his stuffed chair. "Many of the free trappers have joined the trading company to protect their own interests and lives," he informed Hawk. "DuBois has attempted to stifle this competition, but it is attracting more trappers. And the increasing threat of the Blackfoot has forced more men to band together for protection. But it seems the tide has turned." Benjamin sighed heavily. "The popularity of silk hats has crippled the fur market. I fear soon trappers will be forced to look for another profession or they will simply have to settle for living off the mountains they have come to love. There is talk of unrest in the East. Before long, wagon trains will be venturing through the mountain passes on their way to the fertile valleys to the West. I wonder how many of these trappers who prefer to live in the wild will start to lead the caravans west?"

Hawk shuddered at the thought of dusty trails marring the beauty of Wyoming Territory, but he knew emigrants would come. It was inevitable. Settlers were constantly searching for a land of milk and honey. One day they would head toward the grassy plains that lay to the west of the towering Rockies. And how many times would he witness the march westward, searching the faces of the emigrants, looking for a woman who wouldn't be among them? That thought made Hawk's spirits plummet.

Chapter 25

While Rozalyn nibbled on her meal she found herself listening to the wild tales the trappers were weaving. They sounded so convincing that she almost caught herself believing their superstitious nonsense. The men spoke as if their stories were fact rather than legend, as if they were prepared to stand behind their tall tales and proclaim them to be truth.

"Have you ever head of the *Nin-am-beas?*" Wolf-Paw asked as he rambled from one legend to another. Before Rozalyn could respond, the trapper chuckled. "No, I don't reckon you have, being a flatlander. Well, in Shoshone land where I wintered two years ago, one of the squaws"—a slow blush crept into Wolf-Paw's ruddy features when Rozalyn raised an eyebrow—"she and I was friendly, I suppose you could say. As I was sayin' . . . I was in camp when I first heard about *Nin-am-beas*. They're little people like elves, leprechauns, and such. Though they stand only a foot tall, they kin lift a horse by one hoof, whirl him around, and toss him hundreds of feet in the air, as if the critter was as light as a feather."

"An' Lordy, do them *Nin-am-beas* delight in playin' practical jokes," Two-Dogs chimed in, his deadpan expression making Rozalyn giggle in amusement until he eyed her disapprovingly. "Don't you be doubtin' it, girl. There is such things as *Nin-am-beas*." When Rozalyn composed herself, the trapper continued, "That's why Indian squaws place the tenderest meats of the bison and antelope in the crotch of a tree near camp. If *Nin-am-beas* ain't served vittles in generous proportions they fly into a rage and plague the tribe with bad luck."

"A foot tall, you say?" Rozalyn queried, striving for a serious tone.

"No more than that," Fuzzy affirmed. "And you should hear how scared Indians are of gophers. Not that I would cross one myself, but if one of them varmints darts in front of an Indian he starts chantin' prayers to the Great Spirit and offerin' tributes." Fuzzy shook his head and then snickered lightly. "Once I was stayin' with the Sioux and one of them pesky gophers burrowed on the edge of camp. Lo and behold, the news spread like wildfire. Them Sioux pulled down their tepees, packed their belongin's, and moved to a new spot where the medicine man was sure they would be safe from gopher evil. I went to sleep in the middle of a Sioux village and woke up in a deserted camp."

"Is there nothing that brings Indians good luck?" Rozalyn questioned before munching on her meal.

"Why, shore," Trapper insisted, propping his elbows on the edge of the table to peer straight at Rozalyn. "A chickadee twittering near a village is a good omen. The Indians say it was that little bird that discovered the world. Then there are the spirits of the Yellowstone that live in the springs."

Rozalyn pricked up her ears, and her gaze swung to Hawk who lounged at the opposite end of the table, sporting an I-told-you-so smile. "I suppose all of you have been visited by these specters and have indulged in a swim in these boiling springs."

"That's usually the only time we can git Trapper to take to the water . . . 'cept when he lays eyes on a lady as perty as you," Fuzzy chortled, his dark eyes dancing with teasing amusement.

Trapper thrust out an indignant chin. "That ain't so."

Before their taunting raillery led to physical blows, Rozalyn steered her attentive admirers onto another subject. "Is there good trapping in the Yellowstone?" She directed her inquiry to Trapper who instantly mellowed beneath her curious smile.

"We've bin trapping the Yellowstone for several years, after Hawk got us permission from the Crow. But he still ain't found the valley where legend has it beavers are so thick they fight one another to get into a man's trap. I've heard tell there's more game in that hidden valley than the night sky has stars."

That was the tallest tale Rozalyn had yet to hear. The expression on Hawk's face warned her not to scoff at Trapper's remark without insulting her companions. Still, beavers fighting to have their paws lodged in a painful trap? Rozalyn thought these men were prone to believe anything.

Deciding it best to sit back and listen to the trappers fantastic stories rather than contradict them, she found herself assaulted by tales of gigantic avalanches, ground blizzards, and hostile Indian attacks. Finally, the talk of the long-winded trappers turned to the numerous superstitions about the man-eating Wendigo, the giant beaver that prowled the rivers, and to the mysterious Folly of the Woods which crept in during the night to steal men's minds. Rozalyn had thought she had heard all there was of legendary lore while she was under Bear-Claw's care, but it was obvious she had been mistaken. The four trappers she had recently met were filling her head with so many exaggerated tales that she began to wonder if she could again separate fact from fantasy.

More than two hours later, she was hoisted to her feet and shuffled into the open square. There, other mountain men had gathered, bringing their fiddles, harmonicas, and drums to provide music. Rozalyn, along with a few Indian maidens whose white husbands had brought them to the fort, was passed around the boisterous group. Several of the trappers had partaken of so much White Mule whiskey and rum that they were dancing together, seemingly unconcerned that their partners were not of the female persuasion. Rozalyn barely had time to catch her breath before she was snatched from one trapper's arms to be whirled around by another.

Her situation had been tolerable until two drunken trappers had begun to become overly intimate, while dancing. Rozalyn was furious when Dark-Eagle and Yellow-Calf herded her away from the crowd with every intention of molesting her. In no mood to be diplomatic, she attempted to slap some sense into Dark-Eagle and then turned her hand on Yellow-Calf's bristled cheek. Growling at Rozalyn's hostile attitude, Dark-Eagle fastened her hands behind her back while Yellow-Calf attempted to steal a kiss without having the hide lifted from his face. But before the inebriated trapper could see his dream come true, Two-Dogs intervened, jabbing his sharp-bladed knife into Yellow-Calf's ribs.

"The lady came to dance, naught else," he insisted through a tight smile. "If you heathens got other ideas in yore heads, it's best that you forget 'em." Clamping a vise-like grip on Dark-Eagle's arm, Two-Dogs forced Rozalyn's would-be molester to unhand her.

"Go find yer own woman," Yellow-Calf grumbled. "We found her first."

Two-Dogs pressed the stiletto convincingly against Yellow-Calf's tender flesh, evoking a pained grunt. "Maybe you didn't hear me the first time, friend," he gritted out. "Back off before I lose what's left of my temper."

After a strained silence, the trappers retreated, but not without glaring holes at Two-Dogs for interrupting what might have been a satisfying tête-à-tête. After Rozalyn had rearranged the gown that had very nearly been twisted around her neck, she graced Two-Dogs with a grateful smile and allowed him to usher her back to the circle of dancers who were enjoying a lively folk tune. Her gaze circled the rambunctious group in search of Hawk, but when he was nowhere to be found, a troubled frown etched her brow. She knew he had been in a sour mood most of the evening, but would he desert her? Obviously he had or he would have come to her aid when she'd been hustled off by those brutes.

"Hawk ain't here. He went to see his people," Two-Dogs informed Rozalyn when he saw her glancing about the compound. "But don't you fret none. Me and the men will take care of you 'til he comes back."

"He could have told me what he was about before he wandered off," Rozalyn muttered irritably.

"I guess he ain't used to answerin' to nobody," Two-Dogs remarked with a careless shrug. "Hawk is set in his ways, jest like the rest of us. It probably takes some gettin' used to before a man recollects that he can't jest go waltzin' off without reportin' to his wife."

A thoughtful frown creased his brow. Something wasn't right, Two-Dogs mused. He could feel it in his bones. Hawk had behaved strangely all evening, but he wouldn't divulge the source of his trouble. There were a few questions Two-Dogs wanted answered, and he had the sneaking suspicion that what was going on between Hank and Rozalyn Whoever-she-was might not be a simple matter. Two-Dogs was notorious for possessing the curiosity of a cat. Now he wanted to know exactly what a refined young beauty was doing out here. Hawk had lied to his friends, Two-Dogs was prepared to bet his left arm on that.

When Two-Dogs herded her toward her cabin, Rozalyn accompanied him without objection. Her ear had been severely bent and her toes sufficiently trounced upon for one night. She was eager to stretch out on a bed and enjoy a moment's solitude, but it disturbed her that Hawk had strolled off without personally informing her of his intentions.

Two-Dogs noted the melancholy expression that settled on Rozalyn's features, and he gave her hand a fond squeeze. "I suppose you ain't accustomed to all these doin's. Mountain people git a mite uproarious at times, but they don't mean no harm." When Two-Dogs had ushered Rozalyn into a seat, he dragged a chair over in front of her and then plopped down on it. "You ain't really Hawk's wife, are you?" he asked point-blank. "You don't have no ring to prove yore wed. A lady like you would have one because Hawk woulda seen that it was all proper, right down to the gold band. He may seem uncivilized like the rest of us, but he's got the manners of a gentleman. His pa seen to that."

"Did you know Hawk's father?" Long, tangled lashes swept up and Rozalyn's eyes met the crusty mountain man's faint smile. "Do you know why the DuBois and the Baudelairs hate each other?"

"DuBois?" Two-Dogs choked out the name and then stared at Rozalyn for a long, pensive moment. Understanding suddenly dawned on the mountain man. Why else would this lass want to know about the feud if she weren't a DuBois? It was obvious she knew just enough to make her curious. "Lordy, don't tell me yore Aubrey DuBois' daughter!" The bewildered mountain man slumped back in his chair and rolled his eyes. "Hell's bells, don't that beat all."

"I'm afraid I am," Rozalyn confessed quietly.

Two-Dogs raked his fingers through his hair and then let his arm drop loosely to his side. "I'll be damned," he grumbled. "Hawk promised us at last summer's rendezvous that he was goin' to negotiate with DuBois in St. Louis. When he informed us earlier today that he had found a foolproof way to bargain for lower prices, I wondered what he meant. But now the pieces of the puzzle are beginnin' to fall into place. Yore his bargainin' power, ain't you?"

"So it seems," Rozalyn replied. Then she focused penetrating blue eyes on the trapper. "You didn't answer my question."

"I will . . . if you will answer one more of mine," Two-Dogs bartered. "Is Hawk holdin' you for ransom and forcin' you to . . ." The trapper bit his tongue before he blurted out his probing question.

Hesitantly, Rozalyn nodded. "He is not actually my husband, and yes, he abducted me from St. Louis to bargain with my father. But what is between us is not something either of us takes lightly."

Two-Dogs deciphered her delicately phrased message and then frowned thoughtfully. "I reckon stealin' you was the only way Hawk could gain yore pa's attention. But that don't do you and Hawk no good now, does it?"

A sigh escaped Rozalyn's lips, but she met Two-Dogs' scrutinizing gaze. "I have become a pawn and I know I cannot win. I still do not know why my father detests the Baudelairs, or why Hawk and I can never become man and wife. If you could explain, I would be grateful."

Two-Dogs dragged his pipe from his pocket. After lighting it from the lantern, he took a long draw and then watched the smoke rings drift across the shadowed room. "I don't see no reason why you shouldn't know what started this feud," he murmured. "But I ain't sure I'm the one who should be divulgin' the information."

That was not what Rozalyn wanted to hear. She wanted to know the dark secret her father harbored—quickly. But she could tell by the square set of Two-Dogs' jaw that he would not betray a confidence. Dammit, would no one enlighten her? How could she fight when she didn't even know who and what she was battling?

When Two-Dogs bid her good night and closed the door behind him, Rozalyn paced the confines of her quarters, wondering if she would die without knowing what had ignited the feud. Rozalyn had the sinking feeling that her father would retrieve her from rendezvous, cart her back to St. Louis, and never mention the cause of his fierce hatred. And yet it might have been only a simple misunderstanding, something that could be forgiven if both parties would sit down and calmly discuss the matter.

But she knew that wasn't so. She had watched her father fly into a rage at the mere mention of the Baudelair name. He would not rationally discuss what had set him in a frenzy in St. Louis. By the time he reached the mountains he would be so furious at the turn of events that there would be no reasoning with him.

Mulling over that depressing thought, Rozalyn climbed into bed. Blast it, where was Hawk? He knew their days together were numbered. He could have taken her with him to the Crow camp. Don't work yourself into a stew, she told herself. Hawk has his reasons and he loves you. But does he love you enough? the nagging voice of distrust asked. That question continued to torment Rozalyn while she attempted to sleep. She knew Hawk was an adventurer, and no matter what hushed words of endearment he whispered in the heat of passion, he still came and went as he pleased, leaving her without an explanation. It was as if he were proving to her that he still had his freedom, no matter what was between them.

And he will always crave his freedom, Rozalyn reminded herself. He is a restless spirit and love can never truly bind a man like Hawk to a woman.

Oh, why did I fall in love with a man I can't have? Rozalyn asked herself miserably. She might as well attempt to hitch herself to a fleeting cloud. That would be as practical as wanting a future with Hawk. There could be no such thing, even if Aubrey didn't stand like an immovable mountain between them.

A fond smile pursed Hawk's lips when he stepped inside the wigwam to see his grandfather sitting cross-legged before the fire. Although Arakashe was nearing his seventieth year, he was a spry old man with keen, perceiving eyes. His weather-beaten features were framed by braids of silver hair, and his shoulders slumped now as they had not when he'd been in the prime of life.

"You have been gone a long time," the chief remarked in a graveled voice. "I expected you before the season when the buds burst and the owls that hatched from the snow began to take their prey. Could it be that your heart has strayed from the people of the Sparrow Hawk?"

"It has been a busy winter," Hawk defended, sitting down by the fire.

"And a troubling one, I fear," Arakashe said, his scrutinizing gaze working its way over the rugged features of his grandson's face.

Hawk nodded solemnly, knowing it was impossible to put anything past the perceptive chief. "There has been a great deal on my mind. I can find no solution to the dilemma that frustrates me."

Arakashe had seen the same exasperated expression on Hawk's face once before. More than thirty years ago, Hawk's father had come to Arakashe, searching for direction, pondering the truth in his soul. "The past has a way of repeating itself, does it not, Manake?" he questioned, calling Hawk by the name he had been his grandson when Hawk was but a lad. As was the custom, Hawk had taken another name as the years passed, but the chief fondly remembered the boy who had been his constant shadow those many years ago.

Hawk's gaze lifted to survey Arakashe's knowing smile. "You once warned me that it was unwise to make promises I couldn't keep, but I was young and foolish then. I thought I would grow to a man and be able to manipulate the world as it suited me."

"You have not outgrown your fierce desire to control your destiny." The chief chuckled.

"I still have that desire," Hawk admitted with a bitter laugh. "But I lack the power. Bear-Claw has told me of my link with the past. He explained the legend you told to me those many years ago. I wanted to become Morningstar's fiercest warrior, but, too late, I have realized that there are some things in this world a man cannot change, no matter how relentlessly he quests for solutions."

As if the wise chief had read Hawk's mind and plucked out his troubled thoughts, he queried softly, "Who is she, Manake?"

"She is Aubrey DuBois' daughter, a woman of incomparable beauty, and I know I cannot keep her," Hawk declared, his voice revealing his frustration.

Arakashe sat in pensive silence while crosscurrents of emotion passed across his wrinkled features. "Your burden is heavy and the obstacles that cast their shadows upon you are as tall as these mountains. You have followed the tracks of the Longknives for many snows, my son. It is time for you to fast and pray to the Great Spirit for guidance. It is the way of the Crow. I know in my heart what you will ask of Morningstar, as your own father asked before you."

Remorseful green eyes focused on the chief's sober countenance. "I would be wasting my time. How can I search for an answer when there is not one to be found? Don't you think I have considered every possibility? I have spent the winter contemplating alternatives. What purpose will be served by offering tributes to Morningstar when I can see with my own eyes that my future is grim?"

A wry smile rippled across the old chief's lips. "The warrior who casts aside his spear and retreats can never lead his braves into battle. That is not the way of the Absarkoes. The people of the free-flying Sparrow Hawk never back away, Manake. We may give way when the battle does not go in our favor, but we remain steadfast of heart and firm in courage." Arakashe laid his hand over Hawk's and willed his grandson to meet his level gaze. "If a man looses heart, what has he left? Certainly not his life when he must bear it with shame. Let your heart lead you to the place where Morningstar dwells. If no answer comes, you can return, knowing you have done all that is possible. But do not forsake the spirit of your mother's people, of my people. You must search until the last ray of hope follows the sun to the edge of Mother Earth. No man can ask more of himself than that, and no man should admit defeat until he stands in the long shadow." Arakashe gestured toward the northwest. "Go now, Manake. I will bring your woman to you after you have fasted and prayed. We will wait for you beside the boiling river in the land of the spirits."

A low rattle of laughter rumbled in Hawk's chest as he remembered the difficulty of the Sioux chief when he'd attempted to take Rozalyn where she didn't want to go. "You may find dealing with Rozalyn a difficult task if you do not explain your purpose. She is a feisty one, very unlike Crow women."

"I would have expected no less," Arakashe remarked

with a nonchalant shrug. "You have never been satisified with the shy Crow women who would have been proud to invite you to share the wigwams of their families in the custom of our people."

"Do not think to lead her from the fort without explanation," Hawk advised. "Rozalyn is not obedient. She will not hesitate to defy you if she feels she has just cause."

Arakashe chortled. "Then she is much like your own mother, a contrary creature who also had difficulty conforming to the ways of her people."

Hawk couldn't have stated it better himself. Although Rozalyn was flesh and blood, she possessed great inner spirit, something that set her apart from others, a trait that could be annoying and yet endearing. She was a curious enigma, and she intrigued Hawk. He prayed Arakashe wouldn't lose patience with her for his grandfather was in his declining years. Rozalyn was not his own daughter and he might not be as tolerant with her as he had been with his own child. The last thing Hawk needed was for Rozalyn to demolish the Crow camp and invite Arakashe's wrath. She could not know the source of Arakashe's feelings toward her and if she didn't watch her step—

"Come, Manake," Arakashe encouraged, struggling to his feet. "Your ride will be long."

Reluctantly, Hawk aimed himself toward the land of the boiling springs, searching for impossible answers, chasing the rainbow's end, and during his ride he was plagued by the nagging thought that all he was doing was wasting precious time.

Rozalyn strangled on a gasp when a callused hand fastened over her mouth, jerking her from her dreams. As her wide eyes searched the darkness, she saw faces hovering above her, but try as she might she could not free herself from the restraining arms that held her immobile. The two men who had sneaked into her cabin reeked of whiskey and smoke, and panic gripped her when she was hoisted to her feet and then shuffled out into the night. Frantically, Rozalyn prayed that someone would come to her rescue, but she was herded through the shadows toward the stockade gate. Like Indians silently stealing through the night, her abductors stalked into the underbrush that lined the river, and Rozalyn's hope of help faded.

Silently she cursed Hawk. If he hadn't abandoned her this would not have happened.

When the moonlight slanted across her abductors' features, Rozalyn gasped. She recognized the two rowdy men she had met during the festivities that evening. Each man had insisted that she dance with him, and had then mauled her while dancing. But when they had attempted to molest her, Two-Dogs had prevented them from doing so. Now they had returned.

Rozalyn attempted to scream, but she was roughly forced to the ground. Before she could scramble up, one of the men pounced on her, holding her in place while the other chuckled devilishly.

"Since you didn't seem to like our attentions at the dance, we decided to give you another chance," Dark-Eagle said spitefully.

While Yellow-Calf held her down, he drew near to her, grinning like a starved shark. But his anticipatory smile evaporated when the underbrush came alive with Crow braves. Dark-Eagle stopped dead in his tracks and peered up into the old chief's face, which evidenced strong disapproval.

Arakashe had been taking his braves with him to the fort, and when he'd sighted the threesome stealing into the darkness, he'd come to investigate. Hawk had described Rozalyn to him, so he knew it was she who had nearly been attacked by these ruffians.

"Dark-Eagle dares too much," Arakashe growled as he reined his pony toward the drunken trapper. "You and Yellow-Calf are no longer welcome in the land of the people of the Sparrow Hawk. If I learn you have trespassed on the Yellowstone you will pay with your lives."

The intrusion of the powerful chief and his braves had a sobering effect on the trappers. Without uttering a word in their defense they fled, leaving Rozalyn to peer gratefully at the gray-haired Arakashe and his warriors.

When she had risen from the ground she moved toward the chief, who could not help but admire this comely beauty in the sheer nightgown. Arakashe instantly knew why this white woman had captured Hawk's attention. Her unmatched beauty was as rare as that of the rose and her eyes danced with living fire. For a long quiet moment Arakashe merely stared at Rozalyn, recalling another maiden who had once brought joy to his own heart with her undaunted spirit and pleasing grace. There was no fear in this woman's eyes, only a flickering of inner strength that alerted Arakashe to the fact that Hawk's woman did not cower from catastrophe.

"Thank you for your assistance," Rozalyn murmured. "If it were not for you and your braves, I fear I would have met with disaster." She was grateful that it was the Crow who had come to her rescue for she felt she had nothing to fear from Hawk's people.

"You will come with us," Arakashe announced. He gestured for one of the braves to bring the riderless paint pony to Rozalyn.

At that, a wary frown knitted Rozalyn's brow. Although the chief had saved her from the lecherous trappers, she had serious reservations about traipsing off with these Crow braves. She wondered where Hawk was.

Had he really gone to the Crow village?

Rozalyn tilted her chin and refused to budge from the spot. "It is my wish to return to the stockade," she firmly announced.

Arakashe's dark eyes danced with amusement. "No harm will come to you, Mitskapa," he assured her.

"What do you want with me?" Rozalyn demanded to know.

"I have come to speak of the rivalry between your father and my grandson's people."

Rozalyn's frown became deeper. What the devil was going on here? If Hawk had sent the chief for her, why hadn't the aging warrior told her so. "Where is Hawk? Have you seen him?"

Arakashe nodded affirmatively. "He came to me and I have sent him into the land of Morningstar. When the time is right, I will lead you to him, as he wishes."

"How do I know it was Hawk who sent you?"

A low rattle of laughter broke the strained silence. "I am the council chief of the Crow. When Manake was a young boy, living among our people, he followed in my shadow. Even as a mighty warrior he comes to me when his heart is heavy. While he bears the weight of Mother Earth on his shoulders, I have come to take you under my protection." Ever so slowly, Arakashe offered an outstretched hand in a gesture of good will. Then he graced his skeptical companion with a reassuring smile. "Come with me, Mitskapa. You will be safe from harm. It is time you learned the legend of Whispering Falls in the Valley of the Elk."

Another superstitious legend, Rozalyn thought cynically. She wasn't certain she wanted to hear another wild tale. The trappers had already filled her head with enough fantastic yarns to last her a lifetime. She didn't want to hear the old chief weave another farfetched story! She wanted to know why her father detested the Baudelairs!

When Rozalyn remained rooted to the ground, Arakashe became impatient. Hawk is right, he decided. This stubborn white woman is not easily swayed by gentle words. She will be obedient only when a man proves himself worthy of her trust. But the aging chief was weary for he had lost a night's sleep. Speaking the Crow dialect, he ordered three of his braves to forcefully plant Rozalyn on the back of the paint pony. And they did, but not without meeting with resistance.

"I have spoken, Mitskapa," Arakashe told her sharply, reining his steed to the south. "You will come of your own accord or you will be taken by force. The choice lies with you."

Rozalyn glared at the chief's departing back, but when the warriors crowded around her, she reluctantly followed after Arakashe. They rode in silence, past the stockade and along the moonlit trail that led to the Crow camp beside the Yellowstone River.

Hawk has done it again, Rozalyn thought acrimoniously. First he had pawned her off on the Sioux and now the Crow. He kept traipsing off and leaving her in the custody of total strangers. Would he be receptive to such treatment if their positions were reversed? Rozalyn doubted it. She brooded over the annoying thought all the way to the village.

After being deposited in a wigwam around which guards were posted, she paced the small shelter, mulling over her unsettling thoughts. She was beginning to feel that she was insignificant in Hawk's life, although they had not yet gone their separate ways. He was a living, breathing part of this perilous land, and occasionally, he was struck by the impulse to return to it—alone. Loving her simply wasn't enough to sustain him. It never would be, even if they had a future together, Rozalyn thought sullenly. Otherwise, why would Hawk wander off into the wilderness without her? He wasn't going to, suddenly, change his ways and be content as her constant companion. Maybe it was best that they returned to their own lives, treasuring their memories instead of remaining together until Hawk felt too confined by her and fell out of love. When she was haunted by a maddening craving for adventure, she could turn to Harvey Duncan. Once upon a time that had been enough to satisfy her, but Rozalyn realized it would no longer suffice, not after she had blazed a trail through the Mountains of the Wind. Nonetheless, roaming the streets would be all she could turn to when restlessness overwhelmed her.

Perhaps her father's coming was a blessing in disguise. Wouldn't it be easier to leave Hawk while he still loved her than it would to remain by his side and watch his affection wither and die?

Pondering those tormenting thoughts, Rozalyn stretched out on the fur robes. As she tossed restlessly, unable to sleep, she decided that loving a man like Hawk was futile. She couldn't win, no matter what the future held.

Chapter 26

For three days Rozalyn milled about the Crow camp, feeling like a useless stick of furniture for she was ignored. For endless hours she tried to prepare herself to lose the man who had come to mean more to her than life. She had seen very little of Arakashe after he'd deposited her in his village, and although he came to speak with her occasionally, he never mentioned the legend or Hawk. Instead, his conversation was usually centered around the customs of the Crow. He also spoke of the increasing numbers of Longknives and of the Indian migration to the West.

Heaving a frustrated sigh, Rozalyn kicked at the grass, uprooting a clump. How long would she be kept here? she wondered. Until rendezvous? What did Hawk and his grandfather have in mind for her?

"You grow restless, Mitskapa," the old chief chortled as he walked up behind her.

Rozalyn glanced over her shoulder to see Arakashe holding the lead ropes of two mounts packed with supplies and with her belongings which had been retrieved from Fort Cass. Finally, they were departing from the village. Perhaps now Arakashe would lead her to Hawk and she could obtain some answers. And this time

Hawk had better answer her questions. She did not appreciate being treated like a fool, and she had had her fill of secrecy.

"The trappers at the fort have shown concern about your absence," Arakashe commented as Rozalyn climbed onto the paint's back. "They long for the day you will join them at rendezvous."

"I would have bid them adieu, had I been granted the opportunity," she muttered, a hint of sarcasm in her tone.

"You have not been happy of heart among the Crow," the chief surmised. He chuckled softly. "Hawk warned me that you would not be satisfied when you were not in control of your own destiny, but it is now time for you to see the boiling rivers and to offer tributes to the spirits of the springs."

When Arakashe leaned across the distance that separated them to offer her a .50-caliber rifle, Rozalyn's jaw dropped and her eyes widened.

"Our journey is long, the path dangerous. I would not lay a weapon in the hands of a woman if I were not certain she knew how to use it." The grinning chief pulled himself upright on his steed and shot Rozalyn a sidewise glance. "But my grandson told me you were trained by the master trapper himself. I have no worry that you will accidentally make me your target, Mitskapa."

"Do you know Bear-Claw?" Rozalyn asked, nudging her steed into a position abreast of Arakashe's mount.

"I have known him for many snows," the old chief admitted, his dark eyes drifting to the craggy peaks that stretched out before them. "There was a time when he lived as one of our people, content with the ways of the free-flying Sparrow Hawk. But many snows have come and gone since the master trapper has ventured into the Yellowstone. Is he well?" Arakashe's sincere gaze drifted back to Rozalyn who nodded affirmatively.

"He was when I last saw him two months ago," she informed the chief. "And you have appropriately named him the master trapper, although I doubt that he is as wise as the Crow council chief."

Rozalyn wasn't certain why she had blurted out the compliment. She had been standoffish with Arakashe, yet something about the aging warrior compelled respect. She had noticed that the Crow greatly admired their chieftain. Many of the braves sought his counsel regarding their differences, and the gray-haired chief had an aura similar to Hawk's.

Arakashe was as startled by the compliment as Rozalyn was at impulsively offering it. "Your words touch my heart, Mitskapa. It is my wish that we make peace." When Rozalyn gave him the first relaxed smile she had managed in three days, Arakashe knew she finally looked upon him as a friend.

On their two-day ride through ravines and narrow mountain passes, Rozalyn had been entranced by the spectacular surroundings. To the east rose the Wind River Mountains, their bleached and snowy summits reaching into the clouds. These jagged precipices stretched to the northwest until they melted into the rugged mountains of the Yellowstone. In the valleys between the two imposing mountain ranges lived the Absarkoe, or the Crow, a tribe of tall, powerfully built warriors, whose chief rode with Rozalyn. They had made the rugged journey from the foothills to meet Hawk, but Arakashe had had a dual purpose in mind when he'd chosen this particular path. He had come to the place where Morningstar dwelled to lend credence to the legend of Whispering Falls in the Valley of the Elk. From the headwaters of Green River, onto the western slopes that rivaled the grandeur of the Wind River Mountains, Arakashe had guided Rozalyn, letting her marvel at nature's beauty.

Now the old chief's appreciative gaze drifted to the west side of the mountains. It was cloaked in deep purple for dusk was shading those massive rocks while sharp, bright light glittered on the lofty precipices above them. The chief glanced up at the opposite wall of mountains, which still basked in warm yellow light, and he sighed heavily, entranced by these sights he had seen dozens of times before. The colors made a fascinating contrast, shrouding the summits in a rainbow of breathtaking splendor. In the background were the blue mountains of the upper Yellowstone, extending as far as the eye could see.

Smiling at Rozalyn's awestruck expression, Arakashe gestured toward the northwest and began to spin his tale of tragedy. He knew the story would hold this skeptical young woman spellbound for she was overwhelmed by the beauty of the mountains.

"It was one evening in summer, the time of the long day when twilight kisses the summits ruled by Morningstar, the Great Spirit of the people of the Sparrow Hawk." A quiet sigh escaped his lips when he peered back through time to unveil the memories that had long pained his heart. "There was once among us a young maiden the Absarkoe honored with the name of Bitshipe, Rose Blossom. She was neither too short nor too tall. Her waist was trim and her eyes danced with a lively curiosity, much like yours."

Rozalyn's sunburned face turned a darker shade of red when the chief offered her the compliment, but she kept silent for she was anxious to hear where his story would lead.

"The young men of our village respected Bitshipe. The older ones, who had been on the warpath and had earned the right to take a wife, were eager to take her as their woman. Many horses were offered by each suitor, but the beautiful maiden with hair as dark as midnight refused them all.

"Rose Blossom had seen a vision of two men in her dreams. She did not understand its true meaning, but she knew her destiny was tied to both of these men. For that reason she would not consent to any of the braves who approached her. And when these two men appeared in our village Bitshipe's heart was both happy and sad. She feared she was to belong to one man and become the enemy of the other."

A muddled frown knitted Rozalyn's brow while she listened to Arakashe relate the legend. Tears misted the old chief's eyes, and Rozalyn could not help but wonder why the tale evoked such strong feelings in him.

"I have promised to tell you the story of Whispering Falls in the Valley of the Elk. I will repeat the legend as accurately as my memory can permit. Heed its lesson, Mitskapa, and do not forget this story I unfold for you." Arakashe turned his attention to the towering crests that broke the evening sky. "Rose Blossom and Wapike, as this man was known among the Crow, had gone together to hunt on the bluffs in the Mountains of the Wind. At twilight, they stood contentedly in each other's arms, watching the long shadows fall upon the summits, listening to the thundering waterfall that spilled over the slopes to feed the never-ending river. As they whispered their vows of eternal love, Apitsa, the other man from the dark side of Rose Blossom's dream, sprang upon them. Apitsa was angry and bitter because he, too, was drawn to this lovely Crow maiden. He had come to fight for the woman he wanted as his wife. Both men battled fiercely, each firm in his belief that Rose Blossom was to be his destiny.

"But Bitshipe was hopelessly tied to Wapike. Her affection for Apitsa was not as great. Desperately, she tried to force the warring men apart before one of them brought the shadow of death upon the other.

405

"During this hard-fought struggle Bitshipe was flung aside by Apitsa, who was possessed by evil spirits that longed to avenge his crying heart. Rose Blossom stumbled back and her foot faltered on the crumbling ledge above the Valley of the Elk." Arakashe's jaw tensed as the scene flashed before his eyes like a haunting nightmare. "She could not keep her balance. As she plunged from the soaring heights and fell into the falls, her terrified voice mingled with the rushing waters that tumbled over the jagged rocks. Wapike's name was on her lips when she surrendered her life. The deep waters opened wide to accept Rose Blossom, and her spirit was offered to Morningstar as the sun hid its head behind the mountains."

Rozalyn had heard dozens of legends from the trappers, but the one Arakashe had unfolded piqued her curiosity. Although she had vowed to keep silent without interrupting his tragic tale, she could no longer hold back the questions that flew from her lips. "And what of these two warriors?" Her wide eyes scanned the majestic peaks to the northeast. "Did Wapike avenge Rose Blossom's death?"

"No, Mitskapa. It is not the way of our people, though there are many who are eager to adopt the practices of the white man and to change the custom of the peaceful Absarkoe." Arakashe drew his rabbit-skin blanket closely about him to ward off the evening chill. "In Wapike's heart-wrenching grief, the battle with Apitsa was soon forgotten. Swiftly, Wapike scrambled down the bluff in search of his lost love. There, beside the rapids, he waited for two days and two nights. He fasted and prayed for Rose Blossom to appear to him. When she did not come, he mourned his great loss.

"Apitsa, whose own heart was heavy with sorrow, fled from the mountains. He could not look upon the valley without remembering what he had done to the beautiful maiden who had taken hold of his heart. He became an outcast, shunned by the people of the Sparrow Hawk for his vengeful heart had wrought a tragedy and brought death to the woman he coveted as his own. His soul was shattered when he heard Wapike's name on her lips as she fell into the falls.

The aging chief squirmed uncomfortably on his paint pony, his misty eyes taking on a faraway expression that touched his wrinkled features. "It is Bitshipe's sad story and her dying words that whisper in the great falls and echo along the walls of the Valley of the Elk. It was because of this tragic struggle between Rose Blossom and the two powerful warriors who wanted her that this legend came to be. Makhupa, the medicine man and shaman of the Crow, was very fond of Rose Blossom. He had long admired her beauty and lively spirit. When he learned that Bitshipe had perished in the falls his own heart was heavy with sorrow, and he made his way to the ridge that overlooked the valley. Raising his arms and his voice in a plea to Morningstar, he placed a lasting curse on the valley. Makhupa commanded the falls to whisper Rose Blossom's tragic fate to Morningstar so he would be merciful to her wandering spirit.

"Every creature of the earth that lived in the fertile valley now stands in stone. Time does not move beyond the towering peaks where the Mountains of the Wind forge the Yellowstone. The grass, the prairie fowl, the elk, and bear may be seen from the cliffs, as perfect and as natural as they were in life." A tear slid down Arakashe's weather-beaten face. "Even the wild roses, for which Bitshipe was named, bloom in colors of solid crystal. There the birds, even the great sparrow hawk, soar on mighty wings in motionless flight. Only the great falls continues to flow on its course across the colorful rocks, moving forever toward the sea. The air is alive with a sad melody and the mournful voice of Bitshipe continues to call to her lost love. In the Valley of the Elk, the sun and moon shine with petrified light, and because of this curse, our people no longer venture into the region beyond these crests. It is sacred ground. There, the memory of Rose Blossom lives on and the falls murmur Wapike's name."

"It is a sad legend," Rozalyn mused aloud. She peered off into the distance, imagining a place where birds soared in motionless flight, where a waterfall spoke with a human voice that was heavy with sorrow. It was not difficult to be caught up in the tale when she was overwhelmed by the magnitude of the mountains.

Rozalyn found herself wondering if there could truly be such a place where time stood still.

"It is a very sad story," Arakashe agreed. Nudging his pony, he pursued the treacherous path long the lofty crests. "The curse of the shaman shall remain on the Valley of the Elk for many snows. When it is Wapike's time to walk into the spiritual world of Morningstar, he will return to the bluff where he and Rose Blossom once stood. There he will answer the call of Whispering Falls and will search out Rose Blossom's restless spirit. Only then will the sparrow hawk dip and dive and feel the wind beneath its wings. Only then will the elk and antelope melt from stone to graze upon the rich grass that lines the valley."

"Wapike has taken no other woman for his wife?" Rozalyn queried. "But you said it was the custom of your people to live on, to make a new life with another squaw. Does Wapike have no other wives to console him?"

"Wapike will never take another wife. He cannot." Arakashe braced himself when the pony sidestepped along the narrow trail. "He cannot forget Rose Blossom's hauntingly lovely face or the tormented whisper of her voice. He cannot close his eyes without seeing hers shining before him in the darkness. When Rose Blossom perished in the falls she took Wapike's heart with her.

What no longer belongs to Wapike, he cannot offer to another. If he did chose another woman, she would only remind him of Rose Blossom. He would have no love to give her. What could a man offer to another woman if not his heart? A man cannot speak if he has no voice, nor can a man offer love if he has no heart."

Dark penetrating eyes focused on Rozalyn, who had the uneasy feeling there was something about the legend Arakashe hadn't told her. "One must remember that so great a love can sometimes cause great pain. The legend of Bitshipe is one you will not soon forget. The lesson it holds for all of us is one of caution." The faintest hint of a smile rippled across Arakashe's parched lips. "When Hawk was young I brought him to this place to speak of the legend. He bravely announced to me that he did not wish to die while he still lived, that he would never fall so deeply in love that his heart would bleed. But he could not foretell the future, when he was destined to walk among white men and red men alike, calling all of them his brothers. He grew to be a great warrior among the Crow as well as the Longknives. I have prayed to Morningstar that he will find happiness, and that it will not be cut short by another warrior's vengeance."

Eerie sensations skittered up and down Rozalyn's spine. She felt as if the mountains were whispering to her while she and Arakashe blazed a trail along their perilous slopes. Was Arakashe trying to tell her that loving Hawk was a lost cause? She had had that very thought a thousand times in the past weeks.

"Remember well what I have told you, Mitskapa," Arakashe insisted, pinning her to the towering rock wall with a probing stare. "No one has challenged the curse of Whispering Falls. Time has its own way of righting the wrongs of our forefathers. It is the teacher of all things. You must remember the sad legend and avoid the valley of stone. When the curse is lifted, Wapike will walk into the river's waiting arms and life in the Valley of the Elk will be as it once was. Until that day, our people veer away from the mountain overlooking the falls. In the future, you will also speak of this legend. Speak of it with feeling and pass it onto others as accurately as your memory will allow."

When Arakashe had finished, he eased himself from his pony to make camp for the night. Rozalyn peered at the chief who silently crouched to build a fire to ward off the chill.

"I was stirred by the tragic legend," she confessed. "But I think there is more, something you are hiding from me. Has it something to do with the feud between my family and Hawk's?" Rozalyn could not imagine how her father could have had anything to do with the legend since her mother had been white, a descendant of the French aristocracy who had established St. Louis. Yet, Arakashe's remark about a man never being able to love again hit a sensitive nerve. That description seemed to fit her dispassionate father, a man who had made the fur-trading business his life, shutting out his family. Perhaps she was just grasping for some connection, she told herself. This might be just another superstitious tale like the ones she had heard from the trappers. Would she ever learn why her father had such a fierce grudge against Hawk's family?

"You are too impatient, Mitskapa," Arakashe chided lightly. "First you must ponder the legend. Later you will learn its meaning in your life. Not all stories have happy endings. My heart grows heavy when I consider my grandson, and I wonder if Morningstar will smile kindly on him."

Rozalyn prayed fate would smile upon both of them, but she dared not live on false hope. It was as Hawk had said. They had made a space in their lives for love and they could only revel in happiness until it was time for

410

her to return home. She could expect no more than that. Arakashe had made it a point to remind her that happy endings did not necessarily follow when a man and woman fell in love. Was the wise, perceptive chief of the Crow preparing her for the worst? Was that to be her life story? Rozalyn trembled uncontrollably as she stretched out on her pallet by the fire. The more she contemplated the legend and Arakashe's words, the more depressed she became. Why had she dared to fall in love when she knew there was no future with Hawk? It had been easy in the beginning. Rozalyn had convinced herself that she could survive on blissful memories. But now, when the end was near, she wondered if she hadn't been a fool.

When she thought of Hawk, she found herself comparing their affair to a journey down a treacherous river. There had been turbulent rapids along the way, and also peaceful waters. But even from the distance they had heard the thundering of a waterfall, one they must approach. And now there was no turning back, Rozalyn thought disheartenedly. She and Hawk had been swept into a current of passion and there was no place to go but down into the torrents of water to the frothy pool below.

If only Hawk were here with her to chase away her fears . . . But he wasn't and she was left to drown in her dreary thoughts. She kept reminding herself that no one had promised her life would be happy and carefree. She had been existing in a fairy tale for so many months that she had forgotten there was such a thing as reality. Soon she must come to grips with it, and once she had taken the impending fall she would see the world as it truly was—cruel, unjust, and gracious only to a select few. But the worst part of it all was that the man with the dancing green eyes and raven hair would not be there to help her through the rough times ahead, times when the sweet memories of their mountain paradise would be lost to her.

Chapter 27

As Arakashe led Rozalyn through the Yellowstone she became increasingly aware that the fantastic tales of Colter's Hell were true. The sprawling lakes and hot pools that lay before her resembled morning-glory flowers in color and shape, and the sparkling waters that spilled over pastel rocks rivaled the beauty of rainbows. It was like walking into nature's sanctuary.

When the old chief reined his steed to a halt and gestured to the west, Rozalyn's awestruck gaze followed his arm, and she saw a steamy marsh in the distance. "This is the land of the spirit springs. Here, Hawk will come to take you with him on the hunt." Warm brown eyes fell fondly upon her. "I must return to my people to prepare for migration to our spring hunting ground." His tanned finger traced the exquisite features of her face and he blessed her with another smile, one that held a hint of remorse. "You have won a place in my heart, Mitskapa. May the Great Spirit of the people of the free-soaring Sparrow Hawk be kind to you."

To Rozalyn's amazement, the aging chief reversed direction and left her sitting amidst the steamy springs. "You aren't leaving me here alone?" she gasped in disbelief.

Arakashe twisted atop his pony, a confident grin lighting his wrinkled features. "You are a strong, resourceful woman, Mitskapa. Even the name I have given you speaks of your ability to survive the greatest trials. Wild Rose, as it translates in your native tongue, signifies that you blossom like a wild bud, taking root at will in this beautiful but perilous region. Soon Hawk will come for you. But for now, it is best for you to be alone in the land of Morningstar."

When Arakashe disappeared from sight, Rozalyn glanced uneasily about her and then swung from her pony to give her backside a much-needed rest. How long was she to await Hawk's return? What if . . . The thought of attack by a savage or a beast left her with unsettling sensations. She dragged her rifle from its sling and clung to it, just in case such dangers came her way.

Aimlessly, she ambled about, listening to the gurgling streams and the warble of the birds that nestled in the trees. She didn't want to think. It depressed her. Besides, she had done her fair share of contemplating during the journey and she had gained little more from her efforts than a headache.

Rozalyn sank onto the ground to survey the magnificent scenery, keeping a watchful eye for trouble. The last time she had been left alone in the wilds, she had confronted a grizzly. Now she wondered what other creatures were lurking in this vast mountain range, waiting to make her their midday meal.

A low rumble resounded about her, jolting her from her silent reverie. The sound made the ground vibrate beneath, and then a hiss followed, as if a thousand snakes had congregated to serenade her. Rozalyn shuddered. Perhaps an earthquake was about to occur, she thought. But before she could seek more solid ground, the hissing sound grew louder until it very nearly deafened her, and from the peaceful pool near which she sat, a steamy geyser erupted, shooting scalding water two hundred feet into the air. Startled and screaming for all she was worth, Rozalyn bolted to her feet and darted away before the hot mist doused her. When she was safely out of range, she wheeled around to view the bewildering jet, her eyes wide with amazement.

There was indeed such a place as Colter's Hell, where hot springs belched from the earth. She had been skeptical when she had heard the tales of the adventurers and trappers who wandered in the wilderness. But now she was a believer. She had seen and heard the eruption, and she could no longer doubt the existence of geysers and boiling springs.

"Do you still intend to mock me when I insist there is a place where water boils from the earth and rivers of steam hover about the creek beds?"

Hawk's amused voice came from so close behind her that Rozalyn very nearly jumped out of her skin. He had sneaked up on her as silently as a great cat. His stealth and the fact that he had abandoned her earlier had her temper at a roiling boil that matched the heat of the geyser spewing in the distance.

She pivoted around, her blue eyes blazing. Then, without voicing a greeting, she let fly with both barrels. "Damn you, Hawk. Have you not one shred of decency? Couldn't you have had the courtesy to inform me of your intentions before you waltzed off in the middle of the night? You can't store me in a cache in the ground as you do your supplies and pelts and then come retrieve me when the mood suits you. I do not appreciate being taken for granted," Rozalyn's voice was becoming higher and wilder by the second. She was so annoyed with him that she had an urge to hurl something more forceful than words. Hastily she glanced about her, searching for a rock, a club, anything that might serve to pound some sense into the man who, lately, had shown himself to be as insensitive as a pine tree!

When she spotted a weapon and reached for it, Hawk quickly drew her to him, waylaying her attempt to club him with a nearby stick. "A lecture on my faults and a painful beating was not the sort of reception I had envisioned," he murmured huskily.

Rozalyn was too angry to be stifled by the velvety huskiness of his voice. She was furious at him, and had been since Hawk had trotted off, leaving her in a stockade with unruly heathens for company. Forcefully, she pushed away, refusing to be mellowed until he swore he would never pull another such inconsiderate prank.

"Don't think you can coax me into submission, Hawk Baudelair," she spumed, her clenched fists resting on her hips, her wild hair tumbling about her in disarray. "Do you recall the names Dark-Eagle and Yellow-Calf? I certainly hope you don't count them among your friends! While you were waltzing about in the wilds, they sneaked into my cabin to abduct me. Not that you don't approve of such tactics," she added sourly. "After all, if you hadn't kidnapped me, I wouldn't be here in the first place." She was just gathering steam and she intended to erupt as long as the nearby geyser did. "Since I was unable to fend off both lechers, I faced rape. Arakashe came upon me and prevented it. Not that you seem to care a whit."

Hawk had been thoroughly enjoying her tantrum, watching her full breasts heave with every indignant breath she inhaled, and noting the sparks flying from her sky-blue eyes ... until she told him about the aborted assault. At that news, his mouth compressed in a hard line.

"I do care and you damned well know it," he snapped back at her. "I have made mention of the fact several times, or has your memory escaped you?"

"My memory serves me well," Rozalyn flared, her

chin tilting a notch higher so she could stare down her nose at him. "You said we would be together until the end. It is your memory lapse that concerns me, my love." The endearment sounded like a curse, and at the moment, that was exactly how Rozalyn meant it. "You are adoring and affectionate when it meets your whim, but when you crave your freedom you think nothing of stashing me in a corner and prancing off. Damnation, I could have been raped!"

"Well, at least your assailants received retribution," Hawk retored. He knew Rozalyn was right so he couldn't very well argue the point. He had been preoccupied with his troubled thoughts and he had needed the time and space in which to think, not that he had solved his dilemma, but at least he had tried. "I'm sure my grandfather saw to it that your molesters were buried neck-deep in ant hills."

"Like hell! Arakashe didn't bother with torture. He only banished the drunken trappers from the Crow lands. I personally would have had them shot, but I was given no say in the matter. The Crow chief then had me deposited on a horse and herded away although I insisted I had no inclination to accompany him."

A bemused frown plowed Hawk's brow. Arakashe must be growing soft in his declining years, he mused. At one time the chief would have such offenders strung upside down or buried in the ground and left for the ants. It seemed he had become more tolerant of the Longknives. Perhaps that was because Hawk was half-white. Why else would Arakashe have spared the lives of Dark-Eagle and Yellow-Calf?

While Hawk was attempting to analyze the chief's actions, Rozalyn hurried on, refusing to be derailed from her train of thought. "And that is another matter that infuriates me. I do not appreciate being carted off by a party of Indians and detained in a camp in which I can converse with only one member of the tribe. Thank heavens Arakashe speaks English! At least when he spared me the time I could communicate with him, unlike the chief of the Sioux who didn't have the faintest idea what I was ranting about!" Rozalyn inhaled deeply and then plunged on, incensed that Hawk had broken into a smile. "Don't you dare speak of love when you merely consider me a convenient object of your lust! I have had enough of your contradictions. If I truly mean something to you, why did you abandon me for two weeks when you know our days are numbered? Bear-Claw taught me to survive in this wilderness but you leave me behind to traipse off only God knows where!"

"Are you finished?" Hawk raised a dark eyebrow and then bit back a chuckle when Rozalyn glared at him.

"Not quite," she fumed, taking a bold step forward to shake a dainty finger in his face. "I have thought it over, and I have decided to return to the fort to await my father's arrival. You seem to be satisfied with your self-imposed isolation. Far be it from me to make you drag me along with you when you appear content to hunt and trap the Yellowstone alone."

Actually, it was a spur-of-the-moment decision. Rozalyn suddenly realized the future would be easier to bear if she left Hawk while she was angry with him. It had to be less difficult to get over loving him if they parted on a sour note. Besides, it was useless to live on false hope. She had known that in the beginning, and Arakashe's wise words about the scarcity of happy endings preyed heavily on her mind. Perhaps she would be attacked by a bear during her return journey and put out of her misery.

When Rozalyn wheeled around to stalk toward her pony, Hawk's quiet words halted her in her tracks, melting her ire and spoiling any chance of surviving the future without a bleeding heart. "Roz, I do love you. I always have," Hawk told her, his tone so soft and sincere

417

that Rozalyn wilted like a dainty flower in the blistering sun. "Maybe I was inconsiderate, but I had to be alone to attempt to devise a way to keep my promise to the other trappers and still have you with me after rendezvous. I came to the Yellowstone to think, not to avoid you. God, don't you know I would rather be in your arms than staring up at a sea of stars that never shine as brightly as when you send me on a journey among them?" Steadily, he approached her, filling her world, letting her view the raw emotion in his eyes; and his craggy features mellowed in a smile. "Loving you has made me vulnerable, can't you see that? There was a time when I didn't consider the future. I only took each day as it came. But now there's you, and that has made all the difference. I made a bargain with your father, a vow to the trappers. I am obliged to keep both, but my honor is the source of my torment." Hawk expelled a heavy sigh as he lifted a hand and brushed his thumb across the satiny texture of her cheek. "I came here in search of a solution that would allow me to keep my promise without giving you up. But if there is one, I am too blind to see it. Perhaps, I am too emotional where you are concerned to uncover it."

Ever so slowly, his arms surrounded her, molding her soft feminine flesh to his hard, male contours, and for a moment Hawk was content merely to hold her, to fill the emptiness of a fortnight of wanting. "Don't leave me, Roz. There is so little time left when I had hoped for an eternity with you. I prayed during the two weeks I was without you, prayed that a way to keep us together would be revealed to me. But each solution that came to me only created more problems. I considered kidnapping you again after I bargained with your father, but that would only make him furious. He would send the cavalry after me, and we would be forced to live like hunted animals, running, afraid of our own shadows. I even considered sacrificing my friends in a desperate attempt to keep you. They, above all, would understand. But your father will not contemplate any compromise without your return. I doubt that all the money I could offer him would sway him, not if it meant leaving you with a man he despises with every part of his being."

"I'm sorry," Rozalyn murmured, her eyes welling up with tears. "I had no right to hurl petty complaints at you. I was angry and I was lashing out at an impossible situation. Oh, Hawk, make this month we have together last an eternity. Make me forget the world will come to an end at rendezvous."

Rozalyn curled her arms around his granite shoulders, clinging to his solid strength, and when his fiery emerald eyes focused on her quivering lips, she parted them invitingly. Silky ebony strands spilled down her back, as she tilted her head upward, granting him free access to her soft mouth.

"This was the sort of greeting I had in mind," he whispered huskily, his arms tightening about her.

"I only hope I can compete with the mystical mermaids of the spirit springs," she taunted, her body moving provocatively against his and sending delicious sensations trickling down his spine. "No doubt, you have turned to them for comfort these past two weeks."

"There are no such creatures as mermaids," Hawk heard himself say through a cloudy haze of steamy passion.

"Beware, skeptic. I no longer doubt, and now is not the time for you to start," Rozalyn purred as her adventurous hands slid beneath his buckskin shirt to make arousing contact with the lean muscles of his belly. "We stand on the very spot where Hell bubbles up, where gurgling rivers soar into the sky. If underground springs can pour down like rain, one should never question the existence of a creature half-woman and half-fish."

419

When her lips melted against his like a thirst-quenching sip of wine, Hawk lost all interest in conversation. The knot of longing within him unfurled, and desire channeled through his every nerve and muscle. Eager to appease the gnawing craving that had tormented him for two weeks, Hawk clutched Rozalyn to him, overwhelmed by a need as ancient as time itself. Still, he couldn't get close enough to the flame that was burning him alive. His kiss devoured, savored, the intoxicating taste of her. His hands roamed over her flesh, hungry to touch, to arouse, to satisfy. As a muffled groan erupted from his laboring chest, the earth trembled beneath him.

When another nearby geyser erupted, Rozalyn was jolted back to reality. The ground beneath her feet was actually quivering, this was not just a response to Hawk's lovemaking. Her wide eyes followed the path of water that shot into the air like a cannonball, leaving a steamy spray in its wake, and when Hawk's soft laughter vibrated against the trim column of her throat, she smiled.

"And all this time I thought you were the cause of my uncontrollable quaking," she teased, as she laid her head against his shoulder to watch the display of Yellowstone's natural fountain.

"I called upon the geyser to aid me in my attempt to convince you that only my embrace causes the earth to move beneath you," Hawk chortled softly. "The Crow claim these eruptions are the spirits of the springs speaking to the inhabitants of Mother Earth."

"And what are the spirits saying?" Rozalyn questioned while she watched the pool gurgle and then shoot forth another hot stream.

A roguish grin melted Hawk's rugged features, making his eyes sparkle like polished emeralds. "The spirits say only a fool would not take advantage of a lady like you in a place like this." His amusement dimmed and his expression sobered as he tilted her face to peer into her breathtaking pools of blue. "Strange, I thought I had to leave you to come to terms with the future or find a way to change it to suit me. But tomorrow seems a thousand years away when I have you in my arms."

His lips rolled over hers, and their breaths intermingled. Rozalyn was certain it was no freak event of nature that caused the sky to turn as black as pitch and the earth to shudder when Hawk molded their bodies together and kissed her with all the pent-up emotion churning within him. Her mind clouded, and her body arched to seek ultimate intimacy. She knew only that she needed Hawk, that he was a magician who could perform miracles.

Hawk's male body instantly roused to the feel of her shapely curves. His eager hands rediscovered her sensitive places, making her experience the same ardent need that seized him as his lips abandoned hers to blaze a trail of white-hot fire across her throat. All the riches of this westernmost frontier meant nothing in comparison to the rapturous emotions that engulfed him when he lost himself in the feel and scent of the woman in his arms. Hawk soared, momentarily forgetting what awaited him at his journey's end—the agony of loneliness—for here . . . here in the circle of Rozalyn's arms was a euphoric paradise into which reality could not intrude.

A sigh of pleasure tripped from Rozalyn's lips when Hawk divested her of her clothes and drew her to the ground. Breathless, she eagerly explored his sinewy strength. While his wandering hands swam across her bare skin, she returned each tantalizing caress, each fervent kiss, and as their need for each other rose to a crescendo they came together in breathless urgency, hearts thundering in perfect rhythm, bodies singing in harmony with love's precious music.

Their weeks of wanting converged as they scaled

passion's mountain, soaring above the steaming springs and bubbling rivers, and their lovemaking blocked out their apprehensions about the future. While time hung suspended, Rozalyn explored the heights and depths of love, gliding on pinioned wings to pursue each ineffable sensation. Then it was as if a universe of emotions collided, sweeping her up into soul-shattering sensations. Her body quaked as indescribable pleasure spilled over her and trickled into every part of her being.

Instinctively, she clung to Hawk, her nails biting into the corded tendons of his back, as a whimper escaped from her. Then she buried her face against his shoulder, waiting for the wild, sweet sensations to ebb and leave her to mindless bliss.

In the aftermath of love, Hawk reared his head, marveling at the passion that blazed up when he took Rozalyn in his arms. It had always been like this between them, he mused, bending to press yet another kiss to her sensuous lips. Time might dim his memories, but Hawk knew if he returned to St. Louis months, even years, after he and Rozalyn parted, the flame of their love would burn just as brightly. It would take only one glance in her direction to ignite it. How many years would pass before they could be together again without inviting Aubrey Dubois' fury? A score, a score and ten? Would Hawk spend his days, waiting for Aubrey to meet his Maker, waiting until the one obstacle that stood between them had vanished from the face of the earth? Hitherto, Hawk had wished death on only one man—Half-Head, a merciless murderer who had lived and died by the blade. Only a spineless coward would await the end of another human being before he walked in to claim his most treasured possession.

Dammit, why couldn't he think of a way to work out his future? Never in his life had he backed down from adversity. Instead, he had played every situation to his advantage. But at this most important time in his life he was floundering like a witless fool. There must be a feasible way to defeat Aubrey and still grant the hard-working trappers their just reward. He must approach the problem calmly, rationally. Where was the answer for which he so desperately searched?

Flinging aside his depressing thoughts, Hawk focused his attention on the bewitching nymph in his arms. He had pondered for two long weeks to no avail. Now Rozalyn was with him, and he was not about to waste one moment of their precious time. Mustering what was left of his strength, he rolled to his feet and drew Rozalyn up beside him. With her small hand clasped in his, he weaved his way around the bubbling mudpots to a spring-fed whirlpool. Scooping Rozalyn into his arms, he walked into the warm bath.

A soft sigh escaped her lips when the tepid water swirled around her. "Forgive me for doubting the existence of spirit springs," Rozalyn murmured, and twisting free, she eased onto her back to drift with the circling current. "Colter's Hell?" Her easy laughter tickled Hawk's senses and called to him like a siren from the sea. "The name is most inappropriate. This must surely be paradise."

Hawk was certain of it. And, strangely enough, he was sure he was watching a mermaid cut through the water. Among Rozalyn's other unusual talents, it appeared she could swim like a fish. He watched in awe as she disappeared beneath the surface like a bird diving into the water to claim its prey. Then, like a geyser bursting forth from a peaceful pool, she resurfaced, only to dive from his sight.

Never had Hawk felt so whole and alive. When he touched this enticing mermaid's skin and stared into those beguiling blue eyes, he hadn't one dismal thought, and his heart stirred.

When Rozalyn swam between his legs and then emerged to melt in his arms, Hawk's meandering thoughts became fixed on her. He looked into bright blue eyes and saw his world. Following her lead, he dived into the pool, to give chase to the elusive mermaid who had slipped from his arms to return to the spring from which she had come. Like two playful children, they frolicked in the water while the sun made its slow descent across the sky, Hawk plunging into the whirlpool to grasp Rozalyn's ankle and then towing her down with him, his powerful arms enfolding her and his lips seeking hers as they sank onto the spring's bed. When they burst back to the surface for a breath of air, Rozalyn giggled giddily as they bobbed in the tepid pool.

"Do you suppose my friends in St. Louis will think me mad when I tell them of a land of spewing fountains and hot springs?" Suddenly her voice trailed off and the carefree smile faded from her lips.

Her unthinking remark had shattered the spell. She drifted from Hawk's arms and waded ashore. Reluctantly, Hawk followed in her wake to don the clothes he'd discarded in their moment of passion.

"I suppose Arakashe told you the legend of Whispering Falls," he said, assisting Rozalyn onto her paint pony.

She nodded slightly, watching in admiration as Hawk, with lionlike grace, leaped upon his own mount. "But I still do not understand why he brought me to the Yellowstone to relate the legend. Does it have something to do with me and my father?"

"A great deal, I'm afraid," Hawk grumbled. "I forced Bear-Claw to tell me what happened so many years ago."

Rozalyn swallowed the lump in her throat. She could tell by the somber expression on Hawk's face that she wasn't going to like what she was about to hear, yet she had waited a long time to learn the cause of her father's bitterness.

Reining the steed to the north, Hawk led Rozalyn through the winding passes, unfolding the story Bear-Claw had confided in him. "When Lewis and Clark made their first expedition into Louisiana Territory, Lyndon Baudelair and Aubrey DuBois went along to map the region. My father saw the wild, natural beauty of this land, but Aubrey viewed the region as a place where wealth was to be gained from fur trading. During the years Aubrey and Lyndon spent together, they became confidants and friends. It was in the land of the Crow that your father met Bitshipe, my grandfather's only child."

The color seeped from Rozalyn's cheeks. Bitshipe, the lovely maid from the legend of Whispering Falls, was Arakashe's daughter? Her eyes flew back to Hawk and she hung on his every word, fearing the truth was going to be far worse than she had imagined.

"When Aubrey and Lyndon wintered with the Indians, they were accepted into the tribe and given Crow names as proof of their friendship between red man and white. Aubrey fell in love with Bitshipe, but he was not prepared to sacrifice his dream of a fur empire. After the first winter he left my father in charge of Bitshipe, requesting that Lyndon protect her and prevent her from marrying another man until he returned from St. Louis.

"Although Bitshipe admired Aubrey and his ambitious quest, she fell deeply in love with the man who had remained behind to protect her." Hawk's gaze focused intently on Rozalyn who had begun to piece together the legend before he could explain it.

"Both men loved the same woman—your mother," Rozalyn put in.

Hawk nodded grimly. "Lyndon, or Wapike as he was known to the Crow, became Bitshipe's constant shadow. Although my father had promised to keep Bitshipe safe for another man, he was drawn to her by a compelling attraction. A full year passed and Aubrey did not return, nor did he send word that he had safely reached St. Louis to carry out his fur-trading plan. They began to wonder if he had met with disaster as he'd ventured alone through the wilderness. After waiting throughout the summer, my father and Bitshipe gave Aubrey up for lost and they became man and wife as they'd longed to do. They had planned to explain their affection for each other to Aubrey when he returned, but he hadn't come." A faint smile lightened Hawk's somber visage as his eyes drifted to the distant plateau high above the Valley of the Elk. Gesturing to the east, he called Roz's attention to the murmuring falls that could be heard from a distance. "For a year my parents lived and loved as if the sun shone only for them. My father was content to make his home among the Crow, to live off a land that was rich in beauty and bountiful in game. He had no inclination to return to St. Louis, to the refinement of civilization. When Bitshipe bore him a son, he thought his life complete. In the spring Bitshipe coaxed my father into venturing to the Valley of the Elk to ask Morningstar for his blessing. She had grown to love that magnificent area of the mountains, and was certain that particular valley was Morningstar's paradise.

"In the meantime, Aubrey had made his way back to the Crow village. When he could not locate Bitshipe or his trusted friend Lyndon, he sought out Arakashe. Upon learning that he had been given up for dead and that the two he sought had wed and spawned a child, Aubrey was furious. He did not hold Bitshipe responsible, but he blamed my father for betraying him. Although Arakashe tried to stop Aubrey, he followed my parents to the Valley of the Elk, and when he saw the two of them in each other's arms, he was like a madman." Hawk paused a moment, allowing Rozalyn to recall the tragic incident on the precipice above Whispering Falls. "Arakashe told you how the argument ended. The woman Lyndon and

Aubrey truly loved was killed because of their battle over her. It was Aubrey who shoved Bitshipe aside so she plummeted from the towering ledge, and the accident nearly destroyed him as well. He could not forgive himself for taking her life, and he hated my father for marrying her. When he spied Arakashe sitting atop his steed on the summit, he knew he had fallen from the Crow's good graces and he fled back to St. Louis to build his vast fur trade.

"For years your father has harbored a hatred that has poisoned him. He and Lyndon Baudelair have not seen each other in thirty years, but Aubrey has never forgiven my father for that betrayal. And your father has never forgotten Rose Blossom. He even chose for his own daughter the name of the woman he could never have. No doubt, you continue to remind him of her. Rose Blossom . . . Rozalyn." Hawk murmured the names so softly that they could almost have been one and the same.

Finally, Rozalyn understood her father's remoteness, his inability to love her or her mother. Aubrey had married and produced an heir because he'd felt it his obligation to do so. After all, he had established a fur empire. He had married Jacqueline but he had never been able to love her, not the way he'd loved the Crow maiden, so he had thrown himself into his work to try to forget the woman who had died because of his rage. And his hatred for the Baudelairs had festered, while the bittersweet memory of Rose Blossom had lived on in her namesake—Rozalyn.

Her father continued to relive the heart-wrenching tragedy that kept him from loving again, Rozalyn thought. Aubrey had given his only daughter the wealth he could never lay at Rose Blossom's feet, but he'd withheld the love he would have freely given the Crow maiden. Aubrey had wanted it all—loyal friendship from Baudelair, immense wealth, and Bitshipe's vow to wait, no matter how long. But the Crow maiden had loved another and that knowledge had driven Aubrey to the brink of insanity.

Rozalyn pitied her father and yet she felt he was wrong to place the blame on Baudelair. Was Aubrey's hatred for Hawk's father, for the man's entire family, an attempt to soothe his own conscience and his injured pride? Was it Aubrey's way of dealing with the tragedy? Perhaps Aubrey would have been able to live his own life if he had assumed the blame for the incident. But Rozalyn doubted it. Aubrey DuBois was driven by a fierce inner force. He could not tolerate failure, especially his own. It was easier to loathe the name Baudelair than to admit that he might have done the same thing if he had walked in Lyndon's moccasins. Spending each day with a compellingly attractive woman was a great temptation.

Obviously, Aubrey had loved Bitshipe as fiercely as she loved Hawk, Rozalyn thought. Her father would not have behaved the way he had if he hadn't cared so deeply. He was the kind of man who was capable of loving only once in his life, or the tragedy surrounding his early love made it impossible for him to forgive and forget. He had seen to it that the name DuBois was known far and wide, but he had never opened his heart for fear of having it torn asunder again. Aubrey had even taken some revenge on the trappers who inhabited the region where Hawk's father lived.

A muddled frown creased Rozalyn's brow as she stumbled onto another thought. Arakashe had told her the curse of the valley would wane when Rose Blossom's lover followed her into the spiritual world of Morningstar. But if the curse lived on, where was Lyndon Baudelair? Was he still alive, roaming the Rockies, haunted by the same memories that had embittered Aubrey?

Hawk waited, knowing the question she would ask.

Although his father had requested that his identity be kept a secret, Hawk could not keep it from Rozalyn, not now.

"What has become of your father, Hawk? Where is he?"

"He became a part of these mountains until I was thirteen years old. Then, for some reason, he decided to return to the Crow camp to retrieve me. Together, we hunted and trapped and came to know each other as a son should know his father. Since I belonged in the worlds of both the red and white man, he decided to take me back to civilization to learn the ways of my white heritage. I preferred to remain in the mountains, but he would not hear of it. He took me to live with my grandparents in St. Louis, and before he left me with them, he made me promise I would not return to the mountains until I became a man who could be at home in both worlds." Hawk sighed and then squinted in the sunlight so he might view the spectacular terraces over which water gently flowed. "In all our years together, my father never could bring himself to tell me what really happened to my mother. He only informed me that she had died when I was an infant. Never once did he mention the conflict with Aubrey DuBois, and I was at a loss to explain Aubrey's behavior when he learned my true identity." Reining his steed to a halt, Hawk waited for Rozalyn to edge up beside him. "My father is a recluse. He has ventured from these mountains just once in thirty years."

"Have you no association with him? Does he long for no one's company, not even his own son's?" Rozalyn asked, her inquisitive eyes locking with Hawk's. "Has he become as bitter and dispassionate as my father?"

Her rapid-fire questions ignited Hawk's laughter. "You have met him, *chérie*. How do you perceive his torment these past years?"

A puzzled frown carved thoughtful lines on Rozalyn's features. She could not recall meeting Hawk's father. Had Hawk been so long in the light air of Yellowstone that his brain had turned to mush? "I have yet to be introduced to your father," she corrected.

"Ah, no. He watched over you in my cabin," Hawk hinted. "And he became so fond of you that I very nearly had to pry him out of the shack to get him to leave us alone."

"Bear-Claw?" Rozalyn chirped, and her jaw dropped.

Hawk gave his head a positive shake. "Bear-Claw, Wapike, Lyndon Baudelair. My father is known by many names. He requested that his identity be kept from you. He feared your probing questions about the past, just as he feared mine. Although his bitterness has faded, his wound is still tender. Because of Bear-Claw's conflict with your father, he warned me not to become involved with you. He knew how it must end. Aubrey will never forgive, never forget."

Hawk's last remark sent Rozalyn's spirits into a spin. The futility of their love was even more evident after Hawk's explanation. Now she knew for certain Aubrey would not allow her to remain with Hawk, not when he hated Lyndon Baudelair so fiercely. Aubrey would grant Hawk lower prices for supplies at rendezvous, only to ensure that Rozalyn was taken from a Baudelair's custody. Her father's hatred of Lyndon and Hawk might be his only motive for being fair to the trappers, but it was motive enough. Aubrey would see to it that she never laid eyes on Hawk again, at least not in this lifetime. Their love was doomed, just as Rose Blossom's had been. Until this moment, Rozalyn had cherished the hope that her father would listen to reason if she confessed her love for Hawk. She had even been foolish enough to think Aubrey would want his only daughter to find happiness. But if she confessed her affection for Lyndon's son, that would only infuriate Aubrey. She might as well pour salt on a festering wound.

Knowing that separation was inevitable, Rozalyn was even more determined to live a lifetime in the next few weeks. She would cherish each moment she spent with Hawk while he trapped the valleys of Yellowstone and collected pelts to trade at rendezvous.

During the weeks that followed, Rozalyn hunted and trapped by Hawk's side. They explored the vast region of geysers and springs, and Hawk showed her a mountain of black grass that Rozalyn would never have believed existed if she hadn't seen it with her own eyes. Together they roamed their mountain paradise, facing the dangers of an untamed wilderness and marveling at the majestic terraces and at the waterfalls that would continue to whisper of the intimacy between a man and his woman. But the fragile blossom of love that had unfolded in the warmth of spring could not last. Its petals would fall, and be strewn about by the wind. Still, for these glorious moments, amid the snow-capped summits and the roaring falls of Yellowstone, their love blossomed.

Chapter 28

A frown had been stamped on Aubrey DuBois' features since the night he'd discovered that Hawk had abducted Rozalyn. For months on end he had fretted and paced, wondering if his henchman had apprehended the miserable bastard and had retrieved Rozalyn. But Aubrey had received no message from Half-Head or Rozalyn, and even while he organized the caravan he would lead up the Missouri River, he was preoccupied with thoughts of revenge. The very idea that Hawk Baudelair was using Rozalyn made him incensed. But he would expect such skullduggery and betrayal from a Baudelair. Hawk is his father's son, Aubrey often thought.

Although DuBois detested the disastrous turn of events, his hands were tied. It had become apparent that Half-Head had been unsuccessful, and so he was considering several alternatives. He would agree to anything in order to get Rozalyn out of Hawk's clutches, but he knew how difficult it was to track man or beast through the Rockies when the mountains were cloaked in winter snow. Finally, Aubrey had resigned himself to the fact that his henchman had met with difficulty and that any other rescue attempt would be futile in winter. But soon he would reach rendezvous and Rozalyn would be returned . . . she had better be. If his daughter had sustained even a scratch while in Hawk Baudelair's care, Aubrey swore that he would have more than the man's scalp. Hawk had dared too much, and the possibility of intimacy between Rozalyn and Baudelair had Aubrey aboil.

Brooding over the past and it's maddening entanglement with the present, he now stared across the moonlit Missouri. The fleet of keelboats had made good time, despite the fact that it had often been necessary to drag the vessels along, often inches at a time. Aubrey had paused to trade with the *hiverants*, men who wintered in the wilds and who camped in the area that separated the upper Missouri from the lower river. Following his standard procedure, he had also stopped at each stockade he had established for trade with Indian tribes. So, the keelboats, heaped with furs and necessary supplies, navigated the Missouri and then followed the currents of the Yellowstone to Fort Benton.

At dawn on the following morning the supplies would be transferred to wagons to complete the seven-week journey from St. Louis to the rendezvous at Green River. Aubrey was anxious to press onward, to finish his unsettled business with the conniving bastard who had dared to kidnap Rozalyn. Gritting his teeth, he stalked the confines of his cabin, wondering if his daughter had been told the secret he had carefully kept buried for thirty years. He hadn't wanted her to know of his bitter past, of the woman he had loved . . . had never stopped loving, could not forget. Aubrey could only hope that Rozalyn detested Hawk for snatching her from her luxurious St. Louis home to use her in bargaining. If she did not already loathe the Baudelairs as fiercely as Aubrey did, he vowed to remind her of their underhanded dealings.

Soon Hawk would know he had disturbed a vengeful

lion, Aubrey promised himself. Perhaps he would be forced to sell supplies at lower prices this summer and buy pelts at higher prices, but next summer would be an entirely different matter. Hawk would be unable to sell his beaver pelts to furriers anywhere on the continent; Aubrey would see to that. And the price of supplies would soar in years to come, just to prove to Hawk and to the other trappers that they could not dictate policy to Aubrey DuBois.

Mulling that vindictive thought, Aubrey shrugged on his jacket and strode outside to greet the first rays of sunlight. Soon he would set up his encampment on the shore of Green River, amid the tepees of the tribes who had come to trade and the campsites of the white trappers who sought a market for their pelts.

Aubrey could feel his tension mounting. He had seen Hawk's mocking smile every night in his dreams, but the bastard wouldn't be laughing when he learned his goods would no longer be accepted at rendezvous. And if Hawk Baudelair had dared to lay a hand on Rozalyn, he would lose more than a market for his pelts. If it required an army of mercenaries to cut Baudelair down, Aubrey was prepared to pay the price. Rozalyn was no man's whore. She was Aubrey DuBois' daughter. Hawk had made a disastrous mistake when he'd attempted to drive a bargain by ransoming the heiress of the most powerful fur empire west of the Mississippi.

His jaw set in grim determination, Hawk descended from the foothills to the shore of Green River. The loud, uproarious laughter of the trappers who had already reached the meeting place reached his ears. In the past, Hawk had anticipated the raillery, rowdy games, and races that were so much a part of rendezvous. But this summer was an entirely different matter. He was not anxious to face the vengeful entrepreneur. For Hawk and Rozalyn, that meant the end of heaven and the onset of hell.

After stashing Rozalyn with the Crow for safekeeping, Hawk had gathered his pelts from the cache where he had stored them while he'd ventured into Yellowstone. Alone, he had come to confront Aubrey and to ensure that his terms were met. Even from a distance Hawk could see the red-faced furrier pushing bodies out of his way to reach the riverbank. Hawk braced himself for the unpleasant encounter, knowing he had ignited Aubrey's wrath by appearing without Rozalyn in tow.

"Where is she?" Aubrey spat out, dispensing with diplomacy.

Hawk eased his steed through the river and paused in front of Aubrey. A tight smile thinned his lips. "Your daughter is alive and well, no thanks to you. If you were truly concerned about her welfare, you wouldn't have sent Half-Head in pursuit." Before Aubrey inquired about his henchman's whereabouts, Hawk informed him of the man's timely death. "Half-Head has gone to the place he belongs," Hawk declared, his voice carrying no hint of remorse. "The devil is roasting in hell."

"Where is my daughter?" Aubrey gritted out each word.

Hawk threw a muscled leg over the saddle horn and then hopped to the ground to drag his pelts from his pack horse. Turning, he presented the fuming furrier with a taunting grin. "Rozalyn is with the Crow. I knew you wouldn't dare barge into their camp since they bear ill feelings toward you. But you are welcome to retrieve her yourself if you are feeling lucky and think you might walk out alive."

"Damn you," Aubrey hissed venomously. He had not counted on such a crafty tactic.

"I come bearing a message from Arakashe. He asked

me to tell you that he is pleased to find that your daughter is everything her father is not."

As Hawk swaggered past DuBois with the string of pelts slung over his shoulder, Aubrey clenched his fists at his sides, fighting an insane impulse to clamp his fingers around Hawk's arrogant neck. "The bargaining for furs will not begin until I see with my own eyes that Rozalyn has not been mistreated," he declared.

Hawk broke stride and then pivoted to face Aubrey's murderous glower. "I expected your demand. At my request, Arakashe consented to bring his people from the hunting grounds to make their camp on the opposite side of the river. Although he has refused to trade with you in the past, he anticipates reasonable prices this year."

After Hawk's piercing whistle drifted across the river, Arakashe appeared on the winding rock path. Behind him, garbed in a squaw's attire, rode Rozalyn, followed by a procession of Crows. "When the trading is over and the trappers and Indians have received fair compensation for their efforts, your daughter will be returned to you." Hawk's expression was a carefully blank stare. He refused to let Aubrey see how painful it was for him to keep his distance from the raven-haired beauty.

"I should have you cut to pieces for forcing my daughter to live like an Indian," Aubrey growled vindictively.

"There was a time when you lived among the Crow," Hawk goaded. "And I have heard it told that you became overly fond of one of their maidens."

The jibe sliced across Aubrey's soul like a double-edged knife, and he had to exert immense self-restraint to hold his ground and not pounce on Hawk. "It seems your father finally admitted his betrayal after all these years."

"He told me why you bear such a poisonous hatred," Hawk acknowledged. Then he focused a pensive stare on the Indians making their way to the far bank. "I wonder how you would react if your own daughter found herself attracted to one of the Crow braves while she remained with them for safekeeping. It would be ironic, would it not?"

Spewing like a volcano about to erupt, Aubrey stalked back toward camp while the Crows set up their tepees on the opposite bank of Green River. It was obvious Hawk was not about to free his hostage until he had received his profits, and he was not about to ford the river to retrieve Rozalyn, not when Aubrey was held in such low esteem by the Crow chief. "The shrewd scoundrel," Aubrey muttered under his breath. Hawk had plotted and schemed, planned it all right down to the last detail. At least Aubrey was reasonably certain Hawk had not made Rozalyn his whore. She had been living among the Crow, Hawk had implied that.

When Hawk dumped his pelts on the makeshift table of barrels and split logs, Two-Dogs raised a heavy eyebrow and his amused gaze raked over his friend. "Don't you want DuBois to know what's bin goin' on between you and his daughter?"

Piercing green eyes drilled into Two-Dogs. It was obvious that the trapper had discovered the truth about Rozalyn and evidently he'd been eavesdropping on Hawk's conversation with DuBois. Hawk should have known the inquisitive man would pry the information from Roz. Nothing moved in the mountains without Two-Dogs finding out about it.

"No, he doesn't, and I prefer to keep it that way," Hawk insisted. "Rozalyn could suffer if Aubrey learns the truth. There is no telling what he might do if he loses his temper. The last time he became enraged it cost a life."

Two-Dogs knew exactly what Hawk meant. "No need to fret. Nobody here is goin' to enlighten him." His curious gaze tarried on Hawk contemplatively. "Are you really gonna let DuBois take her back to St. Louis? I ain't blind, you know. Yore hooked on that girl."

437

"Do I have a choice?" Hawk snorted disgustedly.

Heaving a heavy sigh, Two-Dogs shook his shaggy head. "No, I s'pose not. You made a bargain with DuBois and yore obliged to keep it. But I don't know exactly how you think yore gonna survive after you fell in love with that girl and was forced to give her up. I'm glad I ain't in yore moccasins."

Hawk's features turned to stone. He didn't know how he was going to survive either. God, tearing off an arm would be less painful than watching Rozalyn climb into the wagon and disappear into the distance with the departing caravan. Even though Hawk had sought solitude to deliberate, his pensive contemplations had led him to this end—saying goodbye to the woman he had come to love more than life.

Rozalyn . . . She rose from the hot springs like a goddess, her exquisite features alive with pleasure, her perfect body glistening with water droplets that sparkled like diamonds. Rozalyn . . . She was lying by his side, her shapely contours making him only too aware of the differences between a man and a woman. Rozalyn . . . She was standing atop a summit, gazing off into the distance, her body silhouetted against the waning sunlight. No matter which way Hawk turned, Rozalyn was there, kneeling by the campfire, riding on horseback, running into his arms with her face uplifted and her blue eyes shining with love. There was nothing they hadn't done together during their passionate sojourn in the mountains of Yellowstone.

A quiet smile rippled across Hawk's lips as he recalled the night Rozalyn had sauntered toward him, wearing nothing but a provocative smile. She had led him beside a waterfall and had made wild sweet love to him until he could not find the strength to move or the will to do so. Then they had lain together, their bodies entwined, letting the fine mist of the falls spray over them until the embers of passion cooled.

"Do you want to sell these pelts or just stare at them?" the fur agent questioned impatiently.

The man's husky voice jolted Hawk from his musings. Turning his attention to the present, he began to barter for top price. "I would think nine dollars a pound would be a fair exchange for these plush furs."

"Nine dollars!" the agent hooted. "Dammit, man, these are beaver pelts, not gold! You ought to know the demand for fur isn't what it used to be. Silk hats are the latest fashion, not fur caps."

Hawk's gaze shifted to Aubrey DuBois who had propped himself in a corner to listen to his agents barter for furs. Their eyes locked for a moment, and after a stilted silence, Aubrey nodded in reluctant compliance.

"Pay him top price," Aubrey grumbled to the agent.

Hawk grasped Two-Dogs's arm, drawing him toward the bargaining table. "My friends also have prime pelts." His intense stare probed into the agent who was set to refuse. "You heard the furrier. The going rate at rendezvous is nine dollars a pound."

The agent compressed his lips and frowned at Hawk's arrogance. He was not accustomed to allowing the trappers to make demands. Heaving an agitated sigh, he looked at Aubrey.

"Prime pelts will receive top price," Aubrey muttered begrudgingly and then wheeled away, but not without flinging Hawk a parting glower.

When Hawk had completed the business transaction, his elated friends led him away, hailing him as a conquering warrior. A mug of rye whiskey was thrust into his hand, and several toasts were made to his success. Never had the trappers received such exorbitant prices for their pelts.

By nightfall the boisterous voices of celebrating trappers echoed through the foothills. One swore he'd discovered valleys crawling with beaver, rivers so thick with the creatures that they couldn't be stirred with a stick. Another said he had been attacked by an entire sloth of grizzlies and had single-handedly battled his way to safety. One drunken trapper and then another tried to top each other.

Aubrey watched the wild goings-on with frustrated anger. He knew he would be forced to endure several days of these raucous festivities before he could retrieve Rozalyn. He wondered if Hawk's rendition of the incident that had occurred many years ago had turned Rozalyn against him. That thought had Aubrey growling like a wounded panther. His confrontation with Hawk had brought back bitter memories, memories he had never been able to bury. Heaving an exasperated sigh, he stalked back to his tent, wishing this were the last day of rendezvous instead of the first.

Rozalyn's longing gaze spanned the distance between the Crow camp and the torch lights of the encampment on the far side of the river. For five endless days the bartering and trading had continued, so had the loud celebrations that echoed far into the nights. She wished she could enjoy the festivities, but she didn't feel like celebrating for this was the beginning of the end. It was all over but the crying. Soon the trappers would scatter and Hawk would deliver her to her father.

A choked sob constricted her throat. With each passing moment she died a little more. Rozalyn had thought she could survive on her sweet memories, but letting go was almost more than she could bear.

"You do love him with all your heart, don't you, Mitskapa?" Arakashe questioned softly. "I can see the mist of longing in your eyes."

Not daring to trust her voice, Rozalyn nodded mutely. Her teary gaze was still fixed on the golden lights across the peaceful river that separated her from Hawk. It might as well be an ocean, Rozalyn thought miserably.

"I have warned you that all stories cannot have happy endings," Arakashe reminded her. "You and Manake have known from the beginning that it would come to this, but nothing can sever the bond of your hearts." A rueful smile grazed the chief's lips. "I have seen many snows and I have seen too much unhappiness. If I could spare you and my grandson this agony, I would. But the way is difficult and the path has become entangled."

Rozalyn's trembling hand folded over Arakashe's. "I know it is futile to want what I can't have, but that doesn't ease the hurting," she said brokenly. "I would sacrifice my past and all the luxuries I had in civilization to remain in these mountains with Hawk."

"Your father will never permit it." Arakashe's dark eyes followed Rozalyn's gaze to the far bank of Green River. "These mountains hold bitter memories of Apitsa. He was once a friend of the Crow, but no more. He can barely tolerate himself, and, because of that, he has become vengeful toward his brothers."

Rozalyn was aware that he spoke the truth, and, grappling with that depressing thought, she turned back to her wigwam. But when she closed her eyes, Hawk's handsome face materialized before her. Would she see his dashing features in her mind's eye for the rest of her days? Rozalyn had never done anything halfway. She had loved Hawk with every fiber of her being, and her unquenchable thirst for adventure had led her to live in ways others of her background only dreamed about. But now, when the sunshine was to be taken from her days, Rozalyn wondered if she would become half a woman, leading an empty existence. Maybe it would have been easier if she had never loved Hawk at all.

Coward, she said to herself. During the months she had spent with Hawk, she had promised herself their winter love would be enough, that she could survive on her sweet memories, but when the moment of reckoning was upon her, she could not help but wonder whether she

441

should have fiercely fought falling in love with Hawk. Now her knot of longing would never ease, not as long as she lived and breathed, not as long as she could look back and remember. . . .

Tears came, a flood of them, and pain channeled through every part of her being. Her body shuddered with tormented sobs. This time she couldn't fight the obstacle that lay between her and the man she loved, Rozalyn reminded herself drearily. Defying her father would only make life impossible. Perhaps Aubrey was at fault, but he was still her father. If she had professed to love any other man, Aubrey would have consented to a match, but he would never allow Rozalyn to live with the son of his mortal enemy, the son of the man who had married the light and love of Aubrey's life. What was unattainable for her father would be inaccessible to his daughter. God, Rozalyn couldn't even allow Aubrey to know how she ached inside. If Aubrey learned of her intimacy with Hawk, he would be enraged. Rozalyn could never divulge the truth to anyone; she must live a lie. Another tear slid down her flushed cheek as a thought struck her. What if . . . No, Rozalyn didn't want to consider the possibility that she was carrying Hawk's child. As much as she would adore a baby with Hawk's captivating green eyes, Rozalyn couldn't bear a child without infuriating Aubrey. There would be nothing but anguish in her future, Rozalyn realized. She could not have Hawk and she could not have his child. If she carried his seed within her she would be forced to flee. But where could she run? She couldn't go into the mountains alone when she was with child. Lord, where on earth could she find sanctuary?

Rozalyn's thoughts swirled together, creating tormented dreams. Fitfully, she tossed and turned, wondering what was to become of her.

Chapter 29

Rousing from another haunted dream, Rozalyn opened heavily lidded eyes to note the silhouette of a man at the entrance to the tepee. Her soul swelled with pleasure when he stepped forward, allowing the scant moonlight to spray across his chiseled features. Like a gigantic mountain lion crouching in his den, Hawk stretched out beside Rozalyn, offering warmth where there had been chilled loneliness.

"Even whiskey couldn't drown my memories," Hawk rasped, his arms instinctively circling Rozalyn's trim waist. "Set my maddening thoughts to flight, sweet nymph. They are tearing me apart."

His lips swooped down on hers with breathless urgency, and Rozalyn welcomed his whiskey-laced kisses, responding to him as she always had. His hands were upon her, gliding over her like ocean waves. Their magical touch erased her troubled musings, and left her swimming in a sea of ecstasy.

Her fingertips scaled the taut muscles of his back to trace the corded tendons of his neck, trailing her worshipping caresses over the rugged terrain of his body, learning this sleek, pantherlike man by touch. In the months to come Rozalyn knew she had but to close her eyes to call upon this memory. Even when Hawk was a thousand miles away she would be able to feel his hair-roughened body beneath her hands, taste his potent kisses, and inhale his masculine scent that now filled her senses.

A tormented groan gushed from Hawk's lips as they flowed over her skin, cherishing the velvety softness of her. Her enticing fragrance enfolded itself around his senses, leaving him aching to become a part of this rare beauty who was as hauntingly lovely as a rose.

Their bodies came into familiar contact, brushing lightly against each other like shadows swaying on the wall, and Hawk found himself burning alive. He wanted this exquisite seraph as his own, craved her more than he had wanted anything else in his life. She was the vital essence that gave him purpose, his reason for being. Over and over again he whispered of his love, his mindless need to lose himself in the rapturous circle of her arms. His hands and lips touched every inch of her satiny flesh, giving and sharing pleasure. He knew that soon these delirious sensations would be beyond his grasp, that he would be floundering in a sea of agony. And knowing that, Hawk was obsessed with making this, their last night together, an interlude of incomparable ecstasy.

Rozalyn died a thousand times over as his skillful caresses swept across her trembling flesh like a gentle whisper of wind, enticing, arousing, satisfying. She was on fire and Hawk was the flame, igniting her passion until she could only respond with wild abandon.

Breathlessly, she drew him to her, whispering of her need to be possessed, to feel his body forging intimately into hers. When Hawk lifted himself above her, he gazed down into her shadowed face. The darkness disguised the passion in her eyes, but Hawk was aware of the expression in them. He had seen it so often in the past few months that he could feel its fire as she arched toward him.

Hawk's raven head moved toward hers, ravishing her with a kiss that carried enough heat to set the night aflame. His hips guided her thighs apart, and he came to her, offering his body and soul.

Rozalyn was assaulted by one wild sensation after another. Her love for Hawk spilled through her, sensitizing her, engulfing her every emotion until her breath caught in her throat. As Hawk's powerful body moved against hers, appeasing the maddening ache that had claimed her, Rozalyn hugged him to her, arching to meet his driving thrusts.

For those blazing moments nothing else mattered except the overwhelming sensations that sent them skyrocketing toward the distant stars. The world stopped spinning as they soared on their intimate journey through time and space, their souls were arching across the black velvet sky like wild, free birds, spiraling higher and higher still. The wind beneath their wings was love and it sustained these graceful monarchs of the sky until they joined as one.

Hawk's tense body shuddered against her and a groan of sheer pleasure vibrated across her shoulder when he buried his head against her. His mind was numb, and his heart pounded in such frantic rhythm that he feared it would beat him to death. For a long, breathless moment he merely held Rozalyn's body to his, loving the feel of her. He could not let her go for this would be the last time he found exquisite peace in a universe far from reality. That shattering thought trickled through his paralyzed mind, and it was nearly his undoing. Sweet mercy, he'd known the end would be painful, but he had anticipated nothing like this! An aching had already begun to swirl in the pit of his belly, and as he drifted back to his senses, the gnawing became intolerable.

"Do you know how very much I love you? Can you,

too, feel the loss, even before it begins?" Hawk choked out.

If only our love for each other could perform miracles, Roz thought dismally. Forcing the semblance of a smile, though her heart was bleeding in her chest, she nodded. "You love me as deeply as I love you, and the pain is indeed intolerable," she whispered back to him, combing her fingers through the crisp, wavy hair that capped his handsome face. "The months we shared were the most precious of my life. I will never forget. . . ." Rozalyn bit her bottom lip, trying to keep her composure.

"I'll come back to St. Louis," Hawk promised.

In five years? It might as well be five hundred, Roz thought disheartenedly. Aubrey would never allow her to see Hawk. They would be forced to sneak away together for a few stolen moments, and then the hurting would begin again. What kind of future would that be? her tortured mind screamed. And yet, the possibility that she might see him again was her only hope.

Hawk propped himself up on his elbows and cupped Rozalyn's face in his hands. "I want you to remember that I love you, that I will go on loving you, Roz. The miles that separate us cannot break this bond. My father has assured me of that. He is living proof that the ties between a man and his woman can never be broken when they have taken such deep root." His lips feathered across hers and then he kissed away the tears that rolled down her cheeks. "There is something you must do for me, Roz. You must never let Aubrey know there was anything between us. When I deliver you to him tomorrow, don't look back, don't let him see what is between us. It will only make your relationship with him more difficult."

Rozalyn was fully aware of the possible repercussions. She knew what she had to do. Raising quivering lips, she looped her arms around his neck, drawing him back to her before he could steal away into the night to return to his own tent on the opposite bank of the river.

"One last kiss," she murmured brokenly. "One that will keep me warm and content until we chance to meet again." If we meet again, she thought.

The sensuous curve of his mouth melted against hers, his questing tongue probing into its sweet recesses to share a ragged breath. They exchanged soft declarations of love and made promises Rozalyn wondered if either of them could keep when their loneliness became unbearable.

When Hawk found the will to drag his lips from hers, Roz swore her heart had shattered into a thousand pieces. She could feel the emptiness closing in on her and she knew the fierce, gnawing sensations of loss would never go away. When she was forced to depart from these majestic mountains, she would leave her soul behind. It would linger on the precipices like a wayward spirit roaming the towering summits in search of peace.

As Hawk silently slipped outside, Rozalyn muffled her choked sobs. When the dawn came to claim the mountains, she knew she would be forever in the shadows of these peaks. Hawk would take the sunshine with him when he returned to the wilderness, and she would trudge back to a civilization that held no allure.

Pained eyes, dulled with heavy regret, peered at her wigwam. Then, Hawk slammed his fist into the palm of his left hand. God, saying goodbye to Roz hurt so he wanted to scream out his frustration.

He had always been in control of his life, but now he had lost that control. For a time he had shared his days with the woman he loved, but, come sunrise, she would vanish . . . and he would never be the same again. Memories would seep from every crack and crevice of the mountain range that had become their secluded paradise, and he would go mad when he remembered how it had been between him and Roz.

If it were not for Aubrey and his stubborn . . . Suddenly, a fragment of the conversation he'd had with Aubrey during the first day of rendezvous flashed through his mind, a careless remark Hawk had overlooked in his frustration. Frowning pensively, he stared across the river and then decided to seek out the sleeping chief. Several questions were looming in his mind and he could not rest until they had been answered.

As if she were riding in a funeral procession, Rozalyn followed several paces behind Hawk as they crossed the river on their mounts. Her expressionless eyes were focused on the man who waited for her on the far bank, and it was with grim determination that she managed a welcoming smile for Aubrey's wrinkled features were stamped with irritation and resentment. Strange, Roz mused. This was only the second time she remembered seeing her father display more than bland indifference to a situation. How could she pretend to be anxious to be reunited with him when he was glaring at Hawk as if he would slit his throat? But, keeping her promise to Hawk, Rozalyn attempted to appear relieved when her father's stony gaze swung to her.

"Well, I'll be damned!" Two-Dogs grunted in disbelief and then strode away from Aubrey's side. "Bear-Claw ain't come down from the mountains in years."

Rozalyn's gaze shifted to the movement on the ridge overlooking Green River, and her breath lodged in her throat. Suddenly panic gripped her. Her wild eyes darted back to Aubrey to view his reaction. What was Bear-Claw doing here? Surely he knew the type of reception he could expect from her father!

Aubrey's narrowed eyes fastened on the crusty mountain man, but it took him a moment to recognize the hermit. When he did, the color drained from his cheeks. "Baudelair . . . ?" The name burst from his lips in a muffled curse. Aubrey wheeled back around to glare mutinously at Hawk. "Why the hell did you send for him? I never wanted to see him again. Damn you. You know how I detest your father."

"I didn't send for him," Hawk snapped back, apprehensive because of Bear-Claw's appearance. If his father did not guard his tongue he could ignite trouble. Thus far, Aubrey had complied wtih the terms of the bargain without making an attempt at revenge, but Hawk knew it would take only one small spark to set Aubrey off. The man was having difficulty maintaining his composure as it was!

As the lone rider steadily approached, his expression somber, the trappers surrounding Aubrey fell away, expecting the feud between DuBois and Baudelair to erupt again.

Cautiously, Rozalyn slid to the ground to take her place beside her father. She would have preferred to stand by Hawk, but that would have made Aubrey suspicious, and it was the last thing he needed when he faced Bear-Claw for the first time in thirty years. She watched Aubrey go rigid when Bear-Claw swung from his saddle and marched toward him.

"What do you want here?" Aubrey spat out.

"To make peace," Bear-Claw said calmly. Then he glanced over to intercept the warning glint in Hawk's eyes. Carefully, he gave Rozalyn a discreet look before again peering at his son. At last he focused his attention on Aubrey. "It has been a long time, Aubrey. Long enough, don't you agree?"

Aubrey wasn't giving an inch. His bitterness and hatred could not be dissolved in a few minutes. "Do you think you can waltz down from the mountains, offer the hand of friendship, and erase the past?" His tormented gaze riveted over Hawk's powerfully built frame. "Do you know how difficult it is for me to look upon your son, the man who abducted my daughter?" Aubrey's voice cracked with barely restrained emotion. "Dammit, he should have been my son . . . my son!" Brooding eyes shot back to Bear-Claw. "Knowing that makes the past even more difficult to bear. I look at him and I see you and her . . ." Fighting for composure, Aubrey turned away, his fists clenched so tightly that his knuckles had become chalky white.

"None of us could help what happened, not you, not me, not her," Bear-Claw sighed. "We thought you had perished."

"Hoped I had perished," Aubrey corrected, his voice carrying a distinctly unpleasant edge. "How long did you wait, a week, a month? You were my friend. I trusted you above all others and you betrayed me." Drawing himself up proudly, Aubrey thrust out his chin and then grasped Rozalyn's arm. He did not want his daughter to hear this conversation; he felt that Hawk had had the decency to keep it from her. "Nothing you can say will make any difference, Baudelair. I never want to lay eyes on you or Hawk again. I kept my end of the bargain and now I'm taking my daughter back to St. Louis." Before hustling Rozalyn along with him, Aubrey flashed Hawk a contemptuous glare. "Don't bother to show your face at rendezvous next year. There will be no market here for your pelts. All the money in the world won't buy your supplies."

As Aubrey's harsh words drifted across the river, Arakashe frowned. He had prayed that DuBois would bury the hatchet and let the conflict die. But it was obvious the man was not willing to forgive for he could never forgive himself. Arakashe turned back to his wigwam, angered and disappointed that Bear-Claw had come to make amends and Aubrey had stubbornly refused to listen.

When Bear-Claw started after Aubrey and Roz, Hawk clutched his arm to detain him. "Let him go. DuBois is too hardheaded to listen to reason," Hawk muttered, his penetrating eyes fixed on Rozalyn's departing back. "The man's heart has shriveled up like a dried acorn. I swear I can hear it rattling in his chest when he walks."

Bear-Claw peered incredulously at his son. "I came down from the mountains to attempt to reconcile the past because Roz means so much to you. Dammit, you know it will tear you in two to let that girl go. I never expected you to give up without a fight."

"A fight?" Hawk pounced on his father's choice of words. "Would you have me pull my pistol and gun DuBois down, risk having Rozalyn caught in the crossfire? Or perhaps we should go at each other with knives on the bluff overlooking Whispering Falls." A melancholy smile surfaced on Hawk's lips when he saw that Bear-Claw's anger was dwindling. "If DuBois and I take arms against each other the incident will explode into a war between his men and the trappers. Would you have me sacrifice even one life for my own personal happiness?"

Bear-Claw's shoulders slumped as he stared after DuBois. "No, I suppose not, but I wanted you and Roz to share what your mother and I—"

"You were the one who told me the time would come when I had to let Rozalyn go," Hawk reminded him. "And I have . . ." His voice trailed off while he watched Rozalyn walk out of his life, for memories suddenly came rushing back to him as Rozalyn and her father marched toward the loaded wagon.

Rozalyn had kept her vow not to look back, but it tore her in two to keep that promise. She ached to break free and run into the protective circle of Hawk's arms. But if she dared, she would invite her father's wrath. She knew

451

as well as Hawk that rendezvous could become a battleground.

Cursing Bear-Claw's unexpected appearance, Aubrey herded Rozalyn toward the wagons heaped with furs and extra supplies. After ordering his men to take their places, Aubrey glanced at his daughter and then lifted her onto the wagon seat.

"If he harmed you in any way, if he abused you, tell me now," he growled. "I'll see him dropped in his tracks."

Rozalyn met her father's smoldering stare and gave her head a negative shake. "Hawk protected me from danger and the Crow chief offered me nothing but kindness," she insisted, her voice devoid of emotion. "The deed is done. Let it be over, Papa. Take me home."

After studying his daughter for a long, calculating moment, Aubrey opened his mouth to utter another remark, then thought better of it. He wheeled around to take his place at the head of the caravan.

An unbearable numbness crept over Rozalyn as the procession made its way along the Big Horn. Aubrey avoided her and she realized that her father's concern was not for her, but for himself. He was obsessed with putting a great distance between him and the man he felt had betrayed him. It was as if Aubrey were driven by demons. He kept to himself, barked orders, and forced his men to spend long hours on the wagons without pausing to eat or rest.

The tiring days blended into weeks, and when Fort Benton finally appeared on the horizon, Rozalyn breathed a sigh of relief. At least she would have the opportunity to rest while the goods were transferred from the wagons to the fleet of keelboats. But Aubrey's plans did not include lounging at the post to recuperate from the overland journey. After their evening meal at the fort, Aubrey ordered his men to load the merchandise and supplies on the keelboats and to be prepared to embark on the Missouri the following morning.

When Rozalyn answered the rap on her cabin door, she found her father, still wearing the frown that had been stamped on his features since the first day of rendezvous. Silently, she stepped aside to allow him entrance, wondering why he had come now when he had avoided her for almost two weeks.

"I don't suppose Hawk and Bear-Claw had the decency to spare you the tragedy of my past," Aubrey blurted out, his eyes failing to meet Rozalyn's.

"Do you think my curiousity would have allowed me to overlook the incident that took place in St. Louis the night I was abducted?" Rozalyn carefully chose her words, attempting to encroach upon the subject without drawing her father into a fit of temper. "I had never seen you upset, Papa. Naturally, I wanted to learn the reason for your ill feeling toward the Baudelairs."

"I consider my feud with the Baudelairs to be well founded," Aubrey muttered self-righteously. "I cared deeply for Bitshipe and Bear-Claw knew that. But, like a coward, he waited until I was out from underfoot before he pursued her. A true friend would have confessed his feelings to my face instead of dallying behind my back. I was scratching and clawing to find financial backers for my fur-trading business, but not a day passed that I didn't wish to be with Bitshipe. An empire could not be built in a day." Aubrey expelled a frustrated breath and then began to pace. "When I was able to return to the mountains, I was prepared to make Bitshipe my wife. I lived for that day. I dreamed of laying riches at her feet."

Although Rozalyn kept silent she wondered if the lovely Crow maiden would have cared about a white man's wealth for it seemed Bitshipe was content to live out her life in the mountains.

453

"You cannot imagine how distraught I was to find my dream had collapsed about me. When Arakashe informed me that the two of them had made a life together and that Bitshipe had born Bear-Claw a son, I couldn't believe it. I had trusted Bear-Claw with my most precious possession and he had coveted Bitshipe as his own. He had slept with . . ." Aubrey's voice trailed off for he was uneasy about discussing this subject with his daughter. "After Bitshipe died, I fled from the mountains, determined to put the past behind me. But after the tragedy and betrayal I lived with nothing but torment."

"Papa, if you don't wish to discuss this, I will understand," Rozalyn interjected, well aware that Aubrey was having difficulty with the sensitive subject.

"I want you to hear my side," Aubrey insisted, without pausing from his pacing to peer at his daughter. "I thought marrying your mother would make it easier to bury the past. She was a fine woman of aristocratic breeding."

"One who could add her prestige to your wealth," Rozalyn blurted out. Then she bit her lip, wishing she hadn't put the thought to tongue.

Aubrey jerked up his head to stare at Rozalyn. After a moment, he let his breath out in a rush and nodded affirmatively. "I thought Jacqueline and I would make a suitable match, that I would come to love her in the years that followed. But each time I looked at her I was reminded that Bitshipe was everything Jacqueline was not. And each time I thought of Bitshipe I remembered what I had done to her in my rage. I tried to live a lie. I tried to offer you and your mother a good life, but part of me could never let go. For that I hold Bear-Claw responsible. Because of his treachery I killed the only woman I have ever loved and I forced your mother to live with a man who had nothing left to give."

A mist of tears swam across Aubrey's eyes, but with a

tremendous effort he composed himself. "Perhaps you can never understand why I react so fiercely to the name of Baudelair. But because of Bear-Claw my life has been hell. I thought by making you Rose Blossom's namesake I could offer you the love I would have freely given her. But you are too much like the free-spirited Crow maiden. Each time I speak your name I think of her, and bitter memories swarm over me. I realize now that it was a mistake to give you a name that is a monument to what I lost."

Rozalyn didn't know what to say. She had known her father had very little to do with her, but hearing him admit the reason brought her pain. Would she and Aubrey ever be able to become close when her entire personality, even her name, caused him inner turmoil?

"I know what you are thinking," Aubrey predicted as he walked steadily toward Rozalyn, but not close enough to offer comfort. "And I despise myself for what I have done to you, my own flesh and blood. I have not meant to be cruel, but neither can I—"

A sharp rap at the door interrupted Aubrey, and Rozalyn thought her father almost looked relieved. When one of his men requested that he see to some matter concerning the keelboats, Aubrey bid Rozalyn a quick good night and took his leave.

Rozalyn wilted onto her cot and heaved a miserable sigh. She had hoped their conversation would lead to a better understanding between them. But it was now clear she could anticipate the same behavior from him when they returned to St. Louis. It seemed she was destined to create crosscurrents of emotion in her father, and an incident that should have drawn them closer together had put even more strain on them.

A tear slid down Rozalyn's cheek, to be followed by another. The world was closing in on her and she was having difficulty boosting her spirits. At one time she had been able to battle depression and emerge the victor, but no longer, not when she was so vividly aware of all she had lost. Her heart twisted in her chest. In the emptiness of her cabin, Rozalyn succumbed to her need to release the emotions she had so carefully guarded.

A painful emptiness knotted her stomach; a haze of despair fogged her mind. The door to the past had closed behind her when she'd left the man with the disarming smile and the sparkling emerald eyes. Living without Hawk wouldn't be living at all. His name echoed through her mind, bringing a vision of windblown raven hair and dark, rugged features. He was there, just beyond her grasp, and Rozalyn knew she would never again experience the happiness she had known in his adventurous world beyond the Mississippi.

Chapter 30

As Rozalyn sat perched in a narrow niche between bundles of pelts and storage barrels, her gaze settled on the horizon, watching the waning light grow dim against the darkening sky. For two days she had studied the gnarled underbrush that choked the shores of the Missouri, wallowing in her own misery. Now the roar of water in the distance caught her attention, and her expressionless blue eyes scanned the river. To the north, where the channel was divided by huge boulders that jutted up in midstream, lay a treacherous waterfall that spilled two hundred feet to a frothy bed below. To the south, a perilous maze of rapids awaited before the channel cut through gentler slopes to form a less dangerous route to the lower levels of the Missouri.

Rozalyn breathed a sigh of relief when Aubrey ordered the fleet of boats anchored. She did not relish the idea of navigating the rapids during darkness. After they had taken their evening meal, while she and her father's men sat around the campfire, a rustling in the thick underbrush caught her attention and her body tensed. Her experiences in the wilds had developed a sixth sense in her, and she could feel the threat of danger in her nerves.

When she turned toward the muffled sound, her heart leaped into her throat as a sharp war cry pierced the night air, bringing Aubrey and his men to immediate attention. Before they could retrieve their weapons, a war party of Crow materialized from the underbrush, surrounding the camp. Aubrey and his men found themselves prisoners of this band of braves that had emerged like a swarm of disturbed hornets.

Instinctively, Rozalyn darted toward the thicket, but before she could flee to safety, a brave manacled her hands. Her frantic gaze lifted to a face smeared with warpaint. She had met the muscular warrior during her sojourn in the Crow camp, but now there was nothing friendly about his appearance. Her wide blue eyes swung to Arakashe who now appeared from the underbrush, poised on his paint pony. Rozalyn swallowed hard when the flickering light of the campfire illuminated the colorful bonnet of eagle feathers that trailed down his back. The chief's weathered face was painted in the traditional colors of red, yellow, and black. He clasped a ceremonial spear adorned with beads and feathers in one hand and a circular buffalo shield in the other. Although his years were evident from his wrinkled features, he looked every bit the proud, invincible chief he had been in past years.

Rozalyn had come to expect a certain warmth in Arakashe's dark eyes. But, this night, only hostility glistened in those deep-set pools. His condemning gaze rivited over Aubrey, who soon found himself tossed on the ground and staked out, spread-eagled, in the grass.

"Apitsa, I have mourned the loss of my daughter for thirty snows. The Great Spirit of the people of the free-soaring Sparrow Hawk bade me to accept the past and let it die its own death. But Apitsa no longer lives by the messages of Morningstar. You have born hatred in your heart like a wounded panther sulking over an injury.

Because your hatred continues to fester and boil, and you refuse to give it rest, I have brought war against you and your people. There was a time when I called you friend and welcomed you into the camp of the Crow, but in your anger you took the life of one of our people, my only daughter." Arakashe pointed his spear at Aubrey as if he meant to hurl it at the sprawled target. "If you could not accept the hand of friendship when your blood brother offered it, I cannot go on forgiving. I have tried to be lenient with you and with the other Longknives who have crowded our lands. But the Longknives take and take, and they refuse to give. Now I will take, as is the custom of the Longknives. You were banished from Crow land, yet you dare to cross our hunting grounds with your caravans. For that and for all the other evils you have committed against the people of the Sparrow Hawk, you will now pay the price."

Returning to the Crow dialect, Arakashe ordered his warriors to confiscate the supplies and the valuable pelts strewn around the camp. When the goods were strapped on the Indian ponies, Arakashe gestured with his spear toward Rozalyn. "You will become the daughter Apitsa's wrath has taken from me. He will know the pain of losing his own flesh and blood." Dark brooding eyes swung back to Aubrey. "Your child will become my child and my people will grow fat on the rations you would have passed among your own warriors. The furs you have bought from white trappers and Indians will be sold to the Rocky Mountain Fur Company to purchase supplies for my people."

Again Arakashe rattled off orders in his native tongue. When Rozalyn had been herded across the camp and placed on the paint pony beside him, Arakashe's condescending gaze fell upon Aubrey. "You and the other Longknives will be set adrift in your boats at sunrise. But you will have no oars or poles to navigate the

459

channel. Let Morningstar decide which rout the Long-knives take." His arms lifted to indicate the roaring falls and then it swung to the hazardous rapids that would capsize a boat unless it was guided by poles and oars. "The Great Spirit of the Crow will decide your destiny, Apitsa. That is more than you allowed Bitshipe when she chose the man she had come to love with all her heart. You would not accept her decision. Now you will live or die by the decision of Morningstar. Your destiny lies in the hands of the Great Spirit. If he is merciful with you, I will not be when you return with your caravans to frighten away the game from our hunting grounds. Hear my words, Apitsa. The people of the Sparrow Hawk will swoop down on you if you dare to trespass on our lands. Only those Longknives who are willing to live in peace with the Crow and his white brothers will hunt and trap in the mountain meadows between Yellowstone and the Wind River. But you, who cannot make peace with yourself, will never by the ally of the Crow."

With that final declaration, Arakashe took up the dangling reins of Rozalyn's steed and disappeared into the underbrush, leaving his braves to stand watch over the Longknives until first light.

Rozalyn managed to keep still until they were out of earshot of the camp, but when they were alone she could not remain silent. Even if her father had wronged Arakashe's family, she could not allow this injustice to take place. The lives of innocent men were threatened. "I had come to look upon you as a friend, Arakashe," Rozalyn blurted out. "I spoke to you from my heart and felt your sorrow when I learned of the loss of your daughter. Will you turn a deaf ear when I dare to plead for my father's life?"

"I am council chief of the Crow," Arakashe reminded her, his dark eyes focusing on her determined expression. "Apitsa, your father, once a friend of my people, was given the chance to make peace and wash away the hatred that poisons his soul. He has long lived in bitterness. I will deal with him in the method he understands. He chose his own way when he denied Bear-Claw's outstretched hand of friendship." The chief peered straight ahead while he led Rozalyn back to the war camp of the Crow. "Do not ask me to forgive a man who will not forgive. Do not ask me to be merciful to a man who judges all others by his bitter past. You waste your breath pleading for his soul. From this day forward you will be the daughter of the Crow council chief and you will obey my wishes, no matter how unfair they may seem to you. It is the way of the Crow woman to heed and obey. Do not anger me with protests. You are no longer white, even though your skin differs from that of our people. You will become one of us, Mitskapa."

Rozalyn could tell by Arakashe's firm tone that the subject was closed. Perhaps the chief thought Aubrey deserved to die, but Rozalyn feared the news of the Crow attack would ignite a war between Indians and whites. If Aubrey died a new feud would begin, one that encompassed more than one family's bitter hatred for another. It seemed an already intolerable situation had worsened. Perhaps she could be with Hawk again, but at what price?

Rozalyn slumped on her steed, and as she did so an another unpleasant thought came to her mind. Perhaps Arakashe had decided to avenge Rose Blossom's death by making Rozalyn suffer through a life without the man she loved. Was the chief that vengeful?

Her eyes swung to Arakashe, whose face was set in a determined frown, and suddenly she wondered if she knew the chief at all. He seemed so distant and remote, so uncaring of her feelings and so preoccupied with his own. Perhaps his bitterness toward Aubrey had surfaced after smoldering for many years. Indians were complex, superstitious souls, after all. Perhaps Arakashe believed he was following the commands of Morningstar. In any case, he had set his mind, and nothing would deter him.

Rozalyn recalled how simple life had been when she'd been flitting about the streets of St.Louis, cavorting with Harvey Duncan and his rowdy friends. Now she stood to lose her father and perhaps even Hawk. To make matters worse, another war between Indian and white could break out on the western frontier. The situation was a dire one. First she had been miserable and lonely without Hawk, but now she was apprehensive of the repercussions that would follow Arakashe's decision to set her father and his men adrift and to force her to live with the Crow.

"Arakashe, you must listen to me," Rozalyn pleaded frantically.

"It is not a Crow woman's place to offer advice," Arakashe snapped, his dark eyes nailing Rozalyn to the tree where he had deposited her. "You will do as I command . . . without question or complaint. If I decide to give you to one of my warriors, then you will accept him as your husband. If you refuse to do my bidding, life with the Crow will not be pleasant for you. You will be called by no other name than Mitskapa. You will dress like the Crow and follow our customs. There can be no friendship between us if you will not accept me as your father and the chief of our people."

Angrily, Arakashe gestured toward the pallet and then sank down on the bedroll that lay beside it. "Sleep, Mitskapa. Tomorrow we will learn the fate of the man you once knew as your father."

Begrudgingly, Rozalyn eased herself onto the pallet, thankful that Arakashe trusted her enough not to tie her down. Although she might face his fury, Rozalyn silently made plans to sneak from camp when the chief had given way to sleep. She wasn't certain how she would go about setting her father and his men free, but she had to try, even if her efforts provoked Arakashe's wrath. Eventually, the chief would apprehend her, Rozalyn knew that, and she wasn't anticipating the confrontation, but there seemed no other way to aid her father for Arakashe wouldn't listen to reason.

Pretending to sleep, Rozalyn lay as still as a corpse until she heard Arakashe's even breathing. Then, carefully, she inched away and climbed to her feet to retrieve her pony. Casting one last glance over her shoulder, she disappeared into the shadows of the night, leaving Arakashe sleeping on his pallet.

Just before dawn Aubrey was nudged awake by one of the Crow braves. With his hands bound in front of him, he was shuffled into a keelboat, along with the rest of his men. The fleet, set adrift, was swept sideways across the swift channel before the boats were caught in a whirlpool and spun around the jutting boulders. When the captainless fleet surged back into the stream, it was drawn into the current that led to the falls, and Aubrey knew he had little chance of surviving the drop to the river two hundred feet below. A knot of apprehension coiled in his belly, but at least the end to his misery was in sight. Perhaps this is what I deserve, he thought to himself.

When the keelboat veered sideways once again before lurching ahead in the powerful current, Aubrey heard the crack of timber on the far shore. To his amazement, a huge tree crashed into the channel ahead of the fleet. When his astonished gaze circled back to shore, his jaw sagged for Hawk strode toward the riverbank, Bear-Claw and four trappers following in his wake. The last two people Aubrey would have expected to save him from disaster were Hawk and his father.

He was jostled from his musings when the keelboat in which he was riding clanked against the fallen timber and clogged on the barricade. But his eyes swung back to Hawk who had bounded onto the monstrous tree and was striding across this makeshift bridge. A wry smile pursed Hawk's lips when he peered down at the entrepreneur who had been bound in his boat.

"You seem to be in a bit of a scrape, Aubrey," he taunted.

"Toss me your knife," Aubrey ordered briskly. As he did so, he glanced toward the end of the log, wondering how many minutes it would take for the current to drag the boat into the channel and send it plummeting over the falls.

"I will be happy to accommodate you if you agree to my terms," Hawk said pleasantly, although he, too, was discreetly speculating on the length of time they would have to barter. He could tell by the frustrated expression on Aubrey's face that the furrier was furious to find himself so compromised.

DuBois gritted his teeth, knowing he was going to be on the short end of Hawk's proposition. "What the hell do you want now?" he queried acrimoniously.

"A market for my goods for as long as rendezvous is held in the Rockies."

When the keelboat slid free of the tangling limbs that had halted its course, Aubrey nodded begrudgingly. "A market," he ground out. "Now toss me your knife so I can free my hands!" Growling when he was upended by another keelboat that rammed him broadside, Aubrey wobbled to his feet and impatiently glared at Hawk, who still had not offered him the key to his salvation—a knife. Aubrey was so annoyed that he considered bounding from the boat, but he feared being squashed between the drifting keelboats before he could reach the fallen tree.

"I have another request," Hawk insisted, a slow grin

working its way across his tanned features.

"Dammit, out with it," Aubrey growled in exasperation.

"Your blessing," Hawk said simply.

A wary frown creased Aubrey's perspiring brow. "My blessing?"

"If you will give your consent to let me marry Rozalyn, I will plead with Arakashe for your life and the return of enough supplies for you and your men to survive the journey to St. Louis."

"No," Aubrey snapped. His burning gaze drilled into Hawk who showed no signs of melting beneath its heat.

Hawk's shoulder lifted in a nonchalant shrug. "Well, it is your life." His unconcerned gaze swung to the end of the tree, toward which Aubrey's boat was steadily drifting. "After you have plummeted over the falls, I won't need your blessing, will I?"

That remark made Aubrey turn pale, and when the keelboat lurched into the current and bumped along the fallen timber, he swallowed nervously.

Hawk grinned. "You haven't much time. Would you like to reconsider?"

When the boat slammed against the tree, toppling Aubrey, he let out a defeated sigh and climbed back to his feet. "Very well, speak to Arakashe on my behalf," he ground out.

"Do I have your blessing?" Hawk prodded.

"You have my consent since I have no other choice," Aubrey begrudgingly corrected.

After Aubrey had forced out these words, Hawk told the other trappers to tie down the keelboats and let them bobble with the current. When the floating caravan had been secured, Hawk hopped ashore and disappeared into the underbrush, leaving Aubrey to wonder if even he could persuade Arakashe to change his mind when the chief was set on vengeance. But it was Aubrey's only hope that the chief's grandson had enough influence with him to do so. Exhausted, Aubrey collapsed in the empty keelboat and then braved a glance at the roaring falls. He could not help but wonder if Hawk's attempt to parley with Arakashe would only prolong the inevitable. If the chief refused to compromise, Hawk would not defy his grandfather. Afer all, what did Hawk have to lose? In that case, the wily trapper would be rid of his nemesis.

His absent gaze drifted to the shore where Bear-Claw stood, staring intently at him. Damn, the man was delighting in his predicament. When the other trappers' backs were turned, Aubrey wondered if Baudelair would stroll across the fallen tree to sever his lifeline. That possibility in mind, Aubrey wondered how long he would be bobbing on the river before Arakashe or Bear-Claw terminated his existence.

When Hawk rode into the clearing and prepared to ford the river at a shallow point, he spied Arakashe galloping toward him, a distraught expression on his face. A troubled frown etched Hawk's brow. Something was amiss. After his last night with Rozalyn, an idea had hatched in his mind, and he had appealed to the Crow chief for assistance. When Arakashe had agreed to intercept Aubrey's fleet and hold him hostage until Hawk arrived to save the furrier from disaster, the scheme had fallen neatly into place. Hawk could retrieve Rozalyn, the Crow would secure supplies which would sustain them, and Aubrey would think he had gotten off lucky.

Arakashe was to have accompanied Rozalyn to camp and to have awaited Hawk's arrival. But the chief was alone. Where was Rozalyn? He suddenly realized he should have explained his plan to her, but there had been no time. Hawk had not slept a wink that night, between making the arrangements with the Crow and then requesting the aid of his fellow trappers.

"Where is Rozalyn?" Hawk asked when Arakashe drew his steed to a halt in front of him.

"She must have fled during the night," the chief explained. Then he frowned worriedly. "I thought Mitskapa would come to the river to attempt to free her father. She pleaded with me to show him mercy. Where could she have gone if not to the river?"

That question was already beginning to haunt Hawk. Dammit, he should have insisted that Arakashe tie her down to ensure she stayed put or explain the plans they had made the last night of rendezvous. Confound it, he should have known better than to think Rozalyn would sit idly by when a disaster was in the offing. She had never been the type of woman who waited to be rescued.

Growling at this unexpected turn of events, Hawk wheeled his steed around and charged back in the direction from which he had come. If Rozalyn didn't appear at the river, he must gather his men and begin a frantic search for her. As the minutes ticked by, Hawk became more apprehensive about Rozalyn's welfare. She was probably unarmed and some catastrophe might have befallen her. Blast it, why hadn't Arakashe tied her to a tree?

When Hawk finally reached the men congregated on the shore, he hastily ordered them to search the woods for Rozalyn. The trappers scattered in all directions, leaving Arakashe and his warriors to stand guard over the floating caravan in midstream.

A sickening dread flooded over Hawk while he searched the woods, calling Rozalyn's name. Had he plotted and schemed to find a way to keep her with him without inciting a war, only to have her meet with disaster? Now that he had found a way for them to make a future together, he didn't want to lose her to a grizzly or a hostile Indian tribe. Dammit, was he not to enjoy any happiness?

Muttering at his lack of good fortune, Hawk fought his way through the thick underbrush. He swore if he was lucky enough to find Rozalyn alive and well, he would never let that unpredictable woman out of his sight again. She attracted trouble. No matter where she was or what she was doing, catastrophe was only a step behind her. Why hadn't he fallen in love with some shy, retiring Indian maiden who would be eternally at his beck and call, instead of a minx who would single-handedly fight off a party of Crow to rescue her father from calamity?

That thought forced Hawk to quicken his pace. If he couldn't find Rozalyn alive he wouldn't care what happened to Aubrey DuBois. It was only because of Rozalyn that Hawk had hoped to make the furrier believe he owed a Baudelair his life.

Suddenly, Hawk began to realize just how difficult life had been for both Aubrey and Bear-Claw. No wonder Aubrey had become so bitter. And no wonder his father had avoided contact with civilization. Each man had lost his life force when Bitshipe died, and each man had reacted to the tragedy in the only way he could. Bear-Claw had mourned his loss and had punished himself with self-imposed isolation. Aubrey had developed an armor of bitterness to survive. How would I respond if I lost Rozalyn? Hawk asked himself. It was one thing to be without her when he knew she was alive and well and living in St. Louis, but it would be an entirely different matter to know he would never see her again, to know that death, not distance, separated them.

Hawk gritted his teeth and blazed a path through the thicket. I will find Rozalyn, he assured himself. And God have mercy on the man or beast that dares to harm her, for I will not.

Chapter 31

A doleful groan bubbled from Rozalyn's lips as she raised her head. It took a moment for her mind to clear, but when she attempted to move she found herself staked to the ground.

What happened? she thought groggily. The last thing she remembered was stealing off from the camp while Arakashe slept. She had been riding through the trees in an attempt to return to the river to rescue her father when . . .

Rozalyn moaned when she laid her head back on the ground for there was a tender knot on the back of it. Had someone leaped from the shadows to knock her senseless? Confound it, she couldn't remember anything except charging through the forest on her paint pony. Yet, here she was in the middle of nowhere, staked in the grass, a gag in her mouth.

With a quick intake of breath, Rozalyn glanced up to see the renegade Blackfoot who had once terrorized the wilderness with the ruthless hunter, Half-Head. Panic flashed through her eyes before she was able to get a grip on herself.

A wicked grin curled the Blackfoot brave's lips as he stalked toward his captive and sank down beside her.

"We meet again, white woman." He chuckled devilishly. "While DuBois fights for his life against the Crow, his daughter will remain my captive."

When the bare-chested warrior laid his hand upon Rozalyn's breast, she flinched and drew herself as far away as the restraining ropes would allow.

"Soon I will learn why so many men fight for you," he assured her in broken English. "Once I have had you, I will sell you to the victors, to the Crow or to the Longknives. They will pay handsomely for your safe return, and I will profit from the goods they will offer for you."

Rozalyn glared at the muscularly built brave who waited, like a circling vulture, to play the situation to his advantage. The warrior counted on the fact that the victor of the feud, Arakashe or Aubrey, would pay dearly to see her returned. But Rozalyn wondered if Arakashe would consider her worthy of ransom after she had fled from the camp to save her father. If the Crow chief had become vindictive perhaps he would consider it fitting for Rozalyn to be abused by this renegade Blackfoot who roamed the wilderness, preying upon the misfortune of others.

Since she had been unable to reach the river, what chance would her father have? He would drown and Arakashe would probably turn his back on her because she had betrayed his trust.

Her musing ceased when the brave crouched above her, his wicked intention stamped on his bronzed features. The thought of what was about to happen nauseated Rozalyn. She had faced the threat of rape at the hands of two drunken trappers at the fort, and she had never forgotten her feeling of helplessness. She detested such abuse, and she itched to claw out the Blackfoot brave's eyes, to spit in his face. But she was bound and gagged and there was nothing she could do but endure his disgusting touch.

Rozalyn swallowed hard when he whisked his knife from its sheath and then severed the laces on the front of her doeskin dress, baring her breasts to his devouring gaze. Then she screamed and writhed when his calloused hand made rough contact with her flesh. Although aware that her muffled cry served no purpose . . . or so she thought.

Like a panther screaming in the night, Hawk issued a warning cry and then pounced. The Blackfoot brave vaulted to his feet wheeling to confront the intruder who flew at him so fiercely he was knocked off his balance before he could bury his knife in Hawk's heaving chest.

Helplessly, Rozalyn watched the two men strain against each other, fighting for supremacy in the forest. She wondered why Hawk hadn't used his rifle to fell his opponent instead of charging in like an angered bull. But giving the matter further consideration, she realized the click of the rifle would have alerted the brave to an intruder's approach. She would not have relished having a blade held against her neck when the warrior realized his only hope was to use her as a hostage.

While Rozalyn was silently analyzing Hawk's tactics, the Blackfoot brave was fighting for his life. Hawk suddenly seemed to possess the strength of two men. A snarl on his lips, he sought revenge while the brave struggled wildly, hoping to inflict a knife wound that would slow his assailant. But Hawk was enraged. The sight of another man, particularly Half-Head's accomplice, attempting to abuse Rozalyn had him breathing fire.

On several occasions Hawk had seen the results of what Half-Head and his Blackfoot companions had done to women. The lingering vision sickened and infuriated him. He thirsted for blood. He wanted to put an end to the maimings and murders of this renegade.

471

When the brave lashed out with his sharp-edged blade, Hawk jerked away, catching the Blackfoot's oncoming arm in midair. Then, like a mountain lion pouncing on its prey, he coiled and sprang. With a pained grunt, the warrior doubled over and fell to his knees, clasping the knife that had found its target.

After Hawk was certain the brave would fight no more, he spun about to survey Rozalyn. Breathing a relieved sigh when he noted her condition, he strode over to cut her loose.

The moment her arms were free, they came around his neck, knocking him off balance, and Hawk chuckled when kisses rained on both his cheeks. "You wouldn't happen to be pleased to see me, would you?" he teased, as he scooped her up into his arms.

"Immensely," Rozalyn breathed, laying her head against his sturdy shoulder.

"If you had stayed put, none of this would have happened," Hawk insisted. Setting her on a mount, Hawk flung her a disapproving frown. "Fright took ten years off my life when Arakashe came charging across the river without you in tow."

When his remark penetrated, Rozalyn was irritated. As Hawk swung onto his steed, she said, "You planned this, didn't you? You persuaded Arakashe to attack my father's caravan and dispose of him."

Hawk nodded affirmatively and then hastened to explain further before Rozalyn jumped to the wrong conclusion. "I did send my grandfather to intercept the fleet of keelboats before they navigated the rapids, but it was not my intent to dispose of your father. I wanted him to think I had bargained with the Crow chief on his behalf so that when I asked for your hand in marriage he would be in no position to refuse. At the moment your father and his men are stranded in the middle of the Missouri, but their lives are not in danger, nor did I ever intend for

472

them to be."

The explanation Hawk offered was meant to cool Rozalyn's temper, but he soon learned it had had the opposite effect. Instead of praising his scheme Rozalyn was glaring at him.

"Dammit, Hawk, this is the last straw! Why won't you ever confide in me before you traipse off into the wilderness or devise some risky scheme that might result in disaster?" Rozalyn fumed.

"There wasn't time. I only thought—"

"Wasn't time?" she echoed incredulously. "We have spent the better part of a year together and you couldn't find the time to reveal this fiasco you conjured up?" Sarcasm dripped from her lips. "Obviously you consider me dim-witted, and think I wouldn't have the sense to play the charade to its end."

"The idea didn't occur to me until the last night we were together." Hawk's voice was testy. "Did you expect me to make the arrangements and explain my intentions during the few minutes it took to ferry you across the river to meet your father?"

"Well, I am not marrying a man who does not have enough courtesy to explain his intentions beforehand. I could have gotten myself killed . . . or worse . . . all because you didn't enlighten me!" Rozalyn countered. Then she turned coldly from him.

"Do you expect me to forewarn you of every move I make?" Hawk snorted derisively. "Upon my word, woman, I swear you would have me tell you when I plan to jump and how high! You would have me so henpecked that, like a hawk, I would molt twice a year."

"You? Henpecked?" Rozalyn laughed at the ludicrous notion. "I have yet to see you follow me around like an obedient pup. Indeed, I am the one who has been led about on a leash and pawned off on one stranger and then another."

When her breasts heaved in indignation, threatening to spill from the plunging neckline of her buckskin dress, Hawk lost all interest in arguing. The fact was neither he nor Roz would tolerate domination. They were destined to clash, but they would always be held together by a strong bond—the compelling attraction between them. Hawk was prepared to compromise occasionally . . . and this was one of those times.

Pulling his steed to a halt, he flashed Rozalyn a roguish grin. Then he deliberately reached out to trail a lean finger over the soft swells of her breasts. "Very well, *chérie,* if you demand to know my every thought, I will reveal it. And as far as my immediate intentions are concerned, I plan to kiss you. Do you have any complaints?"

His wide, boyish grin was her undoing. Suddenly Rozalyn couldn't remember why she was raking Hawk over the coals, and the moment he touched her she melted into a pool of liquid desire. An impish smile pursed her lips, and her blue eyes sparkled.

"Complaints? From me?" she asked innocently. "When have I been known to complain? Surely you must have me confused with someone else, *monsieur.*"

"My mistake."

"Apology accepted."

"Mmmmm . . . this beats the hell out of arguing," Hawk purred, leaning out to close the narrow distance that separated them.

While Hawk was settling down to the arousing business of kissing her senseless, Rozalyn melted into his buckskin shirt. His sensuous lips brushed lightly over hers, teasing her into response, and then his mouth opened on hers and his questing tongue parted her lips. The musky scent of him fogged her mind, transporting her back to another time and place, stirring memories of rapturous pleasure.

After a long, delirious moment, Hawk dragged his lips away and resituated himself on his steed. "As much as I would prefer to continue what we were doing, I'm afraid we have tarried too long already. Your father is probably beside himself, wondering if he is to be marooned in the Missouri for the duration of his life."

While they made their way through the forest, Rozalyn mentally rehearsed what she intended to say to her father. She had to convince him to end his feud with the Baudelairs, and to allow her to remain in the wilderness with the only man who had been bold enough to earn her respect yet gentle enough to win her love. It was time Aubrey faced the truth and accepted Rozalyn's plans for her future. She had been a fool to think she could hide her feelings, return to St. Louis, and live in a vacuum. Her father knew she was spirited and had a mind of her own. It was time she reminded him of that fact and took her destiny into her own hands.

Hawk and Rozalyn returned to the riverbank to find Arakashe and his warriors standing guard over the drifting keelboats. Aubrey growled resentfully when he saw Hawk lift Rozalyn from her steed and then make a quiet comment to her. He loathed being handcuffed and forced to do another's bidding, especially the bidding of a Baudelair.

"Well, what is Arakashe's decision?" Aubrey demanded to know when Hawk strode across the fallen log to confront him.

"The chief has agreed to spare your life and grant me your daughter's hand, but he will not release the furs or the entire stock of supplies," Hawk told him, biting back an ornery smile. It did his heart good to see the powerful furrier in no position to dictate. Perhaps now Aubrey would realize how the trappers felt when they were forced to accept the price the furrier offered them for their pelts.

"That is robbery!" Aubrey fumed, becoming more frustrated by the second. He had already been left adrift for more than two hours while Hawk was retrieving Rozalyn.

"It is no worse than risking the perils of the wild only to receive nominal pay for pelts. Be grateful Arakashe has reconsidered and has allowed you to live—and he is sparing you and your men enough supplies to reach St. Louis."

"Your efforts are astonishing," Aubrey muttered, his tone dripping with sarcasm. "If you could do no better than that, you needn't have bothered."

"Shall I tell Arakashe how ungrateful you are?" Hawk taunted, pirouetting on his toes to swagger back to shore.

"No, dammit. I want to leave here with my scalp," Aubrey growled acrimoniously.

Hawk reversed direction, then gave the sour-faced furrier a mocking smile. "In that case, I suggest you be content with your lot."

The remark cut through Aubrey like a sharp-edged knife. He had often made the same comment to grumbling trappers who were annoyed by the prices they received for their pelts. Hawk had thrown his own words in his face, and they did not set well with the resentful furrier.

Aubrey's narrowed eyes settled on Rozalyn while Hawk and the other trappers filed across the log to dump the meager supplies into the boats. The thought of her marrying this half-breed scoundrel infuriated him. Hawk had declared war on the influential entrepreneur and had emerged the victor, so Aubrey was angry and frustrated. Never had Aubrey been forced to buckle, but now he had been given no choice, not if he hoped to escape with his life.

When the supplies were tossed on board and the poles replaced, Aubrey rose to his feet, his bound hands hanging loosely before him. "Rozalyn, come with me," he beseeched. "Tell Hawk you have no desire to remain in the wilderness. This is no place for you. Hawk won't force you to stay if it is not your want. The scoundrel appears to have a weakness where you are concerned. He will listen to you." When Rozalyn made no move to join him in the boat, Aubrey said excitedly, "Rozalyn, for God's sake, think what you are throwing away. You don't have to stay here!"

Rozalyn stared pityingly at her father. Then she moved to stand directly above him on the fallen log. Aubrey was pleading with her to go with him, only because he could not bear to think of her living with a Baudelair. It was not because he wanted her with him, she knew that. He had said as much. He wanted her to go with him for all the wrong reasons.

"I love him, Papa," she told him simply. "But have you forgotten what it's like to truly care for someone . . . the way you cared for the Crow maiden? You were not able to enjoy the one true love in your life, but in good conscience, can you deny me my love?" For the first time her father really listened to what she was saying, and when his proud shoulders slumped, she knew she had gotten through to him.

"Your wealth has given me many opportunities and it has attracted many suitors who would have married me to link themselves to your fortune and your influence. I wanted to be loved for myself, not because I was Aubrey DuBois's daughter." Her long, thick lashes fluttered down as Rozalyn paused to moisten her dry lips. Then, quietly, she continued. "I have come to respect and admire Hawk during these past months. I have also come to love him, and he loves me because of what I am and what I mean to him. There is no monetary value attached to our affection. Hawk does not need your fortune; he has one of his own." Carefully, Rozalyn stepped over a protruding tree limb to edge closer to the bobbing keelboat. "I love Hawk the way you must have loved his mother," she murmured, allowing a faint smile to graze her lips. "If you had such a compelling attraction to Bitshipe, is it so difficult to understand why I see the same endearing qualities in her son?"

"But you know how deeply I was hurt by his father's betrayal, the cross I bear because of the tragedy," Aubrey said brokenly. "I can't forget Hawk could have been my son."

"He still can be," Rozalyn gently reminded him. "Papa, we cannot change the past. You tried to forget by taking a wife when your heart was tied to another. Would you wish the same agony on me? Could you watch me marry another man to ease my loneliness when it is Hawk I want? I don't think Hawk and I must suffer because of something out of our control, something that happened over thirty years ago."

Aubrey heaved a heavy sigh. God, he had been selfish and bitter. Rozalyn had been right when she'd said he'd paid her little attention during her childhood. What right did he have to give her orders now when he had never offered her love or guidance?

His pained gaze swung to the shore and he saw his one-time friend walking toward him. When Bear-Claw paused to peer down at Aubrey, a rueful smile crossed his lips. "I know you despise me, Aubrey. And I know you think you have every right to. But it is as Rozalyn said. I could no more avoid my compelling attraction to Bitshipe than you could. She was a rare, lovely woman, When she died I, too, was bitter and devastated. For thirteen years I avoided my own son, for fear that looking upon him I would see her. But then I realized that I was running away from the one person I should have been running toward. My son had lost his mother and he desperately needed to know his father, to know that he was loved."

Bear-Claw's misty eyes drifted to Rozalyn, and, sighing, he reached out to trace the delicate line of her jaw. "Look at your daughter, Aubrey. Truly look at her for once in your life. She is remarkably resourceful and high spirited. Rozalyn is an individual, not just Rose Blossom's namesake. I spent time with her this winter, teaching her the ways of the wilderness, and I have come to admire and respect her. I see in her many of the qualities that once drew me to you in friendship." Bear-Claw's solemn gaze swung back to Aubrey who stood as still as a stone statue. "Would you spend the rest of your days in loneliness when you could have the love of your daughter, as I have the love and respect of my son? Believe me, Aubrey, loving helps to ease the pain, to replace the emptiness. I have lived both ways, and reaching out to your own child is far better than holding your emotions inside you, refusing to grant them release. Neither of us can bring Bitshipe back, but I think she would be the first to give her blessing to this match between your daughter and my son."

For a long moment Aubrey stared at Rozalyn as he digested Bear-Claw's words. For the first time he looked past his own heartache and bitterness to see the young woman he had allowed to grow up wild and free, and he realized that Bear-Claw was right. Rozalyn was a unique combination of beauty and resourcefulness, and she was a survivor who could flourish in two worlds. Her zest for life made her fascinating and endearing.

Aubrey had wasted many years, viewing his daughter only as Bitshipe's namesake instead of seeing her as an individual, and as a child he had neglected while he'd wallowed in self-pity. The emotions bottled up inside him flickered like a small flame feeding on a faint breath of wind, and finally a slow, honest smile worked its way across his features when he looked up at his daughter.

"I have been a stubborn, bitter old man," Aubrey ashamedly admitted. "It seems Bear-Claw has been a better father to you than I have been." His beseeching eyes probed Rozalyn's. "Can you ever forgive me for being such a selfish fool? Is it too late, Rozalyn?"

Tears welled up in the back of Rozalyn's eyes. At long last she had a father, one who was no longer afraid to get to know his daughter or to express his emotions.

When Bear-Claw towed the boat toward the fallen tree and secured it, Rozalyn bounded into it and threw her arms around her father's neck. "Oh, Papa, I've wanted this since I was just a little girl. I tried so hard to gain your attention and win your love."

Bear-Claw stepped down into the keelboat to free Aubrey's hands. Then Aubrey fiercely hugged Rozalyn to him. It was the first time she could remember being comforted by her father in all these years together. Although this moment had been a long time in coming, Rozalyn was immensely grateful to have him as a loving, caring father.

Repentant blue eyes lifted to meet Bear-Claw's quiet smile, and without hestitation, Aubrey offered his hand to his friend of many years ago. "I have long owed you an apology, but I suppose I was not man enough to admit it—even to myself—until now."

"Although we have no control over the past, we can look to the future by giving Roz and Hawk our blessing and by renewing our friendship." Bear-Claw glanced up at his son who stood above them on the barricade. "They care a great deal for each other, Aubrey, and I wish them all the happiness we couldn't enjoy."

Clinging to Rozalyn's hand, Aubrey strode to the stern to lift his gaze to the powerfully built mountain man garbed in buckskin. "I will freely give my consent and my blessing to this match on two conditions."

Hawk tensed, wondering what sacrifices he was about to make in order to take Rozalyn as his wife, but whatever Aubrey demanded, he felt that he was going to compromise. "Name your terms, Aubrey. I am not going to live without Rozalyn."

A slow grin rippled across Aubrey's lips. "The first request is that you love my daughter enough for both of us. The second is that you return to St. Louis occasionally to spend some time with me. I have a great deal of compensating to do where my daughter is concerned."

Hawk chuckled lightly and then extended a hand to draw Rozalyn up beside him. "Agreed, Aubrey. Rozalyn will never have cause to doubt my love. And the time is coming when furs will not be in great demand. Though the quest for them will continue, I see myself one day returning to the civilization my father taught me to appreciate. Perhaps Roz and I will decide to make St. Louis our home." A wry smile rippled across his lips, then adoring green eyes fell to the radiant face beside him. "But it will be a decision we make together."

That implication made Rozalyn beam like the summer sun. Hawk had finally come to see her as his equal, perhaps not in all matters, but at least she was to be given a vote instead of being carted about and deposited where he saw fit.

Although the previous night her life had seemed devoid of hope, today had brought a new beginning. Rozalyn had found her father after years of alienation, and Aubrey had reconciled with Bear-Claw and had accepted Hawk. For the first time in her life Rozalyn felt whole and alive; she was bursting with happiness.

Clinging to Hawk and her father, Rozalyn watched the retrieval of the keelboats from the channel. Arakashe and his braves then assisted Aubrey in hauling the caravan overland to the smoother waters of the Missouri. Once the boats were again in the water, Arakashe ordered several of his braves to retrieve the stolen furs and supplies.

"Keep them," Aubrey insisted. "It is the way of the Crow to offer gifts in retributions to a family that has suffered an injustice. The supplies and furs are my offering of apology. We are family now, and I wish there to be no more ill feeling between us."

Dark eyes smiled on Aubrey as Arakashe clasped his hand. "It has been a long time in coming, Apitsa, but the people of the free-flying Sparrow Hawk will once again call you friend and welcome you when you come to trade." The old chief glanced at Hawk and Rozalyn. "And perhaps one day there will be a child to seal the bond between your people and mine, one that will be loved and accepted in both worlds."

"By the look of things, I expect such an occurrence in the near future." Aubrey chuckled softly and then slid Bear-Claw a discreet glance. "They do make a handsome couple, don't they?"

"A fine couple," Bear-Claw concurred.

Hawk's jaw sagged when he saw Bear-Claw follow Aubrey into the keelboat. "Where are you going?" he asked.

Bear-Claw snickered at the stricken expression on his son's rugged features. "Back to civilization." Drawing himself up in a sophisticated pose, Bear-Claw pretended to flick a piece of lint from the sleeve of his buckskin shirt. "Who knows? I may find the trappings of a gentleman to my liking after all these years of wandering in the wild. I dragged you back to St. Louis so you could receive your formal education. Now it's high time I reacquainted myself with my own heritage. I have an estate to manage and it has long been neglected."

"You are never coming back to the mountains?" Hawk was astounded.

The crusty mountain man's gaze swung to the noble chief of the Crow to exchange a silent message before he returned his attention to his son. "I will be back one day," he assured him quietly. "My heart belongs to these majestic mountains."

After the fleet forged from the shore to glide downstream with the current, the trappers headed toward the mountain meadows and the Crow returned to their hunting grounds. Rozalyn and Hawk stood alone on the bank of the Missouri. In silence they watched the keelboats disappear around the bend.

Then a contented sigh escaped Rozalyn's lips. All was well with the world; she was with the man who had come to mean more to her than life. Her happy smile faded when Hawk suddenly turned and walked away, and a smidgen of red stained her cheeks as she glared at his departing back. She was not about to begin the first day of their life together following Hawk's lead without knowing his destination. Had he already forgotten his promise to inform her of his intentions before he wandered off?

"Now wait just a minute, Hawk Baudelair," Rozalyn declared. "I am not following after you until I know where we are going. I can tolerate many things, but I will not tolerate being taken for granted!"

Hawk had anticipated her reaction, but he was not about to divulge his purpose. Without breaking stride, he moved toward his steed to retrieve the gift that had remained in his saddlebag for more than eight months. After extracting the gold band inlaid with emeralds and sapphires, Hawk pivoted around to display his expensive token of love.

"Before we left St. Louis last fall, I sent a letter to your grandmother, informing her that you would be safe in my custody and that her wish would come true." Hawk grinned sheepishly while Rozalyn stood there, staring speechlessly at him. "For a while I thought I had told Lenore a lie." Hawk moved deliberately toward Rozalyn and then placed the ring on her finger. "Although there has been no formal ceremony, we have long been man and wife. In the Crow village, a man has only to enter the tepee of his beloved and consummate their love. In my grandfather's eyes, we have been man and wife since the night I came to you on the shores of Green River." His soft, velvety voice whispered across her cheek, sending a chill through her. "In my eyes, we have been bound together since the first night I came to your room, drawn by a compelling need no other woman has been able to satisfy.

"I love you, Roz, even more now than I did then. Will you be disappointed if we dispense wtih the conventional ceremony until we return to St. Louis?" Hawk asked, his hand cupping her chin to peer straight into the blue eyes that had long captivated him.

Rozalyn gave her head a negative shake. "My grandmother always said I was too unconventional for civilization. I fear she is right. We don't need an audience to speak the words that bind us together."

Hawk stepped back to flash Rozalyn a roguish smile. "And now, *madame,* in answer to your request to know my destination . . ." Recklessly, Hawk peeled off his shirt, exposing his copper skin and the broad expanse of his chest. "I am going to paradise. Are you coming with me or must I make the journey alone." His smile faded, to be replaced by an expression of blatant longing as his hungry gaze ravished her, leaving her to burn in the heat that radiated from his emerald eyes. "Must I remind you how long it's been since we have made love?"

A seductive smile rippled across her lips, and Rozalyn drew the squaw dress over her head, tossed it aside, and then sauntered toward the handsome adventurer who was devouring her with his gaze. "Two weeks and three days," she murmured. Her throaty voice flooded over him like an arousing caress.

When she molded her softness to him and her silky arms glided around his shoulders, Hawk groaned in sweet torment. He had come dangerously close to losing Rozalyn. Now more than ever he realized how much he valued her.

"Though the winds may change and the winter storms may rage, one thing is constant," Rozalyn whispered, raising parted lips. "I will go on loving you forever. There has never been another man, there could never be. You are the one who taught my soul to sing."

When her lips melted like rose petals beneath his impatient kiss, the wilderness faded into a hazy fog. They touched and caressed, silently expressing the love that had blossomed and grown until living separate lives seemed inconceivable. They had become of one in heart and soul, each incomplete without the other.

Hawk moved against her, his body fully aroused and instinctively responding to hers. His worshipping caresses made her tremble, and not once, but over and over again, he tasted and explored the sensitive points of her flesh, evoking passionate responses. And when he came to her, his lovemaking made her cry out his name. As the dark world careened about her, Rozalyn clung to the powerful mountain man who had led her through hell to the rapturous bliss of heaven, and this time she knew she would never have to let him go. They had changed their destiny, had been granted love instead of emptiness. Now they shared emotions that eluded all except a select few. Their strong wills and relentless determination had flung open the gates to heaven and together they walked in paradise. They were one, belonging, possessing, giving and taking the pleasures of love.

Hawk could not imagine that any other man and woman shared such fierce, engulfing emotions, and he knew no man could be happier than he was at this moment. As a quiet thought trickled through his fogged mind, he clutched Rozalyn closer, nuzzling his face against the trim column of her neck, inhaling the subtle feminine fragrance that scented his dreams. Once, many years ago, in the Valley of the Elk, another man and woman had known so great a love, but tragedy had cut their paradise short. Hawk vowed to himself that he and Rozalyn would enjoy what his mother and father had lost, the pleasure Aubrey had spent a lifetime trying to forget. No matter what trials they encountered, they would confront them together, joining forces to emerge the victors. And through it all, a silken bond that even the sharpest of knives couldn't sever would bind them, and it would grow stronger with the years.

"I love you, *chèrie amie,*" Hawk murmured, overwhelmed by the intense sensations holding Rozalyn aroused.

"And I love you, Hawk. In your arms I can soar forever. . . ."

And soar she did. Her hushed words rekindled the flame that nothing could extinguish. It fed on emotions that bubbled like an eternal spring. And somewhere, beyond the wide Missouri, above the whispering Wind River Mountains a new legend of love came to be. It was passed through the bivouacs of trappers who gathered to weave tales of life in the majestic mountains and in the camp of the Crow who were certain that the little bird that discovered the world had spread its wings in flight to lead these lovers onto the towering summit that scraped the clouds of paradise.

Epilogue

John Chadwell looked as if he had been struck by a bolt of lightning when he answered the impatient rap on the front door of the Baudelair mansion. "Lyndon Baudelair, is that you?" he squeaked. His wide, incredulous eyes swung to Mosley who stood beside the man who was garbed in buckskins.

"It is no other," Bear-Claw chuckled, attempting to adjust to his given name, one he had not heard uttered in almost twenty years. "May I come in?"

Chadwell moved out of the entrance to allow the master of the house to brush past him. "I never thought I'd live to see the day you came down from the mountains to return home."

Grinning mischievously, Mosley wedged his way inside. "The master has news about Dominic and the young lass he made off with last year," he informed the bedazzled butler.

Absently, Lyndon Baudelair ambled through the spacious home, reacquainting himself with rooms through which he had strolled as a young man. "My son and his wife are alive and well, living in their mountain cabin in Wyoming Territory," Lyndon explained, as he paused to stroke the plush velvet drapes that hung on the

487

study window.

"His wife?" Chadwell chirped like a sick sparrow. His wild eyes flew to Mosley who was beaming smugly. "Do you mean to tell me young Dominic married Rozalyn DuBois?"

"That is exactly what he is telling you," Mosley confirmed. Then he discreetly stretched out his hand and patiently waited for Chadwell to pay the bet they had made the night Dominic had thundered off with his lovely hostage.

Grumbling, Chadwell fished into his pocket and begrudgingly tossed Mosley a twenty-dollar goldpiece. He silently vowed that was the last bet he would ever make. Never had he expected Dominic Baudelair, that free-spirited adventurer, to take a wife, especially one as feisty and unpredictable as Rozalyn DuBois. But then stranger things had happened, Chadwell reminded himself, returning his attention to the shaggy-haired man who stood peering out the window. Chadwell would have bet his last dollar that Lyndon Baudelair would never return to civilization after such a lengthy absence. But here he was, poised at the window of the study, looking slightly out of place in buckskins that were the worse for wear afer his long trip down the Missouri.

"Fetch me a bottle of our finest wine," Lyndon requested, and after testing the tufted rocker he planted himself in it. Keen eyes scanned the elaborately decorated room that was so unlike the rustic shack in which he had hibernated for so many years. "I would like to toast the newly married couple's happiness."

When Mosley and Chadwell scurried from the study to alert the servants of their former master's return and to retrieve the wine, Lyndon unfolded himself from the soft chair and leaned against the window. He could not quite adjust to the sprawling city and its throng of inhabitants. That would take a while.

As his gaze drifted to the western horizon, a tender smile mellowed his rugged features. In his mind's eye, he could see Hawk and Rozalyn standing on the riverbank while the fleet of keelboats made its way downstream. "Wherever the two of you are, I can rest easy, for I know you have found life's grandest pleasure. May it last forever. . . ."

Before reentering the study, Mosley raised a graying eyebrow and leaned close to the sulking Chadwell. "Would you like to bet the master of Baudelair mansion won't last a year in civilization? Twenty dollars says he will be aboard the next steamer that navigates the Missouri."

"I've sworn off betting," Chadwell grumbled, glaring at the goldpiece Mosley was flipping in the air. "I've already paid the one bet I saw no conceivable way to lose. Go rob some other blundering fool. I can't imagine Lyndon Baudelair remaining in St. Louis. He may be with us for a short time, but a return to the mountains is inevitable."

Mosley tucked the goldpiece in his pocket and poured three drinks. Admiring his long-time friend, he watched Lyndon Baudelair lift his glass in toast.

"To love . . ." Lyndon mumured softly. "And to the mountains where such emotion can flourish without distraction."

Three glasses clinked and then each man took a small sip before Lyndon Baudelair setteld back in his plush chair. He was enjoying a peace he had not felt in years. At long last he and Aubrey had buried their bitterness, and to bring him further contentment, Lyndon had seen the look of devoted affection in his son's eyes when Hawk had gazed at Rozalyn. The pair had found the rare, elusive pleasure that had been Lyndon's for a time. He prayed their life together would be a long, blissful one, and he promised himself if Rozalyn and Hawk did not return before the following summer, he had every intention of setting out to find them.

A low rumble of laughter echoed in his chest as he remembered the two weeks he had spent in Hawk's cabin, forcing the star-crossed lovers to keep a respectable distance. Hawk had been like a man stretched on a torture rack, and Rozalyn had been as nervous as a caged cat. But wherever they were at the moment, Lyndon speculated that neither man nor beast would keep those strong-willed lovers apart. Some things in life could not be changed; Hawk and Rozalyn's fierce need for each other was one of them. Their attraction was so compelling that no amount of adversity could keep them apart. Lyndon would have sworn Hawk was fighting a lost cause, but the young mountain man had never been able to accept defeat. And in the end, Hawk had had his own way, despite the obstacles he had confronted.

Rose Blossom would have been proud of her son and of the bewitching young beauty who had stolen his heart, Lyndon thought. Then, in a silent toast, he sipped the fine French wine and savored memories of another time and of a young Crow maiden who had given meaning to his life. What he and Rose Blossom could not share, Hawk and Rozalyn would. Lyndon sighed contentedly. He knew what Hawk would be feeling while he waded across a clear mountain stream with Roz one step behind him or when, camped in the plush meadows, he fell asleep with his woman in his arms. Lyndon had known the joys of love. And now it was time for his son to begin his life, a life that had been incomplete until Hawk had met the free-spirited sprite with lively blue eyes and shiny raven hair.

Aubrey DuBois trudged up the steps to Lenore Rabelais' home, as he had every night since he'd returned from rendezvous. The conflict between them had evaporated when the *grande dame* had learned that her granddaughter had wed Dominic with Aubrey's blessing. Although Aubrey found a certain comfort in taking up Rozalyn's task of visiting the beldame, he was always assaulted by the same question each time he ventured to the mansion. Tonight would be no different, he predicted.

"Well, have you any news?" Lenore asked the moment Aubrey set foot in the door. "Here I am, practically on my death bed and that inconsiderate granddaughter of mine has yet to return from the mountains. I knew she would be content in the wilderness, but I didn't dream she would neglect her own family! My last wish is to see her and that handsome husband of hers before I retire from this life."

Biting back a grin, Aubrey arched a taunting eyebrow and poured himself his usual drink. "Oh? I thought your last dying request was to hold your great-grandchild. Have you decided to settle for merely laying eyes on Rozalyn after her two-years absence?"

Grumbling, Lenore snatched away Aubrey's drink and downed it herself. "They promised to return to St. Louis a month ago and I have yet to see them walk through my door. I am prone to believe they sent the message only to frustrate me."

"Perhaps you should send word that you may not last another month, that ploy almost worked the first time you concocted it," Aubrey teased, planting himself on the sofa beside his fidgeting mother-in-law. "As I recall, you had Rozalyn convinced that you had reservations on the heavenly chariot and she was willing to do anything to pacify you."

"I was desperate," Lenore muttered, annoyed that Aubrey was mocking her in her present mood. "That child needed a husband to control her. *Mon dieu*, nothing else seemed to hobble her wild ways. And now that she is wed, I have yet to see . . ." Her voice trailed off when she heard the rustling of skirts and quiet murmurings in the hall, and the color gushed form Lenore's cheeks when she swiveled around in her seat to see her long-lost granddaughter appear at the door. "Oh, my . . ." Lenore's breath came out in a rush when she glanced from Hawk's and Rozalyn's beaming faces to the tiny bundle nestled in his father's arms.

"The lad has his great-grandmother's disposition," Aubrey declared, and he snickered when the infant squawked and squirmed in Hawk's arms.

"Pish-posh," Lenore flung at Aubrey before she sprang to her feet to unveil the fussing infant.

While Lenore doted over her great-grandson, Rozalyn looked up into Hawk's handsome face. There, in the colorful depths of his emerald eyes was the warm flicker of love that stirred her soul. She melted against him when he slipped his arm about her and hugged her close, but merely being cuddled in his protective arms was not enough. Their journey down the Missouri upon a cramped keelboat had allowed them no privacy, and Rozalyn had been deprived of his tender touch and passionate kisses during her recuperation from childbirth. She could tell by the expression on Hawk's face that he was suffering from the same deprivation that plagued her.

"Do you suppose Grand'mère would notice if we slipped away to spend a few moments alone?" she whispered against Hawk's cheek.

A grin of roguish anticipation stretched across Hawk's lips, and his wandering hand mapped the shapely curve of Rozalyn's hips. "She didn't notice that I was seducing her granddaughter right before her eyes, why would she notice our absence when she is so distracted by her great-grandson?"

"Why indeed?" Rozalyn purred, already aroused by her husband's skillful touch.

When they had sneaked upstairs and closed the door to one of Lenore's spare bedrooms, Hawk wasted no time doffing the stylish clothing he had donned for his visit to the *grande dame.*

"Really, *monsieur,*" Rozalyn taunted, her gaze flitting over his sinewy torso. "You are much too eager. A gentleman would find a more refined tactic for luring his lover to bed."

Stark-naked, Hawk strutted across the room and snatched Rozalyn to him, his nimble fingers making fast work of unfastening the stays on the back of her pink silk gown. "A gentleman never did stand a chance of getting anywhere with a fesity nymph like you," he growled seductively. "And although I have been everywhere with you, there is one place we have been forced to avoid these past few months." Scooping Rozalyn into his arms, Hawk made a beeline for the bed. "I am not a patient man when it comes to seeking what I want. And what I want at the moment . . ."

Thought deserted them when they tumbled onto the sheets, their bodies eager to express a love that had not dimmed. Their gnawing hunger drew them together in a passionate embrace, and they almost devoured each other. Tenderness returned in the aftermath of love-making, however, and though time had flitted by, Hawk was in no hurry to fly from his nest and return downstairs. Perhaps he was being inconsiderate in keeping Rozalyn to himself when Lenore had not seen her granddaughter for more months than she cared to count, but it seemed forever since he had nestled in the loving circle of her arms.

"We should join my father and grandmother," Rozalyn insisted, her voice heavy from the aftereffect of passion.

"We should . . . ." Hawk agreed, bending to press his lips to her sweet mouth. "And my father will be arriving shortly."

"He is probably already here," Rozalyn commented between feathery kisses. Impulsively, her arm looped around Hawk, bringing his body into intimate contact with hers. She wasn't certain she could drag herself away from the magic circle of Hawk's arms just yet.

"Let them all wait," Hawk growled in mounting frustration. "I can't seem to get enough of you. And until I do, I won't be worth a damn at conversation."

When his lips engaged in something far more stimulating than discussion, Hawk forgot that a houseful of people awaited them. He had always been a man with an insatiable appetite where Rozalyn was concerned and his need was not yet curbed. As flames of passion engulfed him, Hawk felt he was flying into the sun, into a heat so intense he feared he would not survive it.

It has always been like this, Hawk reminded himself. Rozalyn stirred such deep emotions in him that he had not been the same since they'd met. This free-spirited woman had taken a firm hold on his heart, and she had given him a son. Hawk had found a meaning to life that was worth more than all the riches in the mountains. Home was in the glorious blue depths of Rozalyn's eyes, in the sparkle of love in them.

"Don't ever stop loving me," Rozalyn murmured, as she surveyed the ruggedly handsome face hovering just above her. "I couldn't bear it now that I know how wondrous life can be."

Raw emotion tugged at the string of Hawk's heart as he blessed her with a gentle smile. "Never doubt my devotion, *amie*. Without you, I would be only half a man. Ah, how I love loving you . . ."

*   *   *

While Hawk and Rozalyn were entangled in each other's arms, their young son was being entertained by three adults who were cooing at him. Not to be outdone, each of them made faces to gain the infant's undivided attention and to entice him to break into a smile. However, impatient with their childish games, the lad let out a squawk and then found himself cuddled on his great-grandmother's shoulder while she lovingly patted his backside.

"You silly old fools," Lenore grumbled, glaring at Aubrey and Lyndon. "See what you've done. You've frightened the poor child."

"You were making idiotic faces at him as well," Aubrey pouted, his hands folding about the small bundle so he could take his turn at comforting his grandson.

But before Aubrey could nestle the lad in his lap, Lyndon snatched him away to bound him on his knee. The tiny tot gave up his attempt to secure peace and quiet when the threesome crowded around him and again tried to coax him into a smile. This time he gave it. What else could he do? His persistent grandparents would not let him be until he had given each of them a glance and a grin.

"He smiled at me first," Lyndon boasted, swelling with pride.

"Old fool." Lenore sniffed and then turned her attention on the wide-eyed infant. "That one was meant for his grandmother. You just got in the way."

"Give him back," Aubrey grumbled. "It is my turn to hold him."

By the time the tot had been passed among them, he was very nearly exhausted. Wondering at the strange habits of adults, he closed his eyes and drifted off to sleep while his parents renewed the vows of love that had brought him into the world. The young lad slept in first one pair of arms and then another. While he was on the lap of one of his grandfathers, Lenore insisted he was being squeezed too tightly. When she was cuddling him on her shoulder, the men complained that she was smothering him.

Into that scene, Rozalyn and Hawk walked. "I don't think they even realized we were gone." Rozalyn said as they paused by the parlor door.

A wide grin lightened Hawk's dashing features and he arched a rakish brow. "Don't you think it would be most impolite for us to disturb them?"

Rozalyn returned his provocative smile. "I have been so long in the mountains that I had almost forgotten my manners." Her gaze strayed back to the staircase they had recently descended. "I think it only proper to leave them be."

"My thoughts exactly," Hawk concurred, and he ushered Rozalyn back to the stairs. "Besides, there a few more matters I wish to discuss with you while we have the opportunity."

"Do go on," Rozalyn encouraged as she untied Hawk's cravat. "I am hanging on your every word."

"My word?" Hawk's dark eyebrow arched higher when Rozalyn brazenly unbuttoned his shirt on the landing of the stairs. "It seems you are hanging all over me! Shameless wench . . . mmmmmm . . . do that again." Hawk purred like a gentled mountain lion when her roaming hands glided over his bare chest, and when he glanced down into a pair of dancing blue eyes, he wondered if he and Roz would show their faces before the sun rose . . . or their young son roused to demand the bedtime snack he was in the habit of taking before he settled in for a long night's sleep.

"I intend to," Rozalyn promised huskily as she grasped Hawk's hand and led him down the hall. "Just as soon as I get you alone."

And when she did, she did!